Out of a Dark Reflection

by

Lexie Conyngham

First published in 2015 by The Kellas Cat Press, Aberdeen.

Copyright Alexandra Conyngham, 2015

ISBN: 978-1-910926-10-9

Lexie Conyngham

DEDICATION

To Joan, in the hope that she's pleased with the outcome!
And to Mike and Debbie, who have been loyally reading these
from the start.

Dramatis Personae

At Letho:
Charles Murray of Letho
Lady Agostinella Murray, his charming wife
Alester Blair, old friend of the Murray family
Isobel Blair, his daughter, a treasure yet to be claimed
Andrew Grant, cousin of Murray's father
Mrs. Grant, his wife
Robert Lovie, her son

Henry Robbins, faithful retainer, his wife Mary, and family
Mrs. Mack, cook and sugar confectioner
Mrs. Dean, housekeeper
Daniel, a servant who has consistently lived up to his early lack of promise, and his family
William, a servant who has always ambitiously modelled himself on Daniel
Agnes, housemaid with potential
Iffy, kitchenmaid unlikely to progress further
Walter, a solemn house boy

In Letho village:
Rev. Mr. Helliwell and his wife at the manse
Mr. Rintoul, assistant minister, in digs
Dr. Feilden and his wife
Kenny, schoolmaster
Mal Johnstone, and the other upright and virtuous members of the Kirk Session
Charlie, Rab and sundry other committed young scholars
Widow Maggot, a solitary person
Lizzie Fenwick, local midwife and layer out of the dead
Macduff, the sheriff's ubiquitous officer

At Collessie:
Sir John Aytoun
Lady Aytoun, his wife
Matilda Aytoun, their daughter
Sundry servants of lesser quality

Lexie Conyngham

Chapter One

The schoolmaster had had a perfectly good reason for sending the boys out early, and it had not, he reminded them later, been to terrorise the village. In fact they were being sent home to fetch food for their midday meal and warm up, but despite being young lads they were not principally interested in food. Freedom, at this unusual hour on a weekday morning, was at the moment a much more appealing prospect. The village, two main streets on either side of a triangular green, meeting at the top of the hill at the church and schoolhouse, was autumnally peaceful. Most people were at home or in the fields or, for the skilled workers, their workshops. A boy who should probably have been in school dozed as he watched the goats on the green, but they did not disturb him. Instead they surveyed the wondrous opportunities before them, and sized up their chances.

'Chickenelly?' whispered one, tentatively. A bolder boy caught it up.

'Chickenelly!' he announced. 'Right, lads, all together!'

A pause before flight, a brief instant to appreciate the silence – then they were away. Running and skipping and slithering on the muddy road to the east of the green, they rapped hard on the door of every house and cottage, waking dogs, flapping hens, enraging cats, and bringing the inhabitants out with bewildered expressions and shaking fists. Pelting down the road they were too fast for any angry householder, and skied round the corner on to the Dures road where they bent to laugh and catch their breaths, gasping.

'Did you see Ma Fenwick?'

'And Mr. Jack?'

'Come on,' said the bold leader, 'There's more houses here.'

There were a few cottages along this narrow road, and while some held back, puffed, the novelty gone, the keener boys pressed on. No one was in, though, and their speed dwindled, too, until they were kicking leaves and occasionally each other near the last cottage on the road.

This last cottage had something about it they did not quite like. In some ways it did not seem quite to belong to the rest of Letho village, where for the most part the houses were well-kept, the stonework pointed, the windows clean and painted, the gardens productive, even at this tailend of the year. Here there were plants indeed in the little garden but they looked – unusual. The cottage had been thatched, though now what appeared to roof it was a slab of dark mud. The door was crumbling at the lower edge, the latch an old end of string rather than the sturdy metal or wooden ones elsewhere. Just now the cottage did not seem empty, like the others in the row: it had instead an odd absence of life, as if something had been removed.

The boy in charge slowed, and contemplated the run-down cottage. He did not like it, though he did not stop to think why. He folded his arms.

'Rab,' he said, and a smaller boy straightened. 'I dare you to chap old Widow Maggot's door.'

A frisson ran through the group, just as the wind fistled the leaves around their feet. The dark windows of the cottage, thick with cobwebs, stared at them as if through half-closed eyes.

'You canna do that, Rab!' whispered another lad, clutching Rab's sleeve. 'She's a witch!'

'A witch!' The boy in charge was dismissive. 'There's no such thing as witches!'

'Aye, aye, you're right there, Charlie,' several of them agreed hurriedly. 'No such thing as witches.'

'Aye, you're right,' said the boy named Rab. 'No such thing as witches – but she is one, all the same.'

'Aye, well, mebbe so, and mebbe no,' said the boy in charge, prepared to be open on the subject. 'But I still dare you to chap her door.'

All eyes were on Rab. He stared at the ground, and breathed in hard through his nose, then ran a hand back through his hair.

'I'll do it,' he said.

'Rab!' The other small boy still held his sleeve.

'Nah, let me go, Jock, or I'll never do it. Right,' he said, pulling his cuffs down. 'Here I go.'

He took a deep breath, ran a little up the lane to give himself a lead in, then charged at the door of the little cottage. For a moment the others did not grasp what had happened. Rab was at the door, then he had vanished. Then there was one almighty yell, and Rab shot out again as if he had been scalded.

'She's deid! She's deid!' he cried at the top of his voice. 'Widow Maggot's deid!'

Charles Murray of Letho stared out at the autumnal day and thought about gutters.

It was not perhaps a highly academic subject, or indeed one that could give itself up to prolonged and considered debate. Ideally he would have liked to consider reformed farming methods, or the letters of Cicero, or the latest copy of Blackwood's magazine. However, he was responsible for a number of buildings amongst trees in the autumn and that made it an important subject, so he watched with care as some of his estate workers, armed with ladders so long they curved ominously in the middle, tackled the gutters of the two houses that faced each other across his driveway. One was the home of his factor, Thalland, and on the other side lived his manservant, Henry Robbins, with his wife and young child. He had no wish to see either household flooded out because of a mismaintained gutter. Meanwhile above him, he knew, on the leaded flat roof of the main house another team were more securely cleaning leaves away from above, and there was the occasional splat of a wad of half-rotten leaves on the gravel outside the window, and a mumbled curse from the man above who would have to clear it away later. The day was breezy but dry, and he was anxious to be out and away for a walk, but he was waiting for his companion who had no doubt become distracted somewhere, so he stared out of the window and thought about gutters.

The slightest of movements caught his eye and made him jump. He was confused for a second, until he realised that he had seen the movement in reflection, turned back at him by the window glass. He spun round and just saw the tail of a skirt vanish under the arch of the cantilever staircase, powered, it seemed, by the little gust of a giggle. Four long strides, silent even in his high boots, took him across the flagged hall floor to the edge of the staircase, and then he used his considerable height to allow him to peer beneath it without having shown himself to the creature beneath.

'What are you doing there?' he demanded, looking as fierce as he knew how. A little girl, hair as smooth and black as elderberries and with eyes to match, pretended to scream and instead fell into more giggles. There was a scuffle behind Murray and he straightened to find one of his more junior manservants, looking distraught.

'Ah, Daniel. Something the matter?'

'Oh, sir, no, sir.' Daniel stopped abruptly, pulling down his waistcoat over his ample stomach.

'Then don't let me stop you,' said Murray, leaning against the stair rail as if he intended to be there all day.

'No, sir. Of course not, sir.' Daniel looked about him a little wildly, and at last Murray had mercy on him.

'Try under the stairs,' he suggested. Daniel's eyebrows shot up, and he lunged to reach under the staircase, pulling out the little girl by the elbow.

'Maria, how many times?' he admonished her. 'You know you're not to go through that door!' He pointed to the door to the servants' wing, obviously conscious of Murray's gaze on him as he told his daughter off. 'Now, come on back with me – and stay in the kitchen this time, or it's off home with you!' He marched little Maria back through the servants' door and vanished, and Murray, alone again, burst out laughing.

'Oh, what's the matter?' came a voice from the landing above him. He glanced up and saw his old friend Alester Blair, anxiously peering down at him.

'The matter? Nothing that won't mend,' Murray said. Blair scurried down the stairs to join him. 'One of Daniel's multitude of children was hiding under the stairs, but Daniel has taken her back to the kitchens.'

'But you don't mind, do you?' Blair asked, bending awkwardly to scan the area under the stairs, as if looking for proof.

'Not at all: they liven the place up. But as you can imagine, Lady Agostinella would not be pleased if she found them – which given her present condition is ironic, but I have to allow her some indulgence, I suppose.' He managed not to sigh: he knew he spent far too much time sighing these days. 'Are you ready? The good weather won't last many more days, I think. And just now it's perfect for a walk.'

Blair disentangled himself from the stairs and straightened with some effort, at the same time smoothing the little frown that had appeared at the mention of Murray's wife. Instead he beamed at Murray.

'Then by all means let us go!'

Walks with Blair were only fractionally slower now as he was growing older. It had never been a matter of straight lines with him: like a child, he could be distracted by any tiny thing along the way, and absorbed by it for hours. Blair had been a good friend of Murray's late father and a reliable guide to Murray himself since his father's death: he knew Letho and its villagers almost as well as Murray did, and though a walk of inspection around the estate could take four times as long with Blair than without him, it would be a walk worth taking. Blair had no estate himself but took as keen an interest in agricultural matters as he did in everything else: he was a voracious reader and soaked up information on all subjects like a sponge. Murray sometimes thought that his friend had reached the age of ten, liked it, and not bothered to grow further, though in physical terms he must have been past sixty.

Today they took the path to Letho village, crossing the river and climbing the hill, where there was plenty to amuse Blair in fish, birdlife, and the small black cattle that were pastured there. They took the path that led them through a little woodland, bright now in autumn sunlight through bare branches, with the high garden wall of the manse on their right and after a time the lower kirkyard wall on their left. The old sandstone church, perched on the top of the hill, oversaw the village as it sprawled downward from its gate: the schoolhouse and the doctor's house lay beyond it, and the low front wall of the manse, a new, rather smart building, faced the green. The two roads were muddy underfoot and the grass of the green was autumn-faded: a few crows addressed each other gravely in the bare trees. One or two people were out and about on business but otherwise the streets were quiet in the light breeze, and Murray nodded in satisfaction. Most of the houses in the village belonged to his Letho estate, but some belonged to Dures, a neighbouring house, and a few to Collessie, over the hill. Collessie's owner was a naval officer, rarely home, and the house was let out, while the inhabitants of Dures were in Edinburgh for the season. Murray had agreed to keep an eye on their properties as well as his own. Dures had a reliable factor, but Collessie had always been unlucky in its servants. One or two of the Collessie cottages required roof repairs after the October gales, and Murray noted this, speaking to the tenants while Blair shuffled and fidgeted behind him. Murray left the cottages and Blair opened his mouth to speak, but as he did so there came a yelp of irritation from a little further down the hill. A man was standing outside his cottage, staring at an empty hook on the wall with his fists on his hips, half-puzzled and half-annoyed. Murray strolled down to him.

'What's the matter, Mal?' he asked as they came within speaking distance.

'Those boys! Thundering past this morning, waking babies and scaring dogs, and now they've taken my good rope!' The man was small with white hair and a face which from the side would have looked concave, not convex: his small nose did not jut out past his chin and brow. His little mouth was round with annoyance, pinned with two long, narrow front teeth.

'The boys?'

'The lads from the school. It'll be them. It was hanging just here, and I went to get it now to tie the load on my cart round the back,' he jerked his head to where Murray knew he had a rig behind the house. 'Gone! A good new rope, too: I had it at Cupar market last month, for my old one was worn nearly through.'

'I'm sure you'll get it back. Speak to Mr. Kenny: he'll soon have the culprit for you,' said Murray. The boys must have been playing on their way to school: chances were the missing rope was somewhere between here and there. Mal went on staring at the hook as though his rope would magically reappear, and Murray and Blair turned to walk away. As soon as they were clear, Blair burst out,

'I think there's something happening at the inn.'

'Is there?' asked Murray vaguely, thinking of roofs and the invidious task of talking to the Collessie factor.

'Um. I think so. There's a good deal of toing and froing on the Dures road,' he said, waving his hands back and forth to indicate the traffic at the base of the triangular village. Murray peered down the hill: there seemed to be schoolboys running back and forth, which was odd in itself: Mr. Kenny did not often liberate the schoolboys outside school hours, having a keen sense that suffering improved their souls. As Blair was already trotting down the hill with his nose in the air, scenting news, Murray lengthened his stride to catch up.

They reached the Dures road just as the innkeeper himself appeared from the direction of Dures, heading back towards the inn. His face, ridged with anxiety, cleared considerably when he saw Murray and Blair.

'Mr. Murray, sir!'

'Dod. Has something happened?'

'It's Widow Maggot, sir. The boys found her dead in her cottage.'

'Oh, dear, that's a shame,' said Murray. 'We had better tell the Dures factor. Has she any relations around here?'

'Never mind the Dures factor, sir,' said the innkeeper, solemnly. 'I'm off for the sheriff's clerk.'

Blair's eyebrows shot up on his mobile face.

'The sheriff's clerk?'

'Aye, sir. It looks as if someone has killed her.'

The schoolboys, who had been milling around, now gathered around to confirm the innkeeper's story.

'Her heid's been bashed in, sir!' said a tall lad that Murray knew was named Charles after his own father, having been born a couple of years after the old laird's death.

'Did you find her, Charlie?' he asked.

'Yes, sir! Well, Rab found her first,' he allowed generously.

'Can you show me? Yes, Dod, you'd better go for the sheriff's clerk. Have you a horse to hand?'

'Aye, sir, there's one in the stables I can use.' The innkeeper turned away reluctantly, but with an air of importance.

'Now, Charlie – and you're Rab, aren't you?' Murray asked a small red-haired lad who had the wide-eyed look of one in shock. 'Rab, away and get yourself a hot brandy at the inn.' He found a coin and pushed the boy in the right direction. 'Now, Charlie, where did you find her?'

Charlie and the other lads led the way along the Dures road to the last cottage, sitting sullen in its peculiar garden.

'She's in here, sir.' The boys lingered around the gate, eyeing the half-open door warily.

'Why were you visiting her?'

They wriggled collectively, and Blair raised one eyebrow.

'Chickenelly?' he asked, and the boys all jumped.

'Aye, sir,' said Charlie reluctantly. Murray's mouth twisted, but it was not the place for the laird to laugh. He took a careful look at the exterior of the cottage and its garden, noting the state of the roof. As far as he knew, this cottage did not strictly belong to the Dures estate but was one built on feued land, to all intents privately owned, like some of the more prosperous houses in the village. That was all they had in common, though, he thought: Widow Maggot was not a tenant, so Dures would not have been responsible for looking after her roof – or indeed her.

He pushed open the gate and approached the door. It creaked as he touched it, and he cast a shadow into the room as he waited for his eyes to adjust. Blair was right behind him, eager to see inside.

Even as his eyes adjusted, he blinked at the smell. It was almost something solid: a combination of old woman, oily smoke, unwashed laundry, unemptied chamberpot, dust and age. The smell of death did not overwhelm any of these, not at this cooler time of year, but the body was there nevertheless, lying on the sandy floor with her feet to the door, flat on her back as though someone at the door had struck her a terrible blow that made her fall straight backwards. And there was evidence of something like that blow: the centre of her forehead was caved in and black with blood, messy with the gathered edges of a grey lace cap and spikes of hair.

Murray stepped carefully into the cottage and crouched beside the body, gently applying the back of his hand, glove removed, to the old woman's clutched hand and withered cheek.

'Stone cold,' he remarked. 'She's been dead for several hours – maybe since yesterday evening.'

'No sign that there was much of a struggle,' Blair remarked, peering around him. 'The floor is smooth, and there's nothing out of place – as far as one can judge, of course,' he added carefully.

'No other injuries visible,' Murray continued. 'She looks as if she put her hands up to fend the blow off but was too slow, perhaps.' He was experiencing a feeling that was all too familiar to him: here was a dead body, dead through unnatural means, through the desperation or malevolence of another, and he had to do what he could to find out what had happened, to present, as it were, the story of that death on behalf of the dead person, to give this old woman a voice after her death.

He stood and peered up at the bare rafters of the ceiling, and then around at the floor.

'I can't see anything that could have swung down and fallen on her.'

'By way of being an accident, you mean?' asked Blair.

'That's what I was thinking. But I can't see anything.'

'I don't even think that whatever hit her is still here – and that's an indication in itself, I suppose,' said Blair. 'Odd things falling down from rafters don't, in my experience, walk away afterwards.'

'No.'

Murray turned slowly, surveying the contents of the cottage. There was not a cloth clean enough that he would have used it to cover Widow Maggot's face, so he pulled out his own spare handkerchief and used that. Then he returned to his perusal of the cottage.

'Ever been in here before?' he asked Blair.

'No, not at all. Have you?'

'No. Yet … she has been an old woman all my life, living in this cottage like a hermit. I know very little about her.' Fireplace, open fire – long died down, no heat coming from those ashes – a bracket to hold a cooking pot had been swung away from the fire, but there was no pot on it. A table, covered with a cloth, with dishes on it perhaps from last night's supper: breadcrumbs - but she must have had it baked at the village baker, for there was no sign of a bread oven here. There was a smear of butter, he noticed, on the plate, and a bowl showing signs of broth, and hanging from the rafters what had been a decent ham, only that half of it at least had been hacked off.

'Something missing here,' he said suddenly, crouching down again to trace a rectangular shape on the soft floor. 'Some kind of box?'

Blair came and bent over beside him. The rectangle was in the corner, farthest from the fire, sheltered from draughts. Blair sniffed heartily.

'Apples?'

Murray caught it, too, a little bubble of sweetness in the sour room. He nodded, and straightened again, continuing his inspection. A crusie lamp against the wall had burned dry. There was a bed in an alcove: reluctantly he pulled back the curtain and glanced in but the bed was made up and relatively neat. The smell of well-used chamberpot surged upwards, and he let the curtain fall again, trying not to breathe.

'You asked Dod if she had any relatives,' said Blair.

'I did. I can't think that I have ever heard of any.'

'Was she on the poors list?'

'I'm not sure. I don't think so.'

'Butter and ham,' Blair remarked, thoughtfully.

'Indeed, and bread. And her own house, for all I know to the contrary. Was someone looking after her?'

'There are some fine things here, or they look like it, I should say,' said Blair, and pointed to the mantelshelf. Murray leaned over to look. Apart from a large copy of the Bible, rather dusty, there was a prettily-worked box painted with slightly strange patterns, a brass bowl, rather worn, and a hand mirror, of a reasonable size and with an intricate gilded frame.

'If she was poor she could have sold these,' said Murray. 'There is some value in all of them.'

'Which of course begs the question – or it seems to me that it does – why was she killed?' Blair pursed his lips and opened his eyes wide, the picture of bewilderment. Murray finished studying the room, and stood as centrally as the widow's prone body would allow.

'And who killed her?' His mind ran to his tenants, and his responsibility for them. Were they safe? 'As far as I know, and from the evidence here, she was an old woman who lived on her own but had a degree of comfort, from what source I know not. I know of no relatives, and I rarely saw her about the place. She does not seem to have been killed for monetary gain, or the things on the mantelshelf would have been stolen. Instead, the killer – or some opportunist – appears to have taken a box of apples. On the face of it, that's not a strong motive for murder.'

'They'd have to be the apples of the Hesperides,' Blair agreed, nodding deeply.

'We can probably assume that they weren't,' said Murray. He sighed. 'Shall we wait until the sheriff comes?'

'We probably should.'

'Then let's wait outside. But I think I'll tell him I'm taking these three things – the bowl, the box and the mirror – up to the house for safety until someone comes to claim them. Even if there were a lock on that door, it's not much of a defence against thieves.'

They picked up the three items between them: the bowl and box fitted into Blair's bottomless pockets, and Murray carried the mirror carefully, wrapped in a brownish cloth that at least seemed dry and not too noisome. Outside the boys were still waiting, not willing to enter the cottage but at the same time reluctant to leave. If anything they seemed relieved to see Murray and Blair appear safely.

'Charlie,' Murray addressed the chief boy casually, 'none of you picked up a rope this morning in the course of your journey down here from school, did you?'

'A rope?' Charlie reflected. 'I dinna think so, sir. We flew down: I dinna think a'body picked up a'thing.'

'Hm. I wonder who did, then?'

Chapter Two

The main kitchen in Letho House was silent, or as silent as a kitchen can be. Not that it was unpopulated, for William and Daniel were by the fire, tying each other's neckcloths, Walter, the boy, sat under the cap of his chestnut hair on a creepie stool, watching, and Iffy the kitchenmaid was at the kitchen table, as angular and motionless as a fireiron. Mrs. Mack was making a sugar sculpture: it was not going well, and no one had enough of a death wish to speak.

Mrs. Mack, along with most of the staff, had been retained at Letho during the laird's absence in India, and being unchallenged by cooking for the servants had decided to teach herself sugar sculpture. It was a chancy business: sometimes it went beautifully, and sometimes awfully, but she had convinced herself that the mistress, Lady Agostinella, appreciated such sophistication, so any time Letho hosted a dinner, Mrs. Mack tried her hand at another construction. It did not entirely help that as she was a person of diminutive height, she had to stand on a stool to reach the tops of her sculptures. Iffy, who was taller, could certainly not be relied upon for anything approaching sophistication.

A long, silvery thread trailed from her spoon, and she stretched it slowly until it seemed like a concrete form of all the tension in the room. Gently, painfully, she drew it out, until at last it met the peak of the structure. She attached it with pinpoint accuracy, lifted the spoon away, and leaned back.

'Mr. Robbins?' she called, quietly. Robbins, head manservant, appeared at once around the corner of the doorframe. 'It is done.'

The whole kitchen let out a collective breath. On the table was a fair representation of a hare, its long ears woven back and forth, and two berries set in as dark, shining eyes.

'It's lovely, Mrs. Mack!' whispered Iffy reverently.

'At least it looks easy to carry,' Robbins commented. 'Where would you like it?'

'In the dining room, please, Mr. Robbins – as long as you remember to close the doors.'

'Of course.' Robbins eased the hare on its ashet off the kitchen table, and carried it at funereal pace out of the kitchen. At a nod from him Walter hurried after, to open doors.

'Well, that's that,' said Mrs. Mack, suddenly business-like. 'Now we can start on the rest of the dinner. There'll be fourteen at table, so we'll have sixteen dishes.' She started to list them, though it was more as a mnemonic to herself as Iffy's eyes glazed over after about four dishes. 'Oh, and tell that Agnes she can come back in now.'

'Agnes!' yelled Daniel, and everyone jumped.

'I had the idea you might go and fetch her, not summon her like a dog!' said Mrs. Mack with a glare. 'If I find that made Mr. Robbins drop my sugar confection, I'll have you sent to the East Indies!'

'He won't have,' said Daniel, grinning at William. 'Mr. Robbins is far too calm for that. Nothing frightens him.'

Agnes appeared in the doorway.

'Is it all right if I come back in now, then?' she asked. Dead straight ginger hair sat neatly under her white cap, and her dove grey maid's gown, still showing signs of having been taken in and up for her, hung well with the white apron over the top. No one had any complaints about her appearance, anyway.

'Yes, yes: you can help Iffy with the vegetables,' said Mrs. Mack. 'If Mrs. Dean has finished with you for now.'

'Aye, aye, everything's polished and pressed and arranged and swept,' said Agnes cheerfully. She had learned to speak a little more slowly than usual until they accustomed themselves to her Paisley accent. Mrs. Mack considered her, fixing her with her beady gaze.

'Ever make a fruit fool, the last place you were?'

'A fruit fool? Aye, I likely did. See, I always say that the pudding is the best bit of the meal, see, and well I don't much fancy fools myself, for there's not much to the swallowing of them, but aye, yes, I've made the odd fool. See -'

'Right,' said Mrs. Mack, breaking in firmly. 'There's apples in the scullery, so get them ready the way you would for a fool. Iffy, you do the carrots – and dinna peel them till there's nothing left the way you did the last time.' She sighed heavily: any other kitchenmaid would have learned the basics by now. Iffy had been breaking things for ten years already, and was instrumental in rendering Mrs. Mack's hair grey. But Agnes: well, there might be the makings in her, if she could ever stop talking.

'Agnes, what was that letter this morning?' asked William. Daniel made a 'Tch' noise of exasperation, but William shook his head. He was fascinated at Agnes' abilities to talk.

'The letter?' Agnes turned to him with a beaming smile. 'Oh, aye, that was from my friend Dorrie, well, I was the bridesmaid at her wedding, the second one that is, I wouldn't have wanted to be bridesmaid at her first one, you ken? Not that I ever said anything, well, you can't, can you? But I think she knew all the same, even then. And I was there when her brother came and loaded all he'd left her on to a cart and it wasn't much, I can tell you, and took it from Dalwhinnie to Kilwinning and that was that.'

'Aye,' William remarked, which was all that was needed.

'Who's Dorrie?' asked Daniel, unable to resist, despite himself. Agnes took a deep breath.

'Dorrie's my cousin Mina's best friend's sister's neighbour, that's how we met, and we were as close as could be for as I say I was her bridesmaid that time and I stayed the whole month only then her husband very kindly paid my coach back to Paisley which was more than good of him and walked me to the coach himself with my bags –'

'Agnes, dear,' came a new voice from the door, 'that's enough now.'

'Yes, Mrs. Dean,' said Agnes, unabashed. 'I'll do those apples now, Mrs. Mack.'

'Oh, that's good of you,' said Mrs. Mack with sour irony, cutting butter into flour for the pastry. 'All well, Mrs. Dean?'

The housekeeper pattered into the kitchen and began a quick tour of inspection: Daniel and William stood unnaturally smartly while she flicked at their neckcloths, and held their boots out for her to see the shine, even though their presentation was really Mr. Robbins' department.

'Yes, I believe so,' she said to Mrs. Mack. 'All well in your work?'

'Aye, aye. Fourteen to dine, isn't that right?'

'That's what I've been told. The master and mistress, Mr. Blair and Miss Blair, Mr. and Mrs. Grant, Mr. Lovie, Sir John and Lady Aytoun and Miss Aytoun, the minister and the doctor and their wives.'

'We havena met the Aytouns, I think,' Mrs. Mack commented, though as cook she was unlikely to meet them anyway. 'Did I see them at the kirk on the Sabbath?'

'I believe so. Staying at Collessie: they've rented it.'

'Not a bad looking young lassie – lady, I mean,' said Mrs. Mack. 'Why for is she not gallivanting around Edinburgh for the season, looking a husband?'

'I have no idea, Mrs. Mack,' said Mrs. Dean, with a smile. 'Maybe she has hopes of finding one in Letho!'

Both women laughed, and Mrs. Mack added,

'I canna think who that would be, then! The only available gentleman round here is young Mr. Lovie – unless she likes the idea of that creature that's come to help the minister.'

'Mr. Rintoul? Oh, I forgot – he's to come this evening, too. So that's fifteen – so sorry.'

'Not at all, Mrs. Dean, not at all. I can easy stretch at this stage.'

'I'll just go and check that the table is laid for fifteen. I'm glad you asked, Mrs. Mack! Poor Mr. Rintoul,' she said, and vanished from the kitchen with her usual energy.

As if they were swapping with each other, Robbins appeared in the same moment, along with Smith, Blair's man. The servants' wing was full at present, with all the visiting staff as well as the household: it was just as well that Robbins, Daniel and William had all moved out of the wing to nearby houses when they had married. Smith, though, having visited with his master for years, was as close to being household as not.

'There's tea in the pot,' Mrs. Mack called over to the men. 'Not for you two,' she added to Daniel and William, 'you've had plenty. You canna be standing and waiting on table this evening if you've had too much tea, you should ken that well enough.'

'Am I to wait table this evening, too?' asked young Walter, all of eleven or twelve. Robbins regarded him as Smith poured two cups of tea.

'Do you think you're ready?' he asked solemnly. Walter considered.

'I maybe am,' he said with care. 'As long as I don't have to remember too much.'

'Well, that's as close to self-knowledge as any of the three of you is likely to come,' said Robbins, 'and you're a deal more sensible than Daniel. Besides, her Ladyship has asked specially for you.'

'Oh.'

'It's all right,' said Daniel comfortably. 'She'll likely forget. Women in her condition are always forgetting things.'

'Well, you would know,' William put in boldly. 'Since you brought Artemisia home from Naples the poor woman has hardly not been expecting, has she? Anyone would think you're trying to fill Letho with Italians.'

'Aye, well,' Daniel looked tremendously pleased with himself. 'Some of us just can't help –'

'That's enough, Daniel,' said Robbins severely. 'Go home and take your daughter with you – I saw her in the hall again – and don't get your livery dirty. I'll see you back here at half past four. William, you too: go home and see Effy. Walter … you'd better change into your best livery, then, and we'll see how you manage.'

The three menservants left the kitchen, mostly enthusiastically. Smith raised his eyebrows and settled back with his cup of tea balanced against his waistcoat.

'You'd hardly think those two lads were married and all, would you?'

'I doubt they'll ever grow up,' Robbins agreed. He himself had grown up very young, settling into middle age straight away.

'I dinna ken how that Artemisia puts up with Daniel,' put in Mrs. Mack. 'I wouldna.'

'Few of us would,' agreed Robbins.

'How does he manage with your new housekeeper? She seems a sharp one,' said Smith.

'She does, doesn't she?' Robbins, normally discreet about household matters, did not mind discussing them with Smith. 'She seems to take him in her stride. She doesn't seem to be particularly charmed by him, anyway.'

'Oh, young Daniel is very specific who he charms, and I canna say he's ever gone for an older woman. Not that Mrs. Dean isn't fair bonny still,' Mrs. Mack added kindly.

'Aye, you're right there,' said Smith. 'Fair bonny.'

'That's maybe not so good in a housekeeper. But there, she seems sensible. And she has energy, I'll grant her that,' said Mrs. Mack, who in fact was prepared to grant the new housekeeper quite a bit. 'She had the stillroom here turned out within a week of coming here – you can imagine what it was like, with poor Mrs. Chambers so confused the last few years, and then a while without a housekeeper at all. But it wasn't long before she had it all bright and tidy again. She canna sit still for long, that's true.'

'Where was she before?' Smith was a bachelor, and Robbins worried for a moment that he might be interested in taking their new housekeeper away for his own use.

'Glasgow direction,' he said shortly.

'She has no accent.'

'Well, she was from Fife before that. Dunfermline, that way.'

'So she's come home? Or close,' said Smith.

'Near enough, indeed.'

Smith seemed to have run out of questions for the moment, and both men sat and drank their tea. Smith had just poured himself another cup when they heard a bell ring in the passage outside.

'That'll be Mr. Blair,' Smith remarked, and swallowed his tea in a gulp. 'I'd better start getting him ready for dinner.'

'If he's back then Mr Murray will be, too,' said Robbins, draining his own tea cup.

'Aye, but yours won't take half as long to redd up as mine will, will he?' said Smith, with a fond grin. He knew few people had a master quite like his. 'The things I've found in his pockets over the years – it would gar you grue, Mrs. Mack, as I'm sure I've told you before now!'

Mrs. Mack shuddered dramatically, wiggling her fat little shoulders.

'Dinna tell me while I'm cooking, Mr. Smith, for my stomach is delicate nowadays!'

'Well, I'm off,' he said. 'I'll see you later on.'

Mrs. Mack glanced up at Robbins when Smith left.

'I heard there were fourteen this evening but then Mrs. Dean said fifteen.'

'Oh, aye?' Robbins counted in his head. 'Did you remember Mr. Rintoul?'

'I did later. Funny wee man.' Robbins thought Rintoul must be twice Mrs. Mack's height, but made no comment. He was not above the middle height himself. 'Mrs. Dean went then to see if the table was laid for fourteen or fifteen.'

'Fifteen, I'm sure. But she'll sort it out if it isn't.' He sighed. 'It's very good to have a full staff again, isn't it?'

'It is that, Mr. Robbins. I miss Mrs. Chambers, for the pair of us worked together a long time, but I like Mrs. Dean very well.'

'Good, good.' He thought about Mary, who might have been housekeeper instead at one point. Now she was his wife, and he had not seen her since breakfast. 'I'm going to go over home for half an hour, Mrs. Mack, but I'll come back if you need me.'

'Aye, you do that, Mr. Robbins. The girls are here anyway: one of them can run across for you if the bell goes.' She nodded at the scullery. 'Agnes is making a fool, and Iffy still is one.' She sighed.

Robbins stood to go, and just at that moment Mrs. Dean hurried back in. Her face, Robbins thought, was a little pale.

'That's – that's a splendid sugar sculpture, Mrs. Mack. You've outdone yourself, you know!'

'Thank you very much,' said Mrs. Mack, with a little curtsey, her hands coated in dough. Mrs. Dean blinked a few times.

'A hare, is it?'

'That's right.'

'An unusual fancy, for a sugar confection. A hare, eh? What made you think of that?' Robbins, paused in the doorway, thought that Mrs. Dean's voice was also less steady than usual.

'I dinna ken,' Mrs. Mack replied, plump little hands back in the bowl. 'Mebbe I saw one this morning, or something like that.'

'Maybe you did, indeed …' Mrs. Dean seemed to pull herself together. 'Well, splendid, as I say, splendid!'

Robbins nodded in agreement, and went home to see his wife.

Chapter Three

Murray rang the bell for Robbins, and looked around his bedchamber for somewhere to put the mirror he had brought from Widow Maggot's cottage. Blair, as far as he knew, still had the box and the bowl, though by now Smith would probably have excavated them from Blair's capacious and mysterious pockets. He set the mirror at an angle on the mantelpiece, its handle sideways, and began to take his coat off, flinging it down and running his long fingers through his dark hair to rub the cares of the day away. The mirror frame alone was probably worth a few shillings, maybe more. What was the story of Widow Maggot? And why had he never wondered before? She had been there all his life, in her dark little house, in her grey lace cap, only emerging, as far as he ever knew, to terrorise passing schoolboys. Well, the schoolboys had had the last laugh today, though thinking of the look on Rab's face as he headed off to the inn for his hot brandy, Murray wondered if in fact it had been Widow Maggot's last laugh. Why would anyone have killed her, though? It seemed that they would need to know a great deal more about her to find out who might have found it necessary to strike her over the head.

He thought about that. It had been a sure blow, just the one strike – no hesitation? Had she gone to the door and been struck down before she even knew who her visitor was? Or had someone been visiting – even staying with her, and then a quarrel had arisen? Who visited her? It occurred to him that both the minister and the doctor would be coming to dinner, along with their wives, the people in the village most likely to know something of her. Hot broth in the winter, gentle administrations of basic medical treatment, questions as to suitability for admission to communion – all these would be available later. He undid his neckcloth and set it down on his coat, and heard Robbins arriving in his dressing room with his hot water.

In a few moments he was blissfully immersed in his bath, blinking in the steam, washing away the chill of an autumn afternoon out of doors. It had been an unexpectedly fine few days, and he had relished being outside, feeling good clean air in his lungs. Robbins had retreated to his bed chamber and was tidying his clothes, but the connecting door was open.

'What do you know of the Widow Maggot?' Murray called.

'Well, she was found dead today, sir, is that your interest?'

'As usual, news travels on wings of great speed around this parish.'

'Daniel brought word back from the inn just now.'

'He seems to spend a good deal of his time in there at the moment.'

Robbins' mouth twisted slightly.

'Yes, sir.'

'I feel guilty that I don't know much more than that about her. She seems to have been an old woman all my life. What do you know?'

There was a pause. Judging by the sounds, Robbins was brushing at Murray's breeches while he considered.

'As you say, sir, she's been there a very long time. I think I remember seeing her in the kirk once or twice, but years ago now. In the old minister's time, not in Mr. Helliwell's, when I was a boy.'

'I don't think I've ever seen her away from her cottage. Have you ever been inside it, Robbins?'

'I don't think I'd fancy that, sir.'

'No, it was pretty fragrant. Cluttered with stuff, some of it quite valuable, I think. An earth floor and the thatch long past repair.'

'So if she had valuables, was she killed by a burglar, sir?'

'It didn't look like it. There was plenty of dust on things so it was easy to see if anything was missing, and all we could see that might be gone seemed to be a crate of apples.'

'Apples, sir?'

'Yes. There was a rectangular indentation on the floor in a corner and the air smelled of apples.'

'Hm.' A longer pause followed. 'I think she used to be friendly enough with Lizzie Fenwick – the midwife, you know, sir?'

'Oh, yes. That's – reassuring, in a way. In a place like Letho, everyone seems to fit into a pattern – you know, connexions here and there. It's a bit unnerving to realise that there is someone who doesn't have a pattern to fit into.' He pulled himself up out of the bath and reached for a towel, drying himself quickly and flinging on a clean shirt.

'Sir?'

'Yes?'

'This mirror, sir. Where did it appear from?'

'Oh, from Widow Maggot's cottage. As I said, she had some valuable things and the door has a piece of string for a latch, so I arranged with the sheriff's man to bring a few of them up here for safety until we know what is to happen to her belongings.'

Robbins appeared in the doorway, his pale face frowning.

'I'm sorry, sir, I know it's fanciful, but I can't help feeling that it's watching me. I mean, you know when you know someone is watching you? I have that but when I turn around to see, all I see is the mirror.'

Murray raised his eyebrows: that, from Robbins, was a lengthy speech.

'Well, come back in here, now: I'm ready to be shaved anyway. Maybe later I'll move it in here.'

'Yes, sir.'

When he was ready, Murray went to his wife's room and knocked on the door. The little maid, still looking as unsure of herself as she ever had, answered it.

'Is your mistress available?' Murray asked in Italian. The maid nodded and curtseyed, opening the door fully to let him in. With one thing he could not fault his wife, he thought: she rarely denied him an audience, even if he sometimes suspected she only wanted to complain about things to him.

She was at her dressing table, and he approached and dutifully kissed her hand.

'I hope I find you well this evening?' He switched to French, her first language.

'Passable, passable,' she said, and even favoured him with a slight smile. He risked taking a seat on a stool beside her. Her maid returned and took up Lady Agostinella's hair brush, presumably continuing where his arrival had interrupted her. Lady Agostinella's hair was fine to the point of cobwebs, with no shine or silk to it, so fair as to seem grey. Even pregnancy, which in her case was well advanced, did not seem to give her the bloom it did to Daniel's wife, for instance. True, she was worried: they both were. She had never carried a child this long before, and now her time was near. It did not make their marriage any less tense.

'But I hear,' she said suddenly, watching him in the mirror, 'that there has been a murder in the village?'

How on earth had she heard that? As far as anyone knew, she only spoke to Murray and her maid, and her maid only spoke Italian.

'An old woman,' Lady Agostinella continued. 'I do not like this.'

'I'm not sure anyone is particularly pleased by it,' said Murray. 'Though she seems to have had no relatives …'

'It is distressing, a murder so close by. Who knows what else might happen? Once I believed that you sought out such terrible things, but on consideration I wonder if indeed they seek you out instead?'

'I really couldn't say,' said Murray.

'I want to move.'

'To move rooms? Certainly: of course we have all our visitors, but I'm sure –'

'To move from Letho. It is not healthy, murder.'

'Certainly not for the victim,' muttered Murray before he could stop himself. She glared at him. 'Anyway, don't you think it would be even less healthy to move at present? Where would you go? Pitcaithly, for the waters?'

'A common watering spot? I think not.' She reflected, staring now at her own image in the glass. The maid knotted her hair into an elaborate concoction like a grey version of one of Mrs. Mack's sugars, then fixed it in place with a pin decorated with grey pearls. Heavens, did the woman never wear anything cheerful? Murray thought irritably.

'Perhaps you should have a word with Dr. Feilden this evening. I'm sure he will advise you to stay where you are – the house, after all, is not the village – but if he says you are fit to travel then by all means, we shall think of somewhere you would be comfortable.'

He rose, still gazing down at her. Had she ever been attractive? Had there ever been a man who had loved her? He sighed, suddenly inexpressibly sad.

'I'll leave you in peace to finish dressing,' he said. 'I look forward to seeing you downstairs.'

The Blairs, usually prompt, were already in the drawing room when he went down. As he had known Blair all his life, so he knew Isobel, his daughter, who despite a couple of early proposals was still unmarried in her middle twenties, and showed no signs of feeling upset by it.

'Have you and Father been out searching for dead bodies again?' Isobel greeted him with a mocking sigh. 'Surely you have seen enough murder victims to last the lifetime of any sane person?'

Murray took a glass of punch from a tray and went to stand by the fire.

'Well, perhaps you have hit on the problem,' he replied smoothly. 'Perhaps you are accusing your respected father – and indeed your generous host – of insanity.'

'Perhaps she ought to have more consideration of her inheritance,' added Blair solemnly, nodding at his daughter.

'Perhaps I shall find myself a wealthy husband with a less peculiar hobby than solving mysterious deaths.'

'You would find him terribly dull, my dear,' said Blair with certainty, and Murray agreed.

'Oh, perhaps you are right,' Isobel conceded. She sipped her punch with appreciation, though she knew if she had too much her cheeks would go pink: the drawback that went with the reddish hints in her brown hair. 'Anyway, no doubt the fair Miss Matilda would snatch any available husband from me before I had the chance to give him any encouragement. Has anyone seen Tilly Aytoun? Is she fair?'

'You must judge for yourself,' said Murray. 'And you no doubt will.'

'She's a pretty girl,' said Blair, 'but perhaps not a beauty, in the classic sense.'

'Well, she's young: she's bound to have some charm,' said Murray, who was feeling old.

'Does young Lovie have much fortune to his name?' asked Blair suddenly, deliberately not looking at Isobel.

'Father!'

'He has something from his late father, I believe. And he certainly has the charms of youth.'

'Too young, indeed, and callow, for me,' said Isobel firmly. Her father sighed.

'I shall never be rid of her, Charles. Find me a husband for my daughter, dear boy, or I shall never be free!'

The door opened, and all three exchanged a quick look, meaning that they must now behave themselves.

'Charles, dear boy, good evening to you!'

'Good evening, Cousin Andrew.'

Murray bowed to the older man – older and wider, and with rather more worry-lines on his brow. His father's cousin Andrew Grant was a barrister in London, a position that did not seem to do much for one's health or peace of mind. His slim legs and heavy torso gave him the look of an anxious beetle. The woman who followed him into the drawing room was around the same age, with a good intelligent face and a handsome figure, but something of the same illness-at-ease that Murray did not like to see on the face of a guest. Did she fear that coming from London society she would find herself adrift in Scotland? He resolved to do more to make her feel at home, and pay her a little more attention than he had for the first day of their visit. He was not well acquainted with his cousin, and even less so with his cousin's wife, as they were not long married. Robert Lovie, the young man who followed them into the room, had come with the package as a stepson.

'I hope you have had a good day?' Murray asked, guiding Mrs. Grant attentively to a seat by the fire but addressing the question generally.

'Oh, as much as one can when one brings one's work with one!' said Andrew Grant with a friendly smile. 'I had a great deal to read, unfortunately.'

'But Miss Blair and I had a delightful time in the vineries, drawing and painting,' added his wife, who seemed genuinely pleased with her day.

'Too chilly to sit outside, despite the perfect light,' Isobel added.

Murray wondered how good an artist Mrs. Grant was: Isobel, he knew, would have filled her pages with intricate vines, and added telling little portraits of the gardeners where she could snatch them.

'And you, Mr. Lovie – are you an artist, too?' Murray asked. The young man laughed.

'Sadly, not much of one! I spent a good deal of the day with this lovely piano here, practising. It is a beautiful instrument,' he added appreciatively.

'Thank you,' said Murray, pleased. 'My mother was very musical, and the instrument was bought for her.'

'But you play, I believe, sir?' said the boy.

'Yes, indeed – it's far too tempting not to!'

There was a noise of voices and footsteps on the landing and Robbins entered to announce the arrival of the Rev. Mr. and Mrs. Helliwell, and Dr. and Mrs. Feilden, and Murray tried not to interrogate them straight away about poor Widow Maggot. Instead he made himself introduce them to the Grants and saw to it that they had punch in plenty.

'Great good luck we all arrived together,' the doctor was saying. 'Mr. Helliwell left early on foot, while we took Mrs. Helliwell in the gig. Just room for three!'

Mrs. Helliwell directed an apologetic glance at her husband, who glared back. Oh, dear, Murray thought: Helliwell in a temper. But Mrs. Helliwell always did her best to make up for it. Another figure appeared unexpectedly behind Helliwell, ginger hair forming a crispy halo about his head.

'Ah, Mr. Rintoul! I'm delighted you could join us,' said Murray. Rintoul bowed nervously, with a glance at Helliwell: presumably the minister had been lecturing his assistant on the way to Letho House. Helliwell looked as if he was working himself up to rant about something when again there were voices outside, and Robbins reappeared.

'Sir John and Lady Aytoun, and Miss Aytoun,' he announced, with a discreet sweep of the room. Murray guessed he was looking for Agostinella: no point in announcing dinner until the hostess was present. Robbins met Murray's eye and Murray nodded. As far as he knew, Agostinella still intended to join them for dinner. He hoped she would enjoy it for once.

He had only met the Aytouns once since their arrival in Letho the previous week, having gone to pay his respects on Monday. Two tall, slim figures advanced into the room, but were pre-empted by a short, light woman who pattered forward and made her curtsey to Murray with quick grace.

'Dear Mr. Murray! How lovely! So kind of you to invite us to your beautiful home!'

'Lady Aytoun, the honour is mine,' said Murray, bowing. 'Sir John, thank you for coming. Miss Aytoun,' he added, with another bow. Miss Aytoun was looking about her with surprise.

'But this is a lovely house!' she exclaimed, as if she had expected something quite different.

'We do our best,' said Murray drily, then began the task of introducing the rest of his guests. He hoped that Sir John and Andrew would find subjects in common: he had a notion that Sir John had something to do with the law, but when he glanced round to bring them together he was surprised at the look of alarm on Andrew Grant's face. He looked back. None of the Aytoun family seemed to have noticed. Andrew met his wife's eye discreetly – if Murray had not been watching he would not have seen the quick, desperate flash – then turned back to greet Sir John as smoothly as anyone.

They had only just settled to their punch, particularly welcome on an autumn evening, when the door opened wide and Lady Agostinella made her entrance, like something come to haunt them. Lady Aytoun hurried to be introduced, and Agostinella was pleasingly condescending, as much as she saw fit for a de Cumae de Palaeopolitani to be towards the mere wife of a Scottish baronet. She walked heavily to Murray's side and he felt her weight on his arm.

'Shall we go down?' she asked, an instruction phrased as a question.

Lady Aytoun and Mrs. Grant were instantly sympathetic and rose quickly to follow their hostess to the dining room. The guests sorted themselves into pairs, with Blair escorting Lady Aytoun, and Rintoul, almost forgotten, taken under Isobel's wing. Helliwell was left as the odd man, scowling to himself despite his wife's entreating looks.

There was no point in trying to introduce the subject of Widow Maggot over the dinner table: it would only lead to a conflict with Agostinella which would not reflect well on either of them. Instead there was much conversation about the unusually pleasant weather, and what might be done with it for the further entertainment of the party.

'I gather St. Andrews is very close,' said Mrs. Grant. 'A fine university, I believe.'

'Well, I must agree with that, as one of its alumni,' smiled Murray. 'But perhaps the coast would be a little too brisk in October for a pleasant stroll.'

'We went there on Tuesday,' Sir John put in. 'Bitterly cold.' He made an expressive gesture with one slim hand to go with the little scrunch of his handsome face.

'But so lovely!' said his wife, eyes wide.

'Anyway, we always go to St. Andrews,' said Isobel. 'A change would be agreeable.'

'Is Falkland too far? I gather it is very picturesque,' said Andrew Grant.

'It's a little far,' agreed Murray, 'at this time of year, with the length of the day.'

'What about Josie's Den?' said Blair suddenly.

'Josie's Den? I have never heard of it,' said Mrs. Grant with interest.

'It's certainly picturesque,' agreed Isobel, probably packing her drawing materials in her head.

'A fascinating place,' agreed the Rev. Mr. Helliwell, who seemed to have cheered up. 'Rintoul, you should go too. I'm not sure I have time myself, but it would be educational for you.'

'Educational and picturesque and not too far – it sounds perfect!' said Mrs. Grant. 'Will you be able to come, Lady Aytoun?'

'Oh, it sounds lovely!' Lady Aytoun turned wide, pleading eyes on her husband.

'It sounds charming,' said Sir John smoothly. 'And it would certainly be good to make the most of this weather.'

'It won't last much longer,' put in Mrs. Helliwell, who was an experienced gardener. 'Three days at most, I should think.'

'Then shall we say tomorrow?' asked Murray. 'The Grants, the Aytouns, the Blairs – we can talk about carriages. Mrs. Helliwell? Mrs. Feilden?'

Both ladies claimed prior engagements, and their husbands pleaded work.

'Mr. Rintoul, then, if Mr. Helliwell has given you permission?'

'I'd be delighted, sir, if you are sure I shall not be in anyone's way.'

'Of course not. My dear?' He turned to Agostinella, and knew her answer straightaway.

'I shall not be of the party.'

'Of course not – very sensible, Lady Agostinella,' said Mrs. Helliwell.

'Then I shall speak to Robbins about picnics,' said Murray, and all was settled.

The gentlemen did not leave the ladies too long after dinner, though Murray had the impression that Sir John would have been perfectly content to lounge at the dining table with his port for an hour or so, holding forth on several topical subjects with authority. Blair had engaged Rintoul in a conversation on theology, which seemed to encourage the young man. Helliwell and Feilden exchanged complaints about a spate of thefts in the village, which they blamed on the schoolboys, and in which Murray knew he was going to have to become involved at some point: he remembered Mal Johnstone's missing rope. Young Robert Lovie was happy to talk of music and of the season in London, though there was no mention, specifically, of why during the London season he and his parents had decided to visit a distant relative in Fife. Murray did not want to keep Agostinella long in the drawing room if she was tired, so before even his own inclinations he led the men back upstairs where he could hear some cheerful chatter, to his relief.

Isobel had clearly been designated, as next youngest, to keep Miss Aytoun in conversation until the men arrived. Robert Lovie immediately joined them: Andrew Grant went to his wife, and Murray noticed her touching his hand as if in reassurance, though her own face wore an expression of – assessment, he decided, puzzled. Sir John chose to sit by his hostess, and seemed to be explaining to her at some length the characteristics of *Tristram Shandy*. Blair and Rintoul were still in debate and the doctor and minister still grumbling, which left Murray free to make his enquiries.

'Mrs. Helliwell, Mrs. Feilden,' he began affably, pulling a stool over to sit before them as if he were to consult a friendly oracle. 'You'll have heard the sad news about Widow Maggot?'

'Aye, indeed,' said Mrs. Helliwell.

'Murdered, someone said?' asked Mrs. Feilden. 'Now, why on earth would anyone do that?'

'No doubt Mr. Murray will find out,' said Mrs. Helliwell, with a grin. 'No doubt it was a robbery.'

'What do you know about her?' Murray asked, refusing to rise to it.

'Well, she's been there a good deal longer than I have,'

'Or I,' added Mrs. Feilden, who had been born in the village. 'I believe she has always been old, don't you think?' She sounded half serious.

'What of Mr. Maggot? Do you remember him?'

'I'm not even sure there was one,' said Mrs. Helliwell. 'I never heard her speak of him.'

'Or of any other relations?'

Both women looked at each other.

'I'm not sure I was ever even in her cottage - not that I much fancied the idea!' said Mrs. Feilden comfortably. 'We only exchanged a few words if we met in the street – and I'm not even sure I can remember the last time that happened. I haven't seen her for years, I believe.'

'She allowed me to visit her every Friday,' said Mrs. Helliwell, 'but I was only allowed to take her as much broth as would do one meal. And she was never one for chatting when she took it. I don't believe she needed it, or me, at all: it was just to stop me pushing in and interfering, I think.' She gave a self-deprecating smile. 'It made me think about the other people I visit, mind you! Where was I interfering, unwanted, rather than being as useful as I should be? A very salutary lesson. But she always had plenty of food in the house – good food, too – and I don't know where it came from. And I never knew her to be ill.'

'No,' Mrs. Feilden agreed. 'She certainly never called for my husband all the time he's practised here.'

'Interesting …' said Murray. 'Not, on the whole, very useful, but interesting,' he added to himself. Behind him he heard a lighter arpeggio on the beautiful piano and turned in delight. Mathilda Aytoun was waiting to catch his eye.

'May I? Please, Mr. Murray? I have brought my music.'

'Of course you may.'

Mathilda posed herself on the piano stool like a minor Greek goddess, and arranged quite a collection of music books on the stand. Murray looked about for a seat and found one beside Robert Lovie.

'Oh, excuse me, Mr. Murray,' said Lovie politely, 'I was just about to offer my services in turning pages.' He rose and stood attentively by the piano, with an appreciative look down at Mathilda's long white neck.

'Perhaps not quite so callow, if yet young,' said a voice beside him, and he realised that Isobel had been sitting on the other side of Robert Lovie. 'A charming boy, in fact.'

'I hope you're not too charmed,' said Murray, severely. Isobel grinned.

'Still too young for me. I shall appreciate him from a dignified distance, and watch his courtship of young Miss Aytoun with indulgence.'

Miss Aytoun had begun to play and she fell silent, knowing that Murray would hush her otherwise. Mathilda Aytoun was indeed quite pretty: she was tall and willowy, with soft, glossy dark curls and pink cheeks in an ivory face, probably owing more to nature than to powder as her father's complexion was very similar. Her eyes were dark and liquid, and her mouth was a perfect little flower. In fact, thought Murray, if she had deliberately modelled herself on a French fashion plate, she could hardly have done better. Her playing was nothing more than adequate, but she was certainly a pleasure to look at.

'Are you going to delight us this evening?' he asked Isobel as they politely applauded Mathilda's third song.

'Yes indeed,' said Isobel. 'I shall delight you in my usual manner by not playing at all.'

'Excellent,' said Murray. 'That was what I had hoped. Oh, look: you may appreciate this performer.'

Robert Lovie had now taken to the piano with Mathilda to turn the pages, and his performance was significantly better than hers. He played and sang with some talent, finished with a flourish and stood as if ready to leap across the room.

'Mr. Murray, this piano is a delight!'

'I'm glad you like it!' called Murray as everyone laughed, including Lovie.

'Now, Mr. Rintoul,' said Mrs. Helliwell, 'if I accompany you, will you sing your little song?'

'Oh, I'm not sure the company is ...' said Mr. Rintoul, blushing to clash with his ginger halo.

'The company is strong, they can take it,' snapped Mr. Helliwell with a marked lack of charity. It was the minister's job not only to oversee the final stages of his assistant's church training, but also to see him introduced into the kinds of society in which he might have to mingle. On this occasion, Helliwell appeared to be gritting his teeth.

'Of course, Mr. Rintoul,' said Lady Agostinella with unusual grace. 'Sing us your little song.'

Mr. Rintoul stumbled to the piano and waited, fidgeting, while Mrs. Helliwell stretched her gardening fingers into pianist shapes. Though he had to start twice, and apologised with painful fervour both times, in the end the song was apt and his voice pleasant, and no one regretted encouraging him.

'We cannot let the gentlemen have it all their own way, though, can we?' asked Mrs. Grant. 'Miss Blair, surely you will play for us?'

'Oh!' said Agostinella abruptly, '*I* shall play.'

She waded over to the piano, and established herself behind it.

'So what are we to expect at Josie's Den?' Sir John asked Mr. Helliwell as Agostinella flicked through her music.

'I suppose it's very romantic,' said Helliwell heavily.

'In one sense, yes,' added his wife. 'It is supposed by many to have links with the local witches.'

'Witches?' Mathilda Aytoun gave a little squeak.

'Oh, yes, dear, but don't worry. They were all cast out by the power of the Kirk years ago!' She slid a teasing look at her husband, who scowled.

'So romantic! Lovely!' exclaimed Lady Aytoun, and Murray could sense Isobel suppress a giggle.

Lady Agostinella quelled the room with a glance and began to play. Everyone listened, first with obedience, then with appreciation. She really was a consummate musician, even if, Murray thought, she always chose such funereal music. He watched her and wondered if she would ever be happy here. Maybe when she had a child? He offered up a silent prayer, one of many, for that child.

The music ended and everyone applauded enthusiastically, though Isobel leaned over to Murray to murmur,

'Is there a musical direction *dreichissimo*?'

He was about to think of some cutting reply when Mathilda Aytoun screamed.

Everyone jumped, and spun to where she was pointing.

'What? What is it?'

'A face!' she cried, and the pink in her cheeks had vanished. 'I saw a face at the window!'

Chapter Four

It was still dark in the morning when the servants assembled in the kitchen to organise the picnic, but then it was October.

'A picnic at this time of year!' sighed Mrs. Mack, who rarely went out of doors if she could help it. She had been up making pies for a couple of hours already, which at least meant that the kitchen was warm.

'I heard Miss Aytoun from over Collessie saw a face at the window last night after dinner!' hissed Iffy, thrilled. She was picking at the remains of the sugar hare, aided by little Maria, who had an ear in each hand and was sucking them alternately under the firwood table.

'It was likely her own reflection,' said Mrs. Mack dismissively.

'They'd no doubt worked her up with talk of Widow Maggot's death,' remarked Robbins, sensibly. 'There couldn't possibly have been a face at the window, unless someone had a ladder out.'

'Did anyone go to see if anyone had a ladder out?' asked Iffy, breathlessly.

Robbins tutted.

'Everyone had more sense. I closed the shutters and everyone had a cup of tea. Then they had a bit of dancing, and everything was fine.'

Mrs. Dean cleared her throat.

'I'm sure I don't have to remind you, but if you could all avoid talking about poor Widow Maggot in front of Agnes …'

'Oh, aye, of course,' said Robbins.

'Why?' asked Iffy, but squeaked as Robbins trod on her toe. Agnes had arrived in the kitchen. She spotted the hare straightaway.

'Oh, can I have some? It looks pure brilliant. I'm sure it tastes pure brilliant, too. See, an apple fool's all very well, but that, that's dead artistic, that is. And there's some chewing to it, and all.'

'Oh, give her some: maybe it'll stick her teeth together,' muttered Daniel, who was polishing his boots.

'Daniel, give me that straw,' said Mrs. Mack shortly.

'What are you going to weave that into?' he asked cheekily, bringing over a box of fresh straw that some reluctant stableboy had pushed through the outside door.

'It's for round the soup, you impudent child,' she retorted. 'Where are the picnic hampers? Have you found them?'

'I looked most places last night,' said Robbins, 'and I think they must be in the old cellars. Daniel, will you come and help me carry them?'

'Oh, Mr. Robbins, may I do that?' asked Mrs. Dean unexpectedly. 'I think the old cellars are the last place I have to see in this house. Do you know I haven't been able to find them?'

'Ah,' said Robbins. 'Well, I suppose it's not that obvious.'

He lifted and lit a lantern from a shelf, and led the way out of the kitchens and along the stone-flagged, whitewashed corridor of the servants' wing. At one point the corridor shook itself and turned right, the sconces on the walls casting angular shadows across the lantern's beams.

'You know we're in the main house now?' he asked, glancing back at her. The corridor was narrow.

'Yes, I think so.'

'And the servants' stairs are here, of course.' They spiralled upwards, giving access to the upper floors of Letho House. 'But have you been through this door?' He indicated the one at the foot of the stair.

'Yes, yes: it takes you down to a set of cellars – but surely they are the age of the house? And how are there older ones, anyway?'

'Well,' said Robbins, taking a key from his belt and opening the door, 'Mr. Murray's grandfather built Letho House, but he built it on the site of his old house – his castle, I should say. It was the times when the old wars were over, and a lot of gentlemen wanted a – a shatto, like the French, not a draughty fortress.'

'Much easier to keep clean, I should think,' agreed Mrs. Dean.

'But it was simpler to leave the cellars underneath, I suppose, and use them as part of the foundations of the new house. They're strong enough.' He led the way down an extension of the winding stair, through another, lower doorway, into a clean corridor beneath: here the lantern came into its own. It was almost a duplicate of the passage above, stone flagged and white washed, though less used.

'Well, I've been here before,' said Mrs. Dean.

'But did you look behind the door?' Robbins asked. He turned and closed the door they had just come through, to reveal a much older wooden door, lower still, behind it. The door was set behind a sturdy iron crisscrossed gate.

'What on earth did they keep down here?' Mrs. Dean demanded, cross with herself for having missed such a large detail.

'Well, prisoners,' said Robbins. 'It was the laird's prison, for the barony court. And in the days of the old wars, who knows who was down here?' He touched the iron gate gently: the metal was freezing cold. Mrs. Dean seemed to feel it too, and shivered.

'Are you sure the picnic hampers are in there?' she asked, almost in a whisper.

'I canna find them anywhere else,' Robbins shrugged. Even so, he hesitated before unlocking the iron gate, and then finding the heavy key for the inner door. The key turned with a mighty thud, and they both froze to listen, as if they were breaking in.

'Right, let's make this quick,' said Robbins at last. 'I mean, Mrs. Mack will want to have them packed as soon as can be.'

'Yes, yes indeed,' agreed Mrs. Dean. 'We mustn't waste time.'

They pushed the door open, lantern ahead of them like a shield.

'An odd smell,' Mrs. Dean remarked. Robbins had the impression she was trying to sound calm.

'Aye, it's always smelled like that. The damp, I suppose. Though it's out of the way of the old river we had so much trouble with. And to be honest, I wouldn't store the hampers down here if they'd ever shown signs of damp.' He thought he sounded nervous himself, and pressed his lips hard together.

Ahead was a rough stone chamber, with half a dozen or so iron loops in the walls and a sloping floor. There was another door beyond it, a little ajar.

'We'll not trouble with that today, I think,' said Robbins. 'There's nothing I've ever known in there.'

'Right, of course. I'll come down another day to inspect it, shall I?'

Robbins wondered if she would.

'And here are the hampers,' he added. Three large hinged baskets stood on a low stone shelf. 'Can you manage the small one and I'll take the other two, if you hold the lantern?'

'Of course.'

Even the small one was quite bulky, but she hooked her arm around it in such a way that she could manage the lantern with one hand. Robbins stacked the other two hampers and edged through the doorway, setting them down so that he could relock the door and gate when Mrs. Dean was clear. It was a matter of a few seconds before they were back up the stairs to the servants' wing, but it seemed to Robbins that they were both a little breathless, almost as if something had been chasing them. He gave a tiny smile to himself at such a fanciful thought, and followed Mrs. Dean back to the warmth and light of the kitchen.

'So who's going with the cart? It had better be me,' Daniel was saying, 'or I'd never have got up so early.'

'That's true,' remarked Mrs. Mack.

'You, William – when he turns up – and Agnes will go with the cart and get a fire going and a kettle on it,' said Robbins as he entered, setting the hampers down on the floor. Mrs. Dean perched hers on the top. 'Keep the hampers near to the fire – but watch they don't singe this time, eh? Set up the chairs and make sure you keep the cushions dry until the family arrives. I'll arrive with them and I'll see to the rest of the food.'

'You know what to do with the kedgeree, Mr. Robbins?' Mrs. Mack asked.

'Of course, Mrs. Mack. I won't spoil it.'

'Aye, aye,' she conceded.

'Well, where's William?' demanded Daniel self-righteously. 'I'm miles further away than he is, and I can get here on time!'

'I'm here, I'm here,' said William from the doorway, rubbing the tiredness from his face.

'So I'm going?' asked Agnes.

'Yes,' said Robbins patiently.

'And where are we going?'

'Josie's Den.'

'Aye, well, that makes a change, I suppose,' said William, helping himself to a chunk of bread from the food laid out for the servants. 'Though why anyone would want to go there on an October morning I canna think.'

Agnes was more enthusiastic.

'See, I think it's pure brilliant, off to Josie's Den for the day. I've never been to Josie's Den, have you? Was Josie a witch, d'you think? Because I've heard tell it's where witches hold their Sabbaths. Now, that's no good, but it's affa exciting, I think. I think if I met a witch, I'd scream. But then, I'm not sure there are any such things as witches any more, are you? I mean, I think if there were still witches –'

Daniel turned on her.

'Agnes, if you don't keep your mouth shut, I'll find any witch still in Fife and get her to turn you into a frog!'

Agnes considered this for all of a quarter of a second.

'See, I don't really like frogs. I think frogs –'

'AGNES!'

'What? Oh, aye.'

Daniel muttered under his breath.

'Now, behave, you three,' said Robbins: Daniel had a reputation as a womaniser, but he was quite sure that Agnes was safe from his attentions, and William was happily married. He had no concerns that way, but he did wonder if he would find Agnes upside down in a ditch to stop her talking. 'Are the hampers packed, Mrs. Mack?'

'Just this one,' said Mrs. Dean, holding straw back while Mrs. Mack held her breath lifting a pie into the smallest basket. 'That's us, I think.' The pie was smothered in a cloth, surrounded by wrapped warm loaves of fresh bread, and packed with more straw. William, Daniel and Robbins hefted a hamper each and took them out to the cart, which had already been packed with folding stools, rugs, cushions, a basket of crockery and cutlery, and lanterns. Agnes took a light for the cart, and went to have a word with the horse.

'You know your road? Even in the dark?' Robbins checked.

'Aye, aye,' said Daniel and William together: they had been born and brought up in Letho, anyway. 'Agnes,' added Daniel, 'get up and sit in the back and hold those hampers steady.' He caught

Robbins' eye, and added more quietly, 'We'll be less able to hear you from there.'

Agnes hopped up amongst the hampers and cushions, and made her little bony frame comfortable in a billow of winter cloak. William took the lit lantern from her and Daniel, the more confident driver, flicked the long rein to encourage the horse. Agnes waved an enthusiastic farewell until Robbins retreated to the servants' wing and closed the door. He was suddenly visited by a deep desire to return to his own warm bed: he must be getting old, though marriage also helped.

Back in the kitchen, though, Mrs. Dean was in a mood to talk. She and Mrs. Mack had helped themselves to cups of tea, and were taking a rare break.

'I'm sorry to be so anxious about Agnes,' Mrs. Dean was saying 'Will you join us, Mr. Robbins?'

'Where's Iffy?' he asked cautiously.

'Mrs. Robbins came in to help and she's taken Iffy to do the fires and the hot water upstairs.'

'Mrs. Robbins has come in?' asked Robbins, turning away to hide a helpless smile under cover of pouring himself a cup of tea.

'Dinna worry – the bairn's there,' said Mrs. Mack, watching him as she nodded to a settle near the fire. A bundle of blankets moved gently, and Robbins went to stand protectively by his son. He eased himself in beside the little boy's head and sat without waking him.

'I interrupted you,' he said to Mrs. Dean, not wishing to draw attention to himself.

'It's Agnes. I was saying I hope I'm not being over-anxious, but all this talk of Widow Maggot being murdered: I hope it does not upset her.'

'Remind me what happened in Glasgow?' said Mrs. Mack, gently gossipy.

'Well, according to the letter she brought, she saw some tramp murder a poor woman in the street. I cannot imagine what Glasgow must have come to,' she added fervently, 'though I believe it was near dusk.'

'Aye,' said Mrs. Mack.

'You see, the lady she worked for, Mrs. Cowley, she was my mistress a few years ago. Mr. Cowley was a banker in a small way, but when he died there was no money left and the fine house was shut up, and Mrs. Cowley had no more need for a housekeeper and the staff I had under me. She had no family – no children of her own, I mean. There was a brother about, but he was a shilpit character and not fit to take care of her. I decided to come home to Fife and seek a situation here. Mrs. Cowley retired, really, to Paisley, to a small house, with Agnes as a sort of cook – housemaid. She was not one of the staff I had – I think Mrs. Cowley had her through an agency.' She sighed at her old mistress's foolishness. Only those without hope found their servants through agencies. 'Is she any use at cooking, Mrs. Mack? I do wonder.'

'She's no bad, though if she were as good as she thinks she is I could go home now,' said Mrs. Mack sourly.

'Well, that's better than I expected. Anyway, I can only imagine Agnes must have been terribly upset at her experience if Mrs. Cowley sent her up here with no notice, only the letter in her pack and her kist coming after her.'

'Perhaps the tramp recognised Agnes?' suggested Robbins, quietly so as not to disturb the boy. Mrs. Dean's round eyebrows rose.

'There is a thought, Mr. Robbins. There is a thought indeed. Perhaps that is it: she is here for her own safety.'

'I think that's what Mr. Murray thought when he agreed to let her stay,' said Robbins. That, and the fact that he hadn't heard the way the girl could talk, he added to himself.

'Well, this is all very pleasant, but it's no going to get the breakfast on the table,' remarked Mrs. Mack, slapping her cup down on the side table. The boy stirred, and turned over comfortably against Robbins' leg. 'Stay you there, Mr. Robbins, till – till Mrs. Robbins comes back down.' She had never seen eye to eye with Mary, now Mrs. Robbins. Still, he thought, she was good to the boy. Mrs. Dean took his empty cup from him and hurried all three cups into the scullery to wash them. A bell rang from upstairs – Blair's room, Robbins realised, and after a moment he heard Smith stumble past the kitchen door, probably tying his neckcloth as he went. The day begins, he thought. He stroked his son's hair, and thanked his Maker for all his gifts.

Daniel was addressing his Maker, mostly silently, on an entirely different topic, and if his Maker had granted his requests, Agnes would by now be dead in a ditch or at the very least have her mouth miraculously sewn up by merciful angels. She was so distracting that he very nearly drove the horse and cart straight into a shadowy figure, heading the same direction as them on the road. He pulled up sharply.

'Hi!' he cried, unnerved by his own lack of concentration. 'Did you no hear us?'

The figure turned, and the light from the lantern caught his dished, shining face, mouth open in alarm. It was Mal Johnstone from the village.

'Who's that?' he demanded, shielding his eyes.

'It's the cart from Letho House, with Daniel and William,' said William.

'And Agnes!' she called from the back. Daniel rolled his eyes.

'Where are you off to?'

'To Cupar. I need a new rope: some lad from the school has made off with mine,' Mal explained.

'Want to climb up in the back? Mind the hampers, but if you get close to them they're gey warm,' Daniel recommended. 'We're going to Josie's Den.'

'That's a funny place to be going this time of year,' Mal commented, but he was soon up in the back of the cart. 'I must have been walking in my sleep – I never heard you come up behind till you yelled out.'

'See, that's what happened to my friend Mags,' said Agnes, irresistibly. 'She was walking along one morning minding her own business and bang up behind her there's a handcart, and she had no notion of it at all until she was half under the front wheels. And there's her leg, see, never the same again, though it's maybe better than the other one because that's the one that she hurt when she fell into the wee boat along the harbour but that was years ago, and the carter had the cheek to say she must be drunk but I never knew her take any drink at all, or not more than would warm her on a cold evening, as she said to me, and take away the pain of the leg – though maybe that was after she hurt the leg under the cart, or maybe it was the one she hurt falling into the wee boat –'

'So Josie's Den?' said Mal very quickly. 'What's taking you

there at this time of the year?'

'Oh, the high heidyins want a picnic,' said Daniel, with a shrug, though he appreciated the effort to stop Agnes. 'And they didna fancy St. Andrews with the wind off the sea, and there was some talk about how Josie's Den is picturesque. You ken Miss Blair that's always staying, she draws anything that stays still and I fancy she'll have her easel out. The other visitors havena been before so it's for the novelty.' He tried to think of something else to add, but dried up.

'I think they're going because of the witches, Mr. Johnstone!' said Agnes inevitably, slipping into the gap in the conversation before anyone could stop her. 'Do you think there are witches there? Do you think there are witches at all? See, I'm not sure if there are witches or not, and in the daylight when the sun's shining I'm quite happy to say there are no witches at all, and maybe never were, but the minute it gets dark or anything I'm beginning to wonder, and if there's a weird noise or anything then that's it, I'm dead sure there's witches and they're coming to get me!'

'We can only hope,' muttered Daniel.

'Well, lass, aye, I think there's witches all right,' said Mal Johnstone, his hands solemnly on his knees between the hampers. 'There was great trouble with witches in this place maybe twa three hundred years ago, and no doubt they weren't all wiped out then.'

'Wiped out?' Agnes' voice quivered.

'Aye, they burned plenty of them,' said Mal with satisfaction. 'Aye, those were the days when we knew how to give Auld Clootie a taste of his own medicine, like! Burn them or drown them, that way the magic dies with them.'

There was an unusual silence in the back of the cart. Daniel and William found they had moved slightly closer together on the front board, glancing about them at the velvet layers of darkness beyond the lantern's reach.

'But ... but ...' began Agnes at last, 'but you said they didna get all of them?'

Mal tutted loudly.

'They ken how to hide themselves, see? A witch can always conceal herself – or himself – so no one kens they're there, or what they are. In amongst the decent, God-fearing people, living quietly, like, until their time comes again.'

'Och, Mr. Johnstone, you're giving me the creeps! You canna talk like that!' cried Agnes, determined to shake off her fears. 'So there are witches everywhere?'

'That's so, I believe.'

'So is there a witch living in Letho?'

Mal Johnstone paused, as if for effect.

'Well,' he said. 'From yesterday, there's a witch dead in Letho.'

'You mean … what was her name … Widow Maggot?' demanded Agnes.

'That's the one.'

'Widow Maggot was never a witch!' said William unexpectedly. 'I've kenned her all my life!'

'And how would that stop her being a witch?' asked Mal Johnstone. William had no answer to that.

'Here, I think this is our turn,' said Daniel suddenly. 'You'd better hop down here.'

Mal was a little old for hopping, but he took a moment to extract himself from amongst the cushions and rugs.

'Thanks for the lift, lads,' he said from the road. 'And ca' canny around Josie's Den. You never know what might be there – hiding amongst us.'

He turned and in a moment was invisible in the darkness. Daniel kept the horse still for a moment as they sat in silence. Then he puffed out a sigh, and flicked the reins, and on they trudged to Josie's Den.

Chapter Five

The cooking fires were already well-established when the Aytoun and Grant carriages arrived at the roadside above Josie's Den. Murray had ridden: he did not enjoy being cooped up in a carriage, and he always had the idea that it could be useful to have a horse and rider ready. Two spaniels had followed him, sometimes a little too close to the carriage wheels for peace of mind, and were now darting about seeing who descended first. The grooms arranged the vehicles as best they could beside the kirkyard walls of the small mediaeval church on its gentle hummock, and the gentry scrambled down the narrow steps from their doorways into another fine day of autumn sunshine.

'Oh, how lovely!' exclaimed Lady Aytoun, looking about her. Certainly the church was a delightful little bundle of sandstone and leaded glass and slates, set against a background of rook-filled trees, and at once several of the party made their way straight to its door. Blair, never one to hold back, led the way inside, followed by young Rintoul. Murray could hear him talking enthusiastically, apparently in answer to Blair's encouraging questions. Lady Aytoun, after an appreciative examination of the exterior, followed them inside, along with her husband and daughter.

'Oh, it's even colder inside than out!' cried Mathilda, whose slim form was well wrapped in a long spencer, felt bonnet, gloves and muff.

Murray decided to stay outside: he had seen the chapel often enough, and knew it was rather cramped inside. Isobel was explaining the layout to Andrew Grant. Mrs. Grant tugged her son's elbow.

'Robert! Come and see this curious stone. Charles, have you seen this before?'

Murray stepped over to look. The kirkyard had evidently been scythed before the grass died back and the stubble was rough, but for once the few stones in the kirkyard were visible. He did not remember seeing them before. The one Mrs. Grant had found was at a slight angle but looked solidly set, and very old.

'No writing on it, that I can see,' he remarked, having leaned over to see the back.

'No, nothing but this odd circle. I wonder what it signifies?'

Robert knelt before the stone, and traced the circle with one gloved finger.

'I think,' he said, 'that it has a tail, too. See here?'

He stood to let them see clearly. It did seem that the circle had a line coming off it, around the position of four or five on a clock face.

'I can't see anything more than that. An initial, perhaps?' Robert suggested.

'O? or a primitive Q?' said Murray.

'Look, here's another one,' said Mrs. Grant. A few yards away, beyond a perfectly ordinary gravestone with a suitable inscription to a John Clarke, was a stone just as old as the first, with again the tailed circle.

'Hm,' said Murray.

'What have you found?' Rintoul and Blair had emerged from the chapel. Murray pointed to the two stones. Rintoul was down on his knees before the nearer one straightaway.

'How fascinating!' he whispered to it, nose almost pressed against it.

'I hate to tell you,' called Robert from somewhere near the far wall, 'but there's a third.' Mathilda Aytoun, who had drifted out of the chapel with her father, crossed to look at it more closely.

'And a fourth!' called Blair delightedly near the chapel door.

'What is the history of this place, sir?' asked Rintoul, jumping up. His gingery red hair and whiskers stood out at all angles in his excitement.

'It's a chapel of ease, I think, for Cupar,' said Murray. Mrs. Grant looked up, puzzled. 'You know, so that in bad weather the people round here don't have to walk all the way in to Cupar for church.'

'But it was built in Papist times, surely,' said Sir John. 'The age – as Mr. Rintoul was telling us – and the ornament.'

'Oh, yes, it's very old,' Murray agreed. 'I seem to remember being told that there had been a church here since the earliest times – and perhaps some kind of pagan site before that. The den, you see, has a certain atmosphere, and the locals have always felt it must be significant. I'm sure there is more in one of my grandfather's books: I am sorry I did not have the chance to read more about it before we came, but you are certainly welcome to investigate when we go back.'

'If it is Papist, is it dedicated to a saint?'

'To Joseph of Arimathea, I believe,' said Murray. 'Hence Josie's Den.'

'Although,' added Blair who had probably read Murray's grandfather's books, 'some say that the den was named first, for someone else, and the church was called that later either in error or in the hope of, ah, reclaiming the site for the church.'

'The carving is reminiscent of what we call the mirror carving, on certain very ancient stones,' said Rintoul. 'It is supposed to signify a sort of hand mirror.'

'And what does it mean?' asked Mrs. Grant.

'Oh, as to that we have no idea!' said Rintoul, slightly abashed.

'You seem to know a good deal about these things,' said Murray.

'We had a professor – at Glasgow, you know – and he would take us out for walks in the summer term, to see all kinds of things like this. I found it fascinating.'

'Indeed. And did you ever see stones in a graveyard like this?'

'Never! I shall write to him the moment I go home!'

'Just the four stones,' Blair called over, sadly. 'But all very old and worn.'

'Four is plenty, I think!' said Murray. 'Now, we had better go down into the Den while the light is good: it is much more shaded down there and the day will be short.'

'Who's for breakfast?' cried Andrew Grant with enthusiasm. 'Miss Blair, you know where you're going – lead the way!'

Isobel willingly left the kirkyard by the little wooden gate, and set off towards a rough, low outcrop of rock a few tens of yards away. The flatter ground before it was covered in unscythed grass and greying brambles, but Isobel reached the rock and mysteriously began to sink down into the ground: as the rest of the party caught up, they found that she was of course following a set of narrow stone steps, cut into the rock and rounding into its curve. The spaniels hurled themselves down regardless, nearly bowling her off the steps.

'Take care – it can be slippery!' she called back, steadying herself with a gloved finger on the rocky wall beside her.

'Oh, isn't this lovely!' cried Lady Aytoun, as Andrew Grant turned to hand her down the staircase behind him. 'How lovely.'

The den, as it opened out to their right, certainly had its charms. The curving rocky wall, frilled with dusty ivy at the top and browning ferns in its lower joints, curled confidentially around a smooth platform of stone, worn by some ancient river into shapes like well-carved paving stones. There Daniel, William and Agnes had set up the chairs, rugs and fires: some of the cushions were cosily arranged on a higher platform of rock, just about seat-height. Miss Mathilda made her way quickly to the nearer fire, holding her hands out towards it.

Where the curving rock wall dropped away, so did the platform, and they could already hear the beat of a dashing stream some feet below the level on which they were standing. The stream had carved its way through the rock by two routes, which met just here below the platform. Opposite them, between the platform and the far riverbank with its clinging trees and loose rock, was a tall column of an island, a strange spike of dark rock dividing the golden brown water.

'A curious formation,' remarked Mrs. Grant over the noise of the water. 'Can it be of the same rock as the rest of the Den?'

'Geologists say it is a form of granite,' said Murray, pleased with her intelligence. 'The rest of the Den is of course native sandstone.'

'Can one climb it?' asked Robert, eyeing it keenly.

'It's easier than it looks,' said Isobel. 'Come this way.'

She led the way again up a gentle ascent to the level of the seating platform, sure of her footing on the bare sandstone, then higher again to where a small wooden bridge had been constructed to allow easy access to the top of the granite pillar.

'Come along,' she said. 'It's all part of visiting Josie's Den. Come and see Josie's Well.'

She poked at the supports of the bridge briefly, testing to see that the wood was not rotten, and tripped easily across. The top of the pillar was wider than it at first appeared, and soon the Aytouns – Lady Aytoun clutching Sir John's arm – the Grants and Robert were all with Isobel on the rock. She pointed out to them the sight that Murray had seen often enough.

'The pool is never dry, but of course it's not that deep,' she said. He could see in his mind's eye the scooped hollow with its dark water on the top of the rock. He had certainly never known it dry himself. He noticed that Robbins had disappeared behind the cloth screen set up to obscure the business at the cooking fire, and went to see how things were. Behind the screen, Agnes was unpacking ham and hard-boiled eggs and arranging them on to ashets with a degree of artistry, while Robbins poked at the contents of a large shallow pan, stirring in a lump of creamy yellow butter into saffron yellow rice.

'What stage are things at, Robbins?' Murray asked.

'We nearly have tea ready,' Robbins reported. 'I have kedgeree on and there's broth for those who are very cold, sir.' He made a wry face. 'It's not quite picnics in Delhi, is it, sir?'

Murray smiled. Robbins had enjoyed India, for the most part.

'At least we don't have to watch out for snakes, Robbins.'

'True enough, sir.' He went back to his guardianship of Mrs. Mack's precious kedgeree, and Murray went back to his guests.

In only a few minutes they were able to find themselves comfortable places to sit and eat a hearty breakfast. The pies were still warm, in their straw nests, and there was fresh bread to go with the broth, and great bowls of the sweetly fishy kedgeree, salty with butter. Murray always enjoyed eating outside when the weather was colder, and was pleased to see his guests relishing it too, though perhaps Lady Aytoun and her daughter would have preferred something a little more comfortable.

'I'm sure it's a little warmer down here than it is up at the church,' said Mrs. Grant, who looked quite at home perched on the stone ledge on a cushion. 'And it's not just this delicious broth, either!'

'It's a curious thing,' Murray replied. 'Sometimes yes, it is noticeably warmer down here, as if the stone traps the heat. Sometimes, though, it is very much chillier.'

'That's when the witches have been,' said Isobel mischievously.

'Oh, heavens, Miss Blair!' said Mathilda Aytoun. 'Surely there are no witches in Scotland nowadays!'

'Well, if there are this is where they meet, apparently,' said

Isobel. 'And they bathe in Josie's Well.'

'They must be quite small witches, then,' put in Robert Lovie.

'Ah, no, surely it magically expands to accommodate them,' said Isobel.

'Or they shrink themselves down to the right size!' said Robert, and they laughed.

'Isn't there some rumour about a witch in the village?' asked Sir John.

'I don't think Mr. Helliwell would approve of that,' said Rintoul with sudden boldness, as Agnes dropped a pan with a clatter. Rintoul glanced around, frowning, at the curtain.

'No, not at all,' agreed Mrs. Grant. 'It's probably just some elderly woman living on her own, is it?'

'In this case it's an elderly woman who has died on her own, unfortunately,' said Murray. 'A Widow Maggot, who had no known relatives, but seems to have been quite well-to-do.'

'How very sad, to die on one's own,' said Mrs. Grant. Murray met Blair's watery eye: she had not exactly been on her own in her last waking moments. But who would have killed her? And why?

He shook off the thought for now and looked about at his guests, reassuring himself that they were content. It was always a little awkward with comparative strangers. The Aytouns now, they seemed polite and well-bred, so they would likely pretend to be enjoying themselves slightly more than they actually were. Well, perhaps not Miss Aytoun, who was examining the broth suspiciously, but she was at the missish age anyway. He wondered why her parents did not have her off enjoying the season in Edinburgh or elsewhere: she was obviously out in society and did not lack either looks or assurance. Her looks seemed to come from her father, for the most part: his great mop of floppy hair was dark like hers, and her willowy figure followed his slim height more than her mother's petite shape. Lady Aytoun was pretty, too, though, he thought, even now. Some mothers, he was told, did not enjoy the season once their daughters were out, knowing that their own ages and looks would lose by comparison: perhaps this was why they were not in Edinburgh? Sir John was engaged in conversation with Blair, who seemed to be doing his best to appear like a normal gentleman for the occasion. Even so, Sir John had a slight puzzled frown on his high forehead, and Murray wondered, with an inward smile, whether Blair was being any more eccentric than usual. Sir John had a look of convention about him, which even Blair's waistcoat alone was no doubt affronting.

He hardly knew the Grants any better than the Aytouns, even though they were his kin. He had met Andrew Grant a few times when they were younger, but he had been a boy when Andrew had been a serious young legal apprentice, almost his own father's age, or acting it. Again, one would have expected Mrs. Grant and young Robert at least to have stayed in London for the season, to find him an eligible match and enjoy the entertainments a young man tended to like, but here they were begging invitations from relatives hundreds of miles away. He did not like the look of almost perpetual worry on Cousin Andrew's face: was there something about his work as a barrister that was causing him particular stress? Were they here for the good of his health? If so, Murray would do his best to help: he liked the man, and wanted him to enjoy his stay at Letho. He liked Mrs. Grant, too, liked her intelligence and good sense, and Robert seemed an affable boy with a good musical sense, too, which was always an advantage in Murray's books. And then there was Rintoul, sent off by Mr. Helliwell to mix in the kind of society he might be expected to have to deal with as a minister with a charge of his own, though indeed as Mr Helliwell's assistant he would have to blot his copybook not to inherit Letho parish from him. He would need a wife to help him, as most ministers did, and there were few in the parish that might suit. Murray doubted that Miss Aytoun would set her sights so low. Mrs. Grant had for the moment taken him under her wing and was asking him sensible questions about his time at Glasgow University, based on some personal knowledge. He wondered if her first husband or her father had perhaps been a professor somewhere.

Lady Aytoun, catching his eye, distracted him from his thoughts.

'I hope dear Lady Agostinella is quite well today, Mr. Murray?'

'She is keeping well, thank you, Lady Aytoun. But an expedition like this, just now, did not seem wise to either of us. She regrets that she cannot be with us.'

'Oh, of course, of course. Will this be her first child?'

'Ah, yes,' said Murray. Of course, it might well be assumed at her age that Lady Agostinella had been married before and her first family was somewhere else.

'Oh, how lovely for you both! Delightful,' said Lady Aytoun, trying to clap her hands without dropping her plate of ham.

'Well, all being well ...' said Murray, as he found himself saying a good deal these days.

'Oh, indeed, indeed. But she is looking so well – blooming, indeed, as they say! I am sure all will indeed be well.'

Blooming had never been a word Murray had associated with his wife, but perhaps it was so, and it took a stranger to notice what he had failed to see himself. Would Agostinella make a good mother? Would it change her for the better?

When the breakfast dishes had been cleared away and the dogs had been rewarded for their patience with a ham bone each, it was nearly noon and the light in the den was the best it was likely to be. Isobel skipped back up the steps to the Blairs' carriage to fetch her drawing box and easel. Robert seemed to be about to help her but his stepfather had just drawn him over to look at something on the far side of the river. Isobel seemed happy to manage on her own – she would not want anyone to think she was angling for the attentions of a young man. Murray led the others down the second set of steps to the river bank, where the den broadened and there was a charming walk on a generous rocky ledge amidst trees that still clung on to their copper and gold leaves. Where the sunlight tentatively reached the brown river water, it splashed little golden flashes there, too.

'And that is the only piece of this granite rock in the den?' asked Mrs. Grant, fascinated.

'It's the only one anyone has found or marked,' said Murray. 'And I should have thought that any other piece would be as prominent as the column there.'

From where they stood, further down the den, the column rose above them very dark and ominous.

'You know, from here,' said Mathilda Aytoun, 'you could almost think it looks like a figure standing there. See – that bit is an arm, held up like this, bent at the elbow. That's the head, bowed, not looking at us.'

'But just as if it's just about to look at us,' said Rintoul suddenly, and everyone jumped.

'The sun's gone in,' said Murray. 'It does cast a dullness over the den, doesn't it?' Andrew Grant shivered.

'It has turned cold, too,' he said. 'Perhaps the weather is going to break at last.'

'No doubt it will be all the worse when it finally sets in!' said Blair with lugubrious humour. 'As we always say on a fine day, we'll pay for it later!'

Everyone laughed, perhaps a little too eagerly.

'Shall we go back to the picnic place?' asked Murray. 'At least if the rain starts we are not far from the carriages.'

There was general agreement and they turned to climb back up to the sandstone platform. The cooking fire was out and the screen was down: Robbins reported to Murray that he had sent the men and Agnes home with most of the things, but he could still provide tea if necessary. Isobel was serenely drawing with the tails of her cloak bundled beneath her on the rocky ledge. Mrs. Grant went over to see how she was doing, and the others wandered about, examining the various strange features of the den while they could. It was only a moment or so before Rintoul called out 'Mr. Blair! I believe I have found another one!'

Blair, Murray and the Grants strolled over to where Rintoul had a long finger pressed against the rocky wall that curved around the den.

'Oh, but that's the old cross,' said Murray. Rintoul was pointing to a plain cross in a circle, carved into the rock and worn by age.

'It's a cross, yes, but I think it was one of our mirror signs before that. Look,' said Rintoul excitedly. 'First, the cross is not as deep as the circle, wouldn't you agree, Mr. Blair?' Blair nodded enthusiastically, pawing the carving with his bare fingers. 'And then look here – I'm sure there's a line coming off the circle just like the other ones, but it's either worn away or someone has tried to make it look less obvious, Probably at the same time as they carved the cross in the middle. What do you think?'

They all peered at the mark, some with one opinion, some with another, and Blair joined Rintoul to subject the rest of the rock face to minute scrutiny, pulling aside old ferns and grasses to see better. Mrs. Grant looked as if she would have like to join them, but she was talking to Lady Aytoun and her daughter. Murray could hear Miss Aytoun say very distinctly,

'Altogether an odd place to come and visit on an autumnal morning,' and Mrs. Grant gave her a disapproving look. Andrew Grant and his stepson were engaged in some conversation with Sir John about shooting partridges at Collessie. Murray privately wished them luck: the Collessie gamekeeper had been selling partridges in the inn at Cupar for a month or so, under the table.

He wandered over to see what Isobel was drawing, and found, inevitably, that she had two sheets on her easel. The top one showed a picturesque view of the den with the granite pillar dark towards the right. The lower sheet, which he pulled out delicately with a long finger and thumb while she scowled, contained little sketches of the Grants, the Aytouns, and Rintoul, with himself like a guardian heron watching over them. He grinned.

'Pretty view,' he said, pointing to the portrait she had made of Robert Lovie. Her scowl intensified, and she nodded over to the ladies who were examining Mrs. Grant's sketch papers.

'Would you care to take a wager on whether or not Lady Aytoun's next conversation will start with "Oh, how lovely!"?' she asked in a low voice.

'No,' said Murray thoughtfully. 'I don't think I care to take a wager with you.'

'It will, all the same,' said Isobel, just as Lady Aytoun exclaimed 'Oh, how lovely!' over a particularly well studied fern. Isobel rearranged herself to bask in self-satisfaction.

'You are a rude and irritating girl,' said Murray, 'and it's no wonder that your father wants to see you married off.'

'What do you think he is doing with Mr. Rintoul?' Isobel asked after she had sketched Mrs. Aytoun again, making the poor woman smile inanely while feathers floated from her ears.

'Marrying you off, I should think,' said Murray lazily. 'How would you like to be a minister's wife, and the mistress of a manse?'

'I should hate it,' said Isobel calmly. 'There is far too much being nice to people to be done in such a position. And Father knows that far too well to inflict me on any parish – let alone Letho, where I suppose Mr. Rintoul will end up.'

'Well, he had better find a good wife somewhere, though I agree it would not be you,' said Murray. 'I think your father is simply encouraging his enthusiasms. Rintoul seems an intelligent man.'

'He will probably suit Letho well. He would enjoy having a bookish laird,' agreed Isobel. 'Where is he from?'

'Glasgow direction.'

'Oh, aye. Could he not find a parish over there?'

'Presumably not. Or perhaps he wanted a change.'

'Perhaps. The weather will be no change for him, though: I'm sure I just felt a drop of rain.' She folded up her papers quickly.

'Yes, you're right.' He raised his voice. 'I think we have just run out of luck with the weather, ladies and gentlemen.'

'But it has been such a joy,' said Lady Aytoun serenely. Murray could almost see the feathers.

'Nevertheless,' said her husband, taking her arm, 'time to go home.'

The Aytouns' carriage turned off at Letho village to climb over the hill to Collessie. The Blairs and Grants in the Grants' carriage, accompanied by Murray on horseback and the tireless spaniels, continued to the south lodge and up the front drive to Letho House. Already the narrow glass windows of the carriage were thick with rain, and Murray was feeling heavily wet. Robbins, on the top of the carriage, had his shoulders hunched under his hat. As soon as the carriage stopped he had slithered down and marched off to open the front door, and by the time they had all sorted themselves out and gone inside he was ready with Daniel and William to take their coats. Murray was impressed at their speed.

'Shall we meet in the drawing room for tea?' he asked his guests. 'A little something to keep out the damp.'

'A very good idea,' said Mrs. Grant, handing wet shawls to her maid.

'Once we're changed,' added Isobel. 'That's the worst of skirts,' she added, half to herself, as she kicked at her muddy hems.

'Sir, a word,' said Robbins quietly, as the Grants and Blairs headed upstairs. Murray noticed that all three menservants were standing in an anxious row. 'We have a small problem.'

'What is it?' If Robbins was bringing it to him, he must be worried about it.

'It's that Agnes, sir,' said Daniel, in much the same way as he would say 'It's that vase you liked so much on the windowsill ...'.

'The girl from Paisley? What about her?'

'See, sir, she would drive you mad with her talking. She never stops – even if you tell her to.'

'Even if you tell her quite a lot, sir,' agreed William, who was a bit white around the gills, Murray thought.

'So, see, we'd had enough. And we werena that far from home, either, sir. We were only a few yards from the bottom of the drive.'

'Near the south lodge?'

'Well ...' They exchanged looks. 'Quite near the south lodge,' Daniel modified.

'So what happened?'

'Well, like I say, we'd had enough. So we told her to walk the rest of the way.'

'All right – not extreme, perhaps. Assuming you weren't too far from the south lodge.'

They looked at each other again.

'We might have been a wee bit nearer the turn off for the village, maybe, sir,' said William.

'So you put her off somewhere near the village. And then what?'

'Well, that was hours ago, sir. And she hasna come home.'

Chapter Six

'I'm afraid I shall have to go out again straightaway,' Murray put his head in the drawing room door and found all his guests there, drawn in by the lively fire. 'A girl is missing.'

'A girl?' Andrew Grant jumped to his feet. Murray was surprised at his unexpected agility.

'Yes – the maid who was at Josie's Den,' he explained. 'She was separated from the menservants on the way home, and has not appeared.'

He noticed that Grant, who had lost some colour, returned to his normal complexion. Perhaps he had stood up too quickly, then.

'Then you must let us help,' Grant said.

'Oh, yes!' cried Blair. 'After all, we are wet anyway.'

'Yes, of course we must help if we can,' agreed Robert Lovie.

Murray frowned. It would be useful to have three extra pairs of eyes, certainly, even though Cousin Andrew and Robert did not know the place well.

'Very well, but the hot brandy is on its way, so you might as well have a glass first to keep out the damp.'

'Is there anything we can do?' asked Mrs. Grant.

'Nothing at present, thank you. Except perhaps to see that Lady Agostinella is told – one of the maids will tell her maid, no doubt. We shouldn't be long: the girl has probably twisted her ankle or stopped to talk to someone and lost track of the time, but it's growing dark already in this rain and if she is sitting on the dyke unable to walk we'll need to find her soon.'

Robbins brought a jug of brandy and glasses. Murray saw that he had not yet removed his outdoor boots, either. Grant and Blair emptied their glasses straightaway, and Robert Lovie after a sip or two. Murray took one after the ladies had been served, and drained it quickly.

'All well, Robbins?' he asked.

'Aye, sir. Walter has fetched the garden boys and the stable lads. They're waiting outside.'

'Walter had better stay at home, Robbins: we don't want to lose a second person in the dark and he can help here.' Walter was not known for his unerring sense of direction, and was only small. 'Are we ready, gentlemen?' They nodded and he led the way back down into the hall, where they recovered their cloaks and hats – and their sticks, which would be invaluable in the poor light and for poking into ditches and hedges. Murray hurried ahead of them out on to the gravel drive.

'Right, men,' he raised his voice, and the outdoor servants, with William and Daniel, fell silent. Most of them had lanterns ready, he noted, and there were several dogs. The spaniels gravitated to sit at his feet, posed proprietorially. 'We're looking for Agnes – what's her surname, Robbins?'

'Carstairs, sir.'

'Agnes Carstairs. Small made, ginger hair, pale skin. She's new to Letho and may have missed her way, but we'll start by the two routes she is most likely to have taken. Garden staff, with Mr. Blair, William and Daniel, down the drive to the road and left along to Letho village. Ask anyone you meet, in case she's fetched up in someone's house. Dunnet,' he said to the head groom, 'get yourself a horse and ride down the drive and turn right, and go as far as – how long has she been gone? Say the fourth milestone, in case she's been spectacularly unobservant and missed the gate. Talk to Mrs. Gibb at the lodge first: she may have seen her. The rest of the stable staff, come with Mr. Grant, Mr. Lovie, Mr. Robbins and me. We'll take the path to the village and meet you there, Blair. What was she wearing, Daniel?'

'A grey cloak,' said Daniel dismally. Murray sighed.

'Well, keep your eyes open. Check the ditches, check behind the hedges, call her name. Right, we'll meet you in the village. Good luck.'

He watched for a moment as the garden staff spread themselves broadly and set off towards the south gate, taking in swathes of the grass on either side of the gravel drive. One or two darted out from the rest and checked under each shadowy tree: there was not much shelter there, but enough shade to hide a small person. He turned round and nearly fell over Walter, the boy.

'What do you want me to do, sir?' he asked, his chestnut head catching the light from the hall candles. Murray thought for a second.

'Stay here – in the hallway – and be ready to run messages if anyone comes with one. All right?' He prayed he would not have to run anywhere, or who knew when they would see him again.

'Will she be all right, sir?' asked Walter in a serious voice.

'I'm sure she will, Walter. She can't have gone too far, and let's hope if she missed her way she had the sense to sit down and wait for someone to ask. Right, everyone: let's make our way to the village.'

They took the path to the left, passing Robbins' own house. Mrs. Robbins stood in the doorway, holding the boy on her hip, her angular eyebrows concerned. Murray remembered Robbins commenting once that his wife had some patience with Agnes and had listened to her chatter. Murray pictured Mary Robbins seated with her child, the little maid next to her, Agnes gossiping while Mary nodded and made her perceptive remarks. For some reason the thought made him more anxious for Agnes, and he put it from his mind, calling the spaniels to heel.

'Spread out, men,' he called, 'and call out. Keep your eyes open. Cousin Andrew, are you all right?'

'Oh,' said Grant, a little breathless, 'I found, er, one of your cows.'

He swung his lantern to show one of the little black cattle shifting herself unwillingly out of the way.

'My poor father does not find himself at home in the countryside, do you, sir?' called Robert Lovie, with a laugh that was not unkind. Andrew laughed a little in his turn.

'Cows, you know. I'm never very sure about cows.'

'Agnes!' called Robbins, and the gardeners joined in. 'Agnes! Agnes!'

Progress was deliberately slow. They crossed the fields as broadly as they could, trying to make sure that even if Agnes were lying unconscious off the main path they would not miss her. They reached the village path almost reluctantly, as if giving up some little hope, and made their way along it and through the rough woodland to one side. The other side of the path was edged with the high wall of the manse garden. Murray remembered another time when search parties were out and a woman had been found here, and shivered. Surely something like that could not happen again?

He left the men searching and went ahead and round the corner to rattle at the manse door. A maid answered, not far off Agnes' age, and said that Mrs Helliwell was from home and the minister was in the church. No, she had seen no visitor: yes, she knew Agnes by sight, but that was all for she had not been here long, had she?

'Has Agnes made any friends in the village?' Murray asked Robbins, collecting him to go on to the church. He felt he should have asked before.

'I don't think she's been out of the house, sir, except to church with the household. You know Mrs. Dean is very protective of her, and she gives her plenty to do. When she isn't working, she seems content to sit in the kitchen and talk – even if no one is listening,' he added, almost reluctantly. Murray grinned, but he wished they could find her, all the same.

Mr. Helliwell was just emerging from the church and pulling the heavy oak door to behind him.

'Agnes? The wee lass from Paisley? No, I haven't seen her since last Sunday, I believe.'

'No doubt she's missed her way in the dark. If you hear anything, will you send word?'

'Of course, of course,' Helliwell agreed.

'She couldn't be in the church, could she? Did you leave the door open behind you while you were in there?'

Helliwell was about to shake his head, then stopped himself.

'I suppose she might have slipped in,' he conceded, as if someone had been arguing with him. 'Let's look.'

The church was gloomy in the evening dusk, and damply cold.

'Agnes?' called Murray, and the echoes carried it on. They waited, but there was no reply.

'I'd have seen her if she'd come into the other room,' said Helliwell. 'She can't be here.'

'No.'

Helliwell followed him back to the main door and went through the process of closing the door behind them again.

'I hope Rintoul behaved himself this afternoon?' he asked.

'He seemed to enjoy the outing,' said Murray, surprised to think it had not been that long ago. 'He is something of an antiquarian, did you know?'

'He has mentioned it. Good: a minister should have an interest, and all the better if it is a scholarly interest.' He continued down to the manse, muttering, though he sounded pleased.

Robbins and Murray swung their lanterns around the kirkyard, but with no success. Down the hill of the village green, they could hear the other search party making their way up towards them, knocking on doors and asking for any sign of Agnes. Murray divided his own party in two, and sent one half down each side of the green to do the same.

They met in the middle, and Blair scuttled up to Murray.

'Any news?'

'None. You?'

'Unfortunately not,' said Blair, his face drooping under the broad brim of his hat. 'Poor girl: I think the rain is growing heavier.'

'It's certainly getting colder, isn't it?' added Robert Lovie. 'You notice it as soon as the sun starts to go down.'

'I hope she's somewhere sheltered, anyway,' said Murray. 'But where on earth can she have gone?'

They looked about them, as if she would suddenly appear out of the wet dusk.

'We need to broaden the search,' said Murray at last. 'And we need more people. Best go round the houses again and ask for help. You,' he picked out a stable boy he knew was fast, 'run back to see the factor at Dures and explain what's happening. Give him my respects and ask him to start a search on his land. You,' he added to another one, 'off to Collessie and talk to Sir John Aytoun there. Again, my respects, and could he send any of the menservants he can trust to search Collessie lands. Yes, Mal?'

The villager had broken into the circle of searchers, leaving his front door open nearby.

'Mr. Murray, sir, I'm a Collessie tenant, and I can pick out some more to help. We can start at this end and maybe even reach Collessie House before they start there. I ken what the lassie looks like: I met her this morning.'

'Good man, Mal. Have you a hat? It's a wet night.'

'Oh, aye.' Mal patted his white hair and went back indoors for outdoor wear.

Gradually more searchers gathered, and Murray thought of more places to send for help. Mr. Helliwell emerged from the manse again at the sound of all the voices, and agreed to join in. Murray divided them again into parties, including Mal's group of Collessie tenants, and sent them off, before he himself, accompanied by Helliwell, set out for Dures to reinforce the search there. Blair he asked to take Andrew and Robert back up to Letho House to oversee a more detailed search there and to let everyone at home know what was happening: he did not want Agostinella to accuse him of not telling her what was going on.

He and Helliwell and a few others set off down the village street and turned left towards Dures at the foot, knocking on the doors of each of the little cottages as they went. No one had any news and all were happy to have their hen runs and gardens inspected. The last cottage, though, was Widow Maggot's. Murray was startled to see a light in the window.

'Oh, my wife is waking the body,' said Mr. Helliwell, seeing Murray stare. 'The funeral is tomorrow.'

'Oh, of course. Well, we'd still better ask.' He looked at Helliwell, who managed to convey without words that he was thinking about something else and had not even considered going to the cottage door. Murray sighed and stepped through the gate, knocking gently on the door so as not to alarm Mrs. Helliwell and, as an afterthought, so as not to knock the feeble door from its hinges.

Mrs. Helliwell answered the door immediately. Beyond her Murray could see Lizzie Fenwick, the village woman who tended to childbirth and deathbed, sitting by the unkisted form on the box bed.

'Mr. Murray!' said Mrs. Helliwell in surprise.

'I suppose we must pay respects,' said Murray, not grudgingly, 'but we are here in search of my maid, Agnes. Have you seen her?'

'Agnes? The little girl with the ginger hair who talks all the time?'

'That's the one. She was last seen between the inn and the south lodge, but we don't know if she knew the way home. May

I?' He removed his hat and gestured to the box bed.

'Of course.'

Murray crossed the little room in two steps, and Lizzie Fenwick, kind-faced, made way for him. Widow Maggot had been given a decent white cap from somewhere, and death had mysteriously smoothed some of the maze of wrinkles from her face. He removed his glove and touched her hand, as was the custom, then stepped back to allow the minister to do the same. Mrs. Helliwell and Lizzie Fenwick watched in silence, and only when the little ceremony was over did they respond to Murray's query.

'No, there's been no sign of her, and it's been quiet enough here that we would have heard anything bigger than a mouse, wouldn't you say, Mrs. Fenwick?'

'True, true. When was the poor girl seen last?'

'This afternoon, not long before dark. My foolish menservants set her down from the cart as a prank and did not think that she would not find her way back.'

'That'd be William and Daniel?' asked Mrs. Helliwell, sympathetically. 'She's not from round here, is she? She's likely taken the wrong turning, or missed the south gate.'

'Mm. I've sent Dunnet off on horseback down the road, but I haven't heard anything yet. We're working our way over towards Dures.'

'No sign in the village?'

'None, though there's a party going through the kailyards and so on.'

'Well, we'll keep our ears open for the lass,' said Mrs. Helliwell. 'Will you take a cup of ale while you're here?'

'We could take an oatcake in our hands,' suggested Mr. Helliwell, who was no doubt eager to return to his warm manse. Mrs. Helliwell handed them each a warm oatcake from the girdle over the fire, and they nodded farewell, setting out into the evening that seemed much darker already than it had been when they entered the cottage.

'The villagers are worried, you know,' said Helliwell to Murray once they were on the path again. The others in their party trailed their sticks gently along the ditches on the sides of the road, still calling Agnes' name every now and again.

'Worried about Agnes? So am I,' said Murray, frowning.

'Well, aye, maybe. No, they're worried about Widow Maggot.'

'Yes. We have to find out who killed her, as soon as possible. Have you any idea who might have done it, or why?'

'It doesn't seem to have been for money, anyway,' said the minister. 'And you'd hardly think that someone living there, like her, and hardly ever going out, would know anything that anyone would want to kill her for. I've been turning it over in my own mind, of course – we probably all have – but I cannot think of a reason that sounds sensible.'

'I know. We should be asking people if any strangers have been seen in the village – not that it was necessarily a stranger, but if it was a villager, then why now?'

'Anyway, that is not the only reason the villagers are anxious,' said Helliwell after a moment. 'It's … well, there was great talk always about Widow Maggot being a witch. Of course there was, you ken what schoolboys and housewives are like. Old woman living on her own, that's usually enough to set them off.'

'Not just schoolboys and housewives, either. Does anyone know how old she actually was?'

'No idea,' said Helliwell. 'She was old when I came here.'

'Do you know of any family?'

'Neither dead nor alive. But listen – the reason the villagers are worried is that there is great talk that if a witch dies, the rest of the coven, the sisters and brothers, are out to take revenge.'

'Revenge? On the killer …' Murray pondered this, surprised. All this talk of witchcraft in the age of reason, he thought. There had been witch burnings in Fife a couple of hundred years ago, everyone knew that, but that was when men were superstitious and fearful. Surely no one took such things seriously nowadays?

'The thing is,' Helliwell went on determinedly, 'I heard some of the men talking back there before we left the village, and they were – well, they were saying that maybe this was part of the coven's revenge. Taking Agnes, I mean.' Even his voice sounded sheepish, though Murray swung the lantern up to see his face. Helliwell would not meet his eye.

'Agnes killed Widow Maggot, is that what you're saying?' Murray asked, perplexed. As far as he could remember their comparative heights, Agnes would have had to stand on a box to hit Widow Maggot's forehead that way. Or an apple crate.

'No, no, I'm not saying that.' Helliwell stepped out a little, forcing Murray to stride after him. 'I'm not saying that at all. I'm only saying that there are some people in the village that think that once a coven starts taking revenge, there's no saying where it will stop.'

The factor at Dures had reacted quickly to Murray's alert, and as the hour for dinner came and went at Letho and Collessie, the men of the parish went on searching, through Dures' fields and woods and extensive ornamental and vegetable gardens, through sheds and stables, dairies and brewhouses, cellars and even attics, and under every dustsheet over every piece of furniture in the family rooms. It was a minute search. Their heads taken with the idea that Agnes was small, they felt a compulsion to check everywhere, in milk churns, hat boxes, the shallow drawers of the kitchen tables. Everything was as orderly as ever. It crossed Murray's mind that if Agnes had by chance strayed that far, she would have been shaken out, folded and packed away in a cupboard to await the return of the Georges, the owners, in the spring, but that even had that happened, it would have been documented in the housekeeper's scrupulous daybook, and of course there was no sign of such a thing.

The party, with the factor and the well-organised housekeeper, met again in the kitchen to confirm that no one had found anything.

'You'd be best to wait for daylight now,' suggested the factor deferentially. 'It's pitch black out there: even with your lanterns you're no going to see much very clearly, sir.'

'Oh, you're probably right,' said Murray wearily. He looked round at the men in his search party, three quarters Dures men and others from the village. They had worked hard: the initial excitement that came with something out of the routine, however it might be a potential tragedy, had faded now into fatigue and he could see his own tiredness reflected in almost everyone's eyes. By rights their factor should send them off to their beds, whatever Murray said, but they would wait for his word, for it was his servant, his dependent, who was missing. He drew breath, and after a moment's thought turned to open the kitchen door to lead the village men back home. The rain hit his face like a cold slap.

'We can't leave her out there in that!' said Helliwell, surprising himself. 'There's nothing of the girl: she'll be dead in a ditch, if she isn't already!'

'Now there's a cheerful thought,' murmured Murray. 'Well,' he said in a louder voice, 'I'll leave it up to you. Thank you for allowing us to search inside and out here: I think I for one will carry on, at least for a little longer.' He ran a long hand through his hair and settled his hat back on to his head, pulling up his tall collar. 'Do you want to go home for a change of clothes, minister?' he asked Helliwell.

'There's broth here and a bottle of brandy,' said the factor, with a glance at the housekeeper. 'Anyone going out, take a bowl of it first. No sense in anyone catching their death as well, if it can be avoided, sir.'

They took the broth standing, Helliwell and Murray, and the brandy scored down their throats in its wake. A few others, mostly the villagers, did likewise, and with hoods pulled up and gloves tugged tight or sleeves stretched down, they headed back into the October night.

They searched in every place they could think of, and then they searched in them again. At some early hour most of the searchers found themselves once more together on the village green, soaked and exhausted. Several minor scuffles had broken out, misunderstandings over lanterns and hidden obstacles in the dark. Someone had let someone else's hens out and the sleepy birds had had to be rounded up and penned in again, and someone accused someone else of mislaying an old canvas cart cover that, according to the accused, wasn't fit to cover anything any more and was more full of holes than a fishing net. They were cold and fractious, and Murray sent them all home. He and Robbins found Daniel and William and herded them back towards Letho House, depositing Daniel at his cottage in the village and leading William back over the path they had walked into the village hours earlier. They were silent: they could hear the small movements of the cattle about them, and smell their warmth as the rain finally eased. All but one lantern had gone out, but that last one caught a pale shape for a second in the field ahead.

'What's that?' snapped William, suddenly awake. Robbins swung the lantern up. Murray peered hard through the dark. The spaniels, tired at last themselves, sat and panted.

'It's – well, it's not Agnes …' Murray squinted. The dim light made the shape blur and shimmer. 'It's a hare.'

'A white hare?' asked Robbins in surprise.

'A white hare.' All three men stopped on the path, and watched. The hare paused, then moved tentatively towards them, studying them, ears tall and tipped with the faintest grey markings. The dogs did not move. Murray held his breath. It was beautiful.

Then William sneezed, and the hare was gone in an instant. They stared around them but there was no sign of it, and in the end they plodded on down to the river and up the far side, where William headed off towards his cottage, and Robbins and Murray continued to the main house.

'Go home to your bed,' said Murray to Robbins firmly.

'I need to know if there's any news. And anyway, it may be that Mary and the bairn are still in the big house.'

They were: Mary was resting on the settle by the fire with the bairn lying against her. Dunnet the groom sat opposite, his face grim. Mrs. Dean, Mrs. Mack, Jennet and Iffy were around the kitchen table, and by the look of them much tea had been drunk. Walter was asleep with his head on his arms. But there was no sign of Agnes.

The uneasy light of the late autumn dawn outlined the shutters as he reached his room, and he set his candle down to guide him to his bed. He pulled off coat and waistcoat, disentangled himself from his neckcloth, and found that someone had had the time to leave hot water in his room, and not too long ago. He poured it gratefully into the basin and cleaned the weather off his face and out of his hair. He felt old.

He straightened and noticed Widow Maggot's elaborate mirror on the mantelpiece. Did he look any older? he wondered idly, his brain on the point of shutting down. He went to look. No, he seemed much the same age as he had been that morning, he thought, then noticed in the shadowy reflection something move in the room behind him. He swung round. There was nothing there. The candle flame burned straight and still. He looked back at the mirror, studying the room's reflection, but there was nothing there. He must have imagined it.

He tugged off his shirt and breeches, flopped his nightshirt over his head, blew the candle out and flung himself on to the bed. He remembered nothing more.

Chapter Seven

Murray woke late, dragging his eyes open at sounds from somewhere within his bedchamber that he had the impression had been going on for some time. He pushed back the bed curtains, squinting at the wet morning light seeping through the open shutters.

'Sorry to waken you, sir,' said Robbins, who did not look much better than Murray felt. 'I thought you might want to go to Widow Maggot's funeral.'

Murray groaned.

'How are you this morning, Robbins?' he croaked. 'Is there any news of Agnes?'

Robbins was laying out black clothes. They matched Murray's mood.

'Nothing, sir. And it's still raining.'

Murray sat up slowly, wishing he could pull the covers back over his head and make it all go away. He pulled his watch from the watch pocket over the bed and peered at it. It was half past ten. Four hours sleep – less. He groaned again. Robbins would have had less still.

'Where could the girl have gone? I cannot think of anywhere we did not search, can you?'

'No, sir. Collessie, Dures, Letho, the village … unless she was unconscious behind a hedge, and did not hear us calling.'

'Even at that, I think we were behind most hedges ourselves.' He sighed and rose to wash his face vigorously. It must have woken him, for a thought suddenly crossed his mind.

'Robbins, you don't think – could the person who killed Widow Maggot have for some reason taken Agnes?'

Robbins had found something that needed folding: it seemed to be something his hands did while his head considered something.

'I hope not, sir. If that's what's happened, it doesn't bode well at all.'

Murray breakfasted on his own in the parlour, until he had poured himself a second cup of tea. At that point both Grant and

Blair entered: Blair looked irritatingly as if he had been up and busy for hours.

'It's Widow Maggot's funeral this morning, Charles,' said Blair, his wrinkled face drooping mournfully. 'Oh, I see you remembered.' He too was wearing black. 'May I go with you?'

'Of course: no need to ask, you've been an honorary inhabitant of Letho since before I was born.'

'If you don't mind, I shan't, though, Cousin Charles,' said Grant. 'Last night rather took it out of me. I'm not as young as I was, I'm afraid.' His light blue eyes widened alarmingly and then focussed sharply again: he did it frequently, and Murray wondered if he had developed it as a trick to frighten witnesses and had then forgotten it was there.

'I think last night took it out of everyone,' said Murray. 'It would have been different if we had had any degree of success.'

'Indeed ...'

There was a silence, punctuated by Blair's haphazard munching of cold bacon.

'It's not a day for going anywhere unless you have to, I think,' said Murray with a gesture to the window. The rain muddled the panes, smearing the view of trees and park and grey sky.

'Well,' said Blair, wiping his loose mouth extravagantly with a napkin, 'it's at least a good deal more like October than the last few days.'

Murray had been to quite a number of funerals in his life – too many, he sometimes thought – but this one ranked as odd, in his experience. He and Blair arrived at Widow Maggot's toadstool cottage later than he would have preferred, for courtesy, but there were still few there. The cottage was small, of course, but even so it was not packed. Inside, the local carpenter was just about to kist the body, while Mrs. Helliwell and Lizzie Fenwick stood attentively with the doctor's wife and a couple of other women. Mr. Helliwell was adjusting himself to say a quick prayer. There was a pile of oatcake and a keg of ale available, but apparently little inroad had been made on either by the mourners. Blair and Murray removed their hats and bowed their heads as Mr. Helliwell, sounding less sure of himself than usual, intoned something suitable. The carpenter fitted the lid on the black clothed coffin and began to fasten it down, his tools slipping a couple of times to the sound of muttered oaths. As soon as he was done he scuttled out of the cottage with a nod at the minister, and Mrs. Helliwell offered Blair and Murray oatcakes and ale.

'The oatcakes are fresh, Mr. Murray,' said the doctor's wife, 'and the ale comes from the manse, so you've no need to worry!'

'It's fine, Mrs. Feilden,' said Murray, standing awkwardly under the low ceiling. 'Not many here, then?'

'No doubt they'll be here soon,' said Lizzie Fenwick. 'We've the bearers to come, anyway.'

'Here they are,' said Mrs. Helliwell, and Blair and Murray had to leave the cottage to make way for the four men edging their way inside. All were members of the Kirk Session, no doubt pressganged by the minister into serving this role for an unpopular woman with no kin. At least they were evenly matched. Kenny the schoolmaster had a cold, and sniffed bad-temperedly as they manoeuvred the smallish coffin through the rough doorway. Murray wondered about the schoolboys free to commit further mischief, then remembered that this was Saturday. He rubbed his face, trying not to fall asleep on his feet.

The bearers carried the coffin out on to the lane, then stopped to organise themselves and adjust their grip as the coffin swung up to shoulder height. Murray looked about, and was surprised to see that there were suddenly quite a few men there, ready to follow it to the kirkyard. There must have been twenty, thirty – all weary looking, for they had all been out searching for Agnes most of the night. More appeared as they stood there, and as they began the slow walk along to the foot of the village and up the hill to the church, even more appeared, solemn, serious expressions on their faces. They looked like men who had come not so much to pay their respects as to see to it that something was done properly. Murray frowned. He did not like the feel of this.

In the kirkyard, Jocky McClure, a severe-looking man, stood guard over the grave he had helped dig. The bearers, who had all done this before, slipped the coffin down and lowered it expertly towards the grave. It stuck.

There was a moment of very awkward silence. Kenny put out a foot and tentatively pushed down on one end of the coffin, trying to make it fit. There was a hiss of disapproval from the others, and he pulled his toes back quickly. Two of the bearers crouched down along with Jocky McClure to see where the problem was.

'You've dug it too short, Jocky,' said Melville, one of Murray's tenant farmers. McClure was his farmhand.

'I never did,' objected Jocky in the same low voice. 'I always measure twice. And the carpenter been and told me the length, too. So that's three measures.'

'Well, it's too short. We'll have to lift her out and set her aside, and you can take another inch or so off this end.'

'It canna be that end, see,' said Kenny, 'or you'll be in to James Scott's granny's grave.'

'Well, the other end, then. But we'll have to shift her, gentlemen.' Melville took up his rope again. Kenny muttered something in which the words 'old besom' seemed to feature, but took up his own rope. The rain slithered down, lining up in drips on the ropes and on the hat brims of all the men in the kirkyard. Melville counted quietly, the bearers pulled, and with a slither and a scrape the coffin detached itself from the gravecut.

'Where are we putting it?' demanded Watson, one of the bearers. 'We should have said. Melville, you should have said before you made us pick her up again!'

'We'll put her …' Melville looked about. 'Over there?' He pointed to a table stone not far away.

'Or that one?' said Watson quickly, for the one Melville had pointed to was that of Murray's great grandfather. Kenny cast him a wary look, lost his footing on the muddy ground, and slipped into the grave with a cry. The coffin, unbalanced, slid after him, and landed at an angle with Kenny underneath.

'Get me out of here!' yelled Kenny, forgetting any requirement to speak quietly.

'Are you all right?' asked Melville anxiously, as the remaining three bearers scrabbled, with Jocky McClure, for the ropes.

'The bloody thing's landed on my ankle!' came Kenny's voice, muffled by mud and wood. The men hauled the coffin up and quickly laid it on the table stone, while Murray and a couple of other taller men reached down and dragged Kenny out, trying not to slide themselves on the soft earth. Kenny was coated with it, and crumpled to the ground, clutching his ankle.

'Here, sit up on this stone,' said Murray, helping him on to another table stone: they were useful pieces of furniture, really, he thought. 'Put your foot up and rest it a minute.'

Kenny swore to himself quietly and with great fluency, for he was an educated man, while everyone else watched Jocky McClure slither into the gravecut himself, and chop another five or six inches off the end of the hole. Then he sprang back out again with some style, and acted again as fourth bearer to slip the coffin into the grave.

'You cut too much, this time,' said Melville, examining the set of the coffin in the grave. 'It's a good eight inches too long.'

'I tellt you,' said Jocky without much rancour, and began to fill in the grave. The coffin rang hollow under the mudpats as they landed. 'Is there whisky?' he asked.

'Aye, aye, dinna worry,' said Melville, for that was the gravedigger's perk. Melville produced a bottle, and soon everyone had had a reviving dram – Kenny had had two. They stayed to see the grave filled, then began to go their separate ways. Murray and Blair were at the back of the crowd leaving the kirkyard, while the men in front, tongues loosened by whisky, were starting to talk normally again.

'See that,' said one man – Murray thought it was Mal Johnstone. 'He kicked the coffin, and the next thing he's a broken ankle.'

'Aye. It was like the coffin kicked him back, wasn't it?' said his neighbour, nodding ominously.

'It was. And then the coffin wouldn't fit and then it was too small. Like I say, she's still up to mischief. I doubt,' said Mal portentously, 'I doubt she'll lie peaceful there. If she's there at all.'

'She must be there!' said his neighbour in surprise. 'The minister and all was at the kisting of her.'

'Aye, but then we all turned our backs on the coffin to get Mr. Kenny out the grave,' said Mal. Murray grimaced: he had not noticed Mal rushing forward to help. 'What if she got away then, and isna buried at all?'

My, he should write a novel, thought Murray to himself. He met Blair's eye, and they raised their eyebrows at each other, as Mal and his friend headed home.

The mourners resorted themselves, and they found they were walking beside young Rintoul, the minister's assistant. He, like everyone else, was pale and tired-looking.

'How are you this morning, Mr. Rintoul?' Blair asked anxiously.

'Well, Mr. Blair, a little upset, to tell the truth. That was my first funeral here,' he explained. 'I hope they aren't all like that?'

'Ah,' said Murray. 'Well, it was a little unusual, certainly. I've never known Jocky McClure make a mistake before in the size of a grave.'

'Particularly after three measures,' added Blair, making a face.

'But it was very slippery there by the grave,' Murray added. 'Anyone could have lost their footing.' Behind them he could see Kenny being helped home by Melville and Watson, scowling like a fury, his foot high behind him.

'You've quite recovered from last night?' asked Blair with an innocent expression. Rintoul jumped, and his ginger whiskers seemed to sag.

'Last night?'

'The hunt for little Agnes,' Blair explained. 'It was a long night, wasn't it? I hope she's safe somewhere.'

'Oh, oh. Yes, little Agnes … I'm afraid I slept through all of that, all the fuss,' said Rintoul, now as pink as one of Blair's waistcoats. 'Apparently my landlady knocked on my door a few times, but I must have been out cold. I am a very sound sleeper,' he added hurriedly.

'You must be,' said Murray. 'The whole village was up and about, I believe.'

'And has there been any word of the poor girl?' asked Rintoul. 'I hope she is safe.'

'No word, unfortunately,' said Murray. 'She is still missing.'

'That is …' Rintoul cast his gaze down and licked his lips hard as if they were about to crack. 'That is very unfortunate. I shall … I shall go and say some prayers for her safety.' He bowed to them and turned back to the church, where Jocky McClure was now cleaning his spade thoughtfully by the fresh grave.

'You knew he wasn't out with us last night, didn't you?' Murray said to Blair.

'It seemed to me that I knew of no one who had seen him with us, certainly.'

'Do you think he's such a deep sleeper as he claims?'

Blair pursed his lips.

'He may be,' he said, 'when he sleeps. But by the look of him I should say he did not do much sleeping last night.'

'I agree.'

They had been meandering down the hill with no particular purpose, despite the rain, when in the distance they saw Mrs. Helliwell, Mrs. Feilden and Lizzie Fenwick coming towards them. Mrs. Feilden waved at the others and headed off towards the doctor's house near the school. Lizzie lived in the same direction, but instead continued up the hill with Mrs. Helliwell towards the manse. The three women knew each other well, having attended many of the same villagers over the years, and the minister's wife and the midwife walked easily together until they reached Blair and Murray.

'Finished at Widow Maggot's cottage, then?' Murray asked, removing his hat and instantly regretting it as the rain trickled down his collar.

'Yes, for now,' said Mrs. Helliwell. 'The food is cleared away and given to those who need it, and Ninian Jack came and put a bolt on the door for now. The sheriff's man asked if we could wait until he has tried again to find any relatives before the goods are rouped, but I think he's still hoping to find something there that will help him to find the murderer.'

Mrs. Helliwell was a sensible woman, and Murray did not doubt that that was the case. The sheriff's man was not stupid, either.

'So there is no more news of a murderer?' Blair asked breathily. 'Surely she cannot have been killed by a robber?'

'Unless someone tried to rob her, killed her accidentally and fled in a panic,' said Mrs. Helliwell. Lizzie Fenwick nodded: they must have been discussing it through their night's wake. Where Mrs. Helliwell was slight and wiry, Lizzie Fenwick had a more solid build, but it spoke of muscle and endurance rather than fat. Her hair, where it curled from her bonnet, was milk white, but her eyebrows and lashes were black as pitch and her eyes were a striking brown. Her mannish face was full of kindness and good sense and a long, unshockable experience of life.

'Was there no one in the village who knew her well, then?' asked Murray.

'I suppose I was by way of being a friend, sir,' said Lizzie. 'I would call round on her twice or thrice in a week, do what messages she needed, bring any letter from the carrier. Not that she had more than the two or three all the time I kenned her, and none for a few years, now.'

'Do you know where they were from?'

Lizzie tutted, as much at herself as at the question.

'I have no idea now, sir, if I ever did.'

'And she never talked to you of family or friends?'

'I have no notion that she ever did. She was aye interested in what was going on in the village and the big houses, who was walking out with who, who was ill, who was dead, who was born, ken?'

'Did you have the impression,' said Blair, 'if that's the word, for I may be mistaken but I did wonder – was it your impression that you were the only one who visited her and talked with her like that?'

'Well, she certainly didn't say much to me!' put in Mrs. Helliwell with a grin. Lizzie had a long-ago look in her eye.

'Do you know, whiles ago I think someone told me that she would sometimes put up a traveller, if the inn was full.'

'Is the inn ever full?' asked Murray in surprise.

'Oh aye, whiles,' said Lizzie and Mrs. Helliwell together. 'More often in the autumn or the spring,' added Lizzie.

'When you're usually down in Edinburgh,' put in Mrs. Helliwell.

'Farmers moving stock around, that kind of thing. Markets and such,' said Lizzie, as if they were foreign faraway things that were unlikely to have an impact on her life.

'Any word of a traveller in Letho that night, then?' was Murray's inevitable question.

'As to that, you'd best ask Dod Scott down at the inn,' said Mrs. Helliwell sensibly. 'If anyone knows of a stranger in the village that night, it would probably be him.'

'Well, maybe we'll just do that,' said Murray, a little listless. He sighed. 'I don't suppose either of you has heard anything about Agnes?'

'She's still missing?' Mrs. Helliwell was shocked. 'I assumed you would have found her by now. Mr. Helliwell said there had been no sign by dawn, I know, but I thought when you went back to Letho House … oh, dear, poor girl.'

'She's not the kind to run away, then?' asked Lizzie Fenwick.

'Not by any account I've heard,' said Murray. 'I gather she seemed quite content here. Though Daniel and William had just put her out of the cart to walk home.'

'Was she the kind to take offence?'

'The other servants didn't think so, anyway. I hardly know the girl: she's only been with us for a month or so.'

'Of course. Well, Mr. Murray, Mr. Blair, I have digging to do and Mrs. Fenwick has linens to collect for a baby over Collessie way, so if you'll excuse us,' she turned to the manse garden gate.

'Of course. Good day to you both.'

'And to you. I hope you find Agnes soon,' said Mrs. Helliwell, and her concern was genuine.

'Well, the inn, then,' said Murray to Blair, and they continued their meander down the easterly village street. Mary – Mrs. Robbins – was outside Watson's shop, waiting for him to open it after the funeral. Her bairn was rooting about at the edge of the green as Watson arrived still talking with Mal Johnstone, and dug up a particularly large slug to present to his mother. Mary grinned, and ticked him off in Gaelic. Mal Johnstone stared at her as Mary encouraged the lad to replace the slug, and wiped his fingers on a rag. Murray grinned, too: Mary made a good mother, as he would have expected.

Dod Scott, the innkeeper to whom the schoolboys had run for help when they first found Widow Maggot's body, raised his not inconsiderable eyebrows in surprise at their question.

'I havena sent a'body to Widow Maggot this twenty year. Have you no seen the state of that place? I couldna send a'body there.'

'But it's true you used to?'

'Oh, aye, long ago. Times now I have no rooms I'd send them up the village to the Watsons or Mrs. Maitland, but she has that Mr. Helliwell's young assistant biding with her just now. No, I havena sent a'body to Widow Maggot a long, long time.' He shook his heavy head, perhaps contemplating the mortality of all things.

'And were there any strangers here that evening? On

Wednesday night?'

'Aye, aye, the sheriff's man asked me that and all. Naw, there was nobody in that night. The Cupar coach stopped but the three or four on that was on it had their dinners and then back on the coach – I dinna think any of them went further than the midden the whole time they was here, and that was only an hour or so. Like I tellt the sheriff's man.'

'Oh, well …' said Murray. 'Thank you for your help.'

'I don't suppose,' said Blair, who had his head inside the inn's raddled longcase clock, 'that you've seen anything of young Agnes Carstairs?'

'Naw.' The innkeeper shrugged his great shoulders like a resigned ox. 'I couldna go out wi' a'body last night, for I had people here, but I had a crowd back here for warm ale halfway through. And we searched the stables and all the rooms, even the cellar and the attics. No sign of her, poor wee lass.'

'I think I'm going to have to tell the sheriff's man about that too,' said Murray. 'Where could she have gone?'

'Let's walk over to Collessie and round the long way,' said Blair. 'I think the rain must have eased a little by now.' He left the clock and peered out of the inn's small window.

'Good idea,' said Murray, pleased to have a plan, and they took their leave of the innkeeper.

Outside the rain was a little lighter, settling in to a soaking drizzle that seemed to hover in the air rather than be subject to gravity. They were making their way back up the east street again when a group of people at the top of the hill attracted Murray's attention. Several men, still in their funereal black, were standing in a tight circle, focussed on someone in the midst of them. There was something about the set of their shoulders that implied the person in the middle was in trouble. Murray quickened his step, Blair scuttling behind.

'Something the matter here?' Murray asked when he was close enough, in what he thought of as his laird's voice. The group swayed and turned. The figure in the midst was revealed as Lizzie Fenwick, head tilted up defiantly.

Mal Johnstone stepped forward.

'We were just asking her about Widow Maggot, sir,' he said, removing his hat. His little teeth settled back self-righteously into his top lip. 'She kenned the widow well, you ken.'

'And what were you asking her?'

'Oh, just ... how friendly they were, and if the pair of them had any other friends in the village,' said Mal vaguely.

'Mal, if I thought you were in any way suggesting that Mrs. Fenwick – or Widow Maggot for that matter – is a witch –'

'A witch, sir?' Mal laughed but the other men looked stern, and a little frightened. 'No, no. But if she was, sir, that would be a bad thing, wouldn't it?'

'I'm not even going to entertain the idea. Who delivered your sister's babies, Mal? Who helped lay your parents out, after she had attended their deathbeds? Have the decency to show Mrs. Fenwick a bit of respect. Now, off to your work, and no more of your silly ideas. And leave Mrs. Fenwick alone.'

The men had been beginning to edge away even as Mal and Murray were talking, and with a last look at Lizzie Fenwick Mal strode away to join them. Their heads bent quickly together again but Murray watched until all of them had separated to go to their respective homes.

'That's not the end of that, I suspect,' he remarked generally.

'I'm sorry you should have been troubled with that, Mr. Murray,' said Lizzie Fenwick, her face still pale.

'Did they do you any harm?' Blair asked anxiously.

'Not a bit of it, Mr. Blair!' She pulled herself taller. 'They gave me a bit of a fright, that's all. But you're right, Mr. Murray: I don't think that'll be the end of this. You need to find Agnes, and you need to find who killed Widow Maggot. Until you do, I think it won't just be me they'll be at with their bullying. There'll be others they'll accuse. Remember what happened back in King James' times.'

She nodded at them and gathered up the sack of linens from the manse which had fallen at her feet in the confusion. They watched her heading back to her cottage: she had lived alone there for years, and no doubt in the course of her work had used her own herbal concoctions, as most women did, to ease births or deaths. Surely that was not enough for Mal to accuse her, though?

'She talks as if she remembers King James' times herself,' remarked Blair.

Chapter Eight

'No, sir, still no sign.' Robbins was pale, but then that was his natural condition. 'Daniel and William are out searching again, along with most of the garden staff and the mains farm lads that can be spared. Mr. Grant and Mr. Lovie have ridden out along the road this morning to make enquiries.'

'Good of them,' said Murray.

'Well, they have returned with no result, sir.'

'But where on earth is she?' Murray demanded, not expecting an answer. 'She cannot just have vanished into thin air, can she?'

'No, sir,' agreed Robbins, with a frown, just as Blair put in,

'It's like witchcraft, isn't it?'

'Oh, for goodness' sake don't say that in the village!' said Murray, rubbing his hands through his hair. 'Is Lady Agostinella in her chamber, Robbins?'

'No, sir, she is in the parlour.'

Murray stared.

'What? What's the matter?'

'Nothing, I believe, sir. Sir John Aytoun, Lady Aytoun and Miss Aytoun have called, and everyone is in the parlour. The ladies have their needlework, sir, and the gentlemen have been examining your library and found themselves books to read.'

'And Lady Agostinella has joined them?' He tried not to sound too disbelieving: perhaps it was a good sign. Optimism and unease tangled briefly in his head.

'Yes, sir: she has brought her needlework down, too.' Robbins' face was blank.

'Well! Coming along, Blair?'

They made their way to the parlour, a room of little grandeur and great comfort. In the spring and summer, the tall windows were festooned with outdoor greenery and the scents of flowers and foliage flooded through as soon as they were opened. In autumn and winter, the fireplace seemed to have been designed to make the whole room feel like a cosy corner. The sophas were firm enough for support and soft enough for comfort. No item of furniture looked unloved, but at the same time nothing looked as if it would mind a drop of ink or a smudge of mud. The walls were panelled and painted a comfortable light green, and the artwork consisted of paintings of family dogs and horses, mostly done by family members and friends. It had been the room most favoured by Murray's mother, and since Agostinella had shunned it for her miserable chamber upstairs, presumably finding it too plebeian, it had remained unchanged for most of Murray's life, the room he usually thought of at the word 'home'.

Murray's mother had been a good stitcher, and the lamps had been chosen accordingly. Isobel often made use of them for drawing but today all the ladies were sewing. Lady Agostinella, colourless in their midst, was engaged in an item Murray had been told was to be a cot cover, and it was being much admired by Lady Aytoun. Mrs. Grant was working slippers for Mr. Grant, and Mathilda Aytoun and Isobel were presumably furnishing their dowry chests, though Murray thought ungraciously that Isobel's must be fairly full by now. He blinked at the memory of Lady Agostinella's dowry chests, the number of them, and the contents: ancient blue-green tapestries, dusty lace, greying items of clothing whose purpose was mercifully obscure. As far as he knew, most of it still lingered in his wife's chambers upstairs. There had been money, too, a very great deal of money, but he had not touched that, not even when Agostinella's mother, the dreadful Contessa, had died and left the remainder of the Neapolitan estate to her only child. A manager was in charge there: Agostinella had shown no interest in going back, possibly ashamed that she had married so humbly.

The ladies were clustered where the light was best, and with them was Robert, situated neatly between Mathilda and Isobel, reading out loud to them from *Waverley*. He had a pleasant voice, and read expressively, which both Mathilda and Isobel seemed to appreciate. Blair sidled into a space beside Mrs. Grant and joined the appreciative group. Andrew Grant and Sir John had a windowseat each and were indulging in their own reading, Sir John with the latest *Courant* and Cousin Andrew with a volume of local history, in which he seemed comfortably engrossed. He did manage to glance up as Murray came in.

'Just reading about Josie's Den,' he explained. 'Joseph of Arimathea seems to be the man, indeed.' He stood up and set the book down, marking the place carefully. 'Robert and I rode some distance in search of your maid, but with no luck, I'm afraid.'

'So I hear – thank you for trying, anyway. There seems to be no sign of her anywhere.'

'I can't make any suggestions, said Cousin Andrew sadly. 'If I were on my home territory, I might be better able to help …'

'You have done what you can, sir. I am very grateful. Even those who know this parish like the back of their own hands have no idea where she could have gone.'

'She was from Paisley, I believe?' Sir John looked up gracefully from his newspaper. 'Could she have been so upset that she set out for home?'

'I'm beginning to wonder,' Murray agreed. 'Where else could she be? Though how she would have made such progress on her way without leaving a trace and without, one assumes, catching the mail coach, is still a mystery.'

'Someone must have given her a lift,' said Andrew Grant. 'And gone so quickly that they did not hear of the hunt for her. Someone in a private carriage, perhaps.'

'Such a thing had crossed my mind,' said Murray. 'But if so she must send for her kist some time – all her belongings are here.'

'I trust that no one has taken her for …' Cousin Andrew lowered his voice, with a look at the ladies, 'improper reasons.'

'I think we all hope that,' agreed Sir John, folding his paper back on itself. 'A pretty girl, was she?'

'Not noticeably,' said Murray honestly. 'But you know that such things do not always go according to looks. After tea, I think I must ride to Cupar and tell the sheriff, though I am sure he is busy enough with the murder just now.'

'Well,' said Cousin Andrew sensibly, 'there's not much he can do for your Widow Maggot now, and it's still possible he can help young Agnes, so yes, best to inform him.'

Murray smiled at him, grateful for his support.

'I'd be happy to come with you, if you like,' said Sir John. 'I have some experience of these legal matters.'

'How very kind, sir,' said Murray, surprised.

The door opened and Jennet, the older maid, appeared with a tea tray. Walter processed solemnly behind, apparently slightly smaller than the silver urn he was wheeling in. The ladies put aside their embroidery and followed Agostinella to the tea table.

'I do like this work,' Robert remarked, picking up a white cloth as he rose. 'Pineapples, isn't it?'

'Well, they're fashionable,' said Isobel dismissively. 'I liked the idea of doing them as whitework to make the most of the shape rather than the colours.'

'I don't know when I saw work so fine,' said Robert admiringly, holding it out for the others to see.

'Thank you, kind sir,' said Isobel, half-mocking, but pleased.

'How very interesting!' Mathilda hurried back to pick up her own piece of embroidery. 'I've been working pineapples, too!' She waved her multi-coloured cloth in front of Robert, who caught it and seemed to compare the two, one in each hand.

'Beautiful, yes indeed!' he said politely, setting both down with care. 'Oh, is that seedcake? My favourite!' He hurried over to the table to join his mother, stepping away from the mire with some agility. Mathilda looked smug, having perhaps missed Robert's reluctance and only heard the compliment. Isobel managed a kind of graciousness, not even looking back at her work as she went to the tea table. Lady Agostinella gathered her guests around her almost with pleasure, Murray thought, and served tea, and the company joined in general conversation. Agostinella seemed to pay particular attention to Mathilda, drawing her in to talk with interest about her needlework. Murray found himself relaxing very slightly.

When tea was over, Lady Aytoun announced that they had better return to Collessie.

'Very good, my dear, but I shall accompany Mr. Murray to the sheriff in Cupar,' said her husband smoothly. 'I'm sure the coachman will see you safe there.'

'Will you ride, sir?' asked Murray. 'I can lend you a horse.'

Sir John looked mildly put out, but nodded nevertheless. There was a general shifting as the Aytouns made their farewells. Isobel, who had contained her triumph all through tea, found herself beside Murray.

'She's at that awkward age, isn't she?' said Isobel, indicating Mathilda in a superior fashion. Mathilda, oblivious, was hunting for something in her reticule. 'I'm sure I was just the same at that age.'

'No, no,' said Murray with consideration. 'Not at all. Just as unbearable, but in a completely different way.'

'Och, go and boil your heid,' snapped Isobel, and went to stand by Mrs. Grant.

Murray looked at Mathilda thoughtfully: she was indeed quite missish, but there was something else to her, he thought. Robert was helping her with her shawl, which should have pleased her, but instead she was angling under it with unconscious grace. Her focus seemed instead to be on exchanging some kind of silent message with her father. His fine eyebrows rose, and she, with a flicked glance at her mother, shook her head so slightly that if Murray had not been watching her specifically he would have missed it. She nodded at Robert with a smile like an afterthought, then slipped behind her mother and followed her dutifully to the parlour door.

In the hall, the servants appeared with cloaks and bonnets, and again Robert was attentive, brushing past Mathilda, who looked rather surprised, and helping Lady Aytoun with her cloak. Lady Aytoun was vocally appreciative.

'Oh, how lovely of you! What a lovely young man! Isn't he delightful, Tilly?'

'Mother, no wonder I could not find my handkerchief! We have picked up each other's reticules again!' said Tilly, with a smile to cover her exasperation. 'Here – here is yours.'

'Oh, yes, dear – quite right. Perhaps if we had reticules more noticeably different …'

'You mean, my lady,' Isobel was murmuring behind Murray's elbow again, 'that if you had one that was a little less fashionable, and left that kind of thing to your daughter, these mistakes might not arise.' Murray stared at the two reticules, but he was behind enough in reticular fashion not to know whether Lady Aytoun was trying to look younger than she was, or not. Tilly gave her reticule a little shake, and opened it, eventually drawing out the lost handkerchief and giving her nose the slightest of dabs before replacing it. Murray was not sure why, but he felt for a moment like one of the audience in the theatre. But for whom was Mathilda performing? If it was for Robert, he certainly looked appreciative.

'I'm not sure why, but I'd love to know why …' came a murmur from behind his other elbow. He was surrounded by Blairs.

'Why what?' he muttered back.

'You might be able to find out on your way to Cupar, of course,' said Blair with an elaborate shrug.

'Why what?' Murray repeated patiently.

'Why they're here, instead of enjoying the season in Edinburgh and finding that charming young lady a husband?'

Lady Aytoun and the charming young lady were eventually helped into their carriage, sheltered under umbrellas from the door, and the business took so long that as the carriage departed, Dunnet the groom was already bringing Murray's gelding and a grey, rangy mare for Sir John round the corner from the stables. Sir John eyed the horse with some distaste, but swung himself competently enough into the saddle and assumed a seat that was as graceful as one might expect, arranging the reins in one gloved hand like a bouquet. Murray bade farewell to his guests and his wife and promised to be back for dinner, and having done so he led the way at a swift trot down the drive. Sir John pulled himself to attention and followed.

'I find myself still looking in every hole in the hedge for Agnes,' Murray said with a little laugh when they reached the road.

'That way madness lies,' said Sir John, 'tempting though it is. Best to hand over responsibility to the sheriff.'

'How did the search go at Collessie? Did you find the tenants and staff co-operative?'

Sir John made a face.

'Very much so – the first time, in fact, that I had much co-operation from them at all. Of course, the tenants are not my affair, but the staff – well, perhaps you know more about the staff than I do.'

'It has not been a well-run estate in my lifetime, sadly,' said Murray. 'An elderly lady had it, but had lost much of her mental strength for years. Then a nephew inherited, but as you'll know, he's with the navy and rarely comes to see it. And I think he has had little experience of appointing factors or overseeing land.'

'A pity,' said Sir John. 'If it were not a little too far from Edinburgh, I might consider offering for it. It needs a firm hand, clearly, and I enjoy a challenge of that kind.'

'Collessie would certainly benefit,' said Murray noncommittally.

'I had family in Fife many years ago, I believe,' Sir John went on. 'Perhaps it is time to return.'

'I am very fond of the county myself.'

'And I think Collessie would be a decent little estate, with better staff. What say you to the tenants?'

'Mixed,' said Murray. 'About a quarter of the village belongs to Collessie: you may judge quickly from the houses to the north east side, from about the schoolhouse down to Mal Johnstone's or so.'

'The woodland needs much attention ...' said Sir John thoughtfully, and so they rode on to Cupar.

The sheriff's officer, Macduff, met them at the desk of the sheriff's office, and took them politely into an inner room. His limp was as bad as ever, but he greeted Murray with pleased respect, gesturing to the clerk to take their wet cloaks and hats.

'Mr. Murray, sir, have you any news on the Widow Maggot's murder?'

'I'm afraid not – I was coming to ask you the same thing. No news of strangers in the district? Or family of whom we did not know?'

'Nothing, sir. We ken she had been lying there since the night before, and of course her bed hadna been slept in.'

'Did you notice the mark where the apple box had been?'

'Ah, yes, sir – I wondered if you'd have seen that. I wondered if she had had a wee bit money in it or something, but why take the whole box? And there was more money about the place left behind.' He had two chairs in the room and bade them sit, while he himself perched against a table by the small window. Paper and inks were laid out on the table, many with drawings on them: the sheriff's clerk was an accomplished draughtsman, as Murray knew of old. Sir John looked around as if expecting some hospitality, but the sheriff's man was not high enough to have any to offer.

'There is much talk in the village of her involvement with

witchcraft,' said Murray carefully. The sheriff's man lifted his head, alert.

'Stuff and nonsense,' said Sir John sharply.

'How much is much talk, sir?' asked Macduff.

'There was a great deal of dark muttering at the funeral, and afterwards a few men surrounded the village midwife and threatened her.'

'The village midwife? You didn't say,' said Sir John, now thoughtful.

'That'd be Lizzie Fenwick, sir?'

'That's right. A decent woman.'

'Several people mentioned her to me as a friend of the Widow Maggot.'

'She and the minister's wife and the doctor's wife have all done their best over the years to see that the widow was well looked after, particularly when she couldn't get about on her own.'

'Aye, aye.' Now the sheriff's man looked pensive. 'You were at the funeral?'

'I was.'

'I couldna get.'

'You missed a treat,' said Murray drily, and described the events of the morning and the conversations overheard after the funeral. Sir John and the sheriff's man made a gratifyingly rapt audience.

'Good heavens,' muttered Sir John.

'It sounds to me as if we need to keep an eye on matters there,' said Macduff. 'I'd say there are a few there winding each other up.'

'That seems to be the case,' Murray agreed. 'And it doesn't help that – but that's the other reason I'm here. One of my maids has vanished.'

He explained about Agnes' disappearance and outlined what had been done to try to find her since. The sheriff's man took in every detail, nodding steadily as the information was stored in his long head.

'Agnes Carstairs – I don't believe I know her.'

'She's new – only been with us a few months. Apparently she saw something distressing in Glasgow, and her mistress, who knew our new housekeeper, sent her up here for safety, or for a change of air, I'm not clear which. Perhaps she was missing Glasgow and my wretched men's ploy with the cart was the last straw, and she has simply made for home. But we can find no trace of her going, if that is what she did.'

'What did she see in Glasgow?'

'You'd have to ask my housekeeper for the details, I'm afraid. I think the word murder was mentioned, but for all I know it was an accident, or a brawl, or something else entirely.'

'I think I'll have a word with your housekeeper, then, sir, if you don't mind.'

'Not at all: feel free.'

'But surely you must have a list of people in your area who have a history of annoying young females?' asked Sir John. 'Why not just go and question them? No doubt some ruffian has taken her for his amusement.'

Murray looked at him in surprise: Sir John had not mentioned such a conviction before.

'There could be any number of reasons for her disappearance, sir,' said the sheriff's man with respect. 'We'll follow up all kinds of people to try to find her, of course.'

'You don't seem to be doing it very quickly. Or indeed investigating the death of that old woman with any great speed. You seem very comfortable in your office here.'

'He is indeed a very efficient officer,' said Murray quickly, 'and we are lucky to have him in the county. Come, Sir John: we are going to have to leave soon to be back at Letho before dark.' He rose, cross with Aytoun, and nodded his thanks to the sheriff's man. 'Please bring any news you have, of either matter, as soon as you can – and come and speak to my household as soon as you like. You'll be very welcome,' he added, a little over-effusive to make up for Sir John's rudeness.

'These country officials are never quick to do anything unless it pleases them,' Sir John was grumbling as they waited for their horses.

'On the contrary, I have always found him most co-operative,' said Murray. 'Perhaps you find country ways a little slower after living in Edinburgh so long, though: certainly the police offices there are a different matter altogether.' The horses were brought round, saddles covered until they mounted to keep some of the rain off. Murray led the way back towards the Letho road, tweaking his cloak to shield his legs from the steady drizzle. 'So how was the season in Edinburgh this year? Lady Agostinella's condition of course forbade our attendance.'

'The season?' Sir John still sounded a little snappy. 'It was well enough. The usual thing: dances where the windows don't open and the entire room sweats, interminable card games with people who can never make up their mind which card to play or forget the rules halfway through, endless dinners starting with cold soup and finishing with melted ices. I don't know why anyone puts themselves through it.'

'But Miss Aytoun must find it enjoyable? I gather that young girls are the ones who enjoy the season, particularly if they are as much admired as Miss Aytoun must be.'

'I believe she did have a great number of admirers,' admitted Sir John, with just a hint of parental pride. 'She dances well, too … But there, it is all very tiring after a while, and perhaps we all simply needed a little rest from our experience,' he finished firmly. Murray had the distinct impression that the conversation had been declared over.

'So if you took on Collessie,' he changed the subject back to one Sir John seemed to enjoy, 'what would you do about the old deerpark?'

'There is no sign of the maid?'

Agostinella sat in her usual chair in her dim parlour, though for once the lamps had been lit early, giving the room an unaccustomed glow. It almost made her look healthy, but she was lying back in her chair, clearly tired. Her embroidery basket sat unopened by her side.

'No sign at all. It is very strange.' As usual they conversed in French.

'Poor child.'

'Yes. I hope she has found somewhere to shelter, perhaps someone kind to take her in.'

'There is no chance that – that whoever killed the old witch had something to do with this, too?'

'There is no indication of that. Agnes had nothing to do with Widow Maggot, and she was nowhere near the cottage when the widow was killed, if ever at all.'

'It does not bear thinking about,' said Agostinella. 'If there are witches here, and a witch has been killed, what might the other witches do to take revenge?'

Murray frowned: where had he heard that idea recently?

'There are no witches here,' he said, trying to sound soothing. 'Agnes has probably set out for Glasgow, or Paisley, or wherever she came from, heartily sick of being teased by Daniel. Widow Maggot was killed by ... well, I have no idea, really, nor why they might have killed her, but there is no reason to think that whoever did it is looking for another victim. And while I grant that Widow Maggot seems to have tried her best to be mistaken for a witch, I saw inside her cottage and there was nothing remotely peculiar looking or witchlike.' Except the box, said a voice inside his head. Except the box and the mirror. 'Nothing witchlike. And if anyone in the village was a witch, she's the only candidate I can think of. Who else would be one? If there were witches two hundred years ago – and I'm not at all sure that there were even then – then they are all gone now. It's the age of reason, remember? We're very enlightened here, I can assure you.'

'I'm afraid I'm not convinced,' said Agostinella, with the smallest of smiles. 'I'm afraid ... I'm afraid.' Suddenly she looked it, and reached out a thin hand for his. He took it, almost surprised to find it was warm. He slid off his stool and knelt by her chair, holding her hand in both of his.

'Don't be afraid,' he murmured. 'There are no witches.' He looked into her grey eyes, and knew it was not just witches she feared.

'I think I should like the doctor sent for soon,' she said.

'I shall send for him tomorrow.' He felt his heart double its speed, and bent to kiss her hand.

Chapter Nine

'Would Mrs. Robbins be – would I be able to visit her this morning before church? After breakfast.'

Robbins, who was shaving his master, paused to wipe off the blade before answering.

'Aye, sir, I'm sure you're always welcome.'

'Very kind, thank you, Robbins. I'd like to ask her about Agnes.'

'Of course, sir. I'm sure she'd be happy to help any way she could.'

'She doesn't need to go to any trouble – I mean, I don't want to be sorted into the parlour.'

'Sir.'

It was awkward, Murray thought: if only Robbins had married anyone but Mary. But then he would be unlikely to be consulting anyone but Mary. The tall, wild-looking Islander had helped them before, but now that she and Robbins had married – well, Murray always had a sense, however obscure, that Robbins had won.

After breakfast he pulled his waistcoat straight and ran a hand through his thick hair before darting across the driveway in the rain, making for the house on the left hand side of the drive's wide circle. With its twin opposite, it had been built when Letho was rebuilt, intending to make modest wings to the main house, but it was a good size for a senior servant with a growing family. Murray knocked quickly on the front door and only had to wait a moment until a small child, one of the daughters of a tenant on the estate, opened it and curtseyed. She looked about ten: in the Robbins household she would earn a little money, receive some training that would stand her when she was older as a maid in the big house or further afield, and still be home for supper. Frowning with concentration, she showed Murray past the parlour into the kitchen at the back of the house. It was a plain room: Mary had been married twice before and the contents of any dower chest would have been long gone in their travels. It was comfortable, though, and Murray smiled to see a polished wooden elephant on the mantel shelf: he had bought it for Robbins in Calcutta. Mary was seated by the fire, but rose easily as Murray entered.

'Mr. Murray. Will you take a seat?' She was his height, half a head taller than her husband, and dropped only a little as she curtseyed, quite as if she were only doing it as a favour. He bowed, and could not help the grin on his face as he greeted her. She smiled back.

'How are you, Mrs. Robbins?' he asked when they were settled. The very name had been hard for a while, when he always thought of her as Mary. The little maid brought tea.

'Very well as you see, and the bairn as well.' She indicated her son, sleeping soundly on a settle, grown too long like his mother for his cradle. Her voice was liquid with the Gaelic that was her native tongue.

'You never give him his name,' said Murray curiously. 'Why not? It's always "the bairn", isn't it?'

'Aye, well, you wouldn't want to give anyone any notions over him, would you?' Mary looked at him from under wicked brows.

'You mean … the little folk?' Murray felt ridiculous.

'You never know who might be listening,' she shrugged.

'Well, no.' Murray cleared his throat. 'He is a fine-looking lad.' What would his own child be like – if it was born alive?

'All the more reason,' said Mary calmly. 'I hear Lady Agostinella is keeping well this time?'

'So far, so good,' agreed Murray carefully.

'But no sign of Agnes?'

'That's what I came to talk about. No doubt if you had any useful information you would have told Robbins and he would have passed it on, but I couldn't help – I just wanted to hear more about her. I seem to have let her slip by without paying much attention.'

'Well, she isn't fit to wait at a grand table like Letho's,' Mary agreed, 'and it wouldn't be right for a respectable gentleman to paying much attention to the maid laying his fire of a morning. I hear tell she is more fit to be a cook, maybe, in a big household, though she would have been handy enough as a maid of all work in a smaller one, the like of which she was in before.'

'She came here to talk to you?'

'She came here to talk,' agreed Mary. 'Agnes is very fond of the talking.'

'That seems to have been her downfall.'

'Aye, well, Daniel never had much patience. William is kinder to her.'

'And you?'

Mary gave her triangular grin.

'Oh, she keeps me amused enough. I felt sorry for her. There is no one here she really has much in common with, I suppose. Jennet's that bit older and Iffy's daft, and Walter's too young.'

'So what is she like? Did she have interests? Ambitions? A sweetheart?' He had not thought to ask the last question before, and he should have. But Mary shook her head quickly.

'No sweetheart that she mentioned to me. She is young for her age, I should say, but not a fool. A girl from a big town: I should have thought she would be able to look after herself, but sometimes town girls are raivelt by the countryside and cannot cope.'

'Does she not like being here, then?' Murray noted Mary's constant use of the present tense, and it seemed like an anchor of hope that Agnes was still alive, despite all their fruitless searching.

'She seems happy enough. She likes Mrs. Dean, likes her room, seems to think her work is fair, sometimes feels she is not being given interesting enough things to do. She can read and write, you see, and takes that to mean educated. I asked her about her family, but she has none: her parents and an older brother died of the typhus a few years ago, but she was already in Mrs. Cowley's household and was spared. She seems very attached to Mrs. Cowley, though. Sometimes she even weeps a little when she speaks of her,' Mary frowned, as if pitying such weakness, 'and at other times she seems unable to mention her name.'

'Do you think she would have gone home? Back to Mrs. Cowley?'

Mary glanced down at her tea, briefly considering.

'I wouldn't have thought so. For one thing, she seems to me like the kind of person who just makes the best out of wherever she is, and doesn't much consider how it could be made better. And for another ...'

'Yes?'

'Well, something happened in Paisley.'

'I heard that ... well, what happened?'

'I'm not entirely sure. She told me she had seen someone being killed, a man in the street. She said she had seen that the killer had seen her, and would know her again, she thought, so she was very frightened, so much so that her mistress sent Agnes up here to stay with her old housekeeper. That'd be Mrs. Dean, the new housekeeper here.'

'Yes, that's what I heard as well. Mrs. Dean wrote back to Mrs. Cowley to reassure her that Agnes had arrived.'

'I'm not sure that Mrs. Dean ever heard back from Mrs. Cowley. And, well …'

'Yes?'

'Well, it's a strange thing with Agnes. She does love to talk, and she will talk and talk about all kinds of things. Then when we get to Mrs. Cowley and the details of her leaving Paisley, it's as if she swerves away from it. I cannot just put my finger on it,' said Mary, 'but I just have a very strong feeling that Agnes was not exactly telling the truth.'

Morning service was gloomy. The autumn had set in with determination, as if it regretted its charitable sunshine of earlier in the week. In addition, the unsolved murder of Widow Maggot and Agnes's unresolved disappearance had left the village, not unreasonably, uneasy and anxious. Crushed into the Letho pew with Grants and Blairs (not Agostinella, who usually found excuses to stay away), smelling of wet wool, Murray thought about but could not study the villagers ranged behind him. He tried to concentrate on the sermon, which was being delivered, like a particularly ill-wrapped parcel, by Mr. Rintoul. Rintoul's speaking style needed some development: he had a tendency to spring off the point and gallop down odd diversions in a way that reminded Murray of his spaniels. When he found his own argument more exciting than usual, Rintoul's red hair seemed to catch fire, sprouting from his head and chin like rays from a rambling sun.

After the service the congregation left the church unwillingly, glaring at the wet day outside. They were mostly encouraging to the assistant minister, who beamed shyly at each compliment and nodded seriously when anyone made a helpful suggestion. Murray was not sure whether or not Rintoul could hear his proud landlady,

Mrs. Maitland, who was at the kirkyard gate, taking credit for her lodger's improvements.

'That's good Letho air and good Letho cooking, that's what's given him a bit of life!' she was saying to her friends. 'See, his appetite's twice what it was when he came from that unhealthy city!'

'He'll be twice the man, too, if you're no careful,' remarked a friend. 'You dinna want him that fat he'll no fit in the pulpit.'

The women laughed and Murray lingered to enjoy the sound: it was better than looking at the kirk session members, who were lurking about the church door with long faces, waiting for their meeting to start. Watson and Kenny the schoolmaster were heads together, muttering, looking worried. Murray was glad to round up his guests and get away, but as he was about to leave he was surprised to see Rintoul himself hurry up.

'Mr. Murray, sir.' He stretched out a detaining hand like a respectful scholar to his dominie. In his other hand he had a bundle wrapped in sacking. 'I took a walk yesterday towards Josie's Den, intrigued by the place after our visit the other day.'

'I'm glad you enjoyed it,' said Murray with a smile.

'The thing is,' Rintoul went on, 'on my way back I stopped to make a note of something I had just remembered, and in the hedge as I paused I found this.'

He presented the bundle to Murray. Puzzle, Murray unwrapped a corner of it.

'Is it – what I think it is?' asked Rintoul anxiously, raindrops sparkling in his wild hair. 'Is it hers?'

Murray pulled out the hood of a small grey cloak.

'I'm not sure,' he said, 'but I'll ask.'

'We've found Agnes' cloak on the road to Cupar,' Murray explained at tea that afternoon. The Aytouns were returning yesterday's hospitality.

'Surely she knew that was not the way home?' Sir John frowned.

'She may have become confused,' suggested Blair, 'or gone to look for the road through the village and for some reason missed it.'

'It is hard to miss,' said Murray mildly, 'but yes, if she were confused in the dusk.'

'Perhaps she thought it best to return to Josie's Den and start her route again?' said Andrew Grant. He did not seem to have his mind fully on the matter: he had half his attention at least on Miss Mathilda, who was talking with his stepson Robert. Miss Mathilda was indeed pretty, but Murray was sure he would not have exchanged her for intelligent Mrs. Grant.

'In that case – in any case, if she were on that road, why did we not see her?' he demanded, pulling his mind back to the matter at hand. 'I know she was small-made, but for goodness' sake she was looking for us. If we did not see her, in the dusk and the rain, then why on earth did she not call out? She could not have missed us.'

'There's another thing that worries me, Charles,' said Blair, his face a twist of anxiety. 'Why in the dusk and the rain, as you say, did she take off her cloak?'

It did not seem to matter what ideas any of them had: no one could make sense of the cloak, and they seemed not a step nearer to finding poor Agnes.

The ladies were once again sewing in a broad window embrasure, catching the best of the afternoon light as the rain temporarily eased. Miss Mathilda and Robert Lovie were a little apart, tinkering with the box piano, showing each other tunes they knew. Murray glanced at Isobel but she seemed happy enough, only casting them an occasional, deliberately amused look. Mrs. Grant seemed more anxious.

'I must say I tried to persuade Robert not to come with us this afternoon: I am sure he is wearing to catch a cold, and when Robert catches cold somehow he always manages to spread it to everyone around him! I'm sure Miss Aytoun should sit further from him: I should hate her to catch his cold.'

'He looks very healthy to me, Mrs. Grant,' said Lady Aytoun soothingly. 'And Tilly is a very healthy girl: she rarely catches anything unpleasant.' Indeed the only flush on Mathilda's face seemed to be one of pleasure at some compliment Robert had paid her. Truth to tell, they looked a well-matched couple.

'Robert, do come and help me with this pair of scissors, dear,' said Mrs. Grant. 'You know how they always catch, and you're so good at sorting them out.'

'Oh, please, borrow mine!' exclaimed Lady Aytoun, with a benevolent glance at Robert and Tilly.

'No, no, it's very good of you, but I should be bothering you the whole time for them. Robert, dear?'

Robert gave a good-natured sigh and slipped off the piano stool to attend to his mother's embroidery sharps, tiny in his deft fingers.

'There we are, mother,' he said, handing them back. 'All fixed again.' He turned back to Tilly, whose rosebud mouth widened quickly to a smile as he approached. It looked like a match, indeed. Murray's gaze returned to Mrs. Grant who was fiddling with the mended scissors, and noticed a deep gouge on the outside edge of her embroidery hoop. Surely she had not been trying to cut the polished wood with her scissors? That would certainly have made them catch. He must ask Isobel why anyone would do such a thing.

When tea was over, the Letho party gathered their things and began to think about carriages. Murray, still puzzled by Agnes' cloak, excused himself from the carriage party and took his horse back not by the road, but along the paths that led through woods and fields from Collessie to Letho. Blair waved him off, nodding, understanding that he needed time to think, and he allowed his horse to amble along while the spaniels, eager for exercise, covered three times the distance in scent trails around the path.

The Collessie woods were never well-managed, full of fallen trees and untended saplings and thickets of impenetrable brambles. Murray stopped to pick a few late blackberries, shiny in the rain, and the spaniels helped themselves to others on the low-sweeping stems. He looked about him, assessing vaguely whether there was enough work on the estate to keep Sir John interested, or so much that it would put him off offering for the place. The Aytouns as neighbours – well, Letho could do worse, and if Robert married Tilly, then it might bring the Grants more often to stay, and he found he liked both of them.

A little wind suddenly gusted. His gaze sharpened: was there someone there? The spaniels, both dim and friendly dogs, instantly growled, stiff and alert. The horse laid its ears back, and even from behind he could see she was rolling her eyes. He dug his heels in, and she broke immediately into a trot, briskly putting whatever it was behind her, while the dogs darted after. Murray held his seat and wondered whether to try to turn the horse back, but he found that he did not even want to look back, though he could not have said why.

He left the country path and rode into the village along the road by the schoolhouse, with a sense of relief: people were about, even if only a few, and the world felt normal again. He shook himself in much the way his spaniels were doing, and slowed to a walk, waving with uncharacteristic enthusiasm to Kenny the schoolmaster who was at his window. Ahead he could see Mr. Helliwell, the minister, coming out of the front door of the manse. The minister saw him and stopped, then waved.

'I was about to come and see you, Mr. Murray,' he said urgently as Murray approached. He looked so concerned that Murray slid down from his horse and came closer: Helliwell seemed reluctant to raise his voice to be heard too far away.

'What's the matter?' Murray asked.

'It's Lizzie Fenwick,' said Helliwell, glancing about him.

'What about her?'

'Quietly!' Helliwell shook his head as if trying to clear it. 'Sorry, sorry, Mr. Murray. This whole business: the whole village seems to be on edge.'

'Agnes? Or Widow Maggot?'

'Widow Maggot – well, both, I suppose. The thing is, the Kirk Session met after the service this morning as usual, and I tried to talk them out of it but they were so insistent, I had no chance, and in the end I wondered if it would be the safer way to go for all concerned. But now – well, now I'm wondering if I should have been firmer. But they were all determined, all of them – well, maybe not Kenny and Watson, but in the end they went along with the rest, too. But I know it's not right. At least, I think – I must believe – it's not right.'

'Mr. Helliwell,' said Murray, bewildered, 'what is not right?'

'They have apprehended Lizzie Fenwick, and imprisoned her in the old cell in the church tower. They are going to the presbytery as soon as they can, to accuse her of witchcraft.'

'What?'

Helliwell nodded. He looked, Murray suddenly realised, genuinely frightened.

'In the tower. I don't believe that cell has been used in two hundred years – not as a cell, anyway. We sometimes store coal in it … for the stove, you know …' He tailed away, aware that he was drifting off the subject, eyes pleading with Murray to think of something. Murray scowled.

'Can we go to see her?'

'I don't know … I'm not sure …'

'Well, can I go to see her? There's a grille in that door, isn't there? There's nothing to stop me. Is there anyone on guard?'

'Only Mal Johnstone, at the moment. They're taking it in turns, in this weather.'

'I hope they all catch colds,' Murray muttered angrily. 'Fools.' He slipped his horse's reins around the manse gatepost and stalked back to the kirkyard gate, baffled and seething. The door to the old cell was at the back of the church, at the foot of the low tower, with an ancient wooden door facing into a corner of the building so that the cell's inhabitants would have no view and no one casually passing could see in. In the kink of the corner stood Mal Johnstone, plumply to attention, stoically soaking from his hat down. He blinked when he saw Murray approach.

'Mr. Murray, sir!'

'Mal. I understand you have a prisoner here?'

'Oh, aye, sir – we've got her! It's the witch, Lizzie Fenwick, ken. We'll have her up before the presbytery for witchcraft, and nae doubt she'll confess to taking yon maid of yours too.'

'Mal, why would she have taken Agnes? Agnes didn't even know Widow Maggot: she had scarcely even been in the village before. If – and I don't believe it for a moment – if Mrs. Fenwick had wanted to take revenge on anyone for Widow Maggot's death, surely it would have been on someone actually involved in the murder?'

'Oh, witches ken more than we mortals do, Mr. Murray,' said Mal smugly. 'Nae doubt if they've done away with Agnes Carstairs and she had nothing to do with Widow Maggot's end, then it's to be a lesson for us all.'

'But if they've done away with her as a lesson to us, surely it would be more sensible to let us find the body?' He felt he was being tangled in Mal's mad arguments. 'And I thought I heard you say at the funeral yesterday that Widow Maggot wasn't dead, anyway? That she had escaped from her coffin?'

'There's nothing to say there's not the two of them in it,' said Mal.

'Oh, go away and let me speak to Mrs. Fenwick.'

'Do what, sir?'

'Let me speak to Mrs. Fenwick.'

'Och, I canna do that, sir. No one is to speak to her. See, I had her girl's man here ten minutes ago, and I tellt him the same thing. No one is to speak to her at all - that was what we decided.'

'We? You mean the Kirk Session?'

'Aye, sir. In the absence of the minister, the Kirk Session is responsible for the spiritual wellbeing of the parish,' he chanted, as if he had read it somewhere important.

'But the minister isn't absent. He was at the meeting.'

'But the minister isna taking our spiritual wellbeing into account, is he, Mr. Murray? Otherwise he'd be doing something about these witches himself.'

Murray took a deep breath, and made himself step back slightly.

'So do you think these are the only two witches hereabouts?'

Mal's lips twitched.

'Some say aye,' he said tightly.

'But you don't agree?'

'I say that where there's one or two, mostly likely there's more. See, two witches, that's no much of a coven, is it?'

'I wouldn't know,' said Murray with precision.

There was a step behind him, and a scuffle on the stony path. He turned. It was, as Mal had put it, Lizzie Fenwick's girl's man – or Patie White, her late daughter's husband. Lizzie's cottage was next door to his in the village.

'Mr. Murray, sir,' said Patie with a nod. 'Och, Mal, are you still there?'

'Were you hoping there'd be a softer fool than me taking my place to let you see her? Get away home, Patie White, and be glad no one's after you as a witch, too!'

'Right, that's enough,' said Murray. 'Mal Johnstone, move aside out of that corner and let me see Lizzie Fenwick. Give me the key.'

'I've no got it,' said Mal uncomfortably, one hand hovering

over his coat pocket. Murray stepped suddenly across the distance between them and snatched the key from the pocket.

'Go and stand over there,' he commanded, pointing across the kirkyard.

'You canna let her out!'

'I want to see if she's all right,' said Murray. 'Don't make me move you aside.'

For a second, Mal was brave: then he assessed the chances of a man in his condition being able to hold his ground against Murray, and scuttled out of his corner.

'I'm no leaving the kirkyard!' he insisted squeakily. 'I'm no abandoning my post!'

'No one is asking you to leave – yet,' said Murray, his teeth gritted. 'But if you can't be quiet I'll throw you over the wall myself. Now, Patie, what are you doing here?'

Patie had a bundle under his arm.

'I've brought her a blanket and some food,' he explained as Murray opened the cell door.

'Good man. Mrs. Fenwick?'

For a moment there was silence, and it crossed his mind that Mal had gone completely daft and was guarding an empty cell. Then something moved in the corner, and Lizzie Fenwick emerged into the dim light of the October dusk. Murray and Patie gasped.

Her clothes were rumpled, and her face was a little bruised. But more shocking than either was the fact that they had shaved her head. Her snow white hair and sharp black eyebrows had gone.

'What have they done to you, mother?' asked Patie, his voice faint.

'Only shaved me, dinna worry, begoyt boy,' said Lizzie Fenwick, though it was true to say she looked shaken. 'They were looking for witchmarks. I'm to be thankful they haven't thought of pricking me yet, though!' she ended on a slightly wobbly laugh.

'You'd better come to Letho with me,' said Murray. 'We can look after you there.'

'Aye, aye, that's a grand idea,' said Patie, who evidently didn't think much of his chances of looking after her himself. 'You should do what the laird says.'

'I think I'd be better here, no harm to you, Mr. Murray,' said Lizzie Fenwick. 'They're riled enough without me being rescued.

I'm innocent: I'd be as well to stay here and stand my ground in front of the presbytery. They canna all be as doitered as the Kirk Session.'

'But this cell ...'

'I see Patie's brought me a blanket and a pie – I'll be quite comfortable. I've stayed in worse!' She took the blanket from Patie and spread it neatly on a hollow she seemed to have made in the heap of coal, then took the pie from him. Patie drew the end of a candle from his pocket and a small flask from under his other arm, and handed them over. They watched, mesmerised, as she busied herself making the horrid cell as homely as she could, humming to herself as she worked. 'Now, would either of you like a slice of pie?'

'Mrs. Fenwick, I cannot let you –'

'Well, you're going to have to, Mr. Murray! I'll stay here. I tell you, this is palatial: in the last witch hunt, back in King Jamie's time, some of the witches were held in cells in old Letho House. That was not so salubrious, I can tell you! Now, off you go: once I'm fed and watered I'll think of a few choice words to whisper in Mal Johnstone's foolish ears.'

'What could you do with her?' Patie asked with wide eyes when they had allowed Mal to return to his post. 'Thrawn, that's the word for her.'

'Are you worried?' Murray asked him carefully.

'Do you mean do I think she's a witch, sir?' He toed the grass round a grave stone. 'Folks all ken Lizzie Fenwick and I don't always see eye to eye, and indeed many a time we've spent the evening shouting at each other. But I'd no say she's a witch, not at all, and however raist I might be with her I'd never lock her in there, not for a minute!'

'I'd better go and tell the minister,' said Murray with a sigh. 'I think this village is going mad.'

And maybe he wasn't far behind, he said to himself that evening. He stared out of his bedchamber window before closing the shutters. A white hare, paused on the grass below, seemed to be staring back at him, caught for a few seconds in the starlight after the rain. It assessed him, then loped off, winking away into the shadows. He eased the shutters closed and turned to his bed, but something caught his eye on the mantelpiece. He crossed to look, once again, at the mirror there from Widow Maggot's cottage. In the reflection, a shadow, vague but looming, swayed behind him. A cat? There was no sound, and the door was closed. The candlelight, then, no doubt, he told himself, the flame lurching in a draught. He turned, but the candle burned straight and true.

Chapter Ten

Monday morning dawned a little brighter. Murray gazed at the sky through the open shutters, feeling his heart growing more optimistic as the day lightened. He swung out of bed and went into the dressing room for Robbins to shave him.

'How are things, Robbins?' he asked before the razor came into contact.

'Still no sign of Agnes, sir, of course,' Robbins began. 'I do not like the look of the cloak being found, though. I had hopes that she had gone back to Paisley, tormented by Daniel and William, but she would not have left her cloak behind.'

'Everyone is sure it's hers?'

'Definitely. And there's her initials in it, anyway, sir.'

'Yes, it's not a good sign,' Murray agreed, though the part of him that was brightened by the day still fought to be more optimistic. 'But perhaps someone offered her a lift, she took her cloak off because it was wet, and somehow it slipped out of the carriage as she climbed in?'

'Who would be giving a maid a lift inside a carriage, sir?' was Robbins' gloomy response. 'She would be lucky to get a seat up with the coachman, unless the carriage owner had ill intentions towards her.'

'Oh, for goodness' sake, Robbins: how can we ever know what has happened to her?'

'I don't know, sir. I wish I did.'

Blair was at breakfast when Murray entered the parlour, tucking in to an elaborate plateful of ham, eggs, kedgeree and bread, sprinkled with his favourite nutmeg. Isobel sat opposite him, reading an *Edinburgh Courant* from the previous week, apparently using the paper as a barrier to avoid watching her father eating while she sipped her hot chocolate. Murray greeted them with his new-found cheerfulness and they stared at him before returning to their breakfast. Murray shrugged and grinned, and helped himself to kedgeree.

'Plans for today?' he asked generally.

'I hoped to go for a ride, if the rain holds off,' said Isobel.

'Your delightful gardener has promised to show me how the pineapple frames are doing, and the steam device he has invented for heating them,' said Blair, his eyes bright in anticipation. It was just Blair's kind of thing.

'I have to talk to Thalland about the cattle sales at Cupar,' said Murray, 'but after that if you need an escort, Isobel, I'll be happy to accompany you.'

'I don't usually need an escort at Letho,' said Isobel, with a hint of sulkiness, 'and I don't want to delay in case the rain starts.'

'It won't rain before tea time,' said Murray with more certainty than perhaps the situation deserved. Isobel clearly thought so, for she raised her eyebrows cynically at the windows before returning to her paper.

The parlour door opened and the Grants came in together.

'Good morning!' said Murray, still hoping to find a cheerful response. 'How is everyone?'

'Has anyone seen Robert?' Andrew Grant asked at once.

'Not this morning,' said Murray, and looked to the Blairs. Both shook their heads.

'Is he not in his room?' asked Isobel.

'No, nor in the drawing room – we thought he might have been practising at the pianoforte,' said Mrs. Grant, looking more worried than Murray would have expected of the mother of an adult son temporarily strayed.

'No doubt he has gone out for a walk,' said Blair comfortably, 'taking advantage of the better weather. Mrs. Grant, some hot chocolate?'

The door opened again, and the expression on Robbins' face finally extinguished any optimism in Murray's heart for the morning. He carried a note on a tray.

'From Sir John Aytoun, sir.'

'Is the servant waiting for a reply?' Murray asked, reluctant to see the contents.

'He is now: he nearly forgot,' said Robbins sourly, and stood still, watching the note in Murray's long fingers. Murray took a breath, and opened it.

'Dear Murray,' it said. 'My daughter Mathilda has vanished without a sign. Please come as soon as you can. Your servant, J. Aytoun.'

'What is it?' asked Andrew Grant. He seemed to be holding his breath. Murray looked up: everyone was looking at him.

'Send to Sir John to say I'll be there as soon as I can,' Murray said to Robbins. Robbins bowed and left. 'Mathilda Aytoun has disappeared,' he said to the rest.

Andrew Grant and his wife exchanged a hard look, and a nod.

'Charles,' said Cousin Andrew, 'may I speak to you in private?'

The library was across the hall from the parlour, and Murray sat at his desk there. Cousin Andrew was happier to stand.

'You may have wondered,' he said, coming to the point straightaway, 'why we should have begged an invitation to Letho during the season, when most parents of young people are Edinburgh or Bath or London?'

'It crossed my mind, but I was glad to see you,' said Murray, knotting his fingers over his knees, wondering what on earth could be coming next.

'We had to leave London. Robert … my stepson insulted a young lady.'

'Insulted? You mean he –'

'He seduced her,' said Andrew miserably. 'Lured her away from her friends and ah … He claimed her virginity.'

'You could not make him marry her?' It would be the usual solution.

'No!' Andrew flung himself heavily into an armchair and groaned. 'No, we talked endlessly with the girl's parents, Margaret and I. Margaret is so ashamed of him, I cannot tell you. The girl would have married him, I believe, but we would not – we could not abandon the girl to him. You see, he had done it before – when he was at school, he seduced a young lady who lived nearby. They had met at a dance. And then there was another lady he met at the theatre … We only found out about them much later.'

'And the girl in London?'

'Fortunately no child ensued. We helped the parents find a more – suitable husband for her. The girl was not happy with the situation, but it would have been much, much worse for her if their marriage had gone ahead.'

'Let me get this clear: Robert seduces young ladies and abandons them, is that what you are saying?'

'Yes!' Andrew said indistinctly. His chin was in his hands but he met Murray's eye.

'And you think he might have seduced Mathilda, is that it?'

'It seems a strong possibility. We were worried already – you heard us trying to persuade him to stay here yesterday, instead of going to visit the Aytouns. But we had no idea he would work so quickly.'

Murray lay back in his chair and rubbed his forehead. Would it be better or worse for Sir John to think that Mathilda had vanished in the same mysterious way as Agnes, or that she had been seduced by his cousin? But wait – was there a choice?

'What about Agnes?' he asked at once.

Andrew lifted his head.

'We don't think he had anything to do with Agnes. You see, he has never … he has never tangled with servants. It has always been young ladies of good birth.'

'I'm not entirely convinced,' said Murray, coldly. 'It may be that it is only the gently born ladies that have come to your notice. I wish you had told me, at any rate.'

'I'm sorry. Margaret and I discussed it, and we thought he had nothing to do with it. We did ask him, you know, and he denied it. He had no reason to do that, I think.'

'Perhaps not: I should still like to have known. Now I had better go and see Sir John. Will you come with me?'

Andrew swallowed heavily.

'I'd better, I suppose.'

Lady Aytoun was a tearful heap, her anxiety not lessened by their news, merely changed. Sir John Aytoun, by contrast, was furious.

'You let a man like that within a mile of my daughter? You will pay for this, Grant!'

Grant had little answer to make, and stood like an overinflated schoolboy, shoulders hunched in shame. His eyes widened and contracted by turns, like gills.

'Did she leave any message or note? Did she take anything with her?' Murray asked, trying to take the fire out of the conversation.

Sir John glared at his wife.

'No, no, nothing I could see. Only her reticule.'

'Her reticule? Did it contain anything of value?'

'Some jewels, I believe,' said the woman, between sobs.

'And nothing else? She could simply have misplaced the reticule,' said Murray, remembering the muddle over their reticules at Letho a few days before.

'Her cloak,' said Lady Aytoun.

'For heaven's sake, woman, you did not mention that!' snapped Sir John.

'And her bonnet,' added Lady Aytoun.

'I thought she had been snatched from her bed, and instead you tell me that the silly girl went off of her own accord!' Sir John's fury was at least now split between Grant and his wife. 'Gloves? Boots?'

'Yes, yes. Gloves and boots,' Lady Aytoun admitted, tears streaming down her little face. 'Her favourite ones.'

'Damnation!' Sir John yelled, his face chalk-white. His angry eyes were black as soot.

'Right, well, this isn't going to find her. Cousin Andrew,' said Murray briskly, 'is there a typical kind of place you might know that Robert meets his – his female acquaintances?'

'He likes the outdoors,' said Grant helplessly. Murray sighed.

'Woodland? Haystacks?'

Lady Aytoun gave a little squeal.

'Riverbanks? Loch shores?' Murray pressed on relentlessly.

'Not in this weather, surely,' said Sir John, sounding as if he had at least reined in a little of his rage. He was still breathing heavily, and pushed his flopping hair back from his forehead.

'Well, there's a good deal of outdoors to consider here. We should all know that from last week,' said Murray, hanging on to his supplies of patience. Grant had still not convinced him that Robert had nothing to do with Agnes' disappearance.

'Woodland, then, I think,' said Grant, though Murray

wondered if he was picking one at random to give some kind of answer. 'Particularly in this weather.'

'Well, there's plenty of woodland, too. We'd better start looking. Sir John, do you want to start with the Collessie woodland and I'll go back and organise a search of the Letho woods?'

'That's strange,' said Mrs. Dean the housekeeper.

'What's the matter, Mrs. Dean?' asked Mrs. Mack. The kitchen was quiet at this time of day, and she was focussing on boning legs of mutton with precision. Iffy was not allowed near such sharp knives and was washing the breakfast dishes.

'The forks we were using at tea on Saturday: there are two missing.'

'Iffy!' cried Mrs. Mack. Iffy edged out of the scullery, knowing Mrs. Mack's tones of voice very well. 'Missing forks, Iffy. What have you done with them?'

'I dinna ken nothing about any forks, Mrs. Mack, Mrs. Dean,' said Iffy quickly, rubbing her bony hands on her apron. Mrs. Dean and Mrs. Mack met each other's eyes, and Mrs. Dean sprang up to carry out a quick inspection of the scullery. She reappeared in a moment, shaking her head.

'Nothing,' she said. 'Where could they have gone?'

'We've never had a problem with light-fingered servants in this household,' said Mrs. Mack firmly, 'and we dinna want to start now.'

'Oh, I'm sure they've simply been mislaid. Probably my fault, not so familiar with where everything goes,' said Mrs. Dean, but her brow was still wrinkled. 'I'll look again when I get back from the village. I'll maybe check the parlour, see they have not fallen down behind a chair.'

'Off to see friends, then?' asked Mrs. Mack, who liked to know what was going on.

'That's right,' said Mrs. Dean, but did not elaborate.

'Has anyone seen the front door key?' Robbins appeared in the kitchen doorway. 'I've been locking up for two nights with the spare one, and I don't like it.'

'I haven't seen it,' said Mrs. Dean, and automatically sifted through the keys at her waist as if checking it had not hung itself on there without telling her.

'It's not the time to be leaving a front door unlocked at night,' muttered Robbins, then looked up as a bell rang. 'Library,' he added to himself, and turned to answer it.

'Robbins.' Murray waved him in. He was slumped in the desk chair, with his boots still on from his visit to Collessie.

'Sir.'

'We'll have to start a search for Mathilda Aytoun now.' He sighed. 'Apparently we should start with woodland, but I don't know that we'll find her there. Look, you'll need to know this but don't pass it on to the servants' hall just yet. It looks as if Robert Lovie has had an assignation with Miss Aytoun, with dishonourable intentions.'

'I see, sir.' Robbins' pale brows twitched to show he understood entirely.

'He's done it before, apparently.' Murray sighed weightily. 'What else is going to go wrong, Robbins?'

'So we're looking for both of them, sir?'

'That's right. As quickly as possible, before - well, before anything happens.'

'Does that mean he had something to do with Agnes, as well, sir?'

'Mr. Grant says no, that he prefers gentlefolk to servant girls.'

'Is that so, sir,' said Robbins flatly.

'I see your mind runs as mine does, Robbins.'

'Hard not to, sir.'

'Indeed. Mr. Grant is changing his clothes to join in the hunt. Mr. Blair will join us, too. Is there any male servant not already exhausted by this and fit to join us?'

'I think it's the turn of the stable staff, sir.'

'Then we'd better summon them. Again.'

There was no longer an air of excitement in the men assembled on the drive to search for Mathilda Aytoun.

'For those who haven't seen her, she's tall and slim with a pale complexion and dark hair,' Murray addressed them. 'A blue cloak and bonnet, and new blue leather boots. We're starting with the woodland on Letho land, but keep your eyes open everywhere. She may be in the company of Robert Lovie, who has been staying here: we need to find both of them.'

'That's not hard, sir,' said Walter the servant boy suddenly. 'There's Mr. Lovie just coming now.'

Murray spun on the gravel. Robert Lovie came round the corner between the big house and the Robbins' house, his hat back on his head and an expression on his face that almost echoed Murray's own forgotten cheerfulness of that morning. He raised his eyebrows at the search party, and drew to a halt beside Murray.

'Another hunt for Agnes?' he asked. 'Has there been more news?'

'No, nothing on Agnes. Where have you been?'

'I went out for a walk early, enticed by this fine day,' said Robert with a smile. 'Believe it or not I walked all the way to Josie's Den! It is less appealing all wet, though, so I did not linger. I hope my parents have not been worrying you about me?'

'They were anxious, yes. Perhaps you and I had better go indoors for a moment.' He did not want the entire staff of the stable yard witnessing what was likely to be an awkward conversation. 'You men, carry on as instructed – I shall follow soon. Walter, remember to stay close to someone who knows the way.'

'Yes, sir,' came Walter's solemn response as Murray turned and ushered Robert Lovie back into the hallway and through to the library. He rang for Robbins.

'Robert, do you know anything about Agnes' disappearance?' he asked.

Robert looked surprised.

'No more than the next man,' he said. 'Why should I?'

'Robert, your stepfather has told me about the young lady in London.'

'Oh.'

'Yes. And the others.'

'Ah. I see.' Robert stood still, fiddling a little with his waistcoat buttons. 'But that has nothing to do with Agnes. I mean, well, she was a servant. I don't think I saw her more than once, anyway. I had nothing to do with her.'

He seemed plausible, but then he always had. Murray watched him for a moment. Now that he knew, he could see Robert quite easily as a successful seducer. The boy certainly had charm.

Robbins appeared at the door.

'Robbins, can you please bring the Grants here?'

'Sir.'

Murray cleared his throat and turned back to Lovie.

'And now Mathilda Aytoun has disappeared. What do you know about that? She is not a servant.'

'She's disappeared?' Robert's hands dropped from the waistcoat buttons. 'Disappeared? Are you sure?'

The Grants must have been in the parlour: they hurried in, Andrew in his outdoor clothes ready to join the search for Mathilda.

'Robert!' cried his mother. 'What have you done with Miss Aytoun?'

'I don't know what you mean,' said Robert, with an attempt at innocence.

'Robert!' Andrew Grant had pulled himself back from the mortified heap that Sir John had attacked: he was more as Murray imagined him in court with a stubborn witness. His eyes flashed. Robert's face changed.

'I didn't do anything with her, not this time,' he said quickly. 'But I did arrange to meet her.'

'Where?'

'In the woods at Collessie. There's a woodman's hut just off the path near the river, easy to find if you're looking for it. She had seen it so I was sure she would be able to find it even at night, and I had a lantern in the doorway to help her.'

'Last night?'

'That's right. We were to meet at midnight.'

'And elope?' Murray asked. Mathilda had taken no luggage. Robert went a little pink.

'No, no. I had no intention of eloping.' He coughed and flicked a look at his mother. 'Usually one night is enough for me,' he added, in a very low voice.

'You should be whipped,' hissed his stepfather. Mrs. Grant's face was tight and furious.

'So where is Mathilda, then, after your one night?' asked Murray acidly.

'I don't know,' said Robert. To do him justice, he did look worried.

'You let her go back to Collessie on her own? In the dark?'

'No, no!' Robert did not want the crime of a lack of gallantry laid to his door on top of seduction. 'I thought you understood. Tilly never turned up. I waited all night, but she never came. I thought ... I thought she had probably changed her mind. Some of them do ...' he added, then caught his mother's eye again.

'We thought if we brought you here, away from the temptations of London and Bath, you might manage to behave!' said Grant. 'How could you do this again? When you knew very well how upset your mother was the last time? And when you know what effect you have on the girls? What is the matter with you?'

Robert hung his head, but Murray was more interested in the matter of the latest girl.

'So you did not see Mathilda Aytoun last night? She definitely did not appear? Even though you had a firm arrangement to meet?'

'That's right. There was no sign of her. I was a bit put out, to tell the truth: she seemed very interested.'

'That's enough!' yelled Andrew Grant.

'I'll have to go and tell Sir John,' said Murray. 'I think this complicates things. He'll need to know. Please, ah, feel free to make use of this room for as long as you need ...'

He bowed, unnoticed, and left the room. Out in the hall, he paused for a moment, taking in the implications of what they had found out. Then he made up his mind and hurried across the hall to the servants' door, into the half-forbidden territory beyond and along to the kitchen door. As expected, Mrs. Dean and Mrs. Mack scurried to a kind of attention as he entered. He was brisk.

'Miss Mathilda Aytoun has disappeared. I do not want any female to leave this house after dusk and before dawn without a very good reason and an escort. Is that clear?'

'Sir,' said the cook and the housekeeper, and Mrs. Mack, as he was turning away, was hauling Iffy from the scullery and repeating the instructions to her. Robbins, hearing the commotion, appeared in the corridor.

'It seems Robert Lovie had nothing to do with Miss Aytoun's disappearance, Robbins – or at least, he arranged to meet her, but she did not appear. All the women in the household must stay in after dusk unless they have someone trustworthy with them – that probably does not include Daniel and William, by the way.'

'Indeed, sir. Are you going to warn the ladies? I think I heard Miss Blair say she was going to go for a ride.'

'Yes, of course. Go at once and make sure Mary is safe, and the little maid there.'

'Of course, sir. I'll make sure the word is passed on round the tenants, too.'

'Thank you.'

Murray made his way back to the parlour, but he found Isobel in the hall, ready to go out.

'I'm just waiting for Dunnet to bring my pony,' she explained. 'Is there something going on?'

'You're definitely not going on your own,' said Murray. 'Mathilda Aytoun has disappeared.'

'With Robert?' Isobel asked at once.

'No, as it turns out, but not for want of trying. The point is, she has disappeared and so has Agnes, and your father would be mildly upset if the same thing happened to you. But I'm going out just now, too, so if you want to take a ride to the village and to Collessie then feel free to join me.'

Isobel thought for a moment, lips pressed, weighing the options.

'Well, I can't waste the weather,' she said at last.

Outside Murray's horse was still waiting and Dunnet was just bringing Isobel's dappled pony. Murray handed her up into the saddle and swung himself up, waiting for her to settle herself before they set off round Robbins' house to follow the country path to Collessie.

'When did Tilly disappear?' Isobel asked.

'Last night, we think. She took a cloak and bonnet, so she must have left the house of her own freewill.' He chose not to go into Robert's involvement yet. 'But there was no note left, and there's no sign of her today.' He glanced over at the woodland to their right, and saw that the stableboys were quartering it efficiently. At least it was daylight, and not actually raining, but if Mathilda had been lying somewhere all night she would not be in a good state. 'Is there a good reason why someone should try to cut their embroidery hoop with a pair of scissors?' he asked suddenly.

'I imagine she was trying to distract Robert,' said Isobel, and when Murray turned to stare at her added, 'Yes, I saw it, too. I'd say she's done it before. Robert knew what she was doing and she knew that Robert knew, I should say, but she was trying to draw him away from Tilly. Did they have an assignation?'

Murray sighed.

'Yes, they did. I have to go and tell Sir John. Robert says he waited, but Mathilda never appeared.'

'I see.' Isobel was solemn. Murray said nothing. They paced on, Murray's eyes darting about for the least sign of either missing girl. At last she added, 'He didn't try it with me, if you're wondering.'

'I imagine you would have given him short shrift,' Murray remarked.

'Yes,' she agreed, thoughtfully. Murray wondered if she was offended not at least to have been tested for seduction.

'Where are those wretched dogs?' Murray broke the silence, and stopped to look back. 'Come on, Bonnie! Come on, Flash!' The two spaniels scampered after them, abandoning some thrilling scent across the field. A figure in the distance was crossing the field further back, heading for the village path.

'Is that your new housekeeper?' Isobel asked, staring.

'Yes, Mrs. Dean. I hope she's intending to be home before dusk, anyway.'

They could only leave a message for Sir John, with a Collessie servant who did not inspire any more confidence than the rest of them. He at least had the sense to fetch Lady Aytoun's maid when they asked for Lady Aytoun: Lady Aytoun had retired to her chamber in hysterics, the maid reported, but was being looked after. Isobel offered to stay and help but the maid seemed competent, and in the end they turned and remounted and rode for Letho village. On the road, they met Mr. Rintoul, hair and whiskers wine-dark and agitated, hurrying towards them.

'Have you come from Collessie?' he asked, after bowing to them.

'We have.'

'I am just off to join the hunt. Is there any news of Miss Aytoun?'

'None yet, I'm afraid. I'm sure they'll be glad of your help.'

'I missed the whole hunt for little Agnes,' he explained. 'I feel so ashamed. And Miss Aytoun, such a lovely girl. When I think of her out on her own all night – dreadful!' He bowed again and scurried on his way. His hat seemed to bounce on his hair as he went.

'I did think he'd taken a bit of a fancy to her,' said Isobel, watching him go.

'He does seem upset. Well, on to the village: I want you home before dusk.'

'What's your business there, then?' asked Isobel, resignedly.

'I want to see if Lizzie Fenwick is still all right,' said Murray. 'I hope that whoever is guarding her might also release her, since she cannot possibly have had anything to do with Mathilda Aytoun's disappearance.'

But in that he was doomed to be unlucky, or Lizzie Fenwick was. They dismounted at the kirkyard gate and marched up the path beside the church, to find Melville, the tenant farmer who had borne Widow Maggot's coffin, at the door of the cell, propped against the church wall and looking grim.

'Miss Aytoun too?' he asked when Murray told him the news. 'I heard something of the kind.'

'Well, it can't have been Lizzie Fenwick this time, can it?' asked Murray, trying to sound reasonable.

'Ah,' Melville looked knowing. 'Mal Johnstone says a witch can easy do things when she's not even there. And anyway, no doubt there are other witches about. Two witches, that's no much of a coven, is it?' Mal's words from yesterday flowed easily from Melville's lips. Murray knew he was up against more than one man here.

'Has anyone been to see her since yesterday?'

'Her son-in-law came yesterday – oh, that was when you were here, wasn't it, sir? There's been nobody since. She's been quiet enough.'

'Maybe she's escaped,' said Isobel with a straight face. 'There's a tiny gap just under the door here ...'

'What?' squeaked Melville, jumping to the door. 'Ah, no, she's still there. How are you doing, Lizzie? All right?'

'I'm grand, thank you,' came Lizzie's voice from inside the cell. Melville looked relieved.

'We'll take a look, too, though,' said Murray. 'Let us in,

please.'

Melville was more amenable than Johnstone, and unlocked the door, standing just within it to block any rush to escape. He looked as if he did not much like the smell of the place, which was not unreasonable. Lizzie handed him a chamberpot with a cloth over it.

'Here,' she said, 'you can make yourself useful, Mr. Melville. And no emptying it in the kirkyard, either: go somewhere more respectful. You have my word I'll no escape while your back's turned.' She waved Murray and Isobel into the cell. 'You're welcome to my humble abode. I'm sorry I've not much to offer you.'

She had a plate with a blunt knife and a loaf of fresh-looking bread, and what appeared to be a jar of potted meat. It all smelled rather better than its surroundings.

'Are you still determined to stay?' Murray asked. He still found her shaved eyebrows very shocking: they had so defined her face. She pulled her shawl about her warmly, and nodded.

'As I say, I've been in far worse. I had a good news with Mr. Watson last night, and this morning before school time Mr. Kenny told me all about the geography of France and Germany. Every day's a school day,' she added with a smile. Melville reappeared at the door and returned her chamberpot.

'Well, if there's nothing you need, and nothing we can do for you,' said Murray.

'Not at all, but thank you both for dropping in,' said Lizzie comfortably, and came to the door to wave them goodbye before Melville locked her in again.

'She's well provided for, considering,' Isobel remarked as they remounted at the gate.

'Yes ...'

'What?'

'Well, her son-in-law brought her the blanket and a pie, a candle and a little flask, no doubt of whisky. Melville said no one had visited her since.'

'So the potted meat and the fresh bread ...'

'And the plate, and the knife, and the warm shawl. Yes. Where did they come from?'

Chapter Eleven

Robbins met Murray at the front door, assured him that all the women of the household and adjacent homes were accounted for, and informed him that Mr. Blair was in the library. Isobel went upstairs to change for dinner, but Murray asked Robbins for the makings of a toddy for two, and went to the library to see that the fire was lit. It was, and Blair was nested in an armchair in front of it, peering at a book on geology. Murray wondered if there was any subject in the world in which Blair was not interested.

'Good day again, Charles!' Blair greeted him with his usual enthusiasm. 'Have you made any progress? Though I fear I see by your face you have not. Did you bring Isobel back safely with you?'

'I did: she has gone to change. I don't want to lose any other female from the parish.'

'I should miss her, I confess. And progress? Was I right? No progress?'

'Lizzie Fenwick is still in the church cell, though she seems comfortable. The kirk session don't feel that Mathilda Aytoun's disappearance exonerates her at all, apparently. We did not see Sir John, who was out on the hunt for his daughter, and Lady Aytoun had retired to her room.'

'Well, at least we know what the Grants are doing away from town during the season,' said Blair, trying hard to find some advantage they had gained. 'Did you ask Sir John why they were here?'

'I did, and nearly had my head snapped off for my trouble. Apparently they all found the season very tiring, and needed a rest. Sir John is contemplating making an offer for Collessie – or he was. I suppose he might well think differently now, even if Mathilda turns up safe and sound.'

'And there is no sign of where she might have gone?'

'It's about a mile from Collessie house to the woodsman's hut where they had planned to meet – or where Robert says they had planned to meet, anyway. The night was cloudy, if dry, for the most part: she could not have relied on starlight, so I assume she took some kind of lantern. No one at Collessie is likely to know how many lanterns they have or if one is missing. The path is clear enough in daylight, but perhaps not that distinct at night, even with a lantern, if you don't know your way well which I suppose she would not. She might well have lost her way and have wandered in the woods, then decided to sit down and wait the night out. I don't know how far she might have walked before that point, so where she might have gone is not clear.'

'Unfamiliar with the place, after dark, wanders off her path,' Blair summed up. 'Just like Agnes, do you think?'

'I do.' They considered in silence for a moment, before Walter appeared with a tray containing whisky, sugar, lemons, and a jug of hot water. Blair set to to mix toddies as Walter bowed and turned to leave, but Murray called him back.

'Walter, did you have much conversation with Agnes?'

'Well, sir, she had plenty of conversation with me. I wouldn't say I had it back, necessarily,' said Walter solemnly.

'Did she mention any particular friends about here?'

'She never really went out, sir. Only across to Mrs. Robbins, when we couldn't stand her any more in the kitchen. And Mrs. Dean, well, she wasn't her friend, but she took her under her wing, being from the same part of the world. Only Mrs. Dean's from Fife, but she's been away, ken, sir?'

'I think so, Walter. Did you ever get the impression she wanted to go back to Paisley, or Glasgow?'

'Well, she talked about them a lot, sir, but no, I think she was quite happy here. She was like one of those odd cats, sir, that you can just put down somewhere and stroke them a few times and they'll just curl up and stay there, not like the usual kind that you put somewhere and they want to be somewhere else, even if they wanted to be in the first place in the first place. If you see what I mean, sir.'

'Very good: thank you, Walter.'

Walter bowed his shiny chestnut head again and left the room with dignity.

'He's surpassing himself,' Murray remarked. 'Now he even loses himself in his own conversation.'

'It was helpful, though, don't you think?' said Blair anxiously. 'Agnes did not want to leave, and she didn't have any particular friends around here who might be sheltering her, for whatever reason.'

'It's the cloak that worries me. A rainy, cold night: why would she even take her cloak off, let alone leave it somewhere?'

They turned as the library door opened again, but this time it was Robbins.

'Sir John Aytoun, sir.'

'Just in time for toddy, Sir John – and you look as if you need it,' said Murray, standing to usher Sir John to a chair near the fire. Blair handed him a glass, which Sir John accepted wordlessly and emptied in an instant. Murray could not have imagined the elegant, controlled man looking so weary and filthy.

'Is there any news?' Blair asked.

'Nothing,' said Sir John at last, accepting his refilled glass. 'I can only hope that they have eloped together and are safely away by now.'

'Eloped together?' Murray was taken aback. 'But I left a message ...'

But at that moment the door opened again, and Robert Lovie, looking very unsure of himself, edged in. There was a blur of movement and Sir John was out of his seat before the door closed.

'You little – what have you done with my daughter?' he cried in an almost unrecognisable voice, and punched Robert resoundingly in the eye. Robert gave a gurgle and sat abruptly on the floor, just as Murray leapt up and seized Sir John's arms, flexed for a second blow. Sir John's foot twitched as if he was contemplating a kick instead, but Murray hauled him back and pushed him into his chair.

'Didn't you get my message?' he said urgently, as Robert groaned on the carpet. Murray decided he could look after himself for the moment.

'What message?' Sir John scowled like a fury at Robert, not even looking at Murray as Murray pressed him back into the chair.

'They never met. Robert says he arranged to meet Mathilda, yes, but she never appeared.'

'She never appeared?' Sir John allowed himself to think about this for a moment, then deflated slightly. 'Then where is she?'

'I don't know!' Robert shouted indistinctly. 'I was only coming in to apologise to Mr. Murray for causing him all this trouble.'

'They were supposed to meet at the woodsman's hut by the west path through the woods, apparently,' Murray explained. 'He had a lantern out to guide her for a midnight meeting, but she never appeared.'

Robert grunted agreement, and watched Sir John warily with his good eye, clutching the other side of his face.

'Would Miss Aytoun have known her way about the woodland paths, Sir John?' Blair asked timidly.

'No,' Sir John snapped, then swallowed and tried to pull himself together. 'Not very well, I should have thought. We haven't been here for very long, and she has taken her walks mostly in the garden – I believe,' he added darkly, with a glare at Robert.

'I hadn't arranged any meetings with her before last night,' said Robert quickly. Sir John sat back in his seat and helped himself to another hefty glass of toddy.

'Well, if you don't have her – and don't imagine I'm not still blaming you for this, Lovie,' he added through clenched teeth, 'then where is she?'

'We're worried that it might be the same cause for Agnes' disappearance,' said Murray.

'Which neither you nor that insolent excuse for a sheriff's officer has yet resolved,' said Sir John, rudely enough for someone drinking Murray's toddy, Murray thought, but perhaps with good reason. He was spared a reply when Sir John pushed himself out of his chair and bade them an angry good evening, striding out of the library without even glancing down at Robert.

Blair handed Murray a toddy glass, and took one himself. Robert, still pressing his hand over his bruised eye, scrambled to his feet.

'As I said, sir, I was coming to make my apology for causing all this trouble.'

Murray looked him up and down. Even in his current state Robert contrived to charm.

'Well, I think you had your answer,' he said drily. 'Go and ask Mrs. Dean for something to put on that.'

Robert swallowed hard, bowed unsteadily, and left the library.

Dinner that evening was not the most jovial occasion Murray

had ever hosted. Even if he had felt fresh himself, it would not have been easy dealing with Robert, black-eyed and shamed to silence, and Cousin Andrew who seemed unable to look anywhere but at Robert, as if Robert would be off making assignations with the next young lady if Andrew took his eye off him for an instant. The heroine of the hour was, surprisingly, Lady Agostinella, who kept up a determined conversation with Mrs. Grant and the Blairs, demonstrating previously unsuspected knowledge of the works of Byron. Murray was so delighted he was able to rouse himself to join in.

He escorted Agostinella back to her chamber after supper: she looked tired, but somehow more satisfied with the day than she usually seemed.

'Dr. Harker should arrive tomorrow,' said Murray, walking her to her armchair, and nodding to the maid there waiting for her. 'He is an excellent physician.'

'Scots physicians are the finest, they say,' said Agostinella. It was rare for her to praise anything Scots, and he smiled. She leaned back and closed her eyes. 'What do you think has happened to Miss Aytoun?'

He paused: he was not sure if she wanted facts or comfort.

'I think someone has taken her, and taken Agnes, too. I cannot think of a good reason why: I only hope we find them, but I cannot think where else to look.'

'You fear the worst?'

'I do.'

She reached out a hand to him: it was as grey and skeletal as ever, but oddly comforting. The clasp lasted only a moment.

'Mrs. Dean made sure we knew not to leave the house after dark.'

'Yes: I knew you would be safe, but make sure your maid is careful.'

'Of course.'

'Good night, my lady: sleep well.' He took her hand and kissed it as usual. She smiled faintly, and wished him a good night.

He went to his own room. The shutters had been closed but he folded one open, and peered outside into the rain and darkness. Where were Agnes and Mathilda? He hoped they were under shelter, at least, though what that shelter might be he dreaded to think. He offered up a fervent prayer for both of them and stared out into the dark for a long time, until he realised that he was hoping to see the white hare again. No animal with a warm lair would be foolish enough to be out tonight. He closed the shutter gently and lit a candle on the mantelpiece, then jumped back. The shadow in Widow Maggot's mirror had grown: it was as if a large black dog were in the room behind him. He spun, with a sharp yelp. The room was dark and silent.

He rubbed his eyes hard, then lit every candle in the room and left them burning as he undressed and washed his face and hands. Then he blew them out one by one and, resolutely turning away from the mirror, he leapt under the covers like a child dodging monsters under the bed. It was quite a while before he fell asleep.

On Tuesday morning, Macduff, the Sheriff's man, arrived as promised. He looked about as tired as Murray felt, but not ill at ease shown into the library.

'I would have been earlier, sir,' he began, 'but I came through the village and a few people stopped me to say things had been going missing. A canvas and some rope, and food and all.'

'I wonder they didn't just put it down to witches,' said Murray sourly.

'There was mention of witches, sir,' said the Sheriff's man, pursing his narrow lips. 'What's going on at the kirk?'

'Did they not tell you? They have Lizzie Fenwick, the local midwife, locked in a cell there, waiting to take her to Presbytery to be tried as a witch.'

'They canna do that!' exclaimed Macduff, aghast.

'They have. I offered to have her released, but she said she felt safer in there, so I doubt you could do much for her. She thinks the Presbytery will be more sane than the Kirk Session.'

'They might at that,' said Macduff dubiously.

'I'm worried about the village,' Murray confessed. 'There's a hint of hysteria there, and when that kind of thing sets in – well, I suppose I'm thinking of the Edinburgh mob and the Porteous Riots, when crowds go mad together. They're not inclined to wait for justice to take its course.'

'I ken what you mean, sir. If we could find either of the lassies – I mean, Agnes or the lady, Miss Aytoun – then they might be more comforted. I doubt either has been taken by witches.'

'It seems unlikely,' Murray agreed.

'I'd like to talk to Mrs. Dean – that's how she's cried, your new housekeeper, isn't it, sir? – about Agnes, as I said,' said Macduff. 'But then I have a favour to ask of you, sir. Would you mind very much coming with me to Collessie to speak to Sir John about Miss Aytoun? As … ah … as a local representative of the gentry, mebbe, should I say? Or as the laird?'

Murray realised that Macduff was uneasy going to see Sir John when Sir John had not hidden his low opinion of the sheriff's man.

'Of course: I'd want to go and see if there is any news, anyway: though knowing how the Collessie servants gossip I suspect I should have heard by now if there was anything.'

'Aye, they're worse than most,' agreed Macduff. 'I'll away then and speak to Mrs. Dean through by in the servants' wing.' He bowed, and limped away. Murray would have summoned someone to show him the way, but he knew that Macduff was familiar with all the servants' quarters in several parishes: there was not much, in fact, that the sheriff's man missed.

He returned after an hour or so, escorted this time by Robbins, for it was one thing for a sheriff's man to make his way from master to servant on his own, but quite another to go in the opposite direction. Murray found Macduff had been allowed the use of a mule to visit the village, compensating for his limp, so he had his horse saddled and brought round with the mule for departure. They left at an easy pace – easy for the horse, but a smart trot for the mule, with Macduff astride him like an uncomfortable pair of long scissors.

Their path took them along the west road through the woods, past the woodsman's hut where Robert Lovie had intended his ill-fated assignation with Tilly Aytoun.

'Shall we take a look?' asked Murray. Macduff slid off the mule with relief.

The hut was not one used all year round, and in fact as the Collessie woods were so badly managed it had probably not been inhabited even for a season for a few years. It was one low-roofed room, built of wood as befitted its surroundings, green with moss and lichen and half-hidden even though it was only a few feet from the path: in the leafy summer it would disappear almost completely. There was no window for prying eyes to peep through, just a door with a rope latch. Inside someone - possibly the experienced Robert – had lined the floor with bracken for a bed: they might have intended their cloaks as blankets, romantic but uncomfortable. Half buried in the bracken, to be collected later, was the lantern Robert had lit to show Tilly the way. It would have been a good place for a meeting on a dark autumn night: few would come along this path after dark, and even those who did would hardly notice that anything was going on such a short distance from their route. Robert was certainly a well-organised seducer.

Macduff poked and prodded in the shadows of the hut, then froze like a hunting dog.

'What's wrong? What have you found?' Murray tried to see but Macduff's thin body was obscuring the view. Macduff extended a bony arm into the corner under the bracken, and delicately hooked one finger under something which came out of the foliage with a rustle. He turned to the light and to Murray.

'Does this look at all familiar?' he asked.

It was a lady's reticule.

'It does look,' said Murray, 'very like the one she had when she came to Letho the other day. Her mother had a similar one, though: I could not swear to the difference between them.'

Macduff opened the reticule, and spread its jaws wide so they could both see inside. There was a fallen branch outside the hut: they glanced at each other, then set the reticule on it and sat on either side, ready to pick the contents out and lay them one by one on the damp bark.

Macduff drew out a handkerchief, embroidered with an 'M'; two tortoiseshell combs, very little worn; and a small purse of coins. Then, with an expression of surprise, he pulled out two forks and a largish white metal key.

'Planning a picnic?' asked Murray dubiously. 'And what's the key for?'

'It looks like a door key, unless it's for a very large kist,' said Macduff, twisting it in his hand as if trying to picture the door or the chest it would open.

'It looks familiar,' said Murray with a frown. Then he blinked in surprise. 'The forks, however, I do know.' He picked one up. 'See?' There was a heraldic device on the handle of each fork, with little five-pointed stars engraved in it. 'They belong to Letho.'

The sheriff's man stared up at him, a blank look on his face, thinking.

'Could Mr. Lovie have brought them with him, and given them to her?'

'What on earth for?' Murray asked, confused. 'And if he did, here, then he is lying about her not appearing. In fact, if she did not come to meet him, then what is her reticule doing here at all?'

But Macduff was still feeling around in the reticule. His face assumed a perplexed expression, and his fingers slowly drew something else out of the deepest recesses of the bag. He laid it gently on the log beside the cutlery, and they both bent to examine it. It appeared to be a little bunch of things, arranged with a ribbon like a posy – except these were not flowers, but bones.

'Bones?' demanded Sir John, whose mood had not, understandably, improved since the previous evening. 'Why do you imagine my daughter would be carrying bones about in her reticule?'

'Well, we had to ask,' said Murray, trying to sound reasonable. 'Just in case you knew of a good reason. A memento of a pet rabbit, perhaps – though they did look quite recent.'

'And you're sure they are rabbit bones?' asked Sir John, as if he did not feel he could rely on anyone in the parish to be able to tell a rabbit bone from a radish.

'Fairly sure,' said Murray, and Macduff nodded. 'But are you sure that it is Miss Aytoun's reticule?'

'I can't tell the damned things apart. What about you, Ann? Is this Tilly's?'

Lady Aytoun, dabbing at her face with a lace handkerchief, nodded vigorously.

'Well, there you are, then. Lovie was lying: they did meet. So what else is he lying about?'

'Why would he put rabbit bones in her reticule?' Murray asked mildly.

'How should I know? I want to know where he's put her, that's the thing.'

Lady Aytoun burst into renewed sobs.

'Do you have a portrait of Miss Mathilda?' Murray asked, as Macduff had requested him. 'It would be helpful for the search, as she is not well known locally.'

'Well, you're hardly going to confuse her with your maid, are you? Or are you planning to lose more women about the countryside?' asked Sir John waspishly, but he went to a glass topped table across the parlour and retrieved a small item from inside. He handed it to Murray. 'Here: I want it back safely.'

'You will be able to have it back directly,' said Murray, and handed the miniature painting to Macduff. Macduff took it across to the window, drew a sheet of paper from his satchel, inked a pen, and scribbled quickly. In a few moments he handed the miniature back to Murray, who passed it to Sir John. Sir John scowled at the sheriff's man, who showed him the piece of paper like a peace offering. On it was an exact copy of the portrait, in ink, with notes of the girl's colouring. Sir John's jaw dropped.

'Well, we shall leave you to carry on your search,' said Murray quickly, 'and let Macduff here go back to Cupar to spread the word further afield. I shall of course have further conversation with Robert Lovie. We'll go just now …' He edged towards the door, pushing Macduff in front of him: Sir John still looked stunned, the original portrait in his hand, and Lady Aytoun was still sobbing into a sodden handkerchief, as they saw themselves out the front door.

The mule and Murray's horse stood outside, tethered where they had left them: none of the Collessie servants had thought to give them a drink or a rub down. Murray led his horse to a stone water trough to one side of the drive, and Macduff did the same with the mule.

'I'll go back to Cupar now through the village. Thank you for coming with me, sir.'

'I think your skills with the pen may have earned you new respect there, Macduff,' said Murray with a grin.

'Only for drawing, though, I think, sir. Will you indeed have a word with Mr. Lovie?'

'I shall: I can't say I'm looking forward to it. He was very plausible before, and I suspect it will take a great deal for him to admit to anything beyond seduction. But how did the reticule get there if he was telling the truth? You have it safe, and the contents?'

'Yes, sir. Will you take the forks?'

'If you have no need for them: we have all seen that they were there. What about the key?'

'You said it looked familiar, sir. Why not take it, too, and see if you can find what lock it fits? If you cannot find anywhere, then I'll try it elsewhere.'

'Very well.' Murray pocketed the forks and the key. 'Keep in touch, then, and we'll do the same. Good luck, Macduff.'

'You, too, sir.'

Murray swung up and trotted the horse down the drive to where the paths through the woods led off to the right: the drive itself tended more towards the left and the village. He felt he had seen the western route today, so, turning to wave goodbye again to Macduff he took the middle woodland path, keeping his eyes open in case Tilly, too, had come this way. He trotted along, noting again how badly worked the Collessie woodlands were: fallen trees had not been cleared, and there was a dank, dark feel to the place, a sense of unhealthiness. He did not think he himself would have chosen Collessie woods for a romantic meeting, not even in daylight.

As he progressed, it seemed to him that the woods grew quieter the deeper he went. There were fewer birds, the rain pattered more distantly, and the wind had dropped completely. He slowed to a walk, listening. It was absolutely silent for a long moment. Then with a crash like an explosion, the rooks burst out of their roost above him, cawing and crying up into the sky as if someone had fired a gun into their nests. The cries faded, and again there was silence.

He stopped. The horse quivered. He could feel it tremble, then felt something else, too: a vibration, as if it was something rolling behind him. Was it behind him? Or was it underfoot? The horse edged, uneasy, and he pressed it to a walk, then again to a trot. Its pace was uneven, unsteady. The rumbling grew gradually louder.

There was a great crack behind him, like a huge sail smacking in the wind. He ducked, and the horse bolted.

He held on by instinct, as terrified as the horse. His gloves were tangled in the mane, his knees gripping the saddle as if his life depended upon it. He kept his head down: low slung branches swooped across the path, reaching out for him. The horse staggered, but kept the path. Where was the edge of the wood? Surely it must be soon. He dug his heels in, but the horse was already flat out, snorting, and still the rumbling, dark, deep thunder seemed to be gaining on them. The bushes and brambles by the path shook, as if something was lumbering through them, picking up speed. He felt himself drawing up in the saddle, as if something would seize his stirrup, and he almost thought he felt a hand grasp his heel. Then they burst out of the wood and the horse staggered into the fields, stumbling and sprawling headlong, catching itself before it fell, spinning at last, at a good distance, to glare back at the trees. Man and horse panted, sweating. The trees were still.

'What the devil was that?' gasped Murray out loud. The horse whinnied. It had no idea either.

They watched the wood for a few minutes, keeping their distance, until at last a small white shape hopped into sight out of a bush at the side of the field. The hare stopped, ears high, and rose up on its hind legs to regard them with rather academic interest. It was between them and the wood. All at once, Murray felt substantially better. He raised his hat stupidly at the hare, and turned his horse for home.

Chapter Twelve

Murray was shaken, but recovering by the time he reached Letho House. He had almost managed to persuade himself that whatever it was had been the wind. Blowing at an odd angle, perhaps, or pushing through the low bushes just as the leaves were dry and rattling: maybe there had even been a slight earthquake. Such things happened – there had been one in Aberdeen only a couple of months ago - and he had heard that apart from feeling the ground move, people often reported odd sensations in their heads, as if something in the air was shaken, too. No doubt that was what it was.

Robbins brought him a brandy to the empty library, and he sat before the fireplace, waiting and sipping the warm liquor. He had not taken his boots off, feeling that his work was not over for the day, but a good quarter of an hour had passed when Robert Lovie, announced quietly by Robbins, appeared in the doorway. Despite the delay, Lovie gave the impression that his confidence was already coming back: his bruises were developing well but his head was high, his golden brown hair brushed to a shine in the candlelight, and the buttons glinting on his evening waistcoat. He smiled as he approached.

'You wanted to see me, cousin?' he asked.

'Take a seat,' said Murray, gesturing with his brandy glass to the smaller armchair opposite him. Lovie relaxed, crossing his legs, elbows spread across the arms of the chair. Murray pressed his lips together, irritated: the boy seemed not to be able to help charming anyone within range. He knew he had to make a start on his questioning before he, too, fell victim and simply gossiped about the day. He cleared his throat. 'I'd like you to tell me again – from the beginning – about your connexion with Miss Aytoun.'

Robert raised his eyebrows a little, but he could not have believed that the matter was closed.

'Has she been found?'

'Not yet.'

'It's unbelievable. Where on earth could she be?'

'If you could, please, go back to the beginning. Had you two met before you came to Letho?'

'No, not at all. I'd never heard of her. We weren't in Edinburgh this season, you know: we were in London.'

'Yes. So you first met her where? Here, at the house?'

'That's right.' Robert settled back in the armchair, with a little wriggle to make himself completely comfortable. He reminded Murray of a particularly self-satisfied cat. 'It was the evening you invited the Aytouns to dinner here. Last Thursday, wasn't it?'

'Yes. Less than a week ago.'

'My, time flies, doesn't it? So much has happened.'

'Go on.'

'Well, I was impressed. Very pretty indeed, I thought. And bored, which is always helpful. They left Edinburgh very early, with lots of social engagements having to be refused, and I don't think Tilly was very happy about that.'

'Did she say why they had to leave early?'

'No ... no, I don't think so. Why, do you think there was bother with someone there who might have followed her to Letho?'

'Just go on.' Murray refused to rise to any questions.

'Well, I liked her company, and I thought she might make an amusing episode. Mother of course was trying to keep me away from her, but Lady Aytoun was trying to throw us together, and that made me laugh excessively. I don't think Tilly noticed Mother's intentions, anyway. We got along splendidly that evening – didn't she sing beautifully? – and then the next day of course I had a little time in her company at Josie's Den, despite Father's best efforts to keep me under his wing.'

'And you saw her again on Saturday.'

'Oh, yes, Lady Aytoun must have considered me a very promising suitor! Marched her over to see us again. She's a bit of a fool, that lady,' he added thoughtfully.

Murray privately agreed, but did not want to encourage Robert.

'I seem to remember coming in as you snubbed her over her

embroidery,' he pointed out.

'Oh, yes! So I did. Well, frankly, Miss Blair's embroidery *was* far superior. And I always find that when you reach a certain point with a girl, it's best to put their pretty nose just a tiny bit out of joint. Of course I had no intention of trying any assignations with Miss Blair: she is far too intelligent and I know she would see through me right from the start.'

He gazed over at Murray humbly through his thick dark lashes. Whether he thought Isobel intelligent or not, he himself was bright enough to realise that he would have been in even more trouble with his host if he had seduced her instead of Tilly Aytoun. One did not entrap the daughter of one's host's oldest friend. Murray tutted, though he tried not to.

'So you knocked Miss Aytoun back so that she would be much more appreciative of you the next time you paid her a little attention?' he asked.

'Exactly. And she really fell into my lap, so by Sunday evening she was quite ready to accept the idea of a little meeting in the woods. I had noticed the woodsman's hut when I was out on the hunt for Agnes, and it occurred to me at the time that it would be ideal for a spot between here and Collessie: I took the opportunity early on Sunday to make it a little more welcoming, and on Sunday night I collected some food after supper, and a lantern from your stables, and headed off to meet her.'

'When did you send her the note asking her to come?'

'I passed it to her in church on Sunday morning.'

'Good heavens. And she replied?'

'On Sunday afternoon, when we went over for tea.'

'You work fast, don't you?'

'No sense in wasting time!' Robert smiled, keen to include Murray in his delight at a plan well laid.

'Well, you took your picnic, and your lantern, and you headed off – when?'

'Oh, about a quarter past eleven, I suppose. I needed to make sure I got there first, to light her way – and so that she had no chance to dither about changing her mind if she had to wait for me.'

'And you would have arrived at the hut – did you go straight there?'

'Yes, yes. I'm not that confident about prowling about your estate in the dark!'

Pretty confident about other things, though, thought Murray.

'So you arrived when?'

'I suppose about a quarter to midnight. I arranged the food, laid out a rug or two, lit a couple of candles, made it look welcoming.'

'Then what?'

'Then I sat and waited. I had a book with me: I find that they're quite often late, whether they're debating the propriety of coming to the meeting place or whether it's more practical problems, a parent up late or servants flitting around unexpectedly. After an hour or so I began eating the food.'

'And then?'

'Well, much more of the same. I must have fallen asleep at some point: the candles burned down quite a bit, and then I looked at my watch and it was six or so. Well, I ate the rest of the food then, and blew out the candles and the lantern, wrapped myself in the rugs and went back to sleep for a few hours until I thought it was a good time of day to rise and be seen. I tidied up, hid a few things on my way back for picking up later, and came back here.'

'And when you tidied up, is that when you tucked Miss Aytoun's reticule under the heather?'

Robert stared at him.

'Tucked what?'

'Miss Aytoun's reticule. It was found under the heather you had laid in the hut.'

'No!' His gaze fell, and he frowned. 'How could it have been?'

'You tell me. Are you sure she did not appear to meet you?'

'Quite sure. Unless … well, just maybe she came while I was asleep. I'm a sound sleeper.'

'I'm sure you are,' said Murray drily. 'So you suggest she arrived, found you snoring gently in your heather bed, tucked her reticule under your makeshift mattress – in such a way that I'm sure she would have had to climb over you, for it was at the far side of the hut – and then vanished into the night?'

'It does sound a little unlikely,' Robert admitted.

'Doesn't it just?'

'Young Mr. Lovie will not be joining the party for dinner, Robbins,' Murray said when Robbins appeared to shave him before dinner. 'I have persuaded him to enjoy the accommodation on the nursery floor. One of the rooms with bars on the windows and a sound lock on the door.'

Robbins nodded, his pale brows steady.

'You think he's guilty, sir?'

'I don't think he thinks he is.'

'But do you think he might have abducted Miss Aytoun? Or Agnes?'

'I'm not sure, but I put it to him that he might prefer to be somewhere where at least he cannot be suspected if anything further happens. Please do take him any food he requires, and ask Mrs. Dean to make sure he is comfortable, but he is not to charm his way out. His parents are completely in agreement with me, incidentally.'

'Very good, sir. Dr. Harker has arrived, sir: he has been to visit Lady Agostinella, and told me to say that he would like to speak with you after dinner.'

'Right. I'm glad he's here: she'll be reassured, if nothing else. And another thing, Robbins,' Murray went on, flapping into a clean shirt, 'I'd like a word with Mrs. Dean about cutlery.'

'Cutlery, sir?'

'Forks, to be specific.'

'Really, sir? Have you by any chance found some?'

Murray emerged, and eyed him.

'So there are forks missing?'

'Mrs. Dean mentioned it, sir.'

'Those ones?' Murray nodded to the dressing table, where he had laid out the silverware found in Tilly Aytoun's reticule. Robbins extended a pale finger, and examined the forks.

'Aye, sir, I believe so, but Mrs. Dean will know to the last tine, no doubt.'

'I have the impression you approve of Mrs. Dean, Robbins.'

Robbins, as usual in such cases, considered his answer.

'I believe I do, sir,' he said at last. 'She has great energy, and I believe we may have been a little set in our ways - if such a thing would be possible, sir, with so many changes over the last few years. But when Mrs. Chambers went, sir, I believe we tried to keep to the easy path and not try to improve anything. Mrs. Dean will not let us rest, and perhaps that's no bad thing.'

'Do you think she is settling in well?'

'I have seen no sign of her wanting to leave. I'd say she plans to stay here a good while. And of course she's from Fife herself: she hasn't said if she has kin hereabouts, but she seems to have friends. She goes out and about and knows what's going on in the village. I think she has settled, sir.'

'Well, I hope we continue to suit one another, then. What about Mrs. Robbins: what does she think of Mrs. Dean?'

'I think she likes her well enough, sir,' said Robbins, with just the hint of a smile. Dear me, Murray thought, but Robbins had come out of his shell. Before they had gone to India together – and before Robbins had married Mary - it would have taken him a week to draw that much information from him, and a month to see a smile. He grinned, pleased, but Robbins had already turned away, back to the forks. 'Where were the forks, sir, if I may ask?'

'They were in Miss Aytoun's reticule.' This time, Robbins' eyebrows did shoot up, but he said nothing. 'The sheriff's man and I found it in the woodsman's hut where she was supposed to meet Robert.'

'Which is why Mr. Lovie is locked up?'

'Well, that, and the other reason is that if he's locked up I'm in less danger of slapping him.'

'Are you finished with the front door key, then, sir?' Robbins asked after a moment.

'The front door key? What do you mean?'

'The front door key, there on the dressing table. I'd been wondering where it was.'

'Is that what it is?' Murray reached out to examine it again. 'I thought it looked familiar. But what was Tilly Aytoun doing with the front door key for Letho?'

'And the forks, sir,' said Robbins.

'Or was she?' Murray thought for a moment. 'What if Robert took the door key in order to let himself back in again after his little assignation? And perhaps he took the forks, too, for apparently he took a picnic with him.' Robbins' eyebrows rose. 'If he did, it's very close to proof that he did see her. Otherwise how

Lexie Conyngham

on earth did the key end up in her reticule?'

'But the key has been missing since Saturday, sir. Surely Mr. Lovie would not have taken it a day ahead, for then there's more chance it would have been missed.'

'Are you sure, Robbins? Saturday?'

'Aye, sir. I missed it after the tea guests had all gone, before dinner. I used the spare one, and I've been looking for this one ever since.'

Murray sat down on his bed and ran his hands hard through his hair. It was not so much that things were not making sense, as that there were altogether too many things to fit together to make sense, like a book bursting out of its binding.

'I think I need my dinner, Robbins. My head is hungry. Do you remember feeling like that at school? When it was nearly time for dinner, and your head felt as empty as your stomach?'

'It was a long time ago, sir.'

'Too long. I wonder how those schoolboys are, the ones that found Widow Maggot's body. Maybe it's put a stop to all their mischief in the village.'

'I hear not, sir. Mrs. Maitland reckons they've been messing about in her shed. She had apples laid out and they've all been mixed up and disturbed.'

'Apples again …' Murray remembered the marks of the apple box on Widow Maggot's dust floor.

'I'll tell Mrs. Dean to come and see you about the forks, sir,' said Robbins, finishing up. Murray pulled on his coat over his waistcoat, and Robbins helped him to tug the snug-fitting sleeves into place. 'May I take the key?'

'Yes, yes. If it doesn't fit, tell me.'

'It'll fit, sir,' said Robbins, positive, and bowed out of the room.

Dr. Harker joined the party for dinner but of course said nothing in company about the health of the lady of the house. She was absent this evening, and Murray found himself trying to gauge the situation by Dr. Harker's appearance and words in advance of their interview. He had not long to wait when the others went to the drawing room.

'Lady Agostinella is keeping good health, I'm delighted to

142

say,' said Dr. Harker at once, folding his length gracefully into one of the library armchairs. 'Of course with her history of previous losses, she must take very great care, and I have advised her to keep to her rooms until her actual confinement. It will not be long now.'

'Is there anything specific I should do? Particular food, or medicines, or distractions?'

'She is quite inclined to keep herself quiet and that is a good thing. No medicines and few distractions, but if she asks for anything particular to eat it is probably best to procure it, if you can. Some ladies ask for quite extraordinary things, so do not be anxious!'

'And you'll be able to stay for the confinement?' Murray asked, immediately more anxious than he had been.

'That is my intention if it is your will. Is there a local midwife you trust? And have you arranged for a wetnurse?'

'I – I'm not sure. Yes, I trust the local midwife, but unfortunately she is about to be tried before the Presbytery as a witch.'

Dr. Harker's pale brow furrowed right up into his white hair.

'Good gracious. Ah, but that explains something Lady Agostinella said ... Perhaps this woman is best avoided, if her situation is likely to cause distress in the patient.'

'We may not have a choice,' said Murray wrily.

It was next morning when Mrs. Dean made her way to the library and presented herself before Murray.

'I gather you're missing some forks, Mrs. Dean,' said Murray, and handed her the cutlery found in Tilly Aytoun's reticule.

'Mr. Robbins said you had found them. How extraordinary!'

'Well, we have a theory or two for that,' said Murray. He did not feel he knew Mrs. Dean well enough yet to discuss such matters with her. He took the opportunity to observe her for a moment. She did indeed give the impression of being quick and lively, full of energy, and with the kind of sensible, intelligent face that implied the energy would be well applied. A little unsure of herself, perhaps? He wondered: she seemed uneasy, but he did not remember noticing it when he had met her before.

'You have been with us a little while now, Mrs. Dean: do you feel you are settling in?'

'Oh, yes, sir. Everyone is very friendly and helpful, and I hope I am finding my way about the work now. Agnes is a loss, of course, and the manner of her going is very upsetting ...' She tailed away, then caught herself. 'I am very glad to be back in Fife, and the village is lovely. The work is a little behind, of course, the way things have been over the last few years as I well understand, sir. Much of the fruit in the gardens has gone to waste and I look forward to building up what is left of poor Mrs. Chambers' salves and medicines again. But much of that will have to wait now until next year when I can catch the crops, and the little one, well, she'll be up and walking by then, no doubt ...'

Again she tailed away, looking puzzled. Murray frowned.

'The little one?'

'Little Miss Murray, sir,' she said, as though she could not help herself, then blushed. 'I beg your pardon, sir. I don't know what I'm saying. All this worry over Agnes: I have not been sleeping well, sir.'

'Then I had best not keep you from your quarters,' said Murray, more confused than angry. 'You may go.'

'May I just ask, sir: will you be going over to Collessie today at all?'

'I'm not sure. Why?'

'Well, Miss Aytoun and Agnes: I know Miss Aytoun's a lady, sir, but for the two of them to disappear in such a short time ...'

'I know, Mrs. Dean. We're trying our best to find both of them.'

'Thank you, sir,' she said, and this time curtseyed and left.

Murray flung himself back in his chair, baffled by his housekeeper but with a head so full of worries and wonders that he felt he had no strength to ponder on it. He was about to go and find Blair to talk to, when he heard footsteps in the hall outside, and in a moment Robbins announced Mr. and Mrs. Helliwell. They hurried in as if chased: Murray was shocked at their appearance. Mrs. Helliwell was never particularly smart, not being much interested in fashions, but she kept herself clean and neat. This morning she looked extremely flustered, and her shawl was in an unaccustomed tangle around her shoulders as if it had gone on wrong and she had not even noticed. Her husband the minister, though, had aged visibly since last Murray had seen him.

'Mr. Murray, forgive us for calling unexpectedly like this,' Mrs. Helliwell began, but her husband interrupted.

'Lizzie Fenwick has escaped,' he snapped.

'Escaped? But she said she felt safer there.'

'And well she might,' said Helliwell darkly. 'I say she has escaped: she has at any rate vanished from the cell at the church. The Kirk Session are out looking for her.'

'Not, I gather, in kindly concern,' said Murray. What next?

'Not at all,' agreed Helliwell. 'They have stormed round to her cottage, but only found her son-in-law and his children next door. He denies all knowledge: they don't see eye to eye, everyone knows, but I'm sure he doesn't believe she's a witch. But he certainly has a healthy respect for the Kirk Session: I'm positive he wouldn't have let her out.'

'Who do you think did? One of the Session themselves?'

'I wondered if it might be Mr. Rintoul: he's been acting a little oddly recently,' said Mrs. Helliwell, tugging uncomfortably at her shawl. Murray longed to straighten it but did not feel he was in a position to.

'Secretive,' agreed her husband sternly. 'But that wasn't what the Session thought: not that I would have given them his name, the mood they're in. But no, instead they come wheeling over to the manse, thumping at the door and terrifying the maid, and demand to know where we're hiding her!'

'You?'

'That's what they said.'

'Well, to be fair, dear,' put in Mrs. Helliwell, 'that's what Mr. Melville and Mr. Johnstone said. Mr. Watson just looked worried, Mr. Kenny was grumpy, and in the end it was Ninian Jack himself who talked them out of searching the house.'

'I should think so: he's been Session Clerk for years,' huffed the minister. 'If he can't keep himself under control, I don't see what we can expect from the others.'

'I think you've both had a bit of a fright,' said Murray. 'I'll ring for some tea. Pull up to the fire, Mrs. Helliwell, and please, let me take that shawl.' He rang the bell, then unfurled the crumpled shawl and dropped it back down around Mrs. Helliwell's thin neck. She hunched into it at once, needing its comfort. 'When is the

Presbytery meeting to which Lizzie was supposed to go?'

'Tomorrow, in Cupar,' said Helliwell. 'I don't suppose you'd come with me, would you? I'm not sure my fellow ministers are going to believe what has been going on here – and the Kirk Session has already written to them about her, so they'll want to know. Witchcraft, abducted girls, a murder: what on earth has gone wrong with this place, Mr. Murray?'

'I wish I knew.'

Chapter Thirteen

By late Thursday morning, Murray was heartily glad to see the gig brought round to the front door. Blair was ready, too, eager and jittery in the hall, wrapped up wonderfully against the weather which for once was not too bad: the air as they left the house was damp, but could not strictly be called rain. Murray found it refreshing, and relished, too, the fact that stoic, grumpy Dunnett, the groom, seemed unaffected by the nerves that had infected the rest of the staff. Mrs. Mack was in a filthy mood, Iffy was dropping dishes all over the place like overripe apples, Jennet had a sick headache and Daniel and William were uncharacteristically subdued. Even Robbins had slipped back into the silence of his past, apparently worried but unresponsive to any of Murray's concerned queries. Murray noticed that he avoided looking at the Widow Maggot's mirror on the mantelpiece, but then he found he was trying not to look at it much himself. Agostinella was panicky and unable to concentrate as she usually could on her embroidery – her maid had told her that Lizzie Fenwick was on the loose, for which Murray would happily have locked the maid in the same cell. Agostinella had sent the maid instead to ask Murray to come and play for her for a little. A little turned into an hour as she fretted and complained and he tried to think of soothing, calming music, all the time itching to rattle the keyboard from top to bottom. Dr. Harker had eventually given her a small dose of laudanum to calm her nerves, and she slipped into sleep as Murray tiptoed from the room. On the landing he had met Mary – Mrs. Robbins, he reminded himself.

'Mr. Murray,' said Mary with that curtsey that said she only did it because she chose to.

'Are you looking for Robbins?'

'No, sir, I'm over to help. Mrs. Dean has injured her foot, and Jennet is unwell.'

'Good of you. How did Mrs. Dean hurt her foot?'

'She says she turned her ankle when she rose this morning.'

Something about the way Mary said this implied just the least doubt about the honesty of Mrs. Dean's account, but Murray's mind would not take in another mystery just at the moment. He nodded, filing the idea away in his head for later.

'The bairn is well?'

'Aye, sir, he's – er – helping in the kitchen.'

Murray laughed briefly.

'I can imagine!' He felt inclined to talk further, but Mrs. Robbins did not.

'I'd better not leave him too long with Mrs. Mack, sir,' she said with another dismissive bob, and vanished into Mrs. Grant's room with cloths and a brush.

The guests were not much better than the staff, though the Grants certainly had an excuse for anxiety. Robert Lovie was still locked in the old nursery, but his mother and Cousin Andrew were closeted in the parlour, apparently simply pacing and sitting by turns. Isobel was sulking, having been forbidden to go further than the gardens with her sketching and ordered to abandon all thought of a morning ride unless she could persuade both Grants to go with her. Her father and Murray had thought this condition so unlikely to be fulfilled that Isobel was safe enough.

When the gig appeared at the front door, Murray and Blair were out like rabbits from a trap and Murray was already in the seat arranging the reins as Dunnett helped Blair up on the other side. Murray barely let him settle before he gave the reins a flick and they set off at a fair pace down the drive. He managed to slow a little as they turned out on to the road, a wise move as the gig's centre of gravity was quite high. The older he grew, he thought with the melancholy that seemed to be everywhere that day, the more cautiously he regarded gigs. That did not seem to apply to Blair: he glanced sideways and recognised the glee in Blair's wrinkled face as the wind whipped his collar about his ears.

Still irresistibly glancing from side to side for signs of Agnes, he spun the gig along the road to the turn-off for Letho village. As they passed the inn, Blair straightened.

'There's Ninian Jack,' he said, 'and what looks like the greater part of your Kirk Session, if I am not much mistaken. Am I?' he added anxiously.

'No, that's them,' said Murray, slowing even further as he focussed on them sharply. As if they could feel his gaze, a few of them looked across at him and, he thought, twitched a little, their shoulders hunching self-consciously. Sheepish looks passed over one or two faces, though not, he noticed, over that of Mal Johnstone, who walked in the midst of them with his head held high.

'Have they been to Dures?' asked Blair, watching them too as they turned up the hill together. 'Why are they not all at their employments?'

'A good question,' said Murray grimly. He manipulated the reins and set the horse along the Dures road from which the Session had come. In the gig it took only a moment to reach Widow Maggot's hooded cottage. They did not have to leave the gig to see that the door, which had been left fastened by the sheriff's man, Macduff, had been kicked in. It crossed Murray's mind that that was particularly vindictive – after all, Ninian Jack had made the new lock they had used to fasten the door: there would have been no need to destroy it.

'I have never felt this way in Letho before,' said Blair, his sorrow tinged with something else – fear?

'Nor I,' agreed Murray, 'and it's making me very angry. Let's go and collect Mr. Helliwell and see if the Presbytery has any answers.'

He turned the gig awkwardly in the narrow lane, in the end hopping down and taking the horse's head to finish the job, so that by the time they had returned to the green the Kirk Session members had vanished. No one else was about, not even the lad minding the goats in the green – in fact, even the goats seemed to have been kept at home. The green and the streets were empty, with a tense, hollow feel, as if they were waiting for something. The gig's wheels echoed grittily up the street until Murray drew to a halt outside the manse. Helliwell must have been looking out for him: he was at the door in an instant, his hat on his head and his gloved hands shoving papers into his coat pockets, making him bulge about the thighs. Murray hoped he would fit into the gig, but Blair squeezed up to let him slot into the seat. At least, close-packed, they were unlikely to bounce out. Mrs. Helliwell smiled and waved from the door, but she was pale and did not look as if she had slept well. Murray waved back with what he hoped was a reassuring smile, though he doubted it.

'Any sign of Lizzie Fenwick yet?' he asked the minister as they set off.

'Nothing that anyone has told me,' said Helliwell, with a hint of petulance. A minister and his session were supposed to work together. 'The whole village seems to have gone mad.'

'Someone has kicked in the door of Widow Maggot's cottage,' said Blair sadly. Helliwell's shoulders hunched as if of their own accord.

'It doesn't help that all that food is going missing,' he grumbled.

'What food?' asked Murray.

'It was Mrs. Maitland glumpshing about it first,' said Helliwell, pulling himself upright. Murray could feel the readjustments of the gig's balance. 'She said Rintoul was eating her out of house and home – though I think she rather takes that as a compliment to her cooking, if you ask me,' he added. 'Then she said there was food missing from her store – she has an outdoor arrangement, you ken, and she said there was jam and stuff gone from there. Then one or two were blaming all the people running around hunting for Agnes and Miss Aytoun, saying it had put their hens off laying, and now they're thinking the eggs have been stolen. If you ask me,' he inserted again, 'their hens are all in a moult anyway. But then Mr. Kenny the schoolmaster reminded me that he had to send the boys home for food last week, because there was neither food nor fuel in the schoolhouse, and a window had been broken.'

'Food ...' said Murray thoughtfully.

'And wasn't Mr. Johnstone missing a rope?' asked Blair cautiously.

'And someone else had a cart cover gone, hadn't they?' Murray responded. 'Well, gentlemen, I believe – I hope – these might be good signs.'

'Why's that?' asked Helliwell morosely, resistant to any good news.

'Because if someone needs lots of food, and rope and a cart cover, it seems to me that someone is keeping a couple of people, perhaps Agnes and Miss Aytoun, somewhere locally, and feeding them and sheltering them. Don't you think? And if that is the case, then actually there might just be a chance that we will find them both alive and well.'

He finished with a flourish of the reins that made the horse kick up her heels and skip along for a few yards, picking up on his lighter mood. Blair, though, brought it all back down.

'But if someone is keeping the girls alive,' he said anxiously, 'what for?'

Murray was glad when they reached Cupar and it looked normal and busy, with the townsfolk going about their daily affairs and not, apparently, cowering in fear in their houses. Blair's words had echoed in his mind since they had been uttered, playing at the edges of his imagination, conjuring up half-seen images that he did not like at all. Cupar, though, was modern and bright and full of action: the Bonnygate was broad and lined with clean, new houses and businesses, and he was about to turn right into the Crossgate at the market place when Mr. Helliwell roused himself.

'There's something wrong with the stove in the church,' he said quickly. 'The Presbytery are meeting in the Tontine Inn.'

'Easy enough,' said Murray, his spirits a little lighter. He drew back the left rein and they walked instead, mindful of pedestrians and Cupar's ever-changing traffic regulations, along St Catherine's Street, past the fine new county buildings and into the yard of the Tontine Inn. The Inn was almost at the edge of the town, facing the gentle rise of the Castle Hill. The Presbytery had taken one of its private parlours for the afternoon, and the innkeeper showed them to it with respectful efficiency, clearly hoping for repeat business.

Murray wondered what to expect: he had not been to a Presbytery meeting before, which was where the ministers of the churches in the area met to discuss – well, he supposed, church matters. It was a higher court than the Kirk Session, so for moral matters it could be a court of appeal, but what they did otherwise he had no idea. Would there be theological debate? Some keen rhetoric? Detailed and wise pronouncements on matters of church administration? He entered the parlour warily, prepared to retire if his presence was the least challenged.

'Ah, Mr. Helliwell,' said one man mildly amongst the others who greeted Letho's minister. 'Here you are – I received your unusual note. And your Session's – communication.'

The room, tall and modern with full-height windows and several sconces lit against the darkness of the day, was full of about twenty clergymen, a surge of black coats and mostly intelligent faces. The man who had greeted Helliwell was behind the only table, evidently set up to chair the meeting. He was small and emaciated, his face webbed with wrinkles, eyes pale blue and sagging as if from age or long illness.

'Mr. Aitken, sir,' Helliwell acknowledged him. 'I have brought the laird and his friend, if they may be permitted.'

'Is the meeting agreed?' asked Aitken generally. The ministers, who were chatting amongst themselves, gradually quietened as if his soft words had soaked into their conversation, and nodded agreement. 'Then we shall deal with your business first,' Aitken decreed, and the meeting settled to begin with a prayer.

'Now, Mr. Helliwell,' said Aitken when they had resumed their seats. His thin eyebrows were high. 'Your note said something about someone being arrested as a witch?'

'That's only the half of it,' said Helliwell resentfully. 'I think Mr. Murray here, the laird, can tell you the beginning. Mr. Murray, do you want to say something about Widow Maggot and Agnes?'

Murray cleared his throat and stood, thinking back rapidly over the last week.

'I think everything began when the Widow Maggot, an elderly woman living on her own at the edge of Letho village, was murdered in her cottage last Tuesday night.' There was a sharp intake of collective breath, and he knew he had their attention. He outlined the events of the rest of the week, including the growing tension in the village, then sat so that Helliwell could continue with the actions of the Kirk Session and the curious story of Lizzie Fenwick. When he sat down, there was silence. Aitken, sprawled back in his upright chair, regarded Helliwell and Murray for a long moment, then adjusted his sprawl and gazed at the room.

'Does anyone have anything to contribute at this point?'

A sallow-faced man in the corner grunted.

'I'd say this is what happens when our kirk sessions start to lose their powers. See, all these secessions and other fellows – d'you ken there's a Baptist Chapel in Cupar this last year? – and the burgh court taking on all kinds of moral decisions. The kirk sessions are losing control and we have to take it back,' he finished, with the hint of a thump of his fist on the arm of his chair.

One or two of the other ministers sighed, though whether in

sympathy or weariness Murray could not tell. He raised his hand, seeking permission to respond. Aitken nodded.

'I don't think that's the problem here,' he said gently. 'For one thing, there are no other churches or congregations in Letho: everyone belongs to the established church. For another, I don't think the Kirk Session is suffering from a lack of power just at the moment. If anything, they're a bit too powerful.'

A well-built man with thin gingery hair raised a hand then refolded his arms firmly.

'What are the current laws against witchcraft?'

'"Thou shalt not suffer a witch to live", Exodus Chapter twenty-two, verse eighteen,' intoned his neighbour, a powdery-faced individual with half-closed, sanctimonious eyes. Aitken gave a little shrug.

'Thank you, Mr. Usher,' he nodded to the Bible-quoter. 'We are all aware of what the Scriptures say on the matter. The law of the land, however, is more charitable, curiously because the lawmakers no longer believe in witchcraft. The Witchcraft Act of 1735, quite contrary to the Covenanters' legislation of the previous century, makes it solely a criminal offence closest to fraud and begging,' he explained as if he had made a close study of the matter. 'The maximum sentence is a year in prison.'

'A shame,' said the man with gingery hair. 'I doubt we could do with a good witch-burning.' He grinned. 'It would bring the people back into the arms of the Kirk, no doubt about it.'

The other ministers shuffled in their chairs, looking away.

'I suspect, Mr. Arbuthnot, it would more than likely drive the people out of the arms of the Kirk and away to the Episcopalians, or worse,' said Aitken drily. 'Let's have no more talk of burning witches or anyone else here.'

'Anyway,' put in Helliwell in a moment of courage, 'she's not a witch. She's a good and caring woman, who gives her time to looking after women in childbirth and the elderly and sick, even when they cannot afford her payment. My own wife works with her amongst the poor of the parish and would have no one else. If Widow Maggot was a witch I have no evidence of it, and she's dead anyway. There's no point in burning her now.'

Murray wondered if that would stop Mal Johnstone, but put the thought from his mind. Usher was murmuring again, long lashes swooping down devoutly.

'The thing is,' said Helliwell, 'the Kirk Session wanted to bring her here to the Presbytery. If they had managed to do that, what would we have done? As Presbytery, I mean.'

'Well, gentlemen?' Once again Aitken opened the meeting to debate.

'Give the Session back their powers to sentence her,' said the greasy sallow man in the corner.

'We have not the power to give them back their powers, Mr. Henderson,' said Arbuthnot, with an ironic smirk.

'What evidence do they have that she is a witch?' asked a man at the back where Murray could not see him. Several others echoed the question.

'She's a widow who is good at making herbal salves and poultices,' said Murray. 'The same could be said of any good housewife, or my own housekeeper.' Helliwell nodded.

'No one has accused her of any ill will or supernatural behaviour, though no doubt,' he added sourly, 'a few susceptible souls might be made use of if certain members of the Kirk Session felt strongly enough against her.'

'Then I for one would want to assoilzie her,' said the same man at the back.

'I, too,' agreed Usher, the Bible-quoter. 'Matthew Chapter Eighteen, beginning at Verse twenty-one: "Then came Peter to him, and said, 'Lord, how oft shall my brother sin against me, and I forgive him? till seven times?' Jesus saith unto him, 'I say not unto thee, Until seven times: but, Until seventy times seven.'" That's what the Good Book says.'

'There's nothing to forgive,' insisted Helliwell. 'She's innocent.'

'Exodus Chapter Twenty,' began Usher, and several others joined the chorus, nodding, 'Verse sixteen. 'Thou shalt not bear false witness against thy neighbour.'

'Assoilzie her!' called the man at the back again.

'Aye, aye, assoilzie her!' agreed the others, Henderson and Arbuthnot chiming in towards the end. Aitken nodded.

'I think the opinion of the meeting is clear,' he said. 'Mrs. Fenwick would be declared innocent, unless some convincing evidence were later produced. But the problem here is two-fold:

first, the Kirk Session has not brought charges for Mrs. Fenwick to answer and for us to consider formally, and second, Mrs. Fenwick herself has disappeared. There is not much we can do if the Kirk Session has not brought the charges.'

His voice faded in Murray's mind as Mr. Aitken rounded up the discussion and thanked Murray and Blair for their attendance. Mrs. Fenwick had disappeared. He had simply thought that she had escaped, or that someone had rescued her. But she had disappeared, into thin air, just like Agnes and Tilly Aytoun. Where were they going, and who was taking them?

He found himself back in the hallway of the Tontine Inn, with Blair tugging at his sleeve.

'Come along,' he was saying.

'Come along where?' Murray asked. 'We have to wait for the end of the meeting, to take Helliwell back home.'

'Weren't you listening, Charles? Mr. Helliwell has asked if we can borrow the minutes of the Presbytery for the time of the witch hunt in the seventeenth century, and Mr. Aitken said we could go and collect them now. They're at the town manse, apparently. Come along!'

Blair trotted in front of him all the way to the manse of the town kirk, where a resigned-looking woman in an apron who could have been housekeeper or minister's wife brought them into the hall and made them wait while she found the volumes they required. She brought back with her not only two leatherbound books, but also the note they had brought from Mr. Aitken allowing them to take the books, which she spread out between her hard-worked fingers and made a point of studying once more before she handed the volumes over.

'Would you by any chance, madam, have a piece of oilcloth to protect them from the weather?' Blair asked humbly. She frowned, but strode off and returned in a moment with oilcloth and string, and took the volumes back to make a quick and efficient parcel of them. Murray thought she probably did not trust either of them to do anything so practical. She handed the parcel back to Blair, who absorbed it somehow into the layers of his outdoor clothing and smiled at her benevolently. For once, however, his charms did not impress, and she tutted audibly as she showed them to the door.

They began to walk back along Long Wynd to the centre of

the town. The rain was growing heavier, the sky the colour of the slate roofs above the damp honey sandstone walls of the houses. Blair huddled his layers around him, protecting the volumes of minutes.

'Is there anything else we could do while we're waiting for Mr. Helliwell? We could go to see the sheriff's man, for instance,' he was saying. 'I suppose we ought to tell him that Mrs. Fenwick has escaped.'

'But has she?' asked Murray, brought abruptly out of his own thoughts. Blair stopped and blinked at him.

'Has she not?'

'Do we know?' Murray asked. 'Do we know she has escaped? How do we know that she has not been abducted too, just like Agnes and Miss Aytoun?'

He looked about him at the busy street, just as it debouched on to the Crossgate. Ordinary people, shawls over their heads or hats pulled down hard against the rain, hurried about their business, in traps and gigs and carts, on horseback or on foot. The market cross was to their left, where the broad mouth of the Crossgate met the Bonnygate, beside the town house. Grand new houses and older cottages shouldered each other for a view of the business of the day: the cobbles underfoot were wet and muddy, and hens pecked amongst the random rubbish of everyday life. It was so ordinary, so normal – so unlike Letho this morning. What was wrong with his little village? And what could he do to put it right?

'Let's find somewhere dry,' Blair was saying, and he guided Murray gently through the Crossgate congestion, back round the corner to the Tontine Inn. The parlour taken by the Presbytery was not the only one, and soon Blair had them both settled in front of a fresh fire, hot brandy toddies before them and a dish of eggs promised soon. Murray caught Blair eyeing him with a worried expression on his face. 'I think you need something hot to eat,' he explained gently.

'But where are they all going?' Murray asked, as if they had been talking it over since they had left the manse. 'We search and search, and all we have found is Agnes' cloak and Tilly's reticule. There is no other trace. What will we find of Lizzie Fenwick? And how soon?'

'Have you considered that you were perhaps meant to find the cloak and the reticule?'

'How do you mean? The cloak was cast aside by the road – perhaps Agnes had thought to throw it there to help us follow her trail – but the reticule was well hidden, at the back of the hut, under the heather.'

'But you found it the next day – neither so long after that it had lost its relevance, nor so soon that you could definitely say it had not appeared some time after she had disappeared. What if the person taking these girls is laying a trail of breadcrumbs for you?'

'Helping us to find them? But why? Why would he do that?' He reflected, trying to fit that idea into a pattern, any pattern. 'And anyway,' he added crossly, 'if he wants us to follow the trail to the girls, he had better lay a few more breadcrumbs. One by the road and one in a hut, a mile apart at least. Nothing on or in the cloak, and a selection of cutlery and the front door key to Letho in the reticule. And a posy of rabbit bones. If this is some kind of riddle, he has overestimated at least my intelligence significantly.'

Blair pursed his mobile mouth into a bow somewhere between acknowledgement and thought. He had removed several of his outdoor layers on entering the parlour, and the parcel of books lay on the table between them. He poked it with his finger, then tried to undo the knot. The lady at the manse had been thorough: the knot was complex and tight. Blair fiddled for a bit, then watched helplessly as Murray pulled his gloves off and picked the knot apart, shoving the parcel ungraciously back to his friend. Blair pulled out the upper volume, and opened it randomly. The old leather binding cracked loudly, and Murray winced.

'Oh, here we are, straight away!' muttered Blair. '"Jonet Andersone was today brought before the Presbytery accused of witchcraft and being so did ...' the handwriting is extraordinary '... did state that she was in no wise a witch but confessed that she had called Sarah Gunn ane auld fishwife and did beat her about the shoulders and did wish aloud that the said Sarah Gunn's kine should take the pox the quhilk they later did."'

'Even that is not the kind of behaviour I like to have going on in Letho,' said Murray, amused in spite of himself.

'Oh, here comes Sarah Gunn. "Sarah Gunn did compear and did state that Jonet Andersone did beat her about the shoulders and abuse her with wicked words" – that is agreed, then – "and did then curse the foresaid Sarah Gunn's kine, whereupon the saids kine did at once sicken in the pasture and fall upon their knees, and that many did hear the foresaid Jonet Andersone to curse the kine and say that she could draw illness upon tham, and that she could cure the kine moreover but only if Sarah Gunn did say that she was mortally sorry for dallying with the said Jonet's guidman Johne Foular." Ah, the plot thickens! "The Presbytery did attend to this and more evidence and did concur that such case should be referred to the Commissioner for Witchcraft in the County, the honourable Sir John Aytoun."'

'What?'

'Sir John Aytoun. Commissioner for Witchcraft in Fife, in 1640, apparently.'

Chapter Fourteen

Helliwell had stayed to dinner, but that had not made the conversation any more sparkling. Murray wondered if Dr. Harker, pale and elegant at the table, was regretting leaving the sanity of Edinburgh for this strange and uneasy place. After they had talked over the disappearances and the moods of the village again and again, to no more point than previously, Murray and Blair walked Helliwell back to the village and the manse, and stayed a moment to see that Mrs. Helliwell was content before setting out along the path across the fields again to home. Fields and village were silent, as far as humans were concerned: the little wood beside the church was alive with the night time rustlings of animals, and the occasional moth flickered in and out where the bats had played only a month before, between the trees and the high manse garden wall. Beyond in the pasture the little black cows, invisible in the dark, ruminated quietly, and the pale rush of a barn owl made them jump. The lantern Murray carried carved the soft fallen leaves into crisp ash grey and black in front of them, shadows dancing. They walked without speaking, feeling their way along the path by long custom, minds still striving to find some kind of answer to the questions spinning around them.

The spinning did not stop when Murray retreated to his own room and the claustrophobic folds of his high tester bed. If someone was keeping three women captive somewhere nearby, where on earth were they? Where had they not searched in the whole parish, and into the neighbouring parishes? Everyone from here to Cupar would know there were women missing, and would be keeping an eye open for them, in lonely woodsman's shelters or shepherd's huts or disused barns or wherever three women could possibly be hidden, wouldn't they?

And were they together, or apart? He tried to picture the three of them comforting each other in some lonely captivity, but all he could imagine was Agnes talking the other two senseless, which was not helpful.

He slipped in and out of sleep through the dark hours of the night, the pillow too hot and his shoulders too cold, the blankets winding themselves in knots around him. At the first glimmer of damp light around the shutters, he disentangled himself from the bedclothes and curtains and crossed the room to open the shutters and stare out at the trees and lawns, smeared by the wet window panes. He turned away and dressed hurriedly, tugged on his boots and made himself go downstairs, tiptoeing through the quiet house to the front door. The spaniels, who had been sleeping under the stairs, surged up, instantly awake as he passed, and he hushed them with fingers rubbing their soft ears. The great old key was back in the lock, and he turned it carefully so that it made no noise. In a moment he was outside, breathing in the thick, wet air. The tops of the stately trees in the park were fugged and dulled by low cloud, and the distant gates were invisible. For a second, illogically in the damp, he thought there was frost on the ground, but when he looked more closely at the sandstone slab at his feet, he realised that there was some white powder in a line across it. The dogs gave it only a dismissive sniff, so he thought no more about it, and set off with them across the grass to the park, avoiding the noisy gravel where he could.

The spaniels were delighted with an early morning jaunt, and hurtled back and forth fetching sticks and chasing each other through the soaking grass. Rabbits and early pigeons, chancing a dawn breakfast, rocketed out of bushes as if there simply to entertain the dogs who pursued them with insane enthusiasm, ears flapping, but catching nothing. Murray grinned: the spaniels were blissfully simple, unworried by anything much as long as their master was nearby. He wondered how easy it would be to replace the Kirk Session with a pack of spaniels.

He was beginning to chill, having come out stupidly without hat or coat, and he was about to turn and go back when he realised the dogs were unusually focussed on one spot under a tree. He felt a shiver run up his spine. A dead rabbit, perhaps, he told himself firmly, and strode across the silvery grass to see what they had found.

From a distance, he could see it was something white – not a rabbit – and whatever it was, the dogs were keeping well back, noses flat in the polished dead leaves, one on either side and absolutely still. His heart sank as he neared them: on the ground, in a spot cleared of leaves, lay the white hare, on her side. She was panting, her eyes wide, ears laid out behind her like wings, but it was her hind legs that horrified him. They were crushed, the star-white fur bloody and stained. He would have to put her out of her misery.

He crouched beside her, and reached out one tentative finger to touch her head, stroke her along her delicate chin and jawbone. Then he stood, and took a deep breath.

The dogs leaped up and barked, and he spun around to see what it was they had seen. Whatever it was they did not like it: something in the direction of the walled gardens, he thought. He told them to sit, and turned back to finish off the poor hare.

She was gone.

For a moment he looked about him, confused. Where could she have gone? She could not possibly have moved on her own.

He knelt and touched the ground where she had been, sure he could feel a little warmth there still, but there was no blood or loose fur. Stupidly he walked right round the tree, the spaniels waiting for him impatiently, but there was absolutely no sign of her.

'That's it: I am really going mad now,' he said aloud. He rubbed his face and his wet hair, then stared at his hand, the fingers which had touched the soft white fur. He shook his head. 'I'm seeing things. Tired, that's what it is. Tired and worried, and increasingly stupid. Right, lads, what are you after?' he added to the spaniels and gave them the signal to go. They shot off from his side towards the walled gardens, and with a last backward glance at the place where he had thought the hare lay, he followed them.

The walled gardens jutted out at the back of Letho House, askew from the central line of the house because of woodland Murray's grandfather had not wanted to cut into and a stream he had not wanted to divert: he had been a cautious man with the money, whatever his grand building plans for his house. The vegetable gardens lay behind the servants' quarters and kitchen, logically enough, and nearer the woodland which lay on the

Collessie side of Letho. On the right of the house, as you looked at it from the drive, the pleasure gardens lay at the back, the wall partly obscured by the Robbins' house on that side. The dogs had seemed to be staring straight between the main house and the Robbins' house, and true to that line they led Murray back towards the house, skittering over the gravel, eager to find whatever it was that had attracted their attention. As Murray reached the grass in front of the house, the main door opened warily and Andrew Grant appeared. He was surprised to see Murray.

'Cousin Charles!' He closed the door softly behind himself and bowed.

'Good day to you, Cousin Andrew: are you coming out for a walk? I'm afraid it's not the best of mornings.'

'I needed some air,' said Andrew. 'I did not have the best of nights.' His indoor face was indeed greyer than usual, pale eyes wide to make the point. Under the edges of his hat his hair seemed to have receded at his temples even in the few days he had been at Letho.

'I'm sorry to hear that,' said Murray. The dogs had realised he had stopped and had hurried back to circle him, herding him towards their goal. 'The dogs have spotted something they find fascinating over there. Will you come? Or would you rather have some time to yourself?'

'I'll come,' agreed Grant, who had sensibly donned coat, hat and gloves. Murray had forgotten again to be cold.

'Yes, Bonnie, yes, Flash, we're coming,' he told them, and waited until Grant had reached him before following the liver and white backs along the path to the side of the big house. The garden walls rose in front of them, topped by ivy and the bare branches of shrubs and trees reaching out of the garden beyond. At the foot of the wall, the dogs' noses went down and they trailed frantically after some enticing scent, sniffing furiously. Whatever it was, it drew them round the corner of the wall, where they could no longer stay so near the wall's foot because of more bushes and shrubs between the wall and the path. On the other side of the path, light woodland sent out tentative undergrowth from the main woods further on. Amongst the undergrowth Murray could see the bright scarlet of late rowan berries and rosehips, wizening into dots of blood red on the bushes where the daylight caught them.

Then he blinked: it was not blood-coloured berries, but blood.

He called the dogs back quickly, making them sit on the path, away from the ground and the bushes. He turned to Grant.

'Do you see?'

Grant's nostrils were flaring with agitation as he stared at the blood.

'Has – could someone have slaughtered a, a pig? A sheep?' He struggled to think of something rural enough. 'A deer?'

'It would be unusual, to say the least, for them to do it so near the house. Poachers, perhaps – though we have had little trouble with them lately...' He tailed away, stepping carefully towards the ground and examining the grass from side to side. 'See here – whatever it was they have dragged it back into the bushes here.' The grass was pulled flat, and there were twigs and brambles torn, combed backwards with the weight of something hauled through them.

'They wouldn't do that with a pig, I suppose,' said Cousin Andrew, still struggling with his setting.

'No,' said Murray drily, 'and a sheep would have left wool on the branches. No, I think we're looking at a deer – or something worse.'

'Worse?' Cousin Andrew's anxious voice came to him through the undergrowth, as he stayed on the path and Murray pushed further after the trail. He cast about him: there was no more sign of dragging once they were in the bushes. No more sign of any movement: the brambles, grey in the autumn, lay as they had grown, the dead leaves amongst them rotted where they had fallen. He could see no further sign of blood, either. Puzzled, he scrambled back out on to the path further along the garden wall, and returned to where Grant was still standing, staring.

'It looks as though,' said Murray, trying to sum up the picture, 'something quite big had its throat cut. That spray of blood across the bushes: that's strong, and it's bright red, or was. That's lifeblood. And it was not done long ago, either: probably just about dawn, for some of the blood has barely clotted. The blood sprayed out there, and then spilled on to the grass just here.'

'Good heavens, Charles, is this what comes of living in the country?' asked Grant faintly. 'Could it – could it still be a deer?'

'Just about,' said Murray, but he was worried. Then Grant

gave a little yelp.

'Look!' He dived forward, and pulled something shiny out of the nearest bush, then dropped it again when he saw the blood on it. Murray stooped and picked it up delicately in his gloved fingers.

'But those are Margaret's!' cried Cousin Andrew, eyes wider than ever. The thought flashed through Murray's mind that he would never employ Andrew as his advocate for the defence: Mrs. Grant's embroidery sharps, neat little silver blades, were covered in blood.

'The ones she mangled on her embroidery hoop to distract Robert?' Isobel asked at breakfast.

'The same ones, I'm fairly sure.' Macduff, the sheriff's man, had taken them away with him after making an accurate sketch of the bloodstained area under the trees.

'I have never known anyone kill a deer with embroidery sharps,' remarked Blair innocently.

'It would require unusual skill, I agree,' said Murray.

The three of them were alone: Grant had declared himself unable to face breakfast, and Mrs. Grant was not yet down.

'And you said the dragging trail disappeared once you were inside the bushes?' said Isobel. 'Surely that argues that whatever it was then managed to walk away?'

'It was a lot of blood,' said Murray bleakly.

'Oh.'

'Hard to carry a deer,' remarked Blair after a moment.

'In the Highlands, they have special ponies to carry them, do they not?' asked Isobel.

'Garrons, yes,' said Blair, showing a little of his usual excitement. 'Very strong ponies, and not at all, as would be the case with ordinary horses, dismayed by the smell of blood.'

'But a horse carrying a deer would have torn more branches and brambles, and besides, who in Letho has a garron?' asked Murray.

'Then you fear the worst?' asked Isobel soberly. 'For Agnes, or for Tilly?'

'Impossible to say – or it may, indeed, be Lizzie Fenwick. But I think I am fairly sure that one of our missing women died out there in the dawn this morning, only a few yards from the house and safety.'

'I don't like that thought at all,' said Blair, his face solemn.

'No,' said Murray, 'nor do I.'

Nor did Robbins.

'You think it might have been Agnes, sir?' he asked, his lips tight, when Murray had described what he and Grant had found.

'Agnes or Miss Aytoun or Lizzie Fenwick, I'm afraid so, Robbins.'

'Whichever of them, it's an awful thing.' He fell silent for a moment, his pale eyes distant. 'Do you think perhaps whichever of them it was had escaped, and was running here?'

'Maybe so.' Robbins never used to be imaginative: some of Mary's strange mind must have connected with his.

'They must have thought themselves almost in safety,' said Robbins softly.

'They almost were.' Murray shivered. 'Has Mr. Macduff been questioning you all again?'

'Yes, sir. It's no trouble: we're happy enough to do what we can to help, but it happens there was no one outside just there this morning. Daniel and William had walked up before dawn, and you could hardly see into that angle from the main village path anyway. We can't see round that corner from our house, either. It's not a path often used after the summer, unless for blackberries and rosehips, and they're nearly done.'

'If she was indeed escaping … what does that mean? That it was Agnes, for whom this is home? That this was the nearest house, in which case where on earth are they being held? Or that they needed to see someone in this house specifically – but that tells us hardly anything. It could have been Tilly looking for Robert, Agnes looking for home, or Mrs. Fenwick looking for protection. And of course, we don't know if she was escaping at all.'

Robbins seemed about to reply, when the library door opened and Daniel shambled in to announce Macduff, the sheriff's man. Macduff limped behind him, and bowed apologetically.

'I ask pardon for interrupting, sir,' he began. 'I wondered if there was any chance you might be intending a visit to Collessie at all today?'

'There was nothing intended. Are you hoping to tell Sir John about the blood?'

'That was the idea, sir. Only … I felt it might sound better, again, coming from you.'

Murray bit his lips together.

'That makes sense. I know we don't know yet whether or not it was his daughter's blood, but I'm sure he will want to know what has happened, anyway. And since it was on Letho land and I was there, I'll happily accompany you. Well, maybe happily is not the word, but willingly, anyway.'

'Aye, sir. I'm very grateful,' said Macduff with a meaningful look. Clearly he did not quite trust Sir John's faith in him to do his job. Murray did not blame him.

'Do you want to go over right away?'

'That would be best, sir. Before rumours reach the household.'

'Quite right.' He sighed. 'Robbins, please fetch my hat and gloves.'

Blair joined them in the hall and Macduff seemed pleased enough to have another gentleman supporting his visit to Collessie. They set out once again towards the woods, then past the woodsman's hut where Robert Lovie had planned his ill-fated assignation with Tilly Aytoun. Blair had not seen it, and insisted on examining the little structure inside and out, and then viewing it from down the path, and up the path, and from a little distance into the woods on either side. He poked through the bracken bed inside, but did not come up with any other missing Letho cutlery. They continued on to Collessie, Blair unusually silent as he pottered ahead rather like one of the spaniels.

Sir John Aytoun emerged from the library just as Murray was trying to give their names to the servant who answered the door. The servant looked more frightened than usual, and therefore less able to remember simple instructions. Sir John moved with his usual grace, though Murray thought he looked even more tired than he had seemed when he had punched Robert Lovie in Letho library.

'Have you arrested Lovie, then?' he asked, without preamble.

'Not arrested,' said Murray, 'but he is locked up for everyone's protection until we find out what is going on.'

'Then you admit your cousin is dangerous,' said Sir John, though with less fire than Murray would have expected.

'Sir, we've come to tell you about something that happened this morning,' said Macduff quickly. 'Where were you around dawn, sir?'

'Around dawn?' Sir John seemed momentarily distracted. 'Dawn … I was … in my bed, I suppose, like most honest gentlemen.' He pushed his hair back from his face, but did not quite meet Macduff's eyes.

Murray blinked. He had been so wound about in his head wondering who had shed the blood in the bushes that he had not even begun to wonder who had wielded the embroidery sharps. Too little sleep, too stupid, he thought to himself. And had Sir John really been in his bed? It seemed to Murray that Sir John was not a very good liar.

Macduff was telling Sir John about the discovery of the blood at Letho. Sir John's face, porcelain white, turned a nasty shade of yellow at the news.

'You think – you think Tilly …'

'We don't know, Sir John,' said Murray hurriedly. 'It is a substantial quantity of blood, and we found –' He noticed suddenly that Macduff was wiggling his eyebrows urgently. 'We found it likely,' he adjusted what he had been going to say, 'that it came from a human. Of course, Miss Aytoun is not the only person missing in the village at the moment.'

'But if you don't know whether or not it was Tilly, then why did you come to tell me?' Sir John asked petulantly. 'There seems to be no progress at all in this matter.'

'We came to tell you because we did not want you to hear it as a piece of village gossip,' said Murray, trying not to sound cross. 'Mr. Macduff has questioned my servants and he would like to question yours, too, in case they saw or heard anything around dawn.'

'But the blood was found at your house. Are you sure Robert Lovie is securely locked up?' demanded Sir John.

'It was one of the first things I checked,' said Murray, fairly truthfully: he had remembered about Robert after breakfast, but there was no sign that any of his guests had left the house before he himself had. 'May Macduff question your staff?'

Sir John looked as if he might just say no, but pulled himself together in time.

'Yes, yes, why not. He can question them in the library, such as it is. I'll have them sent up one by one.'

Macduff looked pleased and surprised: it was not often he was allowed to use as grand a room as a library for his questions. He nodded to Murray, telling him that he had achieved all he wanted, and Murray and Blair turned to go.

'I hope Lady Aytoun is as well as she can be?' Murray asked.

'Dr. Feilden has given her laudanum. She is better altogether when she is asleep.' Sir John guided them to the front door, as if they might have forgotten their way, and opened it wide for them to leave. Murray nodded to Macduff, and led the way out on to the weed speckled gravel of the driveway.

'Good day to you,' said Aytoun, and closed the door almost on Blair's heels.

'I hope Macduff gets what he needs,' said Murray, stopping on the gravel to stare back at the closed door. 'I can't say I know if Sir John wanted to help or not.'

'Oh, look!' said Blair. 'Isn't that Mr. Johnstone?'

They stayed where they were and watched, as Mal Johnstone, fairly brimming with visible self-righteousness, appeared round the corner from the servants' entrance, and strode off down the drive. He did not seem to have seen them, and they chose not to draw attention to themselves.

'What might he be doing here?' asked Blair.

'Well, he's a Collessie tenant: he was probably visiting the estate office,' said Murray. 'But I must admit, I'm suspicious of almost anything that man does just now.'

'It's that look he has,' said Blair, nodding solemnly. 'Isobel, though I've told her and I know my late sister did too that it's not very ladylike to use Scots words quite so much in her speech, though of course she goes her own way whether I like it or not, would call it pensit.'

'She would, indeed,' said Murray with something like a grin. 'Well, we cannot do much more here -'

He broke off as the air was ripped in two by a scream.

'That came from the house,' snapped Murray, and they turned back to the door. It was not locked, and they burst inside. The hallway was empty, but in a second Macduff appeared at the library door.

'What was that?' he gasped. Even as he spoke, the scream came again.

'This way!' cried Murray, heading for the baize door to the servants' quarters. It swung stiffly on its hinges, and they found themselves in a narrow corridor at the head of a flight of stairs. They were not long: Murray flung himself down to the floor below in three long strides, and nearly banged his head on the low ceiling of the corridor below. Before him were three doorways: one was closed with a wooden door, a window in it barred across the light from at least one candle. Murray stepped up to the window and looked inside the room, just as Sir John's pale face stared back out. He was furious.

'What are you doing here? I thought you had gone!'

'What are you doing here, Sir John?' Murray retorted, and pushed open the door in Sir John's face. They were in a cell, lit as he had thought by three candles in sconces. It was small and strewn with straw, and the candle light was quite bright enough to show them who had screamed. Lizzie Fenwick lay curled up in a twist of straw, her arms around her shaved head, her skirts bundled about her. One bare leg was free of the tangling skirts: it was bloody and twisted, covered in bruises old and new. And in Sir John's long, elegant hands was a sturdy stick.

Chapter Fifteen

'I don't care! She will leave my house, or the child and I will die!'

Agostinella was beside herself at the top of the stairs, her eyes wild in panic. Murray prayed that Lizzie Fenwick, prostrate on a hurdle, had passed out with the pain: he doubted her French was up to Neapolitan aristocracy standards, but Lady Agostinella's meaning was clear and no one could be in doubt that hospitality was not high on her list. A door slammed somewhere upstairs, and Dr. Harker came hurrying along the landing with something in a silver cup. He cast a look of concern downstairs at the miserable little party in the hall.

'I'll take her elsewhere, my lady,' said Murray hurriedly, feeling the doctor's reproach. He wondered precisely where he was going to take Lizzie. He had promised to look after her, and he could not do that if she went back, injured and deeply distressed, to her own cottage. Or back into the custody of the Kirk Session. He glanced at Robbins and saw the man taking a breath, perhaps to volunteer space in his own house, but before he could speak Mrs. Dean came smartly into the hall.

'Sir, bring Mrs. Fenwick through to the servants' wing and we shall see her into Mrs. Chambers' old cottage. I have sent Jennet to light the fire, and I shall tend her myself, with your permission.'

'By all means,' Murray agreed heartily, though he was angry at not being able to deal with the situation himself. 'We'll need a room for Lady Aytoun, too, when you can. Where is Miss Blair, do you know?'

'I believe she's in her chamber, sir,' said Robbins. 'Shall I ask her to come down?'

'If you could, Robbins: I know it's not your place to go fetching guests from bedchambers, but … This is Lady Aytoun's maid, by the way.' He ushered forward the third woman they had brought from Collessie.

'Sir.'

Murray watched as the two stablemen from Collessie manoeuvred the hurdle with unexpected care through the doorway to the servants' corridor, supervised by Mrs. Dean and Blair. Lady

Aytoun's maid followed, ready to receive instructions as to her mistress' quarters. Then Murray turned and guided Lady Aytoun into the parlour, and settled her by the fire. She had not stopped crying since they had woken her, with some difficulty after her dose of laudanum, at Collessie, and told her that the sheriff's man was taking her husband away to Cupar jail. In the circumstances Murray had not felt that they could leave her alone with her maid in a house full of Collessie servants in the midst of a parish infected by insanity. It had taken some persuasion of the said Collessie servants to have the Aytouns' carriage brought round, but the maid had filled the time packing a trunk for Lady Aytoun, and Blair had tended to Lizzie Fenwick, finding blankets and bandages, wet and dry, like the most devoted of nurses. Macduff, the sheriff's man, had already left with Sir John who had nearly to be carried outside: he had collapsed in the straw almost on top of Lizzie Fenwick and could barely walk. Macduff had found a gig and a fairly able horse in the stables and between them they had hauled Sir John into it, and seen Macduff off with his slumped prisoner on the road to Cupar.

He sat opposite Lady Aytoun and thought of taking her hands to rub them, but they were firmly knotted inside her muff: the maid had been unable to slide her fingers into gloves. Still she sobbed: he wondered if she would at some stage run out of tears, but he could think of no words of comfort to give a woman whose daughter was missing and whose husband was in jail for beating another woman half to death.

The parlour door opened and Isobel and her father hurried in, Isobel with a decanter of brandy and glasses in her hands.

'Father said … Lady Aytoun, dear,' Isobel went to her and wrapped her up in her arms. 'Come, now: take a little brandy.'

Murray poured a glass where Isobel had dumped decanter and glasses on the table, and handed it to Isobel. Blair had buried himself in an armchair.

'I asked, I hope it was all right, that Dr. Harker should take a look at Mrs. Fenwick. When he has finished with Lady Agostinella, of course,' he added rapidly.

'How did Agostinella even know who she was?' Murray slumped next to him and ran a hand through his hair. 'And how did she … oh, I don't know. I'm sure I heard her playing the piano

171

when we came in, and in a second there she was on the landing, screaming at us.'

'I hope she has not done herself any harm,' murmured Blair.

'I should hope not. I do hope not, and of course I'm concerned for the child,' Murray almost did not want to say the words, as if they were unlucky themselves, as if Mary was right about taking care over children and speaking about them. 'But Lizzie Fenwick needs urgent attention, too.'

'I only asked that he should look just in case,' said Blair mildly. 'Mrs. Fenwick is in very good hands with your Mrs. Dean. A very efficient woman, and she seemed to care for Mrs. Fenwick. Are they friends, do you know?'

'No idea,' said Murray. By the fire, Isobel had surprisingly managed to soothe Lady Aytoun's tears, and was perched on the arm of the chair with her own arm around Lady Aytoun's shoulders, holding her close. It was a side of Isobel Murray had not seen before, and it took him aback, in the part of his mind that had the leisure to consider the matter.

'Here, another little sip of brandy,' she was saying, and Lady Aytoun swallowed a good mouthful, blinking as the warm spirit went down.

'Have they gone to Mrs. Chambers' old cottage, as Mrs. Dean suggested?' Murray asked. Mrs. Chambers had lived very close to the servants' wing, and it would be convenient. Was it safe enough, though?

'I saw them in,' said Blair. 'Mrs. Dean did indeed have a fire laid and blazing, and the box bed freshly made up, and hot water and cold for more bandages. That woman has a wonderful collection of salves, Charles. But I'm amazed that she had everything ready. Someone from Collessie must have slipped away the moment you offered to look after Mrs. Fenwick, and warned her to make arrangements.'

'She is remarkably efficient. I'm surprised anyone at Collessie was that quick, though.'

'Hm, yes,' Blair agreed. 'Charles, when I arrived she was sprinkling salt around the doorway and windows.'

'Was she?' Murray blinked, and remembered the white powder on the front door step of Letho that morning. 'Salt – would that protect against something?'

'I think I can manage, now, dear. So kind, so kind,' said Lady Aytoun suddenly.

She was already looking better. Her hands had emerged from the muff, and she had hold of her brandy glass on her own now. Isobel was gradually moving back from her, letting her have the chair to herself.

'Can someone please explain to me again,' said Lady Aytoun plaintively, 'what has happened? You woke me and told me my husband was being taken away, but I'm afraid I can remember nothing more than that. Where has he gone?'

'Yes, I'd like to know a little more, too,' said Isobel. 'Why was Lady Agostinella so upset?'

'We found Sir John in the cellar at Collessie, beating Lizzie Fenwick with a stick,' said Murray clearly.

'My husband? Beating someone?' asked Lady Aytoun, though she did not sound altogether surprised, Murray thought. 'But who is Lizzie Fenwick?'

'A local woman who had been imprisoned by the Kirk Session and accused of being a witch,' said Isobel, with only a glance at Lady Aytoun. 'How,' she asked her father and Murray, 'did she end up in Sir John's cellar?'

'I assume it was he who released her from the cell at the church,' said Murray. 'He had beaten her very badly, Lady Aytoun. Did he say nothing to you of this?'

'Nothing … nothing. I have been mostly asleep since Tilly … since Tilly …'

'All right, Lady Aytoun, I understand. You have been given laudanum to calm you, of course.' Murray sighed. 'He must have believed that Lizzie Fenwick had something to do with Miss Aytoun's disappearance.'

'Did she not?' asked Lady Aytoun, then blushed very deeply. 'I mean: surely my husband would not have done such a thing, taken such a woman from such a place and treated her so, unless he thought ...' She rose unsteadily and poured herself another glass of brandy, the decanter chinking against the glass.

'Lizzie Fenwick is the local midwife, and a kinder and more generous person it would be hard to find,' said Murray. 'She was in the cell at the church, guarded by the Kirk Session, when your daughter disappeared. And there are no longer any laws condemning witchcraft, per se, so the Kirk Session were wrong to imprison her. The only laws are against pretending to carry out witchcraft or deceiving people into thinking that you can cast spells or curses. The Presbytery have said that if the charges had been brought, they would have assoilzied her, anyway.'

'Ass-ss-what?' asked Lady Aytoun, whose glass was empty again. She refilled it, spilling some brandy on the table.

'Assoilzied her. Cleared her of all charges.'

'Oh.'

'The sheriff's officer was at Collessie when we found her, so he took Sir John to the jail at Cupar because he had beaten the poor woman senseless. If she dies of her injuries – which I devoutly hope she does not, and not for his sake - he is in very serious trouble.'

'Charles!' said Isobel sharply, her eye on Lady Aytoun, clearly worried that all her calming and soothing might be undone. Lady Aytoun, however, emptied another glass and sat down rather heavily in the nearest chair.

'He always has been a little too ready with that stick,' she remarked indistinctly, put her head back on the chair, and fell asleep.

'A good way to avoid questions,' Isobel observed, back to her more accustomed cynicism. 'Though if he beats her …'

'She might find it a useful strategy,' Murray finished. He rubbed his face with his hands. 'Right,' he said, 'well, we know now where Lizzie Fenwick went, and why, and even more importantly where she is now and that she is safe, if not hale. We don't quite know how, I suppose …'

'Didn't we see Mal Johnstone leaving Collessie? Just as we were about to go ourselves?' asked Blair.

'Mal Johnstone! Wretched man. When this is all over I'm going to do my best to have him removed from the Kirk Session. They were never this peculiar before he joined. Ninian Jack is a sensible man, and so is Kenny. Melville's easily led, that's his trouble, but the others …'

'When a crowd is seized with a notion,' said Blair quietly, 'they will pick it up and run with it, and it's a strong man that can stop them.'

They all shivered at that thought.

'Did Helliwell take the presbytery minute books away with him last night?' asked Murray after a moment.

'I believe he did. I remember him carrying them when we walked him home.'

'Then perhaps we should go and ask to take another look at them. And we can bring him the – relatively good news about Lizzie Fenwick. Mrs. Helliwell will be glad to know she's been found, anyway.'

'Can I come?' asked Isobel. Murray looked at her.

'To be honest, I'd rather you didn't.'

'You think I'll be snatched away in front of you?' Isobel said crossly.

'No, I don't,' said Murray. 'But Agostinella is hysterical, Lady Aytoun's, well, drunk, the Grants are upset, Robert Lovie is locked up and the housekeeper is tending to Lizzie Fenwick. There's only you and Robbins in the house with any sense at all, so I'd be very grateful if you'd stay here in case something else happens.'

'Well, if you put it like that ...' Isobel was not pleased, but she could see the sense of it.

'Lock the front door behind us, though, dear,' added Blair, with a sideways grin. Isobel sighed.

They talked as they walked along the path to the village, knowing they could not be overheard without knowing it.

'I still think that either Agnes or Tilly was killed outside Letho this morning,' said Murray. 'No one kills an animal with a pair of embroidery sharps. And how did the sharps get there? Cousin Andrew was sure they belonged to his wife.'

'I doubt Sir John Aytoun wielded them, anyway, or I'd be very surprised,' said Blair. 'He was too busy with Lizzie Fenwick. And if he had taken a moment to leave Collessie, I wonder if he would have changed weapons like that?'

'I agree. It seems unlikely. And anyway, he took Lizzie Fenwick because he thought she knew something about Tilly's disappearance, so he would hardly have had reason to kill Tilly or Agnes.'

'So we don't think that Sir John took Tilly or Agnes – supposing he would have had a reason to take his own daughter –'

'Perhaps he found out that she intended to meet Robert Lovie and did the same with her as he did with Mrs. Fenwick?' suggested

Blair. 'Has anyone searched Collessie for other captives?'

'Good point – we should find out,' said Murray. 'After all, we know he has a temper. I would not want to be the daughter that defied him. But there is still no link between him and Agnes: I have never heard that they have lived in or near Paisley, for example, or Glasgow. And would he have had any reason to murder Widow Maggot? I can't see one.'

'We still don't know, or at least we aren't sure, why they left Edinburgh in the middle of the season,' Blair added mildly.

'I'll send another note to Macduff. I'm sure he dreads the sight of my handwriting, but we do need to make sure. We'd like him to ask Sir John about Glasgow or Paisley, and we think it a good idea to search the rest of the house at Collessie. Outbuildings too, perhaps, though I'm not sure Sir John would want to take that kind of thing out of the house, not where he can't trust the servants.'

'What about the blood this morning, then?' asked Blair, trotting eagerly on to the bridge over the river and settling in his favourite fish-spotting position. 'How did Mrs. Grant's embroidery sharps come to be there?'

'We need to find out when she last saw them. I can't altogether see Mrs. Grant as a killer, can you? I'm trying to set aside the fact that I like her, though.'

'If she killed Tilly Aytoun, I doubt she would be strong enough to carry her away through the wood,' said Blair thoughtfully, staring at the brown river.

'She would manage Agnes, though,' said Murray. 'Agnes is small.' He kept reminding himself to speak of her in the present tense, like Mary, not to lose hope.

'But what would her reason be? There would be no point, I think, in killing Miss Aytoun to hide what Robert Lovie was doing, since they admitted his faults anyway. Robert has admitted them openly himself, so he does not seem to be protecting anyone else.'

'I heard her talking with Rintoul quite knowledgeably about Glasgow University,' Murray suddenly remembered. 'I remember thinking at the time that she might have been the daughter or the widow of a professor there, but I never had the chance to ask her.'

'Something else to pursue, then?'

'Yes, indeed.'

Blair came up suddenly from his bent position and clutched

the bridge handrail for support.

'Did the Widow Maggot have any connexions with Glasgow, I wonder?'

'Did the Widow Maggot have any connexions with anything or anyone?' said Murray. 'This whole affair, if it is just the one, makes no sense to me.'

Mr. Helliwell was in the manse, and Mrs. Helliwell appeared just as the maid was showing them into his study.

'Have you heard the news of Mrs. Fenwick, Mrs. Helliwell?' Murray asked, pausing in the hallway.

'I have, I have. Mrs. Dean sent a message just now.' Mrs. Helliwell was pale and worried-looking. 'I'm glad she is in good hands, but what possessed Sir John? What a terrible thing to do.'

'We think he might have been led to believe she knew something about Mathilda Aytoun's disappearance.'

'What, on the grounds that she's a witch?' Mrs. Helliwell shook her head in despair. 'Who on earth would have done that?' She blinked. 'Oh, do you know, I think I can guess? Mal Johnstone?'

'That was who we saw there. There's no proof, though: he may just have been visiting the estate office at Collessie.'

'I suppose … I've never much liked the man,' she admitted. 'But now I do wonder if there's something a little bit wrong in his head. He seems entirely obsessed by witches and witchcraft. It's becoming quite frightening.'

'Who's gossiping out there?' demanded Mr. Helliwell crossly from the study, where the maid had been holding the door open. 'Oh, Mr. Murray, Mr. Blair: it's you. Well, come in, then, come in. I hear Lizzie Fenwick has been found, so that's something.'

They settled before the fire in the study and the maid was sent for tea.

'We've come to ask if we may take another look at the presbytery minutes, please,' said Blair humbly.

'Of course: I'd hoped to look at them again myself, this morning.' He rose and fetched the oilcloth parcel from his desk, and perched it on his lap by the fire to untie it. 'This is the earlier volume: it breaks off in the 1640s, I see,' he said, opening it at the back. 'Then this one goes up to … 1755, it seems.'

'Large volume,' Murray commented.

'Small handwriting,' Helliwell countered, showing the clerk's tiny hand in brown ink.

'Oh, that will be fun!' Murray said dourly.

'Well, what do you say that you both set to with reading,' said Helliwell. 'Oh, here's the tea: good. Then when you find anything interesting or relevant, read it aloud and I shall note it down.'

'An excellent plan!' cried Blair. Murray thought it neatly unburdened Helliwell, but he agreed to go ahead. Silence fell in the hum of the fire as they began to read. Blair had the earlier volume, and had to leaf through quite a number of pages before he came to the first reference to witch hunting: Murray was able to start at the beginning of the later volume.

'Oh! I've found a case. 1590,' said Blair suddenly. 'Nan Murit, her name was. That seems to be the earliest one. She was in the parish of ... er, Ebdie?'

'Abdie, on the coast,' said Helliwell, making a note. 'What do they say?'

'They say she makes simples to help people make their neighbours' cattle ill, then offers to cure the cattle for money,' said Blair after a moment. When he concentrated on the writing he stuck the tip of his tongue out and wrinkled his nose as if he were trying to make the two meet.

'That's not unusual,' said Helliwell.

'And not much witchcraft to it,' said Murray.

'There frequently isn't,' Helliwell agreed, sourly.

After a while, Blair muttered,

'Grissell Gairdner, ane wicket woman and ane sorcerer.'

'Really?' asked Murray.

'That's what it says here. 1596, we're in now. There are a few others, too. Hmm ... consorting with the Devil, apparently. Not the usual thing ... An actual coven, meeting at night and dancing and so forth – bare leggit, it seems. I think that's something the kirk session particularly disapproved of.'

'Which kirk session?' asked Helliwell.

'Newburgh.'

'Back on the coast,' said Helliwell with satisfaction, as if you could not expect anything better from the people there.

'This was quite a thing, it seems,' said Blair. 'They really were doing all kinds of exciting things, flying through trees and turning themselves into animals – cats and hares are mentioned particularly – a whole crowd of men and women.'

'What happened to them?'

'Let's see …' Blair turned a couple of pages over slowly. 'They were brought before the Presbytery, of course … found guilty … Oh! They were burned.'

'All of them?'

'No, Grissell Gairdner was defended by her husband, it says. She was allowed to go free: it says that he said she was led into it by her mother but was "innocent of al hairm", according to him. He must have been someone well-respected in the parish: one of the men was burned because his wife was a witch, as far as I can see.'

'I haven't heard of any of our parishioners flying through trees,' said Murray.

'Or changing themselves into hares and cats,' said Helliwell, with a dry laugh. Murray suddenly remembered the white hare, with its crushed back legs. Crushed legs … just like Lizzie Fenwick? Ridiculous, he told himself, and went back to picking through the Presbytery clerk's tiny writing.

'Here's a couple of fugitives in 1645,' he deciphered. 'Bessie Cuper and Jean Buchane, up to witchcraft in … I suppose that's Creich. Mother and daughter, it seems: so perhaps it's another case like Grissell Gairdner's. They've fled the parish, anyway, and the Presbytery is sending out word to all the parishes to see if they can find them.'

'Oh, here's Grissell Gairdner again!' said Blair. 'And again. She can't seem to stop herself: she has a new coven now, and the Kirk Session have reported her for recruiting young people in the parish.'

'What date?' asked Helliwell.

'1599, this one. Her husband's standing up for her again.'

'Brave man,' said Helliwell.

'Perhaps he feared her more than the Kirk Session,' suggested Murray with a grin.

'Well, it didn't last for ever,' said Blair after a moment. 'Here we are in 1610, and the Widow Gairdner is shorn and pricked and burned for "evil doings and sorcery and witchcraft, by habit and repute and according to divers witnesses.'''

'The Session got her in the end,' said Helliwell darkly.

'Then it seems to go a bit quiet,' Blair added sadly.

'Oh, but they've caught Bessie Cuper and Jean Buchane – two years later! Apparently they've been brought back from Lothian.'

'A fair run, I suppose,' Helliwell was grudging.

'They don't seem to know what to do with them, though. No further mention of Jean, it's just Bessie, 'and sindrie ithers lying under the sclander of witchecraft and not yet cleared.' That seems to imply that the Presbytery is more concerned about people spreading slander than about people being witches. There was another case ... the previous year, I think it was. Yes, here we are: two women appealing to the Presbytery to have their names cleared because they'd been accused of witchcraft locally. In Kilmany, that was.'

'Oh, here's one!' cried Blair excitedly. '1600, report sent by the Kirk Session of Letho. Jean Arbuckell, Mary Dan, Johne Arbuckell and sundry others, accused of a Sabbath at Josie's Den with Ann Meggott, a well-kent sorcerer. And using what? Oh, bundles of rabbit bones as witch marks – marking their territory, I suppose.'

'Rabbit bones?' asked Helliwell.

'We found rabbit bones in a little posy in Tilly Aytoun's reticule,' said Murray, suddenly remembering. Then he thought again about what Blair had read out. 'Meggott?' he asked.

'Meggott. Or Maggott, couldn't it be?'

'That's funny,' said Murray. 'There's an Ann Maggott here, too. 1662, it is ... Ann Maggott, of the parish of Letho, long kent to be a witch. The commissioner to try them is Sir John Aitoun of that Ilk.'

'Right,' said Helliwell, 'This is too much. I need something stronger than tea.'

Chapter Sixteen

Despite the minister's sudden generosity with the brandy, neither Murray nor Blair felt much like drinking. The Presbytery minutes had been reassuring, in a way: it seemed that even at the height of the madness in the seventeenth century, Presbytery had kept its head and not burned just anyone at the cry of 'Witch! Witch!'. However, any defence of the Widow Maggot would probably not benefit from mention of her namesake – and the Widow Maggot had also been Ann, as confirmed by the minister – from two centuries ago. Or a century and a half, thought Murray: the name seemed to carry on from generation unto generation, presumably through a series of unmarried mothers.

'There seem to be two kinds of things, two sort of events, in the Presbytery records,' said Blair tentatively as they walked back to Letho House. 'There's either the woman who curses someone else – often for good reason, it seems – and threatens to make their cattle sick, or the full-blown, half the parish dancing round, witches' Sabbath. Which do you think we have here?'

'Well, as yet no one has charged either Lizzie Fenwick or Widow Maggot with cursing anything, or threatening to. It might only be a matter of time, I agree. But Mal Johnstone has mentioned covens, and so did Melville, though he was probably only echoing what Johnstone had said. I think it's the Sabbath style: find a couple of witches, and decide that there must be more. The trouble is that to judge by the Presbytery minutes, those were the ones that ended in burnings.'

'The hysterical ones,' agreed Blair. 'The single witch ones were just individual women causing trouble, I believe.'

'Yes, I think so. Johnstone is determined to make this much more than that.'

They walked on a few more paces, until they were within view of the wood where Murray and his horse had had such a fright on Tuesday. Only three days ago? He had seen the white hare afterwards, too, he remembered. Then he had seen it this very morning with its legs smashed.

He realised Blair had asked him a question, and shook himself.

'What was that?'

'What are you going to do now?'

Murray puffed out his lips, wondering.

'I shall see how Mrs. Fenwick is, then check on Lady Agostinella. Or the other way around, perhaps. Then I want to apply my mind again to where on earth Agnes and Tilly could be, or have been. The blood this morning, if it was indeed the lifeblood of one of them, proves again that they cannot be far away. What have we missed?'

Agostinella, said her maid, was lying down. Murray found Dr. Harker in the parlour, reading an old medical textbook he had found in the library. Murray's grandfather had been a man of eclectic reading tastes.

'My timing was regrettable earlier,' he said. 'I had no idea that Agostinella would hear us coming in the front door. She has never come to greet me before.' He heard a wistful note in his own voice, and cleared his throat firmly.

'Unfortunate, yes,' agreed Harker, who had been Murray's doctor all his life and carried that authority with him. 'She must not be upset, you know, not at all. She is at a very delicate time: you could lose the child, or Lady Agostinella, or both, very easily.'

'I'm sorry,' said Murray, closing his eyes at the pain of the thought. He left it a moment, then went on. 'Have you managed to see Mrs. Fenwick?'

'The accused witch?' There was a tiny laugh in Dr. Harker's voice, and Murray knew he was forgiven for now. 'Yes, I went to see her. Your housekeeper has her very comfortable in old Mrs. Chambers' cottage. She is well-wrapped in salves and bandages. There is a broken leg and a broken arm – I should think she tried to use her arm to protect herself – but I have set them without difficulty and at present I have no fear of infection. She was shaved by the Kirk Session, Mrs. Dean said?' he added, on a note of horror.

'By a faction of them, yes,' said Murray. He still could not believe that Ninian Jack and the other sensible members were really going on with this in their right minds.

'Extraordinary,' murmured Harker. 'I believe your father once told me that in the old times, when witches were burned, several of them were kept here at Letho House – Letho Castle, it was then – as prisoners before their burnings. He said that the prickings and whatever else passed for a trial in those primitive times was often carried out here.'

'In the cells downstairs?' Murray's eyebrows rose. His father had not mentioned it to him, but his father had thought him fanciful enough already, perhaps, and had not wanted to distract him from his exercise. 'That is not a very comfortable thought,' he added.

'Not particularly. I have never been down to the cells myself, and I cannot say they have a great attraction for me.'

Murray thought for a moment. Had anyone else been down to the cellars recently – since Agnes and Tilly had disappeared, for example?

He rang the bell. After a moment, Robbins appeared, looking tired and anxious, but then they all did.

'Robbins, has anyone been down to the old cellars recently? The ones right under the house.'

'I was down there with Mrs. Dean this day last week, sir, for we kept the picnic hampers down there. I can't say I've put them back yet, though, so I daresay no one has been down there since, sir.'

'I'd like to go down there now, if that is not inconvenient.'

'Of course, sir. Do you ... do you want anyone to go with you?' Robbins was not quite meeting his eye. If what Murray remembered of the old cellars was accurate, and he himself had not been down there since he was a boy, Robbins was probably not that keen to accompany him.

'Is there someone who's not too busy at the moment in the servants' hall?' Murray asked, giving him an escape route.

'I'll see, sir. Will you come now?'

'Might as well get it over with,' said Murray, and excused

himself to Dr. Harker.

As it turned out, William and Daniel had been summoned upstairs to move some furniture, whatever that might mean, in Lady Agostinella's rooms, so young Walter was instructed to go with the master and the cellar keys, and to carry the lantern good and high, now, or what use would it be down around the master's knees? Walter had not been to the old cellars before, and he took the instructions philosophically, along with the lantern. Murray received the keys.

'What are we looking for, sir?' asked Walter, for whom shyness in the face of authority had never been a problem.

'I'm not sure I should tell you, Walter. Well, I suppose in fact I should.' Murray reached the door to the staircase and opened it wide. 'I'm not sure,' he said, leading the way through and down the narrow turnpike stair with his head on one side to avoid thumping it on the curl above them, 'that anyone has checked down here for Agnes or Miss Aytoun. I know it might sound daft, but they have to be somewhere.'

'No dafter than anything else that's been happening lately, sir,' observed Walter.

'Then we are of one mind, Walter. Watch that last step there.'

Walter watched it, but only after he had slithered down it in his leather-soled boots. Murray sighed, but only a little.

'Here, better hand me the lantern,' he said, and took it. He fumbled with the keys, and pulled back the stairs door to reveal the iron cage over the door to the cells. He found the right key and opened the grille with a clank. Then he turned the largest key in the lock of the inner door, and the thud as the lock turned echoed down the dark passage. Murray found he was holding his breath, and realised that Walter was, too.

'Ready, Walter?'

Walter nodded, though it was not convincing. His hood of chestnut hair seemed to hug him very close. Murray held the old solid door handle, and pushed the door open, holding the lantern high. Walter shrank in behind him, but followed him dutifully into the cellar.

The swaying lantern showed a bare stone floor, stone walls and stone roof, arching just above Murray's head. To one side of the long, narrow room there was a kind of bench built out of the wall, as rough as if the builders could not be bothered chipping away that one last layer of rock. Above it, set into the wall but rusting now, were iron rings, three or four of them, some distance apart. To stop the witches reaching each other? To prevent frightened women sharing a comforting hug in the darkness? Murray shuddered.

'What's through there, sir?' Walter asked, in a tiny voice that sounded as if he was asking much against his better judgement.

'Same again, I think,' said Murray. The doorway was low and dark, the door that closed it made of some wood that had blackened with age, dull and deep-grained. Murray gritted his teeth. 'I'd better look, though, for the sake of completeness.'

He stepped carefully over to the door, head still lowered away from the roof, with Walter never more than a foot behind him. The door had a large keyhole, and he was not sure that any of his keys would fit.

'Maybe it's not locked,' whispered Walter, and swallowed hard.

'Maybe not.' Murray deliberately did not whisper, but his voice seemed to catch, all the same. He pushed on the dark door. It swung slowly open, noiseless. It took some effort for Murray to move the lantern forward, to see what might be inside.

The inner chamber had a lower floor than the outer one, and shallow steps led down into it. Murray stood in the doorway. The air was cold, cold as December. He made himself move the lantern around, examining the room thoroughly for any signs of recent use.

Here the iron rings were higher on the walls, but there was no stone bench for any semblance of comfort. Other than that, it seemed no different from the outer room. Why, then, Murray wondered, did he find it so much more horrible than the other chamber?

'I've been in far worse,' Lizzie Fenwick had said when he had urged her to leave the church cell, and then she had gone on to talk of the cells at old Letho House. What did she know of them?

'I don't like it, Mr. Murray,' came a small voice from behind him, and he turned to see that Walter was shaking.

'Then let's go.' He stepped back from the doorway, and turned to guide Walter back to the outer door.

'Had you no better shut that inner door again, sir? You

wouldn't want anything … coming out,' said Walter with a shiver. Murray turned to look back at the doorway, intending to shut the door.

'What's that?'

He was not even sure which of them said it. There, on the doorsill, just where he had been standing, was an odd, creamy mist, lying in a little pool. They both jumped back, then watched, fascinated, as the mist grew upwards, slowly, as if something was blowing it from below, forming a column. Then Walter gave a little gasp. The mist, where it touched the floor, was taking on a shape, the shape of two creamy white, angular bare feet – human feet, but made of no human substance. As the column grew taller, so the lower parts took on more of the shape: skirts, down to the bony ankles, hanging in misty folds. The ends of a shawls, defined only by shape as they hung near the vision's waist. Elbows appearing before hands, as if the creature was clutching its face or its throat. The mist trickled upwards, forming the upper arms, the breast, wrapped in the shawl, the cuffs of the blouse …

'Walter, run.'

They spun and shot out of the cellar, and Murray slammed the door and the gate behind them, locking them as if they could keep something like that in. They scrambled up the stairs, Murray pushing Walter in front of him, shoving him back up through the door and into the servants' corridor, crashing and locking that door, too, and running with Walter as fast as they could go to the warmth and light of the servants' kitchen. Then they breathed.

Mrs. Mack and Robbins stared at them.

'Sir, sit down, you're as white as flour,' cried Mrs. Mack, abandoning half-beaten eggs in a bowl to push the kettle over the fire.

'Here, sir,' Robbins gave him his own chair. Walter shivered violently and Murray drew him closer to the fire, and gave him the first cup of hot sugared brandy.

'Thank you, Robbins, Mrs. Mack. I'm sorry to intrude,' said Murray shakily.

'No harm, sir, but whatever has happened? Was there something in the cellar?'

'Something? Something?' Murray struggled for words that made any kind of sense.

'Sir,' said Walter, choking a little on the rich drink. 'Do you ken what it was like? It was like when Mrs. Mack breaks an egg into cold oil, and you canna see the white until it starts to cook.'

'You know, Walter, that's exactly what it was like. Only much, much more frightening.'

'But what do you think it was?' asked Blair, amazed. They were alone in the library: Murray had no wish to tell anyone else about his strange experience at present if he could avoid it.

'I have no idea,' said Murray. 'I don't know if there was a rational explanation for it, but it makes me shake just to think of it.'

'What were you looking for, anyway?'

'I had a notion that there might be something down there that would help. Not something from the original witch hunt: I mean that I realised the cellars had not been searched, and anywhere that has not been searched is worth searching, at this stage.'

'Well, in that case ...' said Blair tentatively, 'it's occurred to me that perhaps – though I may be wrong, indeed, there is another place that has not been searched.'

'Where?' Murray hoped it was away from Letho, but not too far away: he wanted to get away from the house for a bit, but not so far that he would be late for dinner. He had already alarmed the servants' hall: he had no wish to upset them further.

'Josie's Den,' said Blair, his eyes wide.

'Do you know, you're right? I don't think anyone has looked there – it's just that little bit far away. And yet, if Agnes had become confused and and gone back the way she had come ... Oh, wait, though: Rintoul told me he had been there, the day he found Agnes' cloak.'

'But he said that he found that on the way home, did he not?' asked Blair. 'So while he might have visited the Den, he was not necessarily looking for Agnes, was he? Or was he?'

'True, true.'

'And then there's the other question,' said Blair, scowling horribly.

'What's that?'

'Do you really trust Rintoul?'

In the end Blair and Murray went to Josie's Den in the gig, as the fastest way they could both get there. Riding would have been faster, for Murray: Blair, however, despite his affection for animals, had a disastrous seat on a horse and preferred to avoid riding wherever possible. The gig was quick to harness and nippy along the road, and it was not long until the little chapel came into sight amongst its trees. Murray drew up and arranged the reins around the gatepost, and eyed the chapel with calculation.

'I suppose we should try there, first,' he said. 'It's the best shelter around.'

'There's not much to the place: it shouldn't take long,' said Blair, his collar up against the thickening mist. They hurried over to the door, and pushed it open. Inside, it was chilly and not much drier. Most of the flagged floor was bare, with only a few pews at the very front: most people here brought their own stools, or stood at the back. There was a plain desk for the minister, and no choir or gallery. A very few minutes showed them that there was no hiding place.

'Round the back?' asked Murray, and they left the chapel to circumambulate the building. No gravestone was large enough to conceal anything, and there was no other shelter right round the churchyard. They walked out to the stone wall that surrounded it and paced the perimeter, keeping an eye out for anything huddled into the wall's lee, but again there was nothing.

'Well, the Den, then,' said Murray, as Blair scurried round the last of the headstones. But Blair gave a sudden cry, and Murray hurried back to him.

'Look!' Blair was pointing at one of the headstones. 'Another one!'

'Impossible,' said Murray firmly. The stone at which Blair was pointing was ancient, with the mirror mark they had found on the others. 'This must just be one we saw the other day.'

'No, no,' said Blair. 'There were very definitely only four. Look:' he scuttled about the kirkyard. 'Here, and here, there by the wall, I can see it quite clearly, and here by the door. Then this one.'

'But they all look as if they have been here forever!' Murray scowled. 'Could someone have moved one – for repair, or something – and just replaced it after our visit?'

'Maybe, maybe,' said Blair, but he was frowning horribly.

They stared at the stones for a long moment, helpless for something to say. Then they left the churchyard, closed the gate quietly behind them and made their way quickly, for it was close to dusk, over to the head of the steps. Here they slowed dramatically: the steps were covered now in damp leaves, fallen in the rain and wind of the last week. The whole place had taken on a cold, melancholic look that was very different from just a week ago. They stepped with great care, eyes on their feet, hands pressed against the wall beside them, until they were safely down on the relatively bare platform where they had picnicked last Friday. They looked about them.

'There's very little cover here,' said Blair plaintively. 'I had somehow remembered more nooks and crannies.'

'There are a few. Perhaps down by the river?' He led the way, again cautious on the steps, down to the path by the brown stream. The trees shaded them, and made it hard to see, but they peered into any likely bramble patches and holes in the bank, poking gently with their sticks and the toes of their boots. There was nothing, and no sign that there had been anything, in the last few days.

Disconsolate, they turned around and stared back up the Den. The great granite column stood out black against the darkening sky, looming above them. Perhaps, thought Murray, this had not been the most comforting place to come after his earlier shock in the cellar. He wondered how Walter was.

'Is there something up there?' asked Blair.

Murray jumped.

'Up where?'

'There, on top of the column. Where the witches' bathing pool is.'

Murray screwed up his eyes to stare up at the column. It was true: something seemed to be sticking out on one side, the side away from the platform. Something long and thin. He had no idea what it was.

'Oh, let's go up and look,' he said wearily. He let Blair go ahead of him up the first set of steps, back to the platform, then across to the higher level they had used to sit on, and up to the little bridge where Isobel had led the guests across to the top of the column. The bridge was narrow: Murray remembered Robert

Lovie skipping nimbly across it, while Tilly followed more warily, clutching the handrail. The bridge took them a little distance upwards, so it was that they were already halfway across when they could finally see clearly what lay on the top of the column.

With one hand splayed out over the edge of the granite, and the strange black witchpool seeping around her, Tilly Aytoun, damp with the day's mist, lay flat on her back, sightless eyes staring at the dusky sky. In her other hand, like an offering, she held a little bunch of rabbit bones, tied with a ribbon.

Chapter Seventeen

Blair, whose driving skills ranked only slightly above his riding ability, stayed with the body in the dusk while Murray took the gig to Cupar. Macduff met him with a heavy sigh and a thick muffler.

'I should have kent well that my work wasna over for the day,' he said, as he clambered awkwardly into the gig.

'I'm sorry,' said Murray.

'Och, that's no what I meant, sir. I'm pleased the lady's been found, for even a dead body is better than no answer at all for those who cared for her. What made you look at Josie's Den?'

'It was Mr. Blair, actually. He reckoned that no one had really looked at it since Agnes had disappeared.'

Macduff wrinkled his long face.

'The gentleman could be right, at that,' he admitted. 'I think we probably thought it was a bit too far from Letho, if we thought at all.'

'It is a step or two,' said Murray. 'If it was really Miss Aytoun who was killed at Letho House this morning, then it was a long way to take her body.'

'Maybe the fellow is trying to distract us again? I reckon that was what he was up to, sir, with the cloak and the reticule.'

'I'm happy to believe that.' They were out on the open road again and he urged the horse on a little faster. It would be doing Blair's rheumatism no good at all to be sitting in the damp, never mind the company he was keeping. 'How is Sir John?'

'Quiet, sir. He seems to be one of those ones that flares up and then just goes out like a candle.'

'Did he say anything more about why he had done it?'

'Only that he believed she had something to do with Miss Aytoun's disappearance.'

'I assume that at least puts him in the clear for her murder.'

'If we also assume that he's telling us the truth, sir. What if he was beating Mrs. Fenwick because he thought she had seen him doing something suspicious?'

'That's a thought. Well, we can ask Mrs. Fenwick later.'

'How is she doing?'

'The doctor says she'll be fine, physically. As to what the shock might have done to her …'

'Aye, aye.' Macduff braced himself in the seat as Murray turned off at the little chapel. 'Here we are, then.'

This time they took a look down at the dim Den from the top of the steps: Blair and Murray earlier had been too wary of slipping on the leaves to look round, or they would have seen Tilly laid out on the granite column. Blair was still sitting beside her, dangling his chubby legs over the edge and apparently talking to the body, or to himself.

'He's keeping her company,' Murray explained, seeing Macduff's eyebrows rise up his pale face. 'Do you need a hand?'

'I'll manage, no doubt,' said Macduff, and hirpled slowly down the steps. Blair heard them coming and scrambled to his feet, waving. In a moment, all three of them were standing gazing down at the body. Macduff had brought a lantern, and lit it.

'There's a wound in the side of her neck,' he commented.

'Do you think that could have been made by Mrs. Grant's embroidery sharps?'

'I think it very likely,' said Macduff. 'On her right side, I notice. Does that mean that her killer is left-handed?'

'Or perhaps she was attacked from behind?' suggested Murray. Macduff nodded thoughtfully.

'We wondered,' said Blair, 'if she was running to safety at Letho and was stabbed as she ran.'

'That would fit with being attacked from behind, I suppose,' said Macduff. There was a long silence. Tilly lay there oblivious, her long blue cloak easing in the breeze, stained brown with blood.

'I hope,' said Murray at last, 'that she was not running to safety *from* Letho.'

'I'm sure not, sir,' said Macduff politely.

'It's beginning to worry me,' Murray admitted. 'Agnes was from Letho, Tilly was supposed to meet someone from Letho, she had forks and a key from Letho and was killed, it seems, with scissors from Letho. I don't much like the look of it.'

Silence fell again, and Murray did not find it reassuring.

'I have some men coming with a cart to take her back to Cupar,' Macduff said eventually. 'Have you taken a look around, gentlemen?'

'We did look around before we found her,' said Blair eagerly. 'We looked down the den a bit, along the river. But we didn't see anything. Nothing at all.' He tailed away sadly. Macduff knelt at last beside the body and took a closer look at the wound, touching her white skin.

'She's stone-cold. No bonnet, but her cloak and boots in place.' He was half-talking to himself, but Murray and Blair were attentive. 'Would you call this a day dress, do you know?' he asked.

Murray looked carefully.

'I think so. It's a thickish cloth, a round skirt, and long sleeves, as far as I can see. An evening dress would be of finer material and with shorter sleeves. She presumably changed before going out to meet Robert, if she did go to meet Robert. It's very grubby, isn't it? Despite the water.'

'Or because of the water,' suggested Blair.

'No, the dirt isn't following where the water's going,' said Macduff, on his hands and one knee, the other leg stuck out awkwardly. 'I think we can be fairly sure she hasn't been up here on this rock for the last five days. Did the killer bring her back here after she fled as far as Letho? Or was she being kept near Letho and he brought her here to divert us? Or could he have another reason for bringing her here? What's this in her hand?'

'I fear it might be rabbit bones,' said Murray slowly. 'A sign, apparently, of a witch's curse.'

'And Josie's Den is said to have been the haunt of witches,' added Blair. 'This was the pool they were supposed to bathe in.'

'Aye, I've heard all those stories, too. But the rabbit bones: that looks as if someone wants us to think there's a link with witchcraft somewhere. Is it that the killer is a witch, or are they accusing Miss Aytoun of being one?'

'The way things are going around Letho at the moment, it could be either,' said Murray grimly, then heard voices.

'That's my men with the cart,' said Macduff, and called 'Over here! Ca' canny, though.'

Lanterns danced down the slippery sandstone steps, and as the men came closer it was revealed that they had brought some kind of hurdle for the body.

'Can we help at all?' Blair asked.

'Probably best if you left the rock now and went down out of the way, sir,' said Macduff respectfully. 'There's not so much room up here, and they ken what they're doing.'

Blair and Murray waited for Tilly's body to be lifted on to the hurdle and her bearers to balance uneasily back on the narrow bridge. Then they followed the corpse and Macduff up to the chapel and the road. At the top Murray hurried ahead to take his horse's head before the mare scented the body.

'I'll stay here a while with one or two men and take a good look around,' said Macduff. 'Thank you for your help, gentlemen.'

Realising they had been dismissed, Murray helped Blair into the gig. Then a thought struck him.

'Lady Aytoun is staying at Letho House,' he called after Macduff. 'What do you want me to say to her?'

'Nothing, sir, if that is possible,' said Macduff. 'I'll call tomorrow, if I may.'

'Of course.' Murray pulled himself up into the gig, and took the reins. Blair lit the lantern hanging from the side, to help them find their way, though the sky above them was clearing and a little starlight tinged the darkness.

'We might just be back in time for dinner,' Murray commented as they set off. 'I can't believe how much has happened today.'

As it turned out, Lady Aytoun was not available to be deceived. Isobel had left her in the parlour briefly believing her to be sleeping off the brandy, and returned to find she had swallowed the rest of the decanter and was again unconscious. Isobel was inclined to defend her: after all, it was one way of blocking out all that had happened. She was taken away to a chamber prepared hurriedly for her stay, and her maid was looking after her. Agostinella was also keeping to her room, and Robert Lovie was still locked up – Murray wondered about transferring him from the nursery floor to the cells, but decided he would find it hard to hate anyone so much that he could lock them down there. The dinner guests therefore consisted of Isobel and Blair, Dr. Harker, and Andrew Grant and his wife, the owner of the deadly embroidery sharps. Blair and Murray had hurried in with only ten minutes to bathe and change, but they had just about made the dinner table in time so that they did not have to give a full explanation to everyone of their whereabouts that afternoon.

'This is a dreadful account we have heard of Sir John Aytoun,' said Mrs. Grant, exchanging a look with her husband that might even have been a kind of relief: it took the attention away from Robert, anyway. 'Can it be true?'

'He seems to have arranged to have the woman accused as a witch released from the church into his custody and then beaten her, believing she had something to do with Mathilda's disappearance,' Murray explained bleakly. 'She is severely injured, wouldn't you say, Dr. Harker? And Sir John is in the jail in Cupar.'

Dr. Harker nodded agreement.

'A very severe beating,' he added.

'Extraordinary,' said Cousin Andrew. 'Yet I have seen something of the type before: very cool and aloof, until they burst into a terrible rage.'

'You do not think there is a chance that Sir John had anything to do with perhaps your Widow Maggot's death? If he is so very violent?' asked Mrs. Grant.

'I can see no reason why he would even have known Widow Maggot, let alone have struck her. It makes no sense.'

'And the poor woman is here, now? I thought I heard ...' Mrs. Grant tailed away, possibly remembering the circumstances of Lizzie Fenwick's arrival – and rapid departure – from the house.

'My housekeeper is tending to her,' said Murray. He did not necessarily want everyone to know precisely where Mrs. Fenwick was being cared for, not with Mal Johnstone and his friends still against her. If they could deliver her up to Sir John – and who knew how much he had told them of what he intended? – then they could do almost anything with her.

After dinner his first inclination was to go and see how Lizzie Fenwick was, but duty called and he made his way instead up to his wife's chamber and knocked on the door. The maid let him in, though he thought he detected more hostility on her face even than usual. Perhaps it was just guilt on his part.

'Is that woman gone from the house?' Agostinella demanded, as he kissed her hand.

'Yes, my lady, she is not within these four walls.' She was not far away, but it seemed unnecessary to stress that. 'Do not concern yourself about her, or about any gossip you may hear from the village. We are all secure here.'

'Are you sure?' Agostinella's grey face was dark with fear and doubt. He stroked her hand, hoping it would not upset her further.

'Of course. Letho House has always been secure.' Though what had that been in the cellar? he found himself asking, suddenly. He did not think he would ever tell her about that.

Agostinella lay back on her daybed, and pulled the rug over her thin chest.

'Your doctor says I must rest,' she complained.

'He's quite right. You must save all your strength.'

'But I want to do my embroidery.'

'Are you able to? Yesterday it seemed that you found it fatiguing.' He tried hard to sound soothing, not confrontational.

'I do, but I want to do it. I don't want to rest, but it seems I have no choice,' she said fretfully.

'Then do what Dr. Harker tells you, my lady. There will be plenty of time afterwards for embroidery, and strength, too.'

She gazed up at him, willing him to have some extraordinary knowledge that this was true. He did not like to lie, but here it was essential: she needed the reassurance. He did not speak, but met her eyes and smiled, holding her hand gently. Then he kissed it again.

'Good night, my lady. I shall leave you to rest. Please do – for all our sakes.' He gave her hand a little squeeze, and bowed and left her, a fraction easier, on her daybed. The maid saw him to the door. 'She must do as the doctor says, and not agitate herself,' he murmured in Italian. The maid nodded, hostility faded again. He left.

Next he climbed the stairs to the attic floor, and found the nursery where Robert Lovie was being kept. He unlocked the door, sure that Robert would not be able to overpower him if he kept his guard up. Robert was just finishing a dish of syllabub, but stood as Murray came in, waiting politely.

'I just want to ask you a few more questions,' Murray said, sitting on a small, hard chair and waving Robert to return to his pudding.

'Certainly, sir,' said Robert, co-operative as ever. The nursery was white and bare, but the little bed was furnished with warm blankets and there was a small fire in the grate. He had the shutters closed against the night outside. Murray fleetingly wondered if any child of his would ever sleep there.

'Assuming you have been speaking the truth, and that you really did not meet Tilly Aytoun that night, and do not know how her reticule ended up in the woodsman's hut – in your conversations with Miss Aytoun, did you ever have the impression that she was frightened of anyone? Or of anything?'

Robert gave the question some thought.

'I'm not sure that I did, sir. Not that we had any very long conversations: we talked mostly about music.'

'You said before that you did not know why they had left Edinburgh early?'

'That's so.'

'But did you think that whatever the reason, it had something to do with her, or with her mother, or with her father?'

Robert frowned, thinking back.

'Again, I'm not sure. I don't think, though, that it was anything to do with Tilly herself.' He flicked back his shining fringe with one hand, a serious look on his young face. 'Perhaps something to do with Sir John? She's very fond of him, or at least more than of her mother: Lady Aytoun is quite silly. But she said Sir John could be very stern: I imagine if Lady Aytoun had been ill he would simply have told her not to be, and carried on with the season. Only if he were ill himself would he have left, I think.'

'Interesting.' Murray reflected on his conversations with Sir John: he had not seemed like a man ailing. Could his temper have brought him into trouble in Edinburgh society, and he had found it wise to leave? He wondered which of his Edinburgh acquaintances might be able to tell him. A good gossip, that was who he needed.

'Is there any word of Tilly, sir?' Robert was asking. His face was the picture of patient innocence.

'We've heard nothing from her,' said Murray, as strictly accurate as he could be. 'Thank you for your help.' He left, and returned downstairs. His guests, he noted as he passed the drawing room, seemed to have retired for the night. He carried on to the library, the candles in his candlestick flaring out as he hurried. There he reflected for a moment, and then wrote a fairly discreet letter to his old friend Mrs. Thomson, the widow of a prosperous lawyer, who would know of deleterious gossip going the rounds. He wrapped and sealed it, and left it with the extinguished candlestick on the hall table to be collected in the morning. Then he let himself out through the front door – drawing the key with him to lock it behind him again – and marched off round the corner of the servants' wing to the cottage where Lizzie Fenwick was being cared for.

He knocked on the door of the neat cottage, and thought how unlike the Widow Maggot's it was. Inside the main room was warm and bright with candles and whitewashed walls, the shelves lined with dishes and pots that glinted cleanly, the box bed made up with a bright quilt and warm blankets. He could smell bannocks freshly made, and broth, too.

'Mr. Murray, sir!' Mrs. Dean sat up sharply in the chair by the fire. 'There was no need – Mr. Robbins could have sent someone to fetch me had you needed me!'

'I've come to see how Mrs. Fenwick is faring,' said Murray. 'I hope I have not disturbed you?'

'Not at all, not at all.'

There was a movement in the bed, and a hand waved to him.

'Mr. Murray? Is that you, sir?'

'It is, Mrs. Fenwick.' He crossed to the bed, and folded himself on to a creepie stool to come down to her level. 'How are you? Is there anything I can do for you?'

'You are already allowing your good housekeeper to tend to me!' said Mrs. Fenwick. Her voice was not as strong as it usually sounded, and she was washed-out looking, not helped by the lack of those dark eyebrows. Yet there was life in her eyes, still.

'Dr. Harker says your injuries show no signs of infection, though they will no doubt be extremely painful.'

'I can tell you,' she said, closing her eyes as the pain touched her again, 'Sir John Aytoun must be a gifted chiel at the golf, for he has a powerful swing.' She opened her eyes again and smiled at him, a hard-won smile, he thought.

'Can you talk about it? What did he say to you?'

'He wanted to know where his daughter was. I told him I had no idea, that I had been in the kirk cell when she disappeared, but he would have none of it.' She closed her eyes again, and he made to move away but she caught his hand in hers. 'Don't go yet, Mr. Murray. Mrs. Dean's salves are near as good as mine: I need none of your Edinburgh doctor's laudanum here.'

'If you say so …' he said dubiously.

'Aye, aye. But see, he's no a very nice man, that Sir John – like his ancestor, he's no so keen on witches - but that doesn't mean he did any of the other things that have been going on here.'

'I think that's probably right.'

She grinned.

'That Mal Johnstone: he was the one who took me from the cell and brought me to Collessie, and there was a nasty wee grin on his face the while. If you told me he had killed Widow Maggot for a witch, I wouldna be altogether surprised, but I have no proof, see.' She winced again: the pain must have been coming in waves, but she was stronger than he thought.

'Do you think he could have had anything to do with Agnes' disappearance? Or Tilly's?'

'Tilly … I don't know.' She drifted for a second, then pulled herself back. 'But Agnes – for Agnes, I'd say … A mother asked me to come and see her wee lass one time, years ago, when I was just a lass myself.'

Murray cast an anxious glance at Mrs. Dean. Was Lizzie wandering? But Mrs. Dean shook her head and smiled. He turned back to Mrs. Fenwick.

'Go on,' he said softly.

'The wee one was in terrible pain. Five or six she would have been, and in a high fever, rolling about in her truckle bed and clutching her wame.' She made herself breathe a moment. 'I thought her wame was bursting or worse: there's things in your belly that all kinds of bad things can happen to.'

Murray nodded, encouragingly.

'I was going to mix up a draught I had for stopping her up, to hold a'thing in, and the mother was beside herself – it was her eldest one, see, never seen a'thing like it afore. Then the mother left the room to get water, and the wee lassie cried out that she was sorry, she was sorry! She'd been into the kailyard next door to her ain, and eaten all the apples off the tree there. Green, green apples, dozens of the things. No wonder she was ill, the wee rascal! I gave her a different kind of draught, and a'thing came out instead, and she's a grandmother herself now – and doubtless has never touched an apple since!'

Murray laughed, but after a moment he had to ask.

'How does that related to Agnes, though?'

'I just think,' said Mrs. Fenwick, her voice growing fainter with all the effort, 'that when something bad happens, it pays to look into the history.'

'The history? You mean –'

But Lizzie Fenwick's eyes had closed again, and her breathing came more easily.

'She's asleep again: she needs it,' said Mrs. Dean, coming over to take Lizzie's hand gently from Murray's and slide it back under the covers. 'She may not want laudanum, but there's other things will bring rest to a weary body and help it heal.'

'Thank you, Mrs. Dean. Do you need anything? One of the men, perhaps, to stay here and keep watch with you? I imagine the Kirk Session – or Mal Johnstone at least – would still be very keen to have her back in a cell.'

'We'll be ready for them,' said Mrs. Dean definitely. 'And if we need help, we'll come for it.'

It was only as Murray was walking back to the big house in the dark that it occurred to him to wonder who Mrs. Dean had meant by 'we'.

Agnes' history, he thought to himself the moment he awoke next day. What did they know of Agnes' history?

She had worked for a woman in Paisley as a maid of all work, a woman for whom Mrs. Dean had previously been housekeeper. Agnes had lost her family to typhoid, and was alone in the world, but had been fond, he thought he remembered, of her mistress. Could her mistress have taken her back and not told them? But again, it was over a week now and no request had come to send her things back to Paisley.

He heard Robbins come in to open the shutters.

'Good morning, sir,' he said as he rounded the bed to where Murray had the curtains open.

'Good morning, Robbins. How is everything this morning?'

Robbins raised his eyebrows resignedly.

'Much the same, amongst the staff, sir. Mrs. Dean spent the

night over at Mrs. Chambers' old cottage with Lizzie Fenwick, but she popped in this morning and said the night had passed quietly and Lizzie Fenwick is eating porage.'

'A good sign, yes.'

'Lady Aytoun's maid came down and asked for porage, too, but I fancy that was for herself. Lady Aytoun has not asked for anything.'

'Opinions?'

'There's a bottle of brandy missing from the sideboard in the dining room, sir.'

'Oh, dear. Has she been any trouble apart from that?'

Robbins shrugged.

'I haven't seen her, sir. The maid seems a respectable enough body, but she may have a deal of work on her hands there.'

'Well, if you can, help. We don't want any disasters in the house just now: there's enough going on.'

'Very good, sir. I'll have a word with the maid about the fireballs and general matters.'

'Good idea. What about Walter?'

Robbins met his eye.

'I don't know what you saw yesterday, sir, but Walter has decided that it was some kind of scientific phenomenon the like of which they have in Edinburgh, he says.'

Murray grinned.

'I suspect that's a healthy attitude. I wish I could believe it myself.' He ran a hand through his hair, trying not to remember the strange apparition in the cellar. 'Robert still locked up?'

'Aye, sir, I took him his breakfast just now. He asked for a book to read.'

'That's fine, take him one if we have what he wants.'

'Other than that, sir, it seems a quiet enough morning so far. Oh, there's word from the village, sir, that Miss Aytoun has been found dead in Josie's Den.' He gave his master a look, as if judging whether or not this would come as a surprise. Murray nodded.

'Yes: I think Mr. Macduff will be annoyed that that is common knowledge so quickly. I don't suppose you can stop the rumour spreading: it has the virtue of being true, after all, but if you can at least slow it down it would be helpful.'

'I take it she met her death violently, sir?'

'It seems likely she was the one stabbed outside by the garden wall yesterday around dawn.'

'I see, sir.' Robbins looked down at the floor, not happy.

'Robbins,' said Murray, pulling his robe around him and heading for the dressing room, 'remind me what is supposed to have happened in Paisley to Agnes?'

'Well, I'm not entirely clear myself, sir. Mrs. Dean seems to know more of the story. She was out somewhere and saw a man kill another man, and the man who did the killing recognised her – or at least, saw her clearly enough to know her again – and she ran home but was so upset by the event that her mistress sent her up here to Mrs. Dean, with a letter explaining the matter and her kist sent behind her.'

'Can Agnes read and write?'

'Yes, sir. If she hadn't we would be teaching her.'

'Of course.' He considered. 'Do you know if Mrs. Dean kept the letter?'

'I have no idea, sir. I can ask her later.'

'Thank you. So you're not sure if the killer was known to Agnes or not? Actually recognised her and knew who she was, or simply saw her clearly enough to know her again?'

'No, sir. Mrs. Dean might.'

'And the victim?'

'Again, I have no idea, sir. Sorry, sir.'

'Can't be helped. I must speak with Mrs. Dean again.' He washed and dried his face vigorously, and took the clean shirt from Robbins' hands, pulling it on quickly. 'Do you know, is Mrs. Grant from Glasgow or that direction?'

'I believe she is, sir. Her maid mentioned that her father was a Professor of Natural Philosophy at Glasgow University.'

'Ah, I did wonder.' He thought again about the conversation he had overheard between Mrs. Grant and Mr. Rintoul, Rintoul's enthusiastic hair emphasising his love of his antiquities and his enjoyment of his Glasgow student days.

Rintoul had not been on the hunt for Agnes that night, but he did not seem to have slept well, either.

Rintoul's landlady had mentioned Rintoul's irregular eating habits, his suddenly expanded appetite. Why did food come into this matter so often? Apples, jams, schoolroom food … But Rintoul had been eating more than usual, she had said.

Rintoul had brought him Agnes' cloak, on the day he had returned to Josie's Den.

There was a sharp knock on the door, and both Robbins and Murray jumped. Daniel entered, oblivious to Robbins' scowl.

'A message from Mr. Helliwell, sir, he says it's urgent.' He had managed to put the fold of paper on a tray, at least. Murray took it. Helliwell's black bad-tempered writing crackled across the page.

'Mr. Rintoul has appeared at the manse claiming that he has a confession to make. I have summoned the sheriff's man. Can you be here, too?'

Chapter Eighteen

Rintoul was seated in the manse's study by the fire, just as Blair and Murray had sat the previous day to read the old Presbytery minutes. He looked markedly less relaxed than they had. His wiry hair sprayed out around his head, in a dark red fountain, and his bony fingers twisted around a steel pen, as if it would give him some support. So far all it seemed to have given him was inky hands. He sprang up as Murray was shown into the room. Helliwell himself stood more slowly behind his desk, setting down a book with a scrap of paper to mark his place before bowing to Murray. His face was the very illustration for irritable confusion.

'We have only to wait a little for Mr. Macduff from the sheriff's office,' Helliwell announced with little preamble. 'He stayed last night at the inn, apparently, but was not yet awake.'

'He must have had a late night,' said Murray. 'I know he was still busy as Blair and I went back to Letho for dinner.'

'Has something happened?' asked Helliwell sharply. 'Something new, I mean?' he corrected himself.

'But I told you something had,' said Rintoul, his voice nervous. 'I said that … or maybe I didn't get that far. It's all very confusing,' he added helplessly.

'I think we're probably all agreed on that, at least,' said Murray, as Helliwell poured him a cup of tea. Rintoul did not seem to have been offered any: perhaps Helliwell felt there was an etiquette towards those about to confess to unidentified crimes.

They heard a knock on the front door, and then the light steps of the maid skipping to answer it. The footsteps of Macduff, hirpling across the tiles in his boots, were more distinctive, so it was no surprise when he was announced at the study door. Tea was evidently appropriate for sheriff's officers, too, and Macduff took his china cup with a steady hand. He had great dark circles under his eyes, but seemed alert.

'Did – did you already know what happened last night?' Rintoul blurted, then went red.

Macduff looked at him blandly over his teacup.

'What would that be, then, sir?'

Rintoul gulped, and stared wildly at Helliwell. Helliwell gave an exasperated sigh.

'Rintoul, don't play guessing games, lad. Just tell us all whatever it was you felt was important enough that it had to interrupt my breakfast.'

'But where should I start, sir?'

'At the beginning,' snapped Helliwell, just about stopping himself from adding, 'you fool.'

'Well, then … You'll maybe all know I'm from Glasgow, and I did my master of arts at Glasgow University. I graduated this summer.' There was still some pride there: perhaps he was the first of his family to do so well. 'After I graduated, I was allowed to go and work as assistant in the parish in Paisley, just for a wee while because the minister was not so well and needed help.'

'Paisley, you said?' asked Macduff. He had set down his teacup and saucer and was taking notes solemnly.

'That's right. Where the weaving is. Well, in the summer a girl came to see me to say she'd seen something very frightening, and she wasn't sure what to do about it. In fact, she'd seen someone killed. Murdered.'

'Who was this girl?'

'Agnes Carstairs, a maid in the parish. Her mistress was a respectable woman, I believe. I hadn't met her myself.'

'And did you believe Agnes?' asked Murray. Rintoul blushed again

'I – I didn't, really. She talks you into a kind of numbness, and some of the things she says, well … It's not exactly that I think she's a liar. It's more that sometimes I think she tells stories she doesn't entirely understand herself, and because she doesn't really know what has happened, the stories get mixed up in the telling.'

'It sounds as if you knew Agnes quite well,' Murray remarked.

'I do now,' said Rintoul, with a hunted look. Helliwell gestured him impatiently to get on. 'I'd been warned about young women trying to attract the attention of young unmarried ministers – not that I am one yet, of course, but the principle's the same, I think. There's something about the preaching bands that attracts some of them, or so I gather. I believed that Agnes was one of them, and I sent her away.' He swallowed hard. 'I wish I hadn't done that.'

'Hm,' said Helliwell, morosely. Presumably such opportunities had not come his way in his youth.

'And then she disappeared,' said Rintoul.

'She disappeared?'

'Well, she didn't come to church any more. And she didn't come to see me.'

'And what did you do?'

'Well ... nothing,' Rintoul admitted.

'You didn't go to her mistress' house to see if she was all right? Or to her family home?'

'Her family were all dead,' said Rintoul. 'And no, I didn't go to her mistress' house either. I didn't want to encourage her, you know?'

'Yes, we understand that,' said Helliwell in exasperation. 'Your irresistible appeal to the fairer sex must be a terrible burden to you. But what about her mistress? Couldn't you have asked her if her maid was ailing, or away?'

'Oh, but I couldn't, sir,' said Rintoul quickly. 'Her mistress was a Papist, like Lady Agostinella ...' His voice dwindled away to the end of the name, and he focussed on the carpet, like a man who had suddenly realised that a permanent call to Letho parish might no longer be on the cards. Murray tried to frown, though it was hard not to laugh, even in the circumstances.

'So Agnes vanished. What happened next?'

'It's just there are loads of people in Paisley now, sir, and we have enough to do with our own parishioners, without dealing with anyone else.'

'Yes. Next?'

'I did feel bad.' Rintoul seemed to take heart from not having been punched on the spot. 'I felt awful that she'd been going on about this murder and I hadn't really been listening.'

'Did you tell the police office?'

'Well, I didn't really have anything to say. So I decided that I'd just go away as far as I could, so when I heard that Letho parish was looking for an assistant, I made myself available.'

'You had good references, too,' muttered Mr. Helliwell, in a tone that implied he had been deceived.

'Aye, my professors were awful nice about me, weren't they?' Rintoul grinned, forgetting himself for a moment. 'Anyway, it was at your picnic last week, Mr. Murray. I heard Agnes' voice behind that curtain thing you had for the servants. It's not an easy voice to forget: you hear enough of it.'

'And then?' Macduff was still writing busily.

'Well, nothing. I thought to myself I was glad she was safe, but I had no wish to see her. I didn't think she had even seen me. But, well, that wasn't to be. And after I went home that night, back to Mrs. Maitland's house, after dark I heard a tapping on my window. I opened it and there she was, standing on Mrs. Maitland's outhouse roof, grinning in at me. Covered in leaves, she was, like some kind of woodland pixie.'

'But what was she doing there?'

'Well, now, this part is her story, not mine. I don't know how true it is. She said that your servants – is it William and David?'

'William and Daniel,' said Murray, with a grimace.

'Aye, sir, that's it. They'd put her out of the cart on the way back to Letho House, just at the road into the village. She said she just shrugged and started to walk up through the village to take the shortcut home. But she was only just heading into the village when someone grabbed her from behind, and dragged her down a lane, wrapped her cloak around her head, and then carried her off somewhere. She wasn't very clear about where she had gone, but it was obviously woodland somewhere to judge by all the leaves.'

'Did she see her captor?' asked Macduff heavily.

'Yes, she did,' said Rintoul, and they all started. 'It was the man she had seen in Paisley, the one who had killed –'

'Did it not occur to you to tell someone about this?' snapped Helliwell.

'Oh, I wanted to, sir, I did. But she made me promise to protect her – and I felt so guilty that if I'd done something about it back in Paisley, she wouldn't have had to run away to Fife and he wouldn't have followed her and taken her captive.'

'So where is she now?' Murray demanded.

'And where has she been all week, Rintoul?' asked Helliwell sternly. 'If you've been indulging in any kind of immoral activity with this girl …'

'No, sir! I have not!' Rintoul's hair seemed to blaze red with his own innocence. 'She stayed in Mrs. Maitland's outhouse, and I gave her half my dinner each evening. I think she took some of

Mrs. Maitland's apples, too. She was scared to come out until I could assure her that the man had gone – which of course I couldn't. She made me take you her cloak and say I'd found it out on the Cupar road, so that word would go about that she'd left Letho. She's been staying there all week – except I think sometimes she sneaked up into my room while I was out, to avoid being caught in the outhouse by Mrs. Maitland.'

'So she's in the outhouse now?' asked Murray.

'That's what I've been trying to tell you. She was there all week – but he's found her. He took her again last night, and I failed her again.'

'Halfway through your story I wondered if Agnes makes a habit of disappearing,' Murray said to Rintoul as all four of them headed out to visit Rintoul's lodgings. 'How can you be sure that she was taken again, and by the same man that took her before?'

'Well, of course I don't absolutely know,' said Rintoul. The green, as they cut across the top by the church, was empty again, despite the clear, bright morning. 'I heard something in the middle of the night, a noise behind the house – my window faces to the back, of course, otherwise I wouldn't have seen Agnes on the outhouse roof. I thought it was Mrs. Maitland coming home.'

'Mrs. Maitland is keeping late hours? I thought she rarely went out in the evenings,' said Helliwell, ready to disapprove.

'It's only recently. Only since the Kirk Session began asking questions about any woman of her age living alone. So she spends the evenings having supper with her various friends who still have husbands alive, or children about the house, so as not to be taken for a witch. I had no idea all this still went on in the countryside, you know. Glasgow is never this exciting.'

Murray ignored this.

'But you now think it was Agnes being taken again?'

'I think so. She was gone this morning, and she had left her bonnet behind.'

'Truly this time?' asked Murray suspiciously. Rintoul blushed again.

'Truly. I don't know where she would go with neither bonnet nor cloak. She was cosy in the outhouse.' He paused as they reached Mrs. Maitland's house, a newish part of the terrace that started the road to Collessie. The doctor lived next door and the schoolhouse was not far away: it was a well-frequented part of the village. Rintoul, at Helliwell's gesture, led them into the house where Rintoul called out to tell Mrs. Maitland they were there, then took the party on through the house and into the yard at the back. The yard was narrow and long, and to the right of the back door was the outhouse.

'Agnes climbed up on that roof?' asked Macduff, sketching now in his notebook.

'Aye, that was how I came to see her. She's fearless that way. I couldn't do it myself,' he added, with a quick shake of his head. His red hair bounced a little. 'I suppose she climbed on to that barrel and then up.'

'So that's your window,' said Macduff, pointing with the end of his pen.

'Aye.'

Helliwell caught up with them.

'Mrs. Maitland says we're welcome to look in her outhouse if we want to,' he announced, 'as long as none of us disturbs her apples again.'

'Not unreasonable,' Murray remarked. He glanced at the others, and gently unhooked the knot of rope that held the door closed. It swung outwards, and they all peered inside.

The sandy floor was kicked and scuffed, and in a couple of places really gouged, as if there had been a struggle. Helliwell made to go straight in, but Murray put a hand out and stopped him, allowing Macduff to sketch the area quickly before the marks were destroyed. The shed was small, in any case: most of it could easily be seen from the doorway. There was a deep, waist-high shelf around three sides of it, and this held the trays of apples of which Mrs. Maitland was so protective, divided into different kinds for ease of storage and selection. Above this shelf were shallower shelves containing jars of jam and other preserves, and bottles glinting in the darkness. Mrs. Maitland was justly proud of this, if these were all her work, Murray thought. His own stillroom was scarcely more productive. Beneath the apple shelf there were various baskets and wooden crates, and in one corner a pile of sacking. Murray reached in with long arms and prodded the sacking with his stick. The top couple of sacks fell away and revealed a neat little nest behind them, eminently suitable for one very small person in hiding.

'That is where she hid,' said Rintoul, almost unnecessarily. 'I brought food from my meals and laid it out on my window sill, and when she could she would collect it.'

Murray glanced at Macduff, who nodded. Murray stepped across to the sacking, and crouched down, reaching a hand into the nest to investigate further. Agnes had left it fairly neatly, but there were a couple of things tangled in the sacking. He pulled out the first, something wrapped in a thin cloth.

'A piece of cheese,' Macduff announced when Murray handed it to him. 'It's a wonder the mice haven't got that.'

'Oh, there are no mice in here,' said Rintoul seriously. 'Mrs. Maitland wouldn't allow it.'

'A glove, I think,' said Murray, pulling something else out from the nest. 'Yes, a glove. And something else … Oh, just a little bunch of acorns.'

'That must have been tangled up with her,' said Rintoul. 'I said she was covered in leaves the first night, from wherever he had taken her.'

'Not much use, then,' said Macduff, who was still examining the glove.

'No, there are plenty of oaks in the parish.' Murray absent-mindedly tucked the acorns in his pocket, and lifted the top sack to shake it out, but they seemed to have found everything there was to be found.

'Did Agnes describe this man to you?' he asked Rintoul.

'A bit,' said Rintoul. 'She said he was tall, though that could mean anything with someone as small as Agnes, and he had black hair and blue eyes.'

'I haven't heard of a report of any stranger looking like that,' said Macduff.

'I wonder if that is why Widow Maggot is dead?' said Murray suddenly. 'Perhaps she had seen him, and he did not want her telling?'

'Blue eyes with black hair is not so common, around here, anyway,' Helliwell said.

'Lovely blue eyes, she said,' Rintoul qualified. 'She liked his eyes.'

'Good heavens!' said Helliwell.

'I don't suppose she had a name for the man, did she?' asked Macduff, though it was clear he held out little hope.

Rintoul frowned hard.

'No, she named no names,' he said at last.

'A pity. No doubt the sheriff will want to write to the Glasgow police office – which we could have done a week ago, sir, had you come to us with this business.'

Rintoul hung his head.

'And Agnes would be safe home at Letho House by now, I know. I feel terrible. Poor Agnes.'

'Poor Agnes indeed: she didn't find much of a friend in her time of need,' said Helliwell mercilessly.

'She wouldn't let me!' Rintoul complained.

'You let a wee lassie like that tell you what to do?' said Helliwell. 'Surely you knew in your own mind that you had to tell someone.'

'Aye, aye, sir, but she didn't want me to. And I'd let her down before: I didn't want to do it again.'

'Do you believe him?' Murray asked the sheriff's man, as they walked back down through the village to the inn. Murray had fetched his horse from the manse stables, and led it slowly along the grass.

'I don't know, sir. It would be all too easy for him to have done all this kidnapping himself, if you ask me. He could have killed her now, and be covering up for himself before we find the body.'

Murray reflected. It was true: Rintoul's story was convenient, and peculiar.

'What about Miss Aytoun's body?' he asked.

'It's back in Cupar. I stayed here last night because I wanted to make an early start this morning talking to the people in Letho about her, and about anyone who might have been moving her body from Letho House to Josie's Den early yesterday morning. We think she was probably wrapped in her own cloak, which is why the trail of blood stopped in the woodland there. The stains seem to show that, where they haven't been soaked out by the water in that little pool.'

'It was an odd place to leave her, don't you think?'

'With the rabbit bones, too? Aye, as we were saying when my men arrived, did they want us to think a witch had done it, or that Miss Aytoun herself was involved in witchcraft?'

'I think they'd be unlikely to try to accuse Miss Aytoun. She hadn't been in the village long: there were no grudges against her, I wouldn't have thought, and she had shown no sign of being a witch – or the signs these people seem to be looking for, anyway. She hadn't shown an unusual aptitude for healing cattle, or bringing down a love rival.'

'Robert Lovie was attached to her, was he not?'

'He was. I spoke to him about her last night – I did not mention that she had been found – but he seems to have known her hardly at all. He said he thought she was close to her father but not so much to her mother, but that her father could be very stern. He had no idea why they were here and not in Edinburgh for the season.'

'You think that is suspicious, sir?'

'It might be. If Sir John had offended someone, with that temper of his, and they had pursued him here to take some kind of revenge, then Miss Aytoun would make sense as a victim. It would be easier to take her than to attack a man.'

'Aye, aye, it would. We can ask him.'

'Does he know you've found her?'

'Not yet. Nor have I spoken to Lady Aytoun.'

'She's at Letho House. Yesterday,' he thought it best to warn Macduff, 'she consumed a bottle and a half of brandy and passed out twice. I don't know if she makes a habit of it, though: and she was certainly in some trying circumstances.'

'Well, I don't think either of them would have had the chance to kill their daughter and arrange her body at the Den,' said Macduff, lowering his voice as they neared the door of the inn.

'No. And I can't see Mrs. Grant unaided taking the body up on to the platform, even if the weapon was hers.'

'No, sir, she would have needed help. But were she and her husband out at all yesterday?'

'No idea,' said Murray. 'But you're welcome to come and ask them. And we have Lizzie Fenwick, too, who is able to talk now – or did last night. Funnily enough, she thought the answer would be in Agnes' past.'

'Agnes' past? Well, aye, sir: but the way Mr. Rintoul told it, or not?'

Chapter Nineteen

Murray left Macduff at the inn, and turned to look back up the gentle hill of the village green and two main streets to the church. It should have looked peaceful: in some places, this morning's frost had not yet melted, dusting the stones with delicate powder where the sun had not quite reached. In others, the same sun glinted on clean windows, polished metalwork, fresh woodwork, reassuring him that at least Letho had not lost its pride in itself. But as he stood there, he noticed one man emerge from his front door and hurry to another door; a woman scuttle down into a lane and vanish; a face at a window; three people now appear where the man had disappeared and, huddled together, cross the green and enter another cottage where the door was swung quickly to admit them. No one had spoken in all this movement. Perhaps he was over-suspicious, Murray thought, but he could not help feeling that the village was preparing for something.

He pulled himself together and walked up to Mal Johnstone's cottage, well enough kept for a Collessie property, and rattled the risp. He waited, sure he could hear movement inside. He was just about to dismiss it as a cat or a dog when the door opened suddenly, and Mal appeared.

'Mr. Murray!'

'May I come in?'

'Ah …' Mal was blotchy and bleary-eyed, as if he was not sleeping well. He sucked in through his teeth. 'Aye, yes, yes.'

He opened the door wider, ushered Murray in past him, and glanced out nervously at the green before shutting the door. There was no hallway: the door led directly into the main living room, where Murray stood, feeling tall.

The room, like the outside of the cottage, was neat and well kept. Mal was not married, and as far as Murray remembered he had lived alone since the death of his father some years before. The interior reminded Murray a little of a ship: it was a masculine space, without much in the way of ornament, but it was functional and well arranged. A shirt was airing before the fire, presumably to be clean and fresh for the Sabbath, and there were no dirty dishes about or mud on the stone floor. Mal pushed the kettle over the fire reluctantly, and offered Murray a cup of tea.

'It's very kind, but I shan't be staying long,' said Murray, still surveying the room. Above the door and over the two windows he had suddenly noticed sprigs of holly and rowan, bound together. 'That wouldn't by any chance be to keep witches away, would it?' he asked conversationally.

'It would,' said Mal, with unexpected firmness. It may have been because he was standing near the fire, but Murray thought there was a little sheen of sweat over his dished face. He turned again, examining the room. Bible on the mantelpiece, of course, and a couple of books of sermons, all well-thumbed as befitted a church-going man. He thought the silence was making Mal nervous, but actually Murray himself was playing for time: he had come here almost at random, and was trying to think how to make the most of it.

'I saw you at Collessie yesterday morning,' he said at last. Mal did not relax.

'Aye, I daresay. The factor was there.'

No doubt he was, thought Murray, but the phrasing of Mal's reply implied an effort not to tell a lie. Yes, the factor had been there, but had Mal really been going to see him?

'You'll have heard, perhaps, that Sir John Aytoun is in the jail in Cupar?'

'I saw him being taken away by yon sheriff's man, Macduff.'

'Do you know what the charges are?'

Mal shrugged, ashen.

'He was found beating Lizzie Fenwick with a stick. He broke her leg, and covered her with bruises, and left her in a terrible state.'

'Oh, aye.'

'You seem neither shocked nor surprised, Mal.'

Mal did not meet Murray's eye.

'How did Lizzie Fenwick come to be at Collessie? The last I heard she was in your custody at the kirk.'

'She – she escaped. She's a witch: witches can get out of all kinds of places.'

'Then it's not much of a cell to keep witches in, is it? I don't think anyone escaped from it two hundred years ago.'

'Not in their human form, maybe,' said Mal, obscurely.

'And if she's a witch, how did she let Sir John capture her and imprison her?'

'He maybe knew a charm or something. See, last time there was witches, Sir John Aytoun was the commissioner against them.'

'Is that why you took her to him?' Mal was silent. 'Mal, you took Lizzie Fenwick out of the cell, didn't you, and took her to Sir John? Did you tell him you thought she had something to do with his daughter's disappearance? Well?'

Mal's face twitched, and he licked his lips quickly. He looked sick, but he still did not speak, staring at the floor. It struck Murray that he looked very frightened indeed. But was he afraid of Murray, of witches, or of the consequences of his actions?

'Why Lizzie Fenwick, Mal? She's a good woman: she helps many people who are ill or in pain. She's skilled, but her salves are no more than any good woman has about her house. Why did you pick on Lizzie?'

'She's a witch, sir,' said Mal at last. 'I ken she's a witch. She nursed my father on his deathbed, and he thought the world of her.'

'But you didn't?'

'I didna think … I thought he died too quickly. He was in pain, Mr. Murray: he had a lump on his spine the size of my fist, and it ate away at him inside, ken? But there was fight in him yet. And one day I went out with my cart and left her looking after him, and I think he knew what was going to happen, for he looked at me, Mr. Murray, as if he knew he wasna going to see me again this world. But I was busy and I went out anyway, and when I came home he was cold and dead, and her sitting over him with a wee smile on her face, saying he was at peace now. Well, I reckon I know who put him there, and all.'

Murray was silent in his turn.

'That still doesn't make her a witch,' he said eventually. 'And if you thought she was, why did you say nothing at the time? Your father's been dead these eighteen months or two years, is he not?'

'It was when the Widow Maggot died I realised,' said Mal, so softly Murray could hardly hear him. Mal glanced at the cottage windows, and seemed to reassure himself that the holly and rowan were still securely in place. 'Lizzie Fenwick knew her way around that cottage like the back of her hand, and she was busy picking herbs and such from the garden while the Kirk Session were in there with the body. Where there's one witch, there's always more than one, ken? Two witches is no much of a coven.'

'And you're determined to go on with this – ridiculous quest?'

'Witches are against the teachings of the kirk and of the Bible,' said Mal, licking his lips again. He looked terrified.

'But Lizzie Fenwick doesn't go against the teachings of the kirk. In fact, she works with the minister's wife amongst the poor and the sick.'

'Shows how clever she is, then, doesn't it?' said Mal. For a moment Murray had felt sorry for the little man, but now the expression on Mal's face turned his stomach. Hatred and fear scrambled for purchase, neither of them giving way. '"Thou shalt not suffer a witch to live". You wouldn't want to be thought to be going against the Scriptures, sir, would you?'

'If I find you've attacked Lizzie Fenwick again, or any other woman in the village or elsewhere,' said Murray coldly, 'you'll be joining Sir John in Cupar jail. You can't take the law into your own hands – even if you were right,' he added. 'Good day to you.'

Murray rode back up to Letho House deep in thought, and feeling nauseous. He could not shake the idea that Mal Johnstone had been trying to threaten him, and to an extent he had succeeded. But what did he mean? Was it a random threat, warning Murray in a general sense about imperilling his soul? Or was there something more specific? He remembered the silent villagers flitting between one another's houses that morning. Was something afoot? Should he go behind Agostinella's back and bring Lizzie Fenwick back into the main house, where she would be better guarded? He could not decide.

Robbins came to meet him at the door.

'Any news?' Murray asked.

'Nothing here,' said Robbins. 'Has anything new happened in the village, sir?'

'Um,' said Murray, rubbing his hair where his hat had clamped it down. 'Well, a development of sorts, I suppose. Where is Mr. Blair?'

'In the library, when I last saw him, sir. He has been amongst the pineapple frames all morning, and was quite chilled.'

'Is he there alone?'

'I believe so.'

'Everyone else safe and well?'

'As far as I know, sir,' said Robbins, understandably guarded.

'Then if you can spare a little time, I'd be grateful if you would come with me to the library and I'll tell you what news there is.'

In the library, Blair was cosy under a rug with a book slumped on his lap, snoring lightly. He woke before Murray could decide whether it was kinder to rouse him or not, and offered them a beatific smile.

'What's the news? Did Mr. Rintoul confess to everything? For I must say that I did not have him down as any kind of killer: he would be most dangerous, I should think, when he sweeps someone off their feet with his own enthusiasms.'

There was brandy on the table, presumably protected from Lady Aytoun's quests for oblivion, and Murray helped himself, offering a glass to Robbins. He declined, but did accept a seat on a hard chair.

'Rintoul knows, up to a point, what happened to Agnes,' said Murray, collecting his thoughts from the morning. 'He does not, however, know where she is now, and is very concerned for her safety.' He explained what Rintoul had told them in the manse, and what they had found at Mrs. Maitland's house, Rintoul's lodgings.

'Do you believe him, sir?' asked Robbins, whose face had remained impassive through the story of Agnes' safety and her disappearance again into danger. It was the way his face was made.

'I'm not sure. I'm sure that Agnes was there and that she has now left, but whether it happened the way Rintoul says, or whether he himself has been holding the girl captive all this time and she has now escaped, I cannot absolutely tell. I want to believe him, but I can see how convenient the story would be, and why he would tell us now before she reappears, if she does. The thing is, whichever is correct, we need to start searching for her again.'

'Very true, very true,' said Blair sadly.

'And if he is speaking the truth, sir, then at least we know who seized her and why, and roughly what he looks like.'

'That is an advantage, yes,' said Murray. 'If he is speaking the truth.'

'Shall I summon the men again, then, sir?' said Robbins.

'We could at least start with Letho land, anyway,' said Murray, thinking about it. 'If it is the case that she has escaped, rather than been recaptured, I suppose she will be heading back here. Perhaps she is waiting for darkness to give her cover, and that is why she has not yet arrived.'

'You seem a little reluctant, Charles,' Blair remarked, peering at him. 'Are you so weary of searching that this real sign of some hope cannot inspire you?'

'It's not that,' said Murray defensively. 'I think we might have another problem.'

'Another one?' Robbins could not help exclaiming.

'I came back through the village, and I had a distinct sense that there was some kind of plot going on.' He described the secretive scuttlings from house to house. 'I thought I would go and see Mal Johnstone. Obviously he didn't confess all and say they were going to have a massive witch-burning at midnight,' he said, mocking himself, 'but as I left I had the clear feeling that he was threatening me, and I have not been able to shake it off since.'

'But why would he threaten you, dear boy?' asked Blair.

'Local figure of authority siding with the people he says are witches, perhaps?' Murray suggested. 'Or it could be much more specific: we have Lizzie Fenwick here, and he wants her back.'

'Does he know, then, what happened to her?'

'Yes – and I don't think he was particularly shocked. Or surprised. But I have no proof. I told him if he caused any more trouble I'd have him locked up, but I'm not sure we can on what we can prove he has done so far. Nevertheless, it's something that appeals to me more and more.'

'What do you think he would do, sir?' asked Robbins.

'I'm not sure. Perhaps I'm over-reacting, but there's hysteria in the village. Mal Johnstone was full of hate and fear - and when that particular combination comes together, it's wise to keep away from, say, flaming torches. That's why I don't want too many of the servants away from the house, particularly as darkness comes.'

'And what about Mrs. Fenwick, sir?'

Murray blew out through his nose.

'I can't decide. If we leave her out there, in Mrs. Chambers' cottage, she and whoever is with her are very vulnerable. If we bring her into the main house, and Lady Agostinella gets wind of it – which she is alarmingly good at doing …'

Blair patted Murray's arm, understanding his dilemma. Murray nodded acknowledgement.

'Well, we have to think of Agnes, too,' he said, facing the easiest of the problems – though he would not have thought of it that way a week ago. 'Robbins, please let the stable staff know that there is a chance she is out there and on her way to Letho. Just Letho land, though: I don't want them straying too far, even though the day is bright yet. I want them all back by dusk, and if the search has not been too strenuous then maybe we can think of some of them taking turns to guard the cottage. I can't imagine what Mrs. Chambers would have made of this, can you?'

Blair and Robbins both shook their heads, and Robbins rose and bowed, leaving the room to muster his search party.

'Can you really not decide about Rintoul?' asked Blair. 'You're usually good at working out when someone is lying.'

'I want him to be innocent: I like the man,' said Murray. 'Despite his youthful vanity. I'd rather talk to him, convinced as he is that he's at risk of assault from any red-blooded young woman, but not quite sure why, than to Robert Lovie with all his self-assurance and tricks for seducing young ladies. Rintoul will grow out of his notions: I fear Robert will only grow worse.'

Blair thought about that for a moment, lips pursed extravagantly.

'Well, if we take it that he is telling the truth, and that this tall, dark, blue-eyed man from Paisley is the one who tried to take her captive and then succeeded, and that he is the man who committed the murder that frightened Agnes into running to Fife in the first place,' said Blair, and drew breath noisily, 'then does that help us at all with who killed either Tilly Aytoun or Widow Maggot?'

'I think it might,' said Murray thoughtfully. It was easier to analyse this than to decide whether to risk Lizzie Fenwick over his own wife and child. 'The man knew that Agnes had seen him, and followed her up here. He hasn't seen her since he arrived, as she spent almost all her time here, so he kept lying low. I think it's possible that for some reason, he killed Widow Maggot: perhaps because she saw him, or perhaps he was trying to rob her to support himself.'

'By eating apples, perhaps?' said Blair with the ghost of a smile.

'Hm. Perhaps.'

'Then he met Agnes by accident as she walked back through the village after William and Daniel dropped her off?'

'That's right. He might have been out looking for her, anyway. Do you remember the night the Aytouns were here for dinner? Tilly said she had seen a face at the window, and we barely believed her? Perhaps he was peering into people's houses, searching for her.'

'It's better than a ghost or a witch, anyway,' Blair conceded.

'So he snatches Agnes but she escapes, and finds her way to Rintoul's lodgings, for some reason – perhaps because she thought that the man had traced her to this house, and she would be safer taking refuge elsewhere.'

'That seems sensible. I must say, this Agnes is showing a bit of character!' said Blair approvingly.

'I know: quite self-sufficient. It makes me wonder a little that she was so panicky that her mistress sent her up from Paisley so readily.'

'Well, then: you have Widow Maggot dead and Agnes in hiding: what about Tilly?'

'I assume the man would still be looking for Agnes. Perhaps he bumped into Tilly during her midnight meanderings in search of Robert and romance?'

'Perhaps,' said Blair, but he did not sound entirely convinced. Murray felt very tired.

'What am I to do about Lizzie Fenwick?' he wondered aloud.

'Dear boy, you have to decide, I'm afraid,' said Blair, his damp eyes wide in compassion.

'I know. But what?' He pondered, remembering Agostinella's outburst on the stairs, remembering the beaten, bloody figure of Lizzie Fenwick so helpless in the box bed. Was she really a witch? Whether she was or not, had she really killed Mal Johnstone's dying father?

'Right,' he said. 'I've made my decision.' He pushed himself up out of the chair with renewed energy, and headed for the servants' quarters.

He found Robbins in his pantry, alone, which was what he had wanted.

'I want you to bring Lizzie Fenwick in to the servants' wing,' he said, 'and to put her in Agnes' bed. If we find Agnes, that's another problem, but we'll deal with that if and when it happens. Jennet shares with Agnes: she can nurse her. In the meantime, don't let William or Daniel or Lady Agostinella's maid see any of this: that's important. I don't want Lady Agostinella to find out and become – distressed. Let Mrs. Dean – as long as she feels safe – go back and forth to the cottage as before, to make it look as if Mrs. Fenwick is still there.'

'I think that could be managed, sir, if you're sure you want to take the risk.'

'The servants' quarters are barely part of the house itself, Robbins, are they?' said Murray in a moment of defiance. Then he subsided. 'Well, that's what I'm telling myself, anyway. I just want everything to get back to normal, and I'm trying to find some way of making that happen.' He turned to go, but a thought struck him. 'I'll just go and call in on Mrs. Fenwick first, though: I shan't be able to after she is moved.'

Lizzie Fenwick was much as she had been when he had last called to see her, and Mrs. Dean the same. The cottage was cosy, and smelled of bannocks and broth just as before. He explained to them his plans, with which both women had reservations.

'Jennet is not much of a nurse, sir,' objected Mrs. Dean.

'Lady Agostinella won't be too pleased if she finds out,' said Mrs. Fenwick. 'Remember the baby! You cannot afford to upset the lady, sir.'

'I'll take the chance for now,' said Murray firmly. 'As I said to Robbins, the servants' wing is not properly part of the house. A technical detail, perhaps, but an important one.'

'You think the risk from the villagers grave enough to do this?' asked Mrs. Dean, very serious.

'I don't want to be caught out if something does happen,' said Murray, trying to sound relaxed, as if he were just taking extra precautions. Perhaps he was.

When Robbins came to help him dress for dinner, he could report that Mrs. Fenwick had been successfully moved to Agnes' bed, and that Agnes had not yet been found. All the stable boys had reappeared promptly at dusk, some of them with a nervous look about them that seemed to say they had been listening to witch stories, too. Two had been asked to keep an eye on the cottage and were already settled by the fire, enjoying their good fortune. Murray hoped they would have an undisturbed night.

He soaked in his bath while Robbins busied himself as usual in the bedroom, brushing out the clothes he had been wearing since the morning. When Murray went through to the bedroom to dress, he found a few things laid out on the table. Robbins had been clearing his pockets.

'How's Mrs. Robbins?' Murray asked as he came in. 'I hope she's not affected by all this madness – I'm sure she isn't.'

'Not much bothers Mary, you know, sir,' said Robbins with a hint of a smile. 'She's very well, thank you.'

Murray pointed to the things on the table.

'Oh, dear, am I turning into Blair?' he smiled, then put out a hand to one item. It was the little twig they had found in Agnes' hideout that morning.

'If you're carrying it as a charm against witches,' said Robbins with a rare venture into humour, 'I've heard tell that rowan is more reliable.'

Murray explained where it had come from.

'But it doesn't tell us much. There's plenty of oak about the parish.' He picked up the twig and fingered it: he had always liked acorns, smooth nuts in their snug little cups. These acorns sat tight on their twig, like little mushrooms. He fingered them, thinking – or not thinking exactly, but allowing his fingers to think for him.

'What's the matter, sir?' asked Robbins.

'These oaks aren't all over the parish. Not this kind,' said Murray. He showed Robbins the twig. 'Look how the acorns sit on the twig. Usually there's a stem between the acorn and the twig, but here there isn't. Now, there's only one stand of that kind of oak in the parish, as far as I know.'

'Where's that, then, sir?'

'Collessie.'

'There's no guarantee that having taken her there once, and lost her, he'll take her there again,' Murray argued with himself, striding down the stairs while pulling his neckcloth into shape. He doubted the result was a success.

Robbins was hurrying behind.

'Are you sure you want to go now, sir?'

'I think we have to,' said Murray. 'Who knows how long he's been hiding there, on Collessie land, and not a man sensible or reliable enough to find him or notice anything amiss? What if he took someone else? What if he has Agnes, but has not killed her yet?' he added darkly. Robbins' eyebrows rose.

'The men are outside, sir, and they're organising torches. I've sent William over to Collessie to tell the factor – not that he would be likely to notice anyway,' he added with a hint of self-satisfaction.

Once again Murray opened the front door to find a group of determined looking men outside, holding torches and awaiting instructions.

'Who here knows the oak grove in Collessie woods?' Murray asked. There were a few murmurs of acknowledgement.

'Haven't been there for years, though, sir,' said one voice, and several others agreed.

'Didn't know it was still there,' they added.

'Well, we have reason to believe Agnes was there – and may be there again. I don't know why it wasn't searched before, but it's going to be searched now. All right? Stay in twos and threes, no wandering off on your own, and be careful.'

Out of the corner of his eye he saw several more torches, presumably coming to join the hunt, over to his left. He glanced over, waiting to see if he needed to issue his instructions again. The torches did not seem to be coming any closer.

'You there! Who's there?' he called. The torches were jittery, sparking, very near to Robbins' front door. They heard the crack of glass, and the torches disappeared.

Murray whipped round to Robbins. Robbins stood aghast, then as if lightning had struck him he pelted across the gravel and grass to his house. Even as he ran, the flames inside rose. A cry came from within the house, wordless, and then, as if in response, came a shout from outside.

'Burn the witch!'

Chapter Twenty

Murray's legs were much longer, but Robbins shot across the grass like a hare and was at the front door of the house long before him. Murray's heart sank as Robbins, a shadow in the flickering torchlight, quickly assessed the two flaming ground floor windows, and the smoke emerging round the door, and with unexpected power kicked the door in.

'Robbins! No!' Murray cried, but his voice faded almost at once, knowing there would be no stopping him. Robbins disappeared inside. Murray dashed after, pausing only to yell 'Buckets! Water!' over his shoulder. At the dented front door he too paused, quite sure that this was madness. But there were children in there, Robbins' son and the little maid, and there was Mary. He plunged in.

The hallway was full of smoke, and he immediately crouched down, coughing and spluttering. Ahead and to each side he saw only closed doors, the only light dim behind him. Where were Mary and the children likely to be? Where was Robbins?

He remembered the cosy kitchen, and made for the back of the house.

More closed doors. He blundered into someone staggering towards him, and caught Robbins.

'Keep low,' Murray urged him. 'Smoke rises up.'

Robbins squatted down, nodding as he coughed. His pale face was blurry, but his eyes burned.

'Doors all closed,' he shouted. Fires were noisy, Murray thought vaguely, with all their roaring and yelling. Bullies, really. 'Have to get to kitchen.' Robbins scrambled away on his hands and knees, but Murray caught his ankle.

'Look!' he pointed to the foot of the nearest door. Mary had been quick. Each closed door had a blanket or cloth along the bottom, and when Murray felt the nearest one, it was wet. 'She's used the water in the house to stop the fire spreading –' he coughed '– as long as she could.' About and above them they could see

225

smoke sliding from the front of the house to the back, but also seeping round the doors from the back rooms. The devils must have lit all the ground floor windows, front and back. He had a moment of faint anguish as he thought of the poor wooden elephant, burning in the kitchen. They needed air. He grabbed Robbins by the arm, and dragged him back to the front door, both of them clumsy on their knees.

Outside a bucket chain was already forming, clanking and sloshing, bringing water from the pump behind Robbins' house. Murray gulped in the fresh air, holding Robbins up while they took a few seconds.

'Where would she have gone?'

'She must have thought they were outside waiting for her. She would have gone upstairs, waited for rescue.' Robbins' mouth was wide as a skull's, sucking in air.

'Then we'll look.' He glanced back into the hall. 'The fire's very fast.'

'Pitch,' said Robbins, still coughing. 'Smell it?'

Murray sniffed warily. He could smell the tarry scent, and anger surged within him.

'Come on,' he snapped. 'Let's get them.' He was not sure at that moment if he meant they should rescue Mary, or find the arsonists. With Robbins close behind him, he headed for the stairs.

The stairs were wooden but so far untouched. They both pulled their neckcloths across their faces, squinting as their eyes ran, feeling their way along wall and banisters. Upstairs they crawled again. Robbins tapped Murray hard on the back and pointed to the front of the house, and they both edged their way along the landing. Murray had no recollection of ever having been upstairs in this house, and even if he had he thought he would have been lost now. He was beginning to wonder which way the ceiling was, when Robbins pushed through a doorway and into a room with a thin carpet on the floor. They spread themselves out, searching the floor with their fingertips, only just able to see lights from outside through the unshuttered window. They had only gone a pace or two when Robbins gave a cry. Murray shuffled quickly over to him: they had found Mary and the bairn, and the little servant girl. Mary had been holding them tight, their faces pressed into her shawl as they lay huddled together on the floor between the door and the window, the path to safety.

Robbins seized his wife in his arms, and the bairn, and held them close. Murray swallowed hard, kicked a couple of times inaccurately to shut the door of the room behind them, and lunged forward to the window. He pulled himself up by the sill, fumbled, breathless, with the catch, and flung the sash up.

'Ladders!' he tried to call, but broke down coughing. He tried again. 'Ladders!'

Still not loud enough. He hung out of the window, breathing in cold, frosty air, while inside one hand felt around the window. His fingers found a long wooden handle, and he pulled. Something ... what was it? He blinked as he pulled it into the lighter, clearer air. A battered warming pan, metal tray and hinged lid, on a stick. He stuck it out through the window, drew breath, and battered it against the wall below him, at the same time yelling,

'Help! Ladders here! Help! Help!'

At that, someone did hear. He saw Mrs. Grant drop her bucket in the chain and call across to someone – William? Daniel? The ladders for cleaning the gutters were somewhere nearby: in a moment, he saw four men lumbering through the bucket chain with them, manoeuvring them into position. He made sure they knew which window to aim for, then crawled back to help Robbins pull Mary and the children over to the sill. Robbins' face was striped with soot and tears, eyes wild.

The ladders arrived at the window with a wonderful clatter. Two stableboys, shinning up them like lightning, took the weight of Robbins' son between them and slithered back down to the ground, immediately replaced by two gardener's boys who did the same with the little maidservant. Mary was a different proposition, tall and angular, and Robbins scrambled out on to the ladder first to help balance her with exceptional care, guiding the burden of her down gently to the grass. Murray glanced back into the room, but could see nothing but smoke. He levered himself through the narrow sash, found the ladder with his foot, and was down on the ground before he knew it.

Mrs. Grant was already cradling the little maidservant, and Isobel had Robbins' boy in her arms. The children were pale, but the fresh air caught them and licked at them like an exuberant dog, and in a moment they were breathing it in eagerly as if it was a new treat, and the colour came back to their faces, as far as one could tell in the flickering light. The little maid looked about her, realised she was safe, and began to cry.

Robbins saw his son was conscious, and turned his attention back to Mary, holding her and rocking her gently, pushing her wild black hair away from her face and her high, angular eyebrows. Her eyelashes lay sooty across her pale skin. Murray crouched down, not wanting to intrude but needing to know.

'Is she – is she breathing?'

Even as he spoke, Mary's nostrils flared and her mouth opened, and she took a great, gasping breath, then twisted like a seal to curl on her side, coughing helplessly. Robbins thumped her hard on the back, but she coughed on, only gradually managing to control her breathing until at last she was able to roll back into his arms and smile up at him, eyes wet.

'Mary,' said Robbins gently, but she was still wriggling, trying to pull something from inside her shawl. 'What are you doing? Whatever it is, leave it for now.'

'No,' she whispered, and pulled out a dark, heavy object. 'Look.'

Eyes shining, she held out his wooden elephant. Robbins touched it, and her hand.

Murray stood, and moved away to assess the state of the fire fighting, wiping his face with the back of his hand.

The bucket chains were beginning to do their work, but the fire was still blazing in some of the rooms and the smoke from the upstairs windows seemed to be thickening. Isobel and Mrs. Grant took the children back into the main house, the little maid walking unsupported now, but Blair and Cousin Andrew were still active with the buckets and Thalland, the factor, was directing a few of the nimble stable and garden boys to run up the ladders with buckets and fling the contents over the floors of the upper storey, trying to stop the fire from spreading further. Murray joined in, taking a second squad with ladders to the back of the house and doing the same there. A second chain started from the pump behind Thalland's own house across the drive, so that the water from Robbins' pump could be focussed on the rear of his house, and gradually, gradually, the fire began to subside. It seemed like only minutes, but when Murray had the chance to peer at his watch in the light from one of the torches on the drive, he realised they had been there for two hours. He broke up the team at the back of the house, leaving some to watch for flare-ups while the others went to eat, with instructions to take turn about later. At the front of the house, Robbins and Mary had gone, presumably into the main house, and Cousin Andrew, panting but with the air of a man pleased he could meet a challenge, was inspecting the front doorway and testing the temperature there. Blair was doing the same at the windows, and Thalland was overseeing the bringing down of the ladders. Murray told him to make sure the men were fed but vigilant at the front, too, and Thalland nodded, quite competent. Murray stood back and gazed up at the house, darkened and misty with smoke and steam. It was going to be expensive to replace it, in the current climate, he thought distantly, but it had to be done.

He shivered suddenly, and realised how cold the night had grown. On the grass where the firefighters had not been trampling there was already a frost, and his breath mingled with the smoke in the air. He was starving. He glanced up at the main house and noticed a lit window with the shutters open – one of the dining room windows. A figure stood there, strangely shaped. He squinted, his eyes still stinging. It was Agostinella, gazing out at the aftermath of the fire. When she turned away, the candlelight in the room caught her expression: it was a strange mixture of horror and delight, and it stopped him in his tracks. Horror he could understand, but delight? His tired mind scrabbled for an explanation. Could she have thought they were guarding Lizzie Fenwick in the Robbins' house?

He was growing even colder, with his coat and hair wet, and he had no idea where his hat had gone. He collected Blair and Cousin Andrew, and went indoors to change and eat.

He found clean, dry outdoor clothes on his own, not wanting to bother Robbins, and sluiced his smoky hair and face with cold water, probably not improving his appearance at all but simply rearranging the soot on his skin. He scrubbed his hands thoughtfully, examining the thoughts in his head. Lizzie Fenwick, Widow Maggot, Tilly, Robert Lovie, Mal Johnstone, Agostinella, Rintoul, Agnes. He had to keep them all straight.

Back in the bedchamber he glanced at the mantelpiece to see

how sooty he still looked, but the mirror he had rescued from Widow Maggot's cottage had been laid flat, face down. Robbins must have had a moment of defiance, he thought, and he turned the mirror upright.

It flew out at him.

Not the mirror, he realised, though he almost dropped it. Something in the mirror. Something black. The candles in the room swept sideways, and went out.

He was clutching the mantelpiece. He was almost sure he had felt the thing brush the side of his head in its rush to be free. He was breathing fast.

He set the mirror carefully down on the mantelpiece, and turned slowly to face the rest of the room. He could see the edge of the bedroom door, lit against the candles on the landing. He stepped towards it very, very slowly. He was sure he was not alone in the room, and whatever it was, he had no wish to blunder in to it in the dark. He took another step, and another, his hand already outstretched to find the door handle. There was nothing between the fireplace and the door, after all.

His fingers hit something. Not the round, hard, metal doorhandle, and whatever it was whipped away fast. Cloth? Skin? Fur?

He had recoiled but he made himself take another step forward, and lunged for where he knew the handle was. He snatched it, turned it, and ran out on to the landing, slamming the bedchamber door behind him.

Mrs. Dean, who had been on the landing, leapt back in surprise.

'I beg your pardon, sir!' she squeaked.

'No, no, Mrs. Dean, all my fault.'

'Mr. Murray, sir, you look very pale. Are you sure you are quite well?'

Murray sat on a hall chair, rubbing his hands through his hair and catching his breath.

'Mrs. Dean, have you seen that mirror that I brought back from Widow Maggot's cottage? Mr. Blair and I removed two or three things for safety until the sheriff's man should find any relatives to inherit.'

'A mirror, sir? May I see it?'

Murray hesitated. He had no wish to see the mirror ever again, but it would have been discourteous to send her in on her own, to face who knew what.

'Best bring that candle,' he said at last, and made himself stand up. He opened the bedchamber door and much against his better judgement, peered inside.

The room was, as far as he could see, empty.

Mrs. Dean was already crossing it, quite assured.

'This mirror here?' she asked, picking it up from the mantelpiece. 'I'm not sure this would be suitable for a gentleman's room,' she added obscurely. 'Perhaps I should take it away.'

'I think it may be too late,' said Murray, not quite sure what conversation he was having, or why he was having it with Mrs. Dean. 'Something has already come out of it.'

'Something?' Mrs. Dean gave him a quick, understanding look, full of concern.

'I don't know what. It could still be in the room. Behind the curtains, or … or under the bed.' He sounded to himself like an anxious child.

'Best leave the mirror face up, then, sir. You never know: we might be lucky. It might go back in.'

The look on her face, however, implied that she had no expectation of that at all.

'I have to go and look for Agnes,' he said, as if that excused him from any further action concerning the mirror.

'Very good, sir.'

He felt dismissed. He left her standing by the mantelpiece with the mirror in her hand, examining the room with her quick, sharp eyes, and went very willingly to find Blair.

He had decided on a different strategy for Agnes. When he and Blair had taken some food, and he had had a quick word with both Robbins and Lady Agostinella, he and Blair set out for the village inn and collected Macduff. Murray explained about the acorns, and also told Macduff about the fire.

'Did you see any way clearly who did the setting, sir?' asked Macduff, very concerned.

'Not to swear to,' said Murray with regret. 'I'd like to say it was Mal Johstone but I honestly couldn't.'

'And you heard someone shout "Burn the witch!", aye?'

'Definitely. I wondered if they thought we were sheltering Lizzie Fenwick there?'

Macduff considered.

'Your man who lives there, Robbins. His woman's from Lewis or some such, is she not?'

'From North Uist, yes.'

Macduff frowned.

'Does she speak the Gaelic, then?'

'Certainly.'

'I wonder … Yesterday, when I was here in the inn writing down a few things about my investigations into Miss Aytoun, I was in a little private parlour here. I say private parlour, but it's no that private, for anyone in it can hear the conversations in the taproom and I daresay the other way around, too. I reckon there were three or four men there, and I overheard just a few words – not enough really to know what they were talking about – but I did hear something about 'speaking the Devil's language to that bairn of hers', and 'uncanny woman', that made me wonder. But you ken how clumsy I am with this leg: I tried to see who was talking and they had all shifted away when they heard me move.'

'So it was Mary they were after,' said Murray, his voice hard.

'But just now we must look for Agnes,' Blair reminded them. 'It's a dreadfully cold night out there.'

'Aye, aye,' agreed the sheriff's man with a sigh, and went to fetch his hat and gloves, and a thick cloak.

Collessie woods were not inviting at night. Blair and Murray had brought a lantern each, and Macduff had his own, and the light from them sparkled the frost that was growing on every leaf and branch along the way. They took the clearest path they could find, the one that led past the woodsman's hut so favoured by Robert Lovie, and stopped halfway or so along it for Murray to consider his bearings.

'What if the gamekeeper sees us?' asked Macduff. 'Did you tell yon factor up at the house that we were going in here?'

'It's Collessie,' said Murray cynically. 'You're far more likely to meet a poacher than a gamekeeper. I seem to remember it's this way.'

'And this is the only plantation of these funny oaks in the

parish?' Macduff asked a little further on, pausing to cut his way out of an ensnaring bramble. Blair tried to help and only ended up attached, too.

'That's right. I remember my grandfather pointing them out to me and explaining the difference between the two kinds. That was a long time ago but there hasn't been much planting here since, and I know there have been no oaks like that planted at Letho. I think I would probably know if there had been any at Dures, either.'

'I'm happy to follow that line, then,' said Macduff, who had reduced the bramble to a number of very small pieces and finally stepped free. Blair picked bits off his coat, and shook his gloves trying to detach them again.

'The question is, though,' said Murray, who had now encountered another thicket, 'will we ever find it?'

He cut his way through, and all three of them found themselves on a small path, branches trimmed on either side, and not long ago, either. In a moment, they had come to a small clearing.

'Why wasn't this searched before?' asked Macduff, staring around with his lantern high.

'I think I might know,' said Blair, behind him. 'Look.'

He waved his lantern around his head height, and pointed to the tree trunk beside him. Macduff and Murray came closer, and looked. Pinned to the trunk was a little bunch of rabbit bones, tied in a ribbon. Murray held his own lantern up to the next tree. There was an identical posy there.

'Witches?' asked Macduff dubiously.

'Or someone using witch signs to scare away the ignorant,' said Murray suddenly.

'Who searched these woods?'

'Mal Johnstone led the search over this way,' said Murray grimly. 'He said he was a Collessie tenant and knew the ground. But if he had seen these …'

'Do you know, I've had more than enough of witches and witchcraft this last week,' said Macduff abruptly. 'If I dinna find some human criminal soon, I'm going to take ship for the West Indies. Yellow fever canna be worse than all this nonsense.'

He led the way, stumping along on his bad leg, across the

clearing, and waved his lantern up again.

'Is these the trees you were wanting?'

Murray glanced up, and then poked at another trunk.

'These are the ones, yes,' he said. 'Please let her be here!'

They advanced more slowly, poking sticks into the undergrowth, lifting and lowering the lanterns to make the best of their light. Then Macduff tripped, and swore, and fell over.

'What's this?' he demanded, struggling to get up.

Blair and Murray hurried over.

'Some kind of cloth?' A stick was pinning the cloth to the ground.

'It's like a military tent,' said Blair. 'It's canvas of some kind.'

They straightened and looked away from the stick peg. The canvas rose before them, looking exactly like a tent, except that it was so covered in leaves and mud that they might almost not have noticed it if Macduff had not walked into it. They edged around it. Murray could smell smoke on the cold air, but he was not sure if it was still lingering in his nose from earlier.

The canvas had been draped from several trees – oak trees, as it happened – and pinned out to make something the shape of a lean-to shelter, artfully disguised against the forest floor. Inside it seemed to be empty of life: there was indeed a little hearth, made of stones, near the entrance, and though the fire was out the stones were hot. Beyond it was a makeshift bed, made of bundled bracken and a couple of grey blankets, quite comfortable looking. Against the higher side someone had rigged up a framework from branches and rope to form rudimentary shelves, on which a considerable quantity of food was laid out – including, Murray noted with interest, a crate of apples and a tin box which contained a fine looking slice of ham, very much like the one Widow Maggot had had hanging from her ceiling. Beyond the food, another area at the back of the tent had been curtained across roughly. Blair stayed near the entrance, watching out for the camper's return, his breath a white cloud around him in the lantern light, while Murray and Macduff approached the curtain very warily, in case the camper had not in fact left. Macduff reached out one hand to pull the curtain aside, and held up his lantern. Murray moved up beside him.

Beyond the curtain were more bedclothes, and more bracken,

on another little raised wooden framework. It formed a large bed, with several cushions and rugs, and it took them a moment to realise that it was, in fact, occupied. There at the far edge, curled up like a kitten, fast asleep and snoring, was Agnes.

Chapter Twenty-One

'Agnes! Agnes!' Macduff shook the girl's shoulder, but she did not stir.

'She is alive, isn't she?' Murray was sure he had seen her breathing, but she was so hard to rouse he was beginning to wonder. His throat was tight with hope.

'Aye, sir, aye. I think so,' added Macduff abruptly, starting to doubt too. 'I canna get the lantern at the right place here to see properly, and I canna find a pulse.'

'Bring her out here, then,' said Murray. 'Maybe we can revive her.'

They kept their voices low, in case the kidnapper was nearby. The wooden bed platform made everything difficult in the sloping shelter, tripping their feet and chapping their shins. Macduff, leaning at a strange angle to avoid the roof and not put too much weight on his bad leg, lifted Agnes out of the blankets, which were so wrapped round her they seemed to suck her back into the bed like seaweed. He managed to stretch just far enough to pass her to Murray, who was perilously balanced across the edge of the bed platform, wishing Blair would come and grab the back of his coat to counter the dead weight of Agnes. Blair, however, was busy: he had abandoned his sentinel post at the opening of the shelter and Murray could hear him poking around the rustic shelves that formed the shelter's well-stocked pantry. When Murray had successfully taken Agnes from Macduff, and brought her round the curtain and into the front part of shelter again, he laid her on the bed there and glanced around to see what Blair was doing. It was hard to see, so he returned to pulling his gloves off and trying to find Agnes' pulse. Macduff finally extracted himself from the inner room and joined him.

'Nothing in there but blankets and bedding,' he reported, 'of different kinds. I think he must have had them off a few bushes where people were drying them, sir. Any luck with the pulse?'

Murray had given up on finding one in Agnes' thin wrists, and was trying to find the jugular. He grinned: there was the least, faint, regular thud.

'She's still alive. Not much warmth, though,' he added, feeling her forehead. 'She's a bit cold and clammy.' He wondered what age she was: the lantern light caught her reddish gold hair and tiny freckled features, and made her look like a child. What had she been through?

'We should get her somewhere warm and safe,' said Macduff, pushing himself back on to his feet, and Murray agreed. He gathered a blanket up around the tiny form of his maid. 'Blair, are you finished?'

'Can we take these?' Blair asked eagerly. He held out a couple of jars, the lids off to show the contents. One held a mixture of dried seeds, while the other had some kind of sweet-smelling syrup. 'You seemed to be having difficulty waking her: I wondered if perhaps she might have been drugged, and these looked like the most likely drugs – everything else is food,' he added sadly, as if it was a disappointment not to find the shelter brimming with potions and concoctions.

'Can you manage them?' asked Murray. 'If I carry Agnes and you take a jar each, then we should be able to carry the lanterns, too.' Macduff and Blair quickly trimmed the lanterns' wicks while Murray secured the blanket around Agnes so that she would be warm and he would not trip over its tails. Outside the shelter they were surprised again by the chilly night, and their breaths misted the air of the little clearing. Macduff lifted his lantern to show them the way back to the patchy little path they had approached by, and they set off, stumbling and slipping on tree roots and trying to save their hats from low-sweeping branches. They were already some way from the shelter and the clearing before they began to talk again, partly concentrating, partly wary.

'She was well enough treated,' Macduff commented first, easy enough with the two of them now to start a conversation himself.

'Warm and dry, and not bound at all.'

'No need to bind her if she's drugged,' said Blair apologetically. 'It was my impression that her clothes did not look interfered with at all. Would that be right?'

'That's the way it seemed to me,' agreed Murray, who had been worrying about that very thing. What had the kidnapper kept her for?

'Do you think she was kidnapped at all, gentlemen?' asked Macduff, voicing a thought in all their minds. 'Could she just have gone of her own freewill?'

'To meet him in the woods? But then why stay around? If they were eloping, why not just go?' asked Murray. 'And why drug her?'

'Aye, aye,' said Macduff, 'And why would she have hidden at young Mr. Rintoul's and tell him she had escaped?'

'A moment of doubt?' suggested Blair. Murray added,

'We only have Rintoul's word for it that she did any of that. He could have kidnapped her and she fled from him, then he told us about it – or his version of it – so that if she was found he had his story in first.'

They fell silent for a while, considering this. They reached the well-worn Collessie path and were able at last to walk, if not side by side, then at least more closely together. Murray hoisted Agnes up and readjusted his hold on her: she was very light. As he paused, Macduff came over and held his lantern up to examine her face, but she was still out cold.

'Do you think the kidnapper knows we've been in his shelter yet?' asked Blair, a little timid.

'Perhaps he knew we were there all along. The fire was still hot,' said Murray. 'He may have heard us coming, put it out and hidden outside somewhere to watch us.' He almost wished he had not said it, for the very thought made him shiver.

'He could have fled altogether,' suggested Macduff. 'Or he might have been away doing something and we just happened to arrive while he was out. Do you think we should maybe have lain in wait for him?' He seemed struck by a sudden anxiety that he had not done his duty properly. 'Could we have caught him, do you think, sir?'

'I don't know. We needed to get Agnes to safety, didn't we?

And which of us would we have left to tackle him? He might have a gun, or anything.' He managed not to add, 'He might be a witch and attack us with magic,' but the thought skipped through his mind, nevertheless. He shook his head to clear it.

'I should maybe have stayed, all the same,' Macduff murmured, and disappeared into his own thoughts for a while. They were out into the fields before anyone spoke again.

'Rabbit bones here and rabbit bones on Tilly's body,' said Blair. 'All nicely done up in a little bow.'

'And rabbit bones mentioned in the old accounts in the Presbytery minutes,' added Murray. 'Is someone really up to witchcraft of a sort here? Or do they only want to make us think that's what they are doing?'

'Well, whichever it is,' said Macduff with heavy solemnity, 'it's going to have to be stopped.'

Only worry about Agnes kept them striding out as smartly as they could back over the path to Letho House: they were all weary. Murray could still smell smoke from his clothing, then realised that of course there would still be smoke on the clear, frosty air from the fire earlier. As they climbed the gentle slope up to the house, he could see servants still hovering around the Robbins' house with buckets at the ready, keeping warm around a little fire of their own. Someone, he saw, had provided them with broth, and they waved as the party passed with Agnes. In the dark, no doubt, they would only have seen the lanterns, and not recognised the bundle they were carrying. They passed between the two houses and climbed the few shallow steps to the front door, only to find it locked. Blair rang the bell with enthusiasm, and in a moment Daniel opened the door warily.

'Sir,' he said, 'Mr. Robbins says we was to lock the front door and no let a'body in till he said so, sir – is that Agnes?' Caution forgotten, he flung the door wide to admit them, which was just as well: Murray could not imagine Robbins being too pleased to discover that Daniel had tried to bar the way to the laird and his oldest friend.

'Well, lock it again, then, Daniel!' he told him, and waited until he had done so. Then he led the way, leaving Daniel to his vigil in the hallway, through the door to the servants' quarters with

Agnes still in his arms.

He set her down at last in the kitchen, on the settle by the fire, easing his aching arms as the servants clustered round in amazement. Macduff and Blair held back, observing them discreetly. Murray looked about for the housekeeper, but she was already there.

'Mrs. Dean?' he said. 'She seems to have been drugged. Have you any room for another casualty?'

'Of course, sir,' said Mrs. Dean. 'I'll put her in the box bed in my own room. The fire's lit in there just now anyway for the evening.' She squirreled in to the first rank of those around Agnes and pushed them back gently, then took Agnes up in her arms, examining her face closely and taking her pulse at the throat, as Murray had done.

'She's far away,' she agreed. 'Cold and clammy. Has she been outside all this time?'

'We found her in a kind of tent,' said Murray. 'There was a fire: it seemed warm enough, and she was well wrapped up in blankets.'

Mrs. Dean rubbed Agnes' hands gently between her own.

'Well, thank heavens she's alive, anyway. That's a start – something to work with.' She looked about. 'William, can you carry her along to my room, please? Iffy, will you fill a couple of warming pans, and bring them along, too? And I'll need a jug of water, one hot and one cold. Have you any idea, sir, what drugs might have been used?'

Murray nodded to Blair and Macduff, who advanced with their jars and presented them to Mrs. Dean. Murray could not help thinking they looked like a couple of wise men who had lost their companion. Mrs. Dean took the jars with thanks, and hurried after William and Agnes to her room, while Mrs. Mack shooed Iffy off to do what she had been asked to do. Walter, stoic as ever, was left cleaning boots by the back door, eyes wide at all the comings and goings.

'Are you all right, Walter?' Murray asked.

'Aye, sir. It's just all coming once, isn't it, sir? I didna like the fire at all.'

'No, it wasn't my favourite part of the day,' Murray agreed. He turned to Mrs. Mack, who was laying the table for the servants' supper. 'We'll get out of your way, now, Mrs. Mack,' he said, 'but where's Robbins?'

'Oh, he's over at Mr. Thalland's house, sir,' said Mrs. Mack with a curtsey that reduced her almost to the height of the table she was laying. 'Mr. Thalland is going to put them up for the night, anyway.'

'Ah, good idea. Is – is Mrs. Robbins all right?'

'It'd take more than a wee puff of smoke to kill that one,' said Mrs. Mack with a sniff. 'She's grand.' Murray remembered that Mary and the cook had not historically seen eye to eye, and smiled ruefully.

'Don't bother to send anyone over for him,' he said, 'but if he comes back over this evening please let him know I'd like a word.' He doubted Robbins would want to leave Mary and his son tonight, but on the other hand he would not want to leave the household unattended for long. 'When William's free, could you ask him to bring us brandy and perhaps some food to the library? Nothing elaborate, and cold will do,' he added. Mrs. Mack had already had her dinner disturbed today: he did not want to incur her wrath by placing additional burdens on her.

'Aye, sir, as soon as we can,' Mrs. Mack agreed willingly enough, and Murray ushered Blair and Macduff back to the main house.

'I'll leave you in the library for a moment, if you'll excuse me,' he said in the hallway. 'I must just check that Lady Agostinella is all right.'

'Of course, dear boy, of course. Come along, Macduff: there's a fascinating volume in here from old Mr. Murray's great grandfather's time, I believe, concerning the cultivation of tomatoes when they were only just new on these shores, can you imagine? And the illustrations are extraordinary …' His voice faded away as Murray climbed the stairs, smiling at the thought of how enthusiastic Macduff was likely to be about antique horticulture.

Agostinella was sitting up on her daybed, finishing a light supper. She accepted Murray's kiss on the hand with a gracious smile, and looked surprisingly calm.

'Mrs. Dean has given me a kind of tea which I find very refreshing,' she said in response to Murray's compliments on her appearance. 'Your Dr. Harker approved, I might add.'

'Excellent,' said Murray, perching on his usual stool. 'I hope you were not too distressed by all the disruption earlier?'

'The fire? An extraordinary thing. I hope that none of the servants has been hurt.'

'No, no one was hurt at all, except, I believe, Cousin Andrew who twisted his wrist passing a bucket to someone.'

'He should have left the task to someone more adapted to doing it,' Agostinella said dismissively. She probably meant the servants: she had previously expressed her displeasure when Murray himself had helped with any tasks around the estate. 'No one at all hurt? Who was in the house?'

He glanced up at her: she had an unfamiliar, innocent look on her face which he did not quite trust.

'Mrs. Robbins, her child and a servant, that was all. The smoke had affected them, but they are all recovering well.'

'Which servant?'

'One of Melville's daughters. From Hill of Letho farm'

'Oh.' She seemed disappointed. Murray was sure she had believed they were hiding Lizzie Fenwick in the Robbins' house. Had she mentioned that to anyone else? Not in order to have them burned out, of course, but just in passing? He prayed that no one would find out where Lizzie Fenwick really was, if that was what would happen again.

'I have good news, too,' he went on after a moment. 'Agnes has been found.'

'The maidservant? Alive and well?'

'Alive, yes. She seems to have been drugged, but there seems to be no physical harm come to her.'

'Then that is good news.' She yawned delicately, and her eyelids closed for a moment. 'Where was she found?'

'In an oak plantation on Collessie land. It doesn't look as if it was searched the first time round because –' he found himself reluctant to mention the rabbit bones to her, '- because it was extremely well disguised. Whoever took her had stolen ropes and a canvas, and set up a shelter hidden under leaves and branches. But it was warm, and well-supplied, and she was wrapped cosily in a kind of bed. She has, to some extent, been well looked after.'

'Then I hope she will make a full recovery ...' said

Agostinella, but her voice tailed off as she slumped gently back on the cushions. Her eyes fluttered open, and she smiled. 'I feel very comfortable, for once,' she said, 'but very sleepy. I believe I shall sleep well tonight,' she finished on another yawn.

'I'll bid you a very good night, then,' said Murray, rising and kissing her hand again. He gestured the ever-present maid to come and attend to her mistress, who was already dozing. He smiled down at her. Not long to go now, he thought: it was a mercy to see her so serene. Maybe, maybe everything would go well.

Back downstairs, he met Robbins in the hall. Robbins, too, was calm, as if this afternoon's speed and fury were only a dream.

'How are things? Are you in Thalland's house?'

'Yes, sir. Mr. Thalland has been most accommodating, particularly since he is not very used to children,' said Robbins blandly.

'Is there anything you need? Extra bedding, dishes? Take whatever it is.'

'Thank you, sir. I believe we're quite comfortable.'

'And is Mary - Mrs. Robbins – quite recovered? And your child?'

'Yes, sir. I have ordered her to go to bed, but as you can imagine, Mary follows her own orders.' They smiled at shared memories. 'I should rather be with her now, but she told me she was perfectly capable of sorting things out for herself and that I should only get in the way.'

'I'll talk with Thalland tomorrow about rebuilding, and accommodation for you while you have no house,' said Murray.

'Tomorrow's the Sabbath, sir.'

'So it is. There's nothing to stop a little chat, though, and we'll have to take a look at the house in the light of day, anyway, for safety's sake. The Sabbath! I had lost track.'

There was a pause, and then Robbins seemed to feel a change of subject was in order.

'Mr. Blair and Macduff are awaiting you in the library, sir. Walter brought some provisions. I was very glad to find that Agnes is found, though I should be happier if she was awake, even if it meant her talking again.'

'I know. It feels like only a partial victory – especially since we have still not found the kidnapper.' He described for Robbins the shelter, and the chances of the kidnapper still being around.

'Surely he would flee the parish now, sir?' asked Robbins, surprised. 'He has nothing to keep him here: all the women are forewarned, and all the missing women are found, in whatever way.'

'I'm not entirely sure,' said Murray slowly. 'Would he? He kept Agnes alive and apparently untouched. He came back for her when she escaped the first time. Would he stay in the neighbourhood, and come back for her again?'

The library was warm, and Mrs. Mack had found hot pies to send up, the juices sweet and rich to be soaked up with fresh bread. Macduff and Blair were already eating at the library table and Murray joined them, only then realising just how hungry he was. Only when the plates were wiped clean and the food was a luscious memory did the men settle back and consider talking again. They had only just opened up the discussion of Agnes and Tilly and their kidnapper when the door opened and Mrs. Dean appeared, carrying one of the jars Blair and Macduff had brought back from the shelter in the woods.

'Sir, this has me puzzled,' she announced, holding out the jar. It was the one with the syrup in it.

'How so?' asked Murray.

'Well, no doubt this is what the man has used to keep her sleeping. It's a strong sedative, made with valerian and broom and henbane. It has to be used carefully, or it can kill.'

'Do you think he knew that? Did he intend to kill Agnes, or to keep her quiet?'

'I have no idea, sir, but I'd say if he intended to kill her, and she only slept, then why would he not finish her off with something else rather than letting her sleep?'

'Will she come round soon?' asked Macduff.

'Not for a while: she's a long way under,' said Mrs. Dean.

'So what is puzzling you? Are the ingredients strange in any way? Could they help us to find her captor?'

'No, the ingredients are not particularly strange in themselves, sir. But the thing is, this is my own recipe.'

Murray's jaw dropped.

'You made this? It was stolen from this house?'

'It was not stolen from this house, sir. I don't know if I made this batch specifically, for if someone used my recipe accurately it would no doubt turn out the same. But it is my recipe, and it is in one of the jars I used to use.'

'You used to use? Not now?'

'Sir, this is a strong sedative, as I say. I have never made it since I came to Letho, nor did I bring any with me. The last time I used it was during my old master's, Mr. Cowley's, last illness, in Glasgow. It was the only thing that eased him. But whatever was left when he died, I left behind there when I came here. This looks exactly like it.'

'Could Agnes have brought it with her from Paisley?' Blair asked.

'Maybe so,' agreed Mrs. Dean. 'She never mentioned it, but maybe so.'

'We can ask Jennet if she has ever seen it in Agnes' things. Is Jennet still up?'

'I'll fetch her,' said Mrs. Dean. 'She's in her room.' She met Murray's eye firmly at this, reminding him that Jennet was most likely looking after Lizzie Fenwick. The men waited and in a few minutes Jennet appeared, curtseying nervously. She denied flatly ever having seen such a jar in Agnes' possession, and further was able to report that Agnes was as free with information about what was in her kist as she was with information about what was in her head: Jennet had been shown every tiny thing Agnes owned, at least once.

Jennet was dismissed with thanks and vanished back to the servants' quarters. After a few minutes, Mrs. Dean reappeared to collect the mysterious jar. She stood for a moment, twisting it between her capable hands. The men, sensing a moment of indecision, waited without speaking.

'Sir, I found out a little more about Agnes and what happened in Paisley. More than she told us at the start, but she begged me to keep it quiet for her. I'm not sure I should, anymore.'

'I'm sure you shouldn't,' agreed Murray. 'When did you find this out?'

'Not that long after she came.' She set the jar back down on a shelf for a moment, as if she needed all her concentration for what she was telling them. Her fingers knotted together. 'She came here with a letter from my old mistress, Mrs. Cowley, and it had the same story Agnes told, that she had seen a murder and the murderer had looked at her and she was afraid, so Mrs. Cowley was sending her into my safe keeping until she felt better. Her kist followed in a day or two, presumably sent at the same time as she left. I think that was the end of the matter, as far as Agnes was concerned. But of course I wrote back to Mrs. Cowley to tell her that Agnes had arrived safely and had a position here, as anyone would. I never received a reply.'

'Perhaps the letter miscarried?' suggested Blair, his eyes wide as he listened.

'I don't believe it did, except in one particular way,' said Mrs. Dean gravely. 'It never reached Mrs. Cowley, because she was dead.'

'Dead? How do you know?'

Mrs. Dean sighed, her face twisting in dismay.

'I wondered that she did not reply, for she was a great letter writer. So I sent a note to a neighbour I remembered, to ask if all was well. You understand, Mrs. Cowley moved around the time I left, so that most of my acquaintance there would no longer know her.'

'Yes.'

'Well, the reply came fast enough. The murder Agnes had witnessed, the one that had distressed her so – it was Mrs. Cowley's.'

The men gasped.

'She saw her mistress killed?' demanded Macduff. 'Then why did she no tell the police office?'

'I asked her that,' said Mrs. Dean quickly. 'She hadn't really seen the murder, but she had come on her mistress' body, and she knew, she said, who had done the deed. She told me she tried to find help locally, but in the end she fled to me, having heard of me from Mrs. Cowley. Bless her, she thought Fife was further than any sane person would ever travel: she would be beyond any danger here, she thought.'

'And did she tell you who Mrs. Cowley's murderer was?' asked Murray, struggling to take in more information, though he felt it was already answering some questions.

'No, she did not. She was too frightened, for the murderer had fled and never been caught.'

'So the murderer followed her to Letho – further than any sane person would travel – bringing a jar of sedative syrup from the house where he had killed Mrs. Cowley?' Murray suggested. 'And yet, when he finds Agnes, he does not kill her. What is he up to?'

Chapter Twenty-Two

The atmosphere in the sandstone barn of Letho Kirk was mixed the following morning. Mr. Helliwell took as his theme the betrayal of Jesus in the Garden of Gethsemane by Judas Iscariot, and preached in a pointed fashion for a good hour and a half, while certain members of the Kirk Session hung their heads and one or two notable people folded their arms and avoided his eye. There was a distinct nervousness about most of the congregation, though they must have felt safe enough on holy ground. There was a poor representation from Collessie. By contrast, the Letho House contingent was large – of the household staff only Jennet had pleaded another of her sick headaches, and Mrs. Dean had stayed behind to look after her. In reality the two of them were keeping an eye on Lizzie Fenwick and Agnes, but no one at the kirk needed to know that. Mr. Murray led his guests, Mr. and Mrs. Grant and the Blairs, well kent in Letho Kirk, into the front pew. Lady Agostinella was near her time, everyone knew, so her absence was not remarked upon. If there was any comment made about the absence of young Robert Lovie, it did not come to Murray's ears. Mr. and Mrs. Robbins were particularly prominent, heads held high, smiling to their acquaintances and intent on their devotions, leading the staff into the Letho staff pews as if no one had had the nerve to burn their house down last night. After the service, the guests and staff from Letho House were uncharacteristically noisy in their gossip, and very keen to let everyone know that Agnes was back and safe, and ready to be restored to her duties after she had spoken to the sheriff's man. Anyone remotely surprised at her recovery was loudly reassured that no, Agnes was very much back on her feet and fully intended to walk over to Cupar that afternoon, after a rest and a good meal, to meet Mr. Macduff.

Mr. Helliwell greeted Murray after the service, his wife by his side. Mrs. Helliwell was beaming.

'I'm delighted to hear about Agnes. Where on earth was she?'

'In the woods at Collessie, in a kind of shelter there. She seems to have been well looked after.'

'That is welcome news,' said Mrs. Helliwell. She looked puzzled. 'Unexpected, but welcome.'

'And her abductor?' asked her husband.

'No sign: we wondered if he might have been hiding nearby and watching us, but we were able to take Agnes away unmolested. But we have more evidence of links with her life in Paisley.' He stopped there, unwilling to say more at the moment.

'So if the man came from Paisley and he has lost Agnes, perhaps he will go back there?'

'He's taken her twice: I don't think she's safe yet. But she's determined to go to Cupar this afternoon to see Macduff. He went back this morning before she was awake.'

There were eager footsteps behind him, and Murray turned to find Rintoul hurrying up.

'You found her, sir! Agnes is well?'

'Very well, Mr. Rintoul. She was well looked after. She's fit enough and determined enough to go into Cupar this afternoon and tell all to Macduff, the sheriff's man.'

'Extraordinary! And wonderful!' Murray could almost see Rintoul's glowing hair bushing out with the sheer power of guilt lifted. Could he be her captor and look this pleased at her release? He had to admit that, like Blair, he found Rintoul an amiable man, and did not want him to be guilty. Robert Lovie was definitely out of the picture, safely locked in Letho while Agnes was being tended in the woods. Sir John Aytoun could have had nothing directly to do with it, either. It seemed more and more likely that Agnes' captor was the man she had seen murder her mistress in Paisley. But if he had pursued her all the way to Fife, why had he not simply killed her while he had the chance? And why kill Tilly instead? And what had it all to do with witchcraft?

He turned back to Mr. Helliwell, trying to remember to keep a happy, confident expression on his face for the benefit of the villagers. Agnes was fit and well, he reminded himself firmly.

'Have you heard about our other drama yesterday, though?' he asked.

'The fire? Yes, dreadful!' said Mrs. Helliwell at once. 'Mrs. Melville told me her daughter was unharmed but quite shaken.' Murray had arranged for a small gang of servants to walk the little maid back to her parents at Hill of Letho: Melville might be annoyingly keen to follow Mal Johnstone's notions, but that was no reason to let his daughter come to harm. Had Melville known

Mal was setting fire to the house where his daughter was working? Surely not. Did that mean that Mal had not set the fire?

'Yes: the house is destroyed but mercifully no one was injured.'

'How did it start?' asked Mrs. Helliwell, concerned.

Murray glanced around him to see who was within hearing. Melville himself was nearby, along with a few other members of the Kirk Session, but not Mal Johnstone.

'A few people set fire to the house. They threw torches with pitch through the windows and shouted "Burn the witch!".' He watched the Helliwells' jaws drop.

'That's terrible!' Mrs. Helliwell was the first to speak. Mr. Helliwell was white with shock and anger.

'If I find which of them did it ...'

'If we find which of them did it,' said Murray soberly, 'they'll hang at Cupar.'

'How could they do such a thing?'

'I wondered if someone thought that we were sheltering Lizzie Fenwick there,' said Murray, 'but apparently Mrs. Robbins had already crossed swords with Mal Johnstone. I went to see him yesterday,' he remembered suddenly. 'To my mind, he seemed scared.'

'Scared? Well may he be!' muttered Mr. Helliwell furiously.

'He seemed genuinely scared of witches, though. Where would that come from?' Again he glanced around, but he could no longer see Melville, or Watson or any other members of the Kirk Session except Ninian Jack, stubborn and settled, shaking out pew cushions at the church door. Helliwell noticed him, too.

'I'll not be long, Ninian,' he called over.

'No rush, sir,' said Jack sourly. 'The rest of them have headed off somewhere – said they'd no be long.'

'But it's the Kirk Session meeting!' It was always the Kirk Session meeting after the morning service. Where else could they possibly be going? Helliwell shook his head hard, as if he could no longer work out at all what was happening in his parish. He was looking old, Murray thought: he would be glad enough to have Rintoul to help him. Murray drummed his gloved fingers thoughtfully on the handle of his stick. The Kirk Session disappearing mysteriously just before a meeting? He hid a smile and summoned the carriage to take his guests back to Letho. Their work here was done.

'Now, Walter, are you quite sure about this?'

Walter, his chestnut hair polished on his head like a helmet, considered for a moment, then nodded.

'I think so, sir.'

'You do realise what you'll be doing?'

'Aye, sir. But I didna like that that carlie took Agnes away, however good it might have been to have a bit of peace. I'm happy to give a bit of hand to catch him.' He stood in front of Murray, Blair and Robbins, undaunted, a man amongst men, for all his twelve years.

The men exchanged looks. This had seemed like a good idea this morning, but now they were not so sure.

There was a knock on the door and Mrs. Dean hurried in.

'Excuse me, sir, but I thought you would like to know: Agnes has opened her eyes and she's speaking.'

'Speaking?'

'Aye, sir, but she's not making a word of sense yet.'

'Nothing at all?'

'Barely even words, yet, but she's trying. I think it's a good sign, sir.'

'I'm delighted to hear it. And Lizzie Fenwick?'

'We're helping her cope with the pain, sir, and she's certainly improving.'

'Wonderful: well done, Mrs. Dean.'

The housekeeper curtseyed and left.

'By the time Agnes has really come back to her senses, sir, the fellow could be long gone,' said Robbins. 'And we don't even have a very good description, let alone a name for him.'

'I know. And we've done all the preparation work this morning. I think word will have travelled well.'

'Oh, definitely, definitely,' said Blair. 'All kinds of people were talking about it as I went around the kirkyard.'

'Yes. But still … You do know the road to Cupar, Walter, don't you?' Murray asked anxiously. Walter had been known to lose himself before he had left the servants' wing. Walter frowned.

'I think so, sir.'

'Walter, you've lived in Letho all your life, and you must have been to Cupar dozens of times,' said Robbins in unusual frustration. 'Surely you know the road to Cupar? At least the beginning of it.'

'Aye, sir, aye. At least, if someone points me in the right direction.'

'Oh, we'll do that, Walter, don't worry. And there will be people watching you. All you have to do is walk along looking tired, a bit slow, maybe, then stop at the milestone to rest.'

'The milestone near the woods, you said, sir?'

'That's right. He seems to like woods, this fellow, even if these ones are Dures woods and rather better looked after than the Collessie ones he's been calling home.'

'Aye, sir, I can do that fine.'

'I hope so.'

'Well, then, go back to the servants' quarters and get yourself something to eat, then go and see Jennet and she'll help you get ready.'

Walter bowed and left, and the men exchanged looks again. It could not be said that they felt confident, but it was hard to see how else they could flush out Agnes' captor. Robbins offered to fetch some food for them, too, and tea while they were waiting. Blair and Murray settled by the fire. Murray slumped back in his chair.

'I hope this works,' he muttered. 'And I hope Walter doesn't come to harm. Or lose his way. Do you know he has an aunt in the village who could apparently take on any man in a fight and better them?'

Blair smiled beatifically.

'Oh, yes, I've met Walter's aunt. If anything happens to Walter you have no hope,' he added calmly. Murray grinned, though it was a little forced.

'Well, then, perhaps the best we can hope for is everyone home safely by nightfall.' He sighed. 'Once this is all over, I hope never to have to live through a fortnight like it again.'

'There we are in complete agreement, dear boy,' said Blair with feeling, jiggling his knees. 'And if we have to keep Isobel from her morning rides for much longer no doubt there will be murder done in this house, too.'

'Don't joke about it!' pleaded Murray. 'I've had enough!'

The library bracket clock was hesitantly striking half past three when there was a gentle knock on the door and, at their summons, it slowly opened. Robbins pushed in first, then turned to present the character following him. A neat little demure maiden appeared, wearing a grey cloak and bonnet and some kind of skirts underneath, perhaps not of the conventional kind but presenting a fair outline of a girlish form. The creature glanced winningly out from under the bonnet, and became Walter, wary but dutiful, ready for action.

'How do you feel, Walter?' asked Murray, doing his best not to laugh. He could feel the first tendrils of hysteria clutching his chest.

'Quite well, thank you, sir. Tell me, though, sir, how do women move with all this cloth about them? It's like being caught up in an eiderdown, and about as warm.'

'Then be thankful it's October, and not July,' said Murray.

'And bonnets, sir: why would you want to go around with your head peeking out of a box?'

'That I don't know, Walter, not being in the habit of doing so. Are you otherwise ready?'

Walter sighed deeply.

'I believe so, sir.'

'Then off we go.'

Murray's reasoning, late last night with Macduff and Robbins and Blair, was that if the abductor knew Agnes was on her way to Cupar alone to meet Macduff and tell him all about her experiences, he would want to stop her again on the way and presumably abduct her again, whatever his mysterious reason for keeping her safe and warm and drugged out of her senses in the oak grove. Murray prayed that the man would want to abduct Agnes again, and not just finish her off.

A girl walking from Letho House to Cupar would go by the village path and pass through the patch of scrubby woodland beside the church, but as she would be there while it was still daylight they thought that an unlikely place to try to catch her. Then she would walk down through the village, past the inn – all fairly safe in daylight and normally, Murray thought crossly, through the night as well. Then she would turn left on to the Cupar road and carry on, past the turning to Josie's Den, and eventually come to the market town. Near the turning to the Den the roadway passed again through woodland, well kept but older and with reasonable undergrowth in places, particularly near the road where a rough and prickly hedge, made to look orderly by the addition of well-clipped beech, had been used by the Dures estate in place of a wall. Along this stretch the land rose and fell again, and at the highest point, where a smooth bank of grass rose to one side of the road, there was a milestone and a worn stone beside it which had been used for many years as a handy resting place for folks returning weary – or confused – from market. Anyone seated on it would have their back to the hedge, and low hanging branches overhead, and in the dusk would be in deeper shadow. It was a dark bit of the road at the best of times, the place the mail coach driver was most likely to flick up his reins and speed the horses on, where lonely travellers hesitated and looked about to see a likely person to walk with for a little human company. They reckoned that Walter would reach it around half past four, as the low sun was starting to set. He was then to wait there, and see what happened, keeping his head down and moving as much like Agnes as possible.

'Should I talk to myself, sir?' Walter asked just before setting out.

'I don't think so,' said Murray. 'We don't want people thinking you've gone mad.'

'It's just, I don't know. But she never stops talking when there's people around. I thought maybe she just never stops talking at all.'

'Let's say she's tired, Walter, and has finally run out of things to say.'

'All right, sir. I'm glad, for I don't think I could talk all that way myself.'

'Remember your road?'

'Aye, sir, through the village and right at the inn.'

'*Left* at the inn,' chorused Robbins, Murray and Blair. 'Right would bring you *right* back to the front gate,' added Robbins helpfully.

'Left at the inn,' Walter nodded, unperturbed. As far as he was concerned, his lack of any sense of direction was just one of those things, and nothing to worry about: he left that to everyone around him.

He picked up his skirts and teetered off along the path, down towards the village.

'At least he's started in the right direction,' muttered Robbins.

'Right, give him ten minutes and then off we go, too,' said Murray briskly. They went back inside to find outdoor clothing: the sun was shining but the day was bitingly chill.

Ten minutes later, Robbins and Blair appeared at the front door and closed it carefully behind them, then passed between the main house and the stinking remains of Robbins' own house towards the village path.

A moment or so later, Murray trotted round from the stables on his favourite mare, the spaniels at his heels, and clipped down the drive towards the front gate.

Walter trudged on across the fields and on to the village path, relieved to find it where he expected it. He kept his head down, and practised walking like Agnes, or what he thought might look like Agnes. It was probably fortunate that he did not meet anyone between Letho and the village.

The shadows lay long and dark across the autumn brightness of the village green, sombre with Sabbath quiet. There were few about, and he pattered down the east side to the inn at the bottom, and hesitated. Left or right? What had Mr. Robbins said? Left would have you left at the front gate? Did that make sense? He considered. No wonder Agnes had got lost, he thought. It was very confusing.

No, he suddenly remembered, right would take him right back to the front gate. He imagined Mr. Robbins would not be amused if he did that. He turned left.

Robbins and Blair reached the village a little later, and ambled down the west street as if they were out for a stroll. It was not unusual for Blair to keep company with servants of all kinds, so if anyone had been looking they would probably not have thought anything of it. At the bottom of the hill they, too, hesitated, bidding each other farewell. Blair squirreled off towards Dures House, past Widow Maggot's empty cottage, and Robbins made for the main road to Cupar. There he turned right, against all his previous advice, but in a moment ducked into a field on the far side of the road and doubled back, towards Cupar.

Murray, carrying out an impromptu but apparently thorough inspection of his estate wall, followed some way behind, walking his horse unhurriedly along the Cupar road. If he glanced ahead a little more often than was usual, perhaps he had his mind on other things.

Walter was tiring now, and he did not find it particularly difficult to imitate the gait of a weary girl who had spent the last few days drugged in a wood. His feet were dragging, and he felt the weight of the skirts very much, and the bonnet kept sliding on his head and perching at odd angles, much more felt by him than seen from the outside. His fingers were cold, and he spent some time praying that he was on the right road, interspersed with occasional anxiety that made him hope he was not. He reached the edge of the woodland: not a definite edge, but occasional trees and shrubs that seemed gradually to mesh together around the road. He shivered. Not far to go, he thought, and hauled his heavy skirts a little further.

Once on the drive beyond Dures gates, Blair caught sight of the factor and greeted him enthusiastically. He explained, in his usual rambling way, what he was up to, and the factor, always a sensible man, offered to come with him as a guide. He led Blair further up the drive and beyond the near edge of the woods that Walter was at that point approaching, and then showed him how to turn back into the woods again from the far, Cupar, side. Blair beamed, and followed him, brandishing his stick with enthusiasm.

Robbins made good time through the Letho fields beyond the hedges on the Cupar road. They had been ploughed and sown but the edges were grass and easily and quietly navigated. The road here marked the border between Dures land to the north and Letho land to the south, so the woods, when he reached them, were Letho woods on his side. He kept low and found a place where he could crouch comfortably and watch the road, and the milestone and resting stone on the other side of it. He had worn, like the others, his darkest clothes, and had pulled his collar up to hide his white neckcloth. With his hat tugged down to disguise his pale face, he made himself close to invisible. He waited.

Murray tried to pace himself, not too fast, not too slow, and eventually dismounted and led the horse along the grass at the edge of the road to dull the sound of her hooves. The spaniels were breathy and excited, but he managed to keep them behind the horse. Ahead he could see the woods, and in the dimming light he could just make out the little grey form of Walter, wearily scrambling up the bank to the resting stone and sinking on to it, bonneted head slouched.

Blair and Robbins could see it too, each from their vantage point in the woods. Walter was motionless, and so were they. Murray held his mare's muzzle and murmured soothing words to the spaniels. Nothing moved.

Blair saw him first. The man was tall and thin, with jet-black hair and a face that might have been pale had it not been quite so grubby. He came creeping through the woods from the direction of Dures, just as they had expected – or hoped. He looked like a man well used to creeping through woods, Blair thought, and was glad that he was lying low with the factor, well hidden. The man did not even glance in their direction.

Robbins saw him next: a vague face, one he could not even have identified, peering over the hedge within the woods, a few yards from where Walter was still slumped on the stone seat. His breathing tightened. The man leaned forward delicately, not wanting to brush against the hedge and make a sound, presumably. Walter did not even seem to be aware of him. Then the man disappeared. Would he be off to find a way around the hedge?

Blair watched the man as he pulled something from under his coat, and fiddled with it. What was it? The light in the woods was failing fast and it was hard to see. Then the man straightened, and leaned out again over the hedge. Blair gasped.

Robbins's breathing stopped. The man was making sure his captive would not run this time: he had a noose.

He dropped it skilfully so that it slipped right over the bonnet, and pulled hard back. Walter let out a yell, and from four sides men ran to him. There was a scramble, a cracking of hedges, a slither of boots on mud, and the spaniels barked fit to burst. In a moment, the dark Glaswegian was being held firmly by the Dures factor and Robbins, with Murray at his back with a hand in his collar, and Macduff informing him of his arrest.

Blair scuttled over to Walter, who was pulling the rope off his neck with an expression of disgust. He turned to face the Glaswegian.

'I dinna like you, sir. I dinna like you at all,' he announced. The Glaswegian's jaw dropped.

'But where is Agnes?' he demanded. 'You're no Agnes!'

'Dead right I'm not,' said Walter.

'You were right about the place, then, sir,' said Macduff to Murray, as they manhandled their captive down the slope to the road. Just around the corner, they could see now, was Macduff's little mule cart, as arranged.

'Thank goodness,' agreed Murray.

'But where's Agnes?' cried the Glaswegian. 'Where is she? I need to see her!'

'Whyfor would we let you see Agnes? No doubt you want to kill her, for she kens well all you've done,' said Macduff sourly. 'In Glasgow and here, too.'

'I'd never kill her!' cried the man. 'She's my very heart! Whatever I've done, that angel will forgive me!'

'Good heavens,' said Murray. 'Is that why you took such care of her?'

'Of course it is! And they said she was fine, she was better, and now it's not her at all, it's him!' He jerked his head at Walter, unable to point as his hands were being bound. 'Is it true? Is she all right?'

'You nearly killed her with your drugs,' said Murray coldly. 'No, she's not all right.'

The man set up a howl so dreadful and loud that they almost did not hear the approaching hooves until the horse was nearly upon them. It was Murray's groom, Dunnet.

'Sir!' he said, leaping down and giving Murray the trace of a bow. 'Sir, Dr. Harker says you're to come at once. It's Lady Agostinella, sir: her time has come.'

Chapter Twenty-Three

For a wonder, Daniel was waiting to open the door for him, and a stablelad was ready for the horse as Murray and the mare skidded to a halt outside Letho's low front door. Murray shot inside and galloped up the curving staircase three at a time. At the doorway to Agostinella's chambers, he was stopped abruptly with a hand to his chest. It was Isobel.

'No entry, I'm afraid,' she said coolly, though her face was flushed. 'Rest assured, Dr. Harker is here, Mrs. Grant is here, Mary is helping in the background, and Mrs. Helliwell is on her way, too.'

Murray could hear constant sobbing coming from the chamber beyond.

'What is *that*?' he hissed. Isobel rolled her eyes.

'Oh, that's just the Italian maid,' she said. 'She doesn't seem to have any function other than to sob. I offered to put her in a kist and leave her there, but it had no effect.'

'Apparently she doesn't understand English.'

Isobel raised her eyebrows, cynical.

'Is Agostinella all right?' he demanded.

'She's doing well so far,' said Isobel. 'Dr. Harker is pleased with her: her time hasn't come too early. You'll just have to be patient, I'm afraid.'

'How long does it take?'

Isobel laughed, not particularly kindly.

'Five minutes? Five hours? Five days? Who knows?'

Murray gave a sigh of exasperation. He wanted to shake her.

'Well, I'm home now and I'm not going out again. Call me if there's anything I can do.'

'Of course,' said Isobel, in a tone that implied there would be very little useful he could do. He restrained himself from further comment, and stamped back down the stairs. For a moment he paced along the hall, then back again, satisfied and irritated at once by the sound of his boots on the stone flags. He found he was knotting his fingers behind his back. He flung his hands out to his sides, tutted, and marched over to the door to the servants' quarters. Then he thought better of it, returned to the body of the hall, and rang for someone to come to him. Then he realised his mistake. Where was Robbins when he needed him? Presumably still on the Cupar road, taking part in the arrest of the Glaswegian – whose name he did not even yet know.

Daniel appeared at last.

'Sir?'

'Ah ...' Murray had to think of something. 'Brandy, please, Daniel, to the library.'

'Sir.'

Daniel vanished back into the servants' quarters, but now Murray could not go in until there was no chance of meeting Daniel coming out. He tapped his feet on the stone floor, and for a moment took pleasure in slowly kicking the bottom step of the stairs, quite hard, feeling the shock in his toes. Then he thought it was a little uncouth to be standing there waiting for Daniel, so he went to the library.

The fire was warm, too warm, really, and he realised he still had most of his outdoor layers on. No one was in there: Blair, of course, was also still on the Cupar road. He pulled off his cloak and muffler: he had no recollection of where he had tossed his gloves on his way in. After a moment, Daniel appeared with the brandy, and found Murray still on his feet, perusing the bookshelves as though he had never seen them before. Daniel left him to it.

Murray took a glass of brandy neat, and made himself sip it, while still scanning the bookshelves. There was nothing he was looking for, except for the solace of seeing old friends on the shelves. He heard Daniel retreat across the hall. His wife had produced – how many bairns now? They seemed to pop out like piglets. It couldn't be that hard, could it? But then Daniel's wife was plump and healthy and designed, it seemed, to do nothing but cook and give birth. Agostinella, though ... What had she been designed for? He could not imagine Agostinella giving birth: he shuddered at the thought, and the glass of brandy was suddenly empty.

The way must be clear now, if he was lucky. He left the glass, and tiptoed back across the hall, through the servants' door and up the stairs. He hesitated for a moment at the top of the stairs. Which way? Then he remembered, and in a moment was knocking gently on a door. Jennet's nervous voice answered.

'Come in?'

Murray stepped inside.

'I hope I'm not intruding,' he said. 'I wanted to see how Mrs. Fenwick was.'

Jennet had squeaked and turned pale at the sight of the laird in her humble room, but Mrs. Fenwick was more self-possessed.

'I'm improving all the time, thank you, sir, but you'll forgive me if I dinna curtsey.'

'I'd be alarmed if you did,' said Murray. He kept his voice down, hoping that no one else had yet worked out where Lizzie Fenwick was being sheltered.

'But what are you doing here, sir? You should be through in the house, not dandering around here! You could be needed at any moment.'

'I'll go back in a minute or two,' said Murray. 'Are you really feeling better?'

'Aye, indeed.' Her face was a healthier colour, though the lack of those black eyebrows was still discomfiting. 'Your housekeeper brews a good calming syrup.'

'So I hear,' said Murray wryly, thinking of the syrup that had been used on Agnes. 'Did Jennet tell you about the fire?'

'I did, sir,' said Jennet with unexpected nerve. 'I bring her all the news.'

'Good girl,' said Murray, seeing that she expected a pat on the head.

'Do you think it was me they thought they were after?' asked Lizzie. 'If that's the case, I should be away and make it clear I'm away. I dinna want Letho burned down and laid to my account.'

'We think,' said Murray carefully, 'that the men from the village may have thought Mary Robbins had something to do with witchcraft, too.'

'Mary Robbins?' Mrs. Fenwick was incredulous. 'Not a bit of it! She wouldna do a thing like that!'

'That was my feeling,' said Murray, 'and anyway, I trust Mrs. Robbins. It was a bad fire, though: they were lucky to get out alive.'

Lizzie Fenwick squirmed a bit in the bed, and her eyes showed pain. Jennet jumped up to attend to her.

'I'll heat some more of the syrup, Mrs. Fenwick,' she said, tucking the blanket over her.

'Aye, aye, do that, lass.' Lizzie Fenwick wriggled into the pillow. 'Itchy new hair,' she explained. 'But you'd better be getting back, Mr. Murray. You need to be there. You dinna ken when you'll be needed.'

'Needed! Ha,' said Murray, remembering Isobel's expression.

'Aye, aye, you'll be needed soon enough.' She had closed her eyes tight, and her voice grew thin as she gritted her teeth. 'Go on, now.'

'Well, I'll leave you in peace, at any rate,' said Murray, and turned to go. 'Good work, Jennet.'

'Thank you, sir,' said Jennet, eyes wide as a frightened rabbit. Murray checked the passage outside, and left quietly by the same stair, and in a moment was back in the library with his brandy.

Had he said thank you to Dunnett, the groom, for fetching him? He was not sure: he only remembered slithering into a stirrup and hauling himself up on to his mare's back and then the gallop back to the house. It was lucky he had not met any other traffic in the dusk.

Dunnett had been the one to bring him news of his father's accident, ten years ago now and more. Good old grumpy Dunnett.

He wondered if he would ever have a child to be told if he had an accident. What was happening upstairs?

He had still not managed to sit down, pacing about the bookshelves, when the door opened and Robbins appeared. He was wearing an old pair of boots he kept in his butler's room in the house for emergencies: presumably the boots he had been wearing were muddy and he now had no others.

'What news?' Murray demanded.

'Walter's back here safely: I brought him back myself in case of mishaps,' said Robbins. 'The collar of his cloak – Agnes' cloak – protected him from that noose, so he's fine.'

'And the Glaswegian?' Murray asked. He had expected news of Agostinella, but was trying to hide his surprise at Robbins' response.

'We got him into Macduff's cart. It was a good thing Macduff had brought one of his men with him: we had a fair struggle to keep him there, and in the end we had to tie his hands to the body of the cart. The man sat in the back with him, and Mr. Blair went with them, sir. He said to tell you he hopes that everything will go well, and he will be back as soon as he can.'

Murray grunted. Robbins gave him a guardedly sympathetic look: he too had done the pacing and worrying through the night.

'Sir, about dinner …'

'What about it?'

'You asked for it to be served late, sir, but it's late now and the dinner is ready. Mr. Grant and Lady Aytoun are waiting in the drawing room.'

'Oh, are they?' Murray struggled to remember what either of them was doing in his house. 'Then I suppose … I'm not the least bit hungry. Oh, now I say that, actually I'm starving. Yes, Robbins, dinner, by all means.'

'Should I ask Mrs. Grant and Miss Blair to come to the drawing room too?'

'Why?'

'It would not be quite proper, sir, for Lady Aytoun, otherwise.'

Murray considered. Dining with two men to whom she was not related: no, of course it would not be proper. Where was his head?

'Yes, yes, of course. Fetch them along. No reason why they should starve.'

'And I was to tell you, sir, that Mrs. Helliwell has arrived and is with Lady Agostinella, too.'

'It must be like a ball in the Assembly Rooms in there,' said Murray testily. 'Oh, tell the ladies no need to change, or we'll be here all night.'

'Very good, sir.'

Murray set down his brandy glass and went up to the drawing room, and greeted Lady Aytoun and Cousin Andrew absently. After a few minutes Mrs. Grant and Isobel joined them, and they went quickly through to the dining room. William and Daniel dispensed mulligatawny soup as if they had been waiting for some time. Murray had no sympathy for them.

The soup plates vanished, and William and Daniel began to replace them with the various dishes of the main course, arranged in the usual lozenge. The centrepiece was a side of beef, which

Cousin Andrew greeted with enthusiasm, fingers twitching on his cutlery. Murray, too, had a couple of healthy slices on his plate along with a dish of potatoes, and was helping himself to purple and yellow carrots when there was a sound of mild consternation from behind the screen that concealed the servants' door. Robbins appeared.

'Sir, Lady Agostinella would like you to attend her,' he said. Murray leapt up, trying to read his face. Good news? Bad news? He could not tell.

'Excuse me,' Murray said generally to his guests, and bolted out of the room.

'Mrs. Helliwell begged to say that both Mrs. Grant and Miss Blair were not to disturb themselves at present,' he heard as he left. Was that a good sign? A bad sign?

He ran up the stairs to the bedroom floor, back to Agostinella's chambers. His heart seemed to be beating in his ears as he burst through the door. The little Neapolitan maid was just inside the door, and shrieked. Mrs. Helliwell hurried out of the bedroom to see what was the matter.

'Oh, Mr. Murray! Thank you for coming. You're a wee goose, lass,' she added to the maid. 'She'll not stop greeting, and I've told her if she doesn't stop I'll give her something to greet about, but it does no good at all.'

'She only speaks Italian,' Murray explained automatically. Mrs. Helliwell favoured him with much the same cynical look as Isobel had done earlier. He followed her across the room.

'Thank you for coming so quickly,' she said again.

'But what's the matter? Is there news? What?' He knew he was gabbling but he could not seem to help himself.

'No, no, no news. It's only that Lady Agostinella wanted to speak to you.'

It was such an ordinary explanation that he felt quite taken aback, but he found himself shortly in Agostinella's bedchamber. Dr. Harker nodded to him from his position by the head of the bed, and Mrs. Dean was attending to a kettle of water over the fire. Murray looked about him for any sign of childbirth that a man without medical training ought not to be witness to, but Agostinella was well covered with bedclothes. She had her eyes closed and one skinny hand to her grey forehead, as if she was taking a rest in between whatever was happening.

'Mr. Murray, my lady,' said Mrs. Helliwell. Agostinella's eyes snapped open.

'How dare you bring that witch into this house! How could you do it?'

Dr. Harker jumped.

'Do not distress yourself so, my lady!' he cried. Murray wondered how she went from silence to screaming in so short a time. He knew Dr. Harker also spoke French, but was not sure if Mrs. Helliwell did.

'What witch?' he tried.

'The witch Fenwick!' She pronounced it 'Fenn-wig'. At this Mrs. Helliwell did blink, so he supposed she had not understood up to now. Mrs. Dean also seemed to freeze at her work. Everyone seemed to be waiting for what he would do next. He had never been so frightened in his life, he thought. Had anyone actually told her that Lizzie Fenwick was in the house, or was she guessing?

'But my dear,' he regained his nerve, and stepped forward to take her hand gently in his, 'you told me to remove her. How could you imagine I would have brought her back in?'

'Well,' she said, still loudly but less hysterically, 'she was not in the Robbins' house, was she? It was only Mrs. Robbins and the child, no witch. I was watching: you could not have deceived me.'

'Nor would I wish to, my lady.' It was typical of her, he thought, not to mention the little maid who had also been rescued: mere maidservants did not count. Witches, however, clearly did. 'Lizzie Fenwick is safe away from you.' Which of them was safe in this equation he was not quite sure: both, he hoped. 'But she is not a witch, you know: she attends women in childbirth, and lays out the dead –'

'And women who die in childbirth?' she gasped, pulling the two duties together much faster than he had hoped she would when he heard himself say the words.

'I daresay: we both know it happens. But it will not happen to you: not here, not tonight.' He made his voice soothing, giving up on the matter-of-fact practical line he wanted to take. 'Dr. Harker assures me you are fit and well. You have looked after yourself so well this time, and see how well you are doing!' He could hear how patronising he sounded, but already she seemed to be soothed, as if all she needed was his willingness to try. 'My lady, I am sure that all the strength of the de Cumaes and the de Palaeopolitanis are with you tonight: they will see you through.'

He watched as she drew something from this idea. Her eyes grew distant, no doubt thinking of her lines of dead ancestors, all the way back, she had often told him, to the ancient peoples who had hospitably allowed the Romans into Italy - never would she admit that they might have been persuaded in battle, for surely the de Cumaes and the de Palaeopolitanis could never be beaten! She pulled herself a little higher on the bed. Generations of her family had no doubt faced down much worse than witchcraft and childbirth. She would do the same.

'My dear,' he said, 'do you wish me to stay?'

'No,' she said, for he was a mere Murray of Letho: she had no need of that. 'These people seem to be very capable. I shall send word if I require you again.'

He bowed and kissed her hand as if it were a normal evening, and left the room. Dr. Harker discreetly followed, and caught up with him in the outer chamber.

'I hope she will not be excited again in that way, Mr. Murray,' he said, 'but we felt it necessary that you should reassure her in person. This witchcraft business has unnerved her, but now we can encourage her to relax a little more and see the matter through.'

'And will she be all right?' Murray asked. Dr. Harker smiled reassuringly.

'We can never be absolutely sure,' he said honestly, 'but I can tell you that thus far she has given me no cause for concern.' He nodded to emphasise it. 'Go and enjoy your dinner, Mr. Murray: Mrs. Dean will make sure none of us goes hungry, I'm delighted to say!'

'Very good: I'm glad to hear it. Call for me if there is anything at all I can do,' said Murray. He felt somewhere between flat and relieved, but still tense. His feet found the way back down to the dining room, slithering a little on the stair carpet, holding the banisters for support. Witches, childbirth, fire raising, seduction, kidnap, drugs and beatings: his head was spinning and the last thing he wanted to do was to rejoin his guests for dinner. But he found himself opening the dining room door, nevertheless, and at his appearance Daniel produced his plate from under a cover and replaced it at his place. He sat and began to eat, as if he had never gone away.

The pudding course was brought in, surmounted by Mrs. Mack's latest creation, a sugar swan. Murray was unaware of any conversation on any sensible level: if asked later, he would have said that no one spoke at all. He wondered vaguely why Lady Aytoun was dressed in mourning, and then distantly remembered that someone must have told her about Tilly. Daughter dead and husband in prison: good enough reason to wear black, he thought. Mrs. Grant was looking anxious. On Agostinella's account? Or on her own son's? Children were a bit of a liability, he thought. Perhaps it was almost better not to have them, not to lay oneself open. A bit late now, perhaps: by the end of the night he might indeed be a father.

Lady Aytoun stood up abruptly, swayed, and clutched at the table, toppling the sugar swan which fell, with considerable grace, into a blackberry fool. Mrs. Grant rose and seized her about the waist, and led her out of the room. Murray and Cousin Andrew had not even had time to stand.

'What?' asked Murray generally.

'She was drinking too much wine, I believe,' said Isobel. 'It was her first time down to dinner: I think she just found it all too much.'

'I was trying to make her ease off, but I couldn't quite manage,' said Cousin Andrew who had been sitting the other side of her. Murray, on her left, had not even noticed.

'A shame about the swan,' Isobel remarked, and leaned forward to break off a piece of its golden wing, flavoured with blackberries.

No one bothered with the drawing room in any formal sense, except that the best fire was there. Cousin Andrew sat with a book and Isobel toyed with the piano, but not for very long. Mrs. Grant reappeared.

'I've left her with her maid. Such a pity,' she said quietly. 'She has no strength of character to cope.'

'Very sad,' agreed Cousin Andrew, with a wry face. Murray wondered how much strength of character the two of them required to cope with Robert Lovie. What were they to do with him?

'You have the miscreant who took Tilly in prison, I believe?'

Mrs. Grant asked Murray. He tried to pull himself together.

'I believe so: we trapped someone who was certainly interested in taking Agnes back into captivity, and the sheriff's man has taken him to Cupar. I don't even know his name.' He told, briefly, what they had done on the Cupar road.

'Gracious!' said Mrs. Grant. 'I hope your servant boy was unharmed.'

'Very cross, but yes, unharmed,' Murray assured her.

'Splendid. Well, I'm afraid I should just like to retire for the night, if you will excuse me,' she said, which of course meant that Isobel had to retire, too. Cousin Andrew sat reluctantly.

'Do you want company, cousin? I've never been in the position you are in, but if you want someone to talk with …'

'It's fine, thank you very much,' said Murray with a smile. 'I shall retreat to the library and await news.' He felt better now, anyway: the food seemed to have helped and even he was reassured by the thought of Agostinella's ancestors all cheering her on. Well, no doubt they would never have done anything so undignified as cheering, but the sentiment was there.

The library was still cosy, and he stoked up the fire and poured himself another brandy, and settled in one of the armchairs with a book almost randomly selected from the shelves. He read a chapter or two, then laid the book down and stared, glazed, into the fire for a few minutes. He picked the book up again, and started on the next chapter. He had read three pages before he realised that he had no idea what was on any of them. He sighed, pushed himself up out of the seat, and took a turn around the room.

And that was how he spent the hours of the night. He paced about the library, dozed in the chair, stared into the fire, allowed his eye to run down pages of incomprehensible text, and occasionally wandered, soft-footed, into the hall and stood at the bottom of the stairs, straining to hear any possible noise from anywhere above him. The servants left him alone: indeed, they had probably long gone to bed, Robbins over in Thalland's house with Mary and the bairn, the rest of them cosy in the servants' wing, along with Lizzie Fenwick with her calming syrup and Agnes fighting to recover from something similar. He sighed, and poured another glass of brandy.

He must have dozed off more completely for he woke to see

the fire had died down to a glowing cave amongst dark wood ash, smelling smoky. A noise had roused him, and he straightened and looked about him, blinking in the dim light. The candles had all burned down. He was just replacing one and lighting it from the fire when the door opened and Blair appeared, bouncing with horrible energy.

'My dear boy, no news?'

'Nothing yet,' Murray assured him. He assumed they would have woken him. 'Are you just back from Cupar?'

'That's right. Have you been asleep? It's around half past six, you know.' There was a faint reprimand in Blair's voice: he never slept long.

'Half past six? Then the staff are up and about?'

'Oh, yes. Daniel let me in just now.'

'Have you spent the night in Cupar, then?' Murray asked stupidly. His mind had not quite caught up, fogged with too much night time brandy.

'Yes, yes, well, most of it. The inn we were at for the Presbytery furnished me with a bed for part of the night, certainly. And a very fine broth, I must say, very fine indeed.'

'Any news of the Glaswegian?'

'There was nothing for a good while,' said Blair sadly. 'I went with Macduff and his man, as Robbins no doubt told you. The Glaswegian was wild, quite unreasonable. It was undoubtedly him who took Agnes: he sees it in a different light, of course, but does not deny it in the least.'

'He seems to think they were in love?' Murray remembered.

'That's right. Though he is not able to explain why, then, she had to be drugged, or why she might have left him and hidden at Rintoul's landlady's house. He becomes a little confused over points like that.'

'Is he calmer now?'

'Well, he's asleep. He raved for most of the night – or not raved, exactly, for he made some sense if you didn't know that there was another version of events.'

Murray heard footsteps outside on the hall flags, approaching the door. His heart wobbled.

'Did you find out his name, in the end?' he asked, trying to ignore them.

'Oh, yes, yes!' said Blair. 'He is a Peter Cahill.'

At the same moment, the door opened. It was Mrs. Dean. She stopped on the threshold.

'I beg your pardon, sir,' she said, 'but I know that name. It is the name of my old mistress' brother – the lady for whom Agnes also worked.'

'Is it? Is it indeed?'

'Not that common, either,' said Murray rapidly. 'Mrs. Dean, did you want something?'

'Yes, indeed, sir. You're wanted upstairs, sir, straightaway.'

For the third time, Murray leapt up the stairs and ran to Agostinella's door. What would it be this time? Soothing music? More rants about witches? He hurried inside.

The room was oddly silent. Then he heard a cry – a young, tiny cry.

Mrs. Helliwell came to meet him, holding a small white bundle. She offered it to him with a look he could not read.

'Your daughter, Mr. Murray.'

His legs seemed to lose all strength, but he gently took the bundle. Inside it was of course a baby: he gave a stupid grin at his own daftness. What had he expected?

'Is she – is she all right?'

The baby looked up at him with wide blue eyes. Little lips pursed contemplatively.

'She's perfect,' said Mrs. Helliwell. 'And she has been yelling fit to burst, so there is nothing wrong with her lungs, either. But …' She backed to one side, and Dr. Harker approached. Murray's heart sank. Mrs. Helliwell took hold of the baby and relieved him of her as he went forward towards Agostinella's bedchamber.

'She doesn't have long,' said Dr. Harker quietly. 'She has lost far too much blood. I'm so sorry.'

'That's … that's …' He knelt down by Agostinella's side, and took her hand. She was breathing, but so shallowly he could hardly see. The maid was sobbing so hard it was difficult to hear anything else. 'My dear,' he said.

She half-opened her eyes.

'The child – it is alive?'

'Alive and well. A daughter. A beautiful daughter.'

Agostinella's breath hushed out in a little sigh, and there was the least smile on her lips.

'Another generation,' she breathed, her eyes closed. He waited for her to breathe in again, waited until he had to breathe himself, but she did not. Dr. Harker leaned past him, and tried her wrist and her throat, and shook his head.

'She is gone. Charles, I am so very sorry.'

Murray kissed Agostinella's hand for the last time, then stood.

'I think she knew it was going to happen,' he said quietly. 'She knew.'

He looked down at her, grey and thin amongst the tormented bedclothes, then turned away and took his daughter back from Mrs. Helliwell. She was so light, so tiny: he prayed that she would be strong, not a replica of her mother. He walked to the window, where the curtains and shutters had been flung wide to the sight of the dawn. She lay thoughtful in his arms, staring up at him as if memorising him. Suddenly she had a look of his father about her, and he grinned down at her. Another generation, he thought, but not only of the de Cumaes and the de Palaeopolitanis. Another generation of Murrays, too.

He held her close and gazed out at the frost-spiked lawns outside. Then he blinked. There was a movement amongst some bushes, and as he watched, the white hare loped out and paused, staring up at the window, at him, at his daughter. He could have sworn she nodded. Then she stretched, and leapt away – not as smoothly as she had once done. She was limping badly, he saw, so he had not imagined her terrible injuries. But at least she was active: he liked the idea that she was around, somehow. It felt safe.

Chapter Twenty-Four

Scuff, scuff, thump. Scuff, scuff, thump.

Mrs. Mack was working pastry, spinning and pressing it with her capable little hands. It was not going well.

She sniffed, and blinked her beady eyes. For once she was alone in the kitchen: it would be a busy day, and the rain was on, melting the early frost. Scuff, scuff, thump: she sniffed again, and batted her button nose with the back of her sleeve. She had barely known her Ladyship: seen her at church, perhaps, when she went, but never had her Ladyship set foot in her kitchens. But Mrs. Mack was a lover of order, a fearer of change. A death meant change. Scuff, scuff, thump. She stopped and inspected the pastry, and lifted it from the floury board. It flaked away like the autumn leaves outside, damp in some places and crumbling in others. Never had she made a worse batch of pastry. She folded it and scrumpled it into a ball, and began working it again. Scuff, scuff, thump, scuff, scuff thump. And Mr. Murray's poor wee bairn, an orphan after only a few minutes' life: a father was never the same as a mother. A daughter, too: poor wee lamb. Not the son Mr. Murray must have longed for.

Scuff, scuff, thump. She stopped and peered at the lump again. She seemed to have been working at it for hours. It looked like it, too: it had taken on a grey hue, lumpy, cracking. She sighed, scraped it off the table and slipped off the stool to deposit it in the pig bin in the scullery. She waddled back to the table, poured more flour into a mixing bowl, cut the end off a dish of butter, and started again.

'Aye, seems like they've got someone! That Mr. Blair from Letho House, Dod down the inn saw him coming back from Cupar at the skraik of dawn, in one of yon Macduff's carts, looking gey pleased with himself. And Dod says Mr. Blair was down at the inn yesterday having a crack with the sheriff's man, and then Macduff headed off back to Cupar very smartly.'

'Well, maybe yes and maybe no,' said Mal's friend Watson, always cautious. 'Who do they say has been arrested?' Mal had a sick feeling in his throat, though he could not have said why, but

Melville who had brought the news was full of the thrill of gossip. Despite the rain, he was holding them captive by the green.

'I don't know, but I know they found Agnes alive yesterday and she was well enough to tell everything she knew.'

'Yes,' Mal snapped, 'we all ken that. She was to go off yesterday afternoon and tell Macduff all about it.'

'That's right.' Melville subsided a little: he had forgotten that that was general knowledge. 'But I reckon the kidnapper went after her and they caught him trying to kidnap her again.'

'Why would he want to kidnap her again?' asked Mal, though even to himself he sounded wabbit, truculent. He was tired, he thought: it had been a stressful couple of weeks. And the rain was growing heavier.

'Well, that's a good question,' said Watson. 'Why would he want to kidnap her again? She's no rich nor anything.'

'She might have seen him murder Mathilda Aytoun?' suggested Melville in a moment of inspiration. 'In that case he might have been trying to kill her, too?'

'Ach, who kens a'thing?' said Mal bitterly. 'Some of us have work to do, Melville. I'm away to get on with it.'

Lizzie Fenwick opened her eyes and blinked at the dawn light shivering through the cracks in the shutters. Jennet was snoring inoffensively on a mattress on the floor, blankets heaped over her. Lizzie's hand came up slowly from beneath the covers and her strong fingers stroked her bristly head, still curious at the unfamiliar feeling. She rubbed her eyebrows, hoping, with a silent laugh at herself, that it might encourage the regrowth. She touched her bruises, and tentatively felt the worst injured parts of her broken leg. Then she smiled broadly: she could feel her strength coming back. Now she needed to talk to Mrs. Dean.

Mary Robbins was making the bed in her temporary accommodation, upstairs in Thalland the factor's house. With practical serenity, she flicked and stretched sheets and blankets, making everything neat and tidy, keeping up an easy commentary to the bairn who sat on the floor beside the window. The bairn was marching the precious wooden elephant back and forth, but he glanced up to interrupt her.

'Tha an t-uisge ann.'

'Tha,' she agreed, hearing the rain on the window. 'Aye, it's raining.'

'Tha an t-uisge ann!' the bairn said again firmly, bashing the elephant on the wooden floor to emphasise his point. Mary looked round. Drips of water were descending on the bairn's head from a growing crack in the ceiling. Her face in a twist of disbelief at their run of luck, Mary picked up the bairn and the elephant, pushed the bed back as far as it would go from the crack, and went downstairs to find Thalland and a bucket. She heard the plaster crash behind her.

'Augusta,' said Murray, still gazing at his daughter, memorising her face, her eyes, her tiny curling hands.

'Augusta? Not bad,' said Isobel.

'You're so kind,' said Murray, with a faint grin. Augusta pursed her lips and blew a very faint raspberry.

'The wetnurse is here,' said Mrs. Helliwell, with a hand on Murray's arm. Reluctantly, he handed little Augusta over to her. 'She's lovely,' she assured him. 'A wee darling.'

'The wetnurse?' queried Isobel.

'The wetnurse is Ninian Jack's daughter Sarah,' said Mrs. Helliwell. 'Neither wee nor particularly darling, I agree, but decent and clean and reliable.' She gave Isobel a look that was designed to remind her to behave herself, and took Augusta out of the room. Murray watched them go, and then jumped: something dark had moved at the corner of his eye. He looked about, half expecting one of Daniel's galloping infants, but he and Isobel were alone in the parlour, and even the spaniels were flung motionless on one armchair, where they had no right to be.

Isobel settled back to her drawing: she had a quick sketch on the paper of Augusta in Murray's arms, but felt it could be improved upon. Murray sagged on to a sofa, elbow on the padded arm and chin in his hand, his eyes almost too tired to close. He was exhausted, and he had a funeral to organise. How he felt about that funeral he was not yet prepared to say, even to himself.

He dozed for a little, comfortable and warm, and was eventually woken by Robbins' polite throat-clearing. Murray opened leaden eyes and glared at him.

'Sir, I have your mourning black laid out upstairs, when you are ready.' Murray shuddered. Mourning for two years, full mourning for one, and no dancing. Oh, well. 'And there's a small problem, sir. If you don't want to know we can deal with it, but I thought you would probably like to know what is going on.'

'A small problem? That sounds like a refreshing change. No murders, witch hunts, houses burning down, deaths of wives?' He tried to smile, and managed something like one. 'You might as well tell me: I'll need to know some time.'

'It's Mr. Thalland's house, sir: the roof is leaking badly.'

'Is that a new thing? I don't remember anyone mentioning last week when the gutters were being cleared.' He pulled himself upright and looked around. Isobel had gone, and he had been sleeping alone in the warm parlour.

'I think the gutter clearing might have been a contributing factor, sir. The men were interrupted clearing Mr. Thalland's gutter and didn't have the chance to look at the roof, and when they came back to finish the job the ladders had gone, apparently.'

There was the least emphasis on the word 'apparently' that made Murray think.

'Weren't they there when we needed them during the fire?'

'That's right, sir.'

'That's a bit odd – if true.'

'Mm.'

'So – well, now where are you staying?'

'Well, we were wondering, sir, if it would be all right if we took two rooms up on the nursery floor for now? The ceiling has come down and the house is soaking. And with Mrs. Fenwick in Mrs. Chambers' old cottage, there isn't another house free nearby.'

'Thalland too? Of course.'

Fleetingly he thought this was not a bad thing: he had drawn Lizzie Fenwick into the house, and now the Robbins and Thalland, too. He felt the least bit like Noah, gathering people into the ark. Even the spaniels came in twos. The rain helped, too.

For a moment the only sound in the room was the crackling of the fire, and the constant purring of the rain on the windows, turning the grey-brown world outside into sliding vertical stripes. It was mid-morning, he discovered, looking at the mantelpiece clock. It looked like dusk. At last he stood up and stretched.

'Mourning, right, then. Is there any hot water?'

'Of course, sir. I'll just be a few minutes.' Robbins bowed and went out, and Murray stared for a few seconds at the rain before heading upstairs to his chamber.

On the mantelpiece lay the mirror, still on its back as presumably Mrs. Dean had left it. He had hardly been up here since: Saturday night had been spent mostly in the library with Blair and Macduff after they had brought Agnes back, and Sunday night too he had based himself there. He approached the mirror very warily, and almost skimmed over it with a glance, as if anything more direct would find him trapped in the reflection. He saw nothing. He picked it up between two fingertips, and set it upright again, wiping his fingers as if the thing was contaminated. It reflected the room, coolly, challenging him to find anything wrong with it. Soon it would be covered anyway, like all the other mirrors in the house, until after Agostinella's funeral. He shivered. What on earth was wrong with him, scared of a mirror? Whatever it was, he did not feel easy about taking a catnap in the room, which had crossed his mind. He blew out through loose lips to make a resigned noise, and thought he had been spending too much time with Blair. Blair had taken the box and the bowl from Widow Maggot's house: he wondered if there had been any trouble with them?

Blair had removed his outer layers to snooze for a couple of hours, and then he was ready to take on a new day. His man Smith shaved his mobile face and brought him the dish into which each night Smith decanted the inanimate contents of Blair's capacious pockets, and allowed him to select what would be placed in the pockets of today's coat. It was usually, in Smith's experience, around nine-tenths of what had been removed from yesterday's coat. Smith was strangely proud of Blair's eccentricities and his own manner of dealing with them.

Smith had already seen to it that the sheriff's man's man, as he thought of him, the fellow who had brought Blair back from Cupar at dawn, had been woken and given sustinence to console him for a lack of sleep. When Blair bounced down the stairs and out the front door, conceding to events by wearing a darker than usual waistcoat, the man was already waiting outside with the cart, discreetly munching on a heel of hot bread. He did not really mind being put out for Mr. Blair: the old gentleman was always interested in the opinions of lesser folk like him, and the man liked talking. He set the bread down to hoist Blair on to the cart, and off they went at a trot.

Macduff was an early riser, too, and was already in the room he used as an office when Blair arrived.

'Ah,' he said without preamble. 'That's grand. I was going to take another look at the prisoner. Peter Cahill, that is.'

'I bring you a little news on that score,' said Blair eagerly. 'Though I do not know indeed if it is significant or even a genuine connexion, nevertheless it is a possibility and I feel you should know.' He stopped with a satisfied look, his loose lips meeting in a smack.

'And what might the news be, then, sir?' asked Macduff after a patient moment.

'Oh! Oh, well, it is that the brother of the woman that Mrs. Dean and then Agnes worked for in Glasgow, Mrs. Dean only until the husband died and then Agnes afterwards not in Glasgow at all of course but in Paisley, was called Peter Cahill.'

'The husband?' Macduff was lost.

'No, no, the brother.'

'Right,' said Macduff, finding his way again. 'So a Peter Cahill, not necessarily this one, but possibly this one, was the brother of Agnes' mistress in Paisley that was murdered and she came on the body?'

'Yes!'

'And this one certainly has a voice that would make you think he was from that part of the world, though he has not said so.'

'He does, doesn't he?' Blair said in delight.

'Anything else, before we go and talk to him again?'

Blair pursed his lips.

'I don't think so. Only that Lady Agostinella has died giving birth to Murray's daughter, so he won't be able to come here today.'

'Oh!' Macduff made customary sympathetic remarks, though he thought it a little strange that these facts had just been tacked on at the end. No doubt about it: Mr. Blair was an oddity.

The prisoner was in a cell that even after a night of occupation smelled fresh and scrubbed. The prisoner himself had a light fragrance of leafmould and mud mixed with sweat, though his coat had been taken away to be examined and he was wrapped in a grey blanket. He rose politely when they entered, until Macduff waved him back down to the low wooden bed. His face was naturally fair under the layer of dirt from outdoors living, his hair and brows almost black, and his eyes a startling blue under dark lashes. He looked, Blair thought, friendly, and just a tiny bit vacant.

'Have you any food about you?' he asked. 'I'm gey hungry.'

'You've had your breakfast,' said Macduff in surprise.

'Oh.'

The man looked disappointed, but Macduff was unconcerned.

'So you admit you took Agnes Carstairs and hid her in the woods at Collessie?' the sheriff's man began.

'Aye, that's right,' said Cahill, quite content. 'She's my best girl.'

'You gave her some drugs? Some kind of syrup?'

Cahill frowned, but it turned out to be concern for Agnes rather than for himself.

'Aye, you asked me that afore. She wasna sleeping well and I had the stuff from – from before.'

'You gave her a terrible amount of it, man,' said Macduff.

'Did I? Maybe it gets stronger as it gets older,' he said innocently, though it seemed to Blair that he knew what he was about more than he was admitting.

'Who made the syrup?'

'Och, an old woman I used to know.'

'An old woman in Glasgow, perhaps?'

Cahill met his eye.

'Those parts, aye,' he said eventually.

Macduff cleared his throat, and tried to ignore Blair jiggling next to him.

'Did you give the same syrup to Mathilda Aytoun, then?'

'Who?' Cahill looked blank.

'The other young woman. The tall one with dark hair.'

Cahill laughed ruefully.

'Oh, aye, she was a right pain! But the syrup didna seem to work on her.'

Mathilda Aytoun was clever enough, thought Blair: no doubt

she had managed to spit it out rather than swallow it. Macduff may have thought the same for he did not pursue that point.

'Why did you take her to the woods? She wasn't your best girl too, was she?'

Cahill laughed again at this whimsical thought.

'Naw, Agnes is the only girl for me. And I didna take the other lassie into the woods. She came to us. In the middle of the night, too. She said she was lost, but I dinna ken. Anyway, I tried to help her sleep, too, for it didna seem right for a lady to be wandering round in the woods in the middle of the night when she should have been safe and warm in her ain bed.'

'True enough. But the syrup didn't help her sleep. Is that why she left?' asked Macduff, trying to sound casual. Cahill frowned, as if he was trying to remember.

'I'm no sure. I came back early one morning and she was away, but I followed her and I found her. She said – she said something about telling, telling people she'd found Agnes ...' He drifted off, staring past them at the wall. His eyes were glazed, and it took a moment for them to clear.

'And what happened then?' asked Macduff softly.

'I – she was – she was lying on the ground, so I wrapped her up in her cloak. I wasna sure what to do with her: I mean, it wasn't like the witch down in the village, she was in her ain home and all. And then when I thought of the witches, I thought maybe that would be the best place for her. That place where the witches are supposed to go. Someone told me about it. I took her there.' He sounded very vague all of a sudden.

'How did you get her there? It's a long way: you must be very strong.' Macduff's voice was soothing, as if Cahill were a sick man, a dying man. As well he might be.

'Someone lent me a cart, I think. A handcart. Would that be it? I dinna ken ... And I laid her out for the witches, for I thought it would please them.'

'With rabbit bones?'

Cahill nodded, still miles away. They let him sit for a minute, and then Macduff leaned forward and laid a heavy hand on his shoulder. Cahill jumped, and looked up, focussing abruptly. He put a hand to his forehead, as if wiping away a weariness that lingered there. His sleeve slipped.

'That's a nasty cut,' said Macduff sympathetically. The gash was on the lower side of his forearm, where the skin was bare and pale. The upper side was thick with black hair. Cahill fingered the cut: it was a couple of inches long, and looked deep, but was already healing well.

'Aye ... I tellt you the syrup didna work on her.'

'Mathilda Aytoun did that to you?'

'Aye, wi' a wee tiny pair of scissors. I didna even ken she had them there. They were wicked. Well ...' he tailed away again, perhaps not quite remembering what had happened to the wicked pair of scissors after that. Macduff and Blair knew: they were locked in a drawer in Macduff's room.

'Do you have a sister at all?'

Cahill hunched, and dropped his gaze.

'Naw, naw, I dinna.'

'Did you ever?'

There was a long pause.

'See,' said Cahill at last, 'she didna approve of Agnes and me. It was none of her business.'

'But Agnes worked for her, didn't she? As her maid?'

'What does that have to do with it? Agnes was my best girl, whatever she was in my sister's world.' He reflected for a moment. 'Katie had no right to butt in.'

'That'd be Katie Cowley?'

'Aye, aye.' He seemed unsurprised that they knew. On the other hand, he must have thought that Agnes was awake and talking. He was much more alert now himself.

'Tell me,' said Blair at last, 'how did you find out that Agnes would be on the Cupar road last night?'

Cahill's face broke into a wide, clever smile, his blue eyes shining.

'Oh,' he said, 'my friends told me.'

'What friends? Who do you know around here?'

'I have all kinds of friends,' said Cahill, cunning. 'All fine upstanding citizens. Members of the Kirk Session, even!'

Blair had been there as the Kirk Session had vanished from the churchyard on Sunday morning.

'People like Mr. Johnstone?' he asked quickly, 'And Mr. Watson?'

'Aye!' Cahill looked gleeful. 'Mr. Johnstone's my particular friend. He listens to everything I say!'

Macduff and Blair exchanged a look.

'Even when you tell him about witches?' asked Macduff, quite as if he did not care.

Cahill crowed with laughter.

'Isn't it a great joke? I tell a few folk about witches, and the whole village is in a panic! And I only thought of it by chance – but I was gey clever to use it like that,' he told them seriously.

'Yes, yes you were,' said Macduff, as if impressed. 'You had us all running around looking for witches. Tell me, what made you think of it?'

'That old woman at the end of the village,' said Cahill instantly, keen to show off. 'She was a witch, you know. That's why I went there.'

'Was that why you killed her? Because she was a witch?'

'Naw, I've nothing agin witches. But she could find out who I was and where I came from easy enough, and that was no good.'

'How could she find out? By witchcraft?'

'She's pals with Mrs. Dean that's the housekeeper where Agnes is, and Mrs. Dean worked for Katie.'

'Mrs. Dean and the Widow Maggot were friends?'

'Aye, aye. The Widow kenned Agnes was at the big house, so that was useful. I kenned where to start looking for her, and as soon as it was dark I went up for a keek through the windaes.'

'Up a ladder?' asked Blair thoughtfully.

'Well, there was one lying there, I thought I might as well use it,' said Cahill reasonably.

'What made you go to the Widow in the first place?' Macduff did not see how ladders were relevant.

'Och, Katie kenned her frae years ago. She would stay there if she was ever up this way. Like I always say, all witches together! How do you think I had the syrup for Agnes? It's brilliant!'

Macduff and Blair exchanged glances again. Was he saying his dead sister was a witch? Witches everywhere.

'I have something I need to do just now,' said Macduff thoughtfully. 'We'll be back later, Cahill.' He stood up, easing his bad leg. Cahill nodded, still grinning, then a fresh anxiety seemed to strike him. He seized Macduff's arm, his blue eyes darkening.

'Tell me why you tricked me? Why did you send that wee lad instead of Agnes?' He was abruptly almost in tears, Blair saw in surprise.

'Well, we couldn't send Agnes,' said Macduff, in a hard voice. 'She's still unconscious. Your brilliant syrup nearly killed her.'

Chapter Twenty-Five

When Murray was washed and changed, he made himself go to Agostinella's chambers. The maid had disinterred, from some hidden chest, a shroud that Murray wondered for a moment if he had seen before. So many of Agostinella's clothes had looked like something from a graveyard that it would not have surprised him, but the maid confided, in tear-strewn Italian, that she and her ladyship had stitched it together before she had departed Naples for India, and they had kept it close since. Dust and ashes, he thought, looking down on his dead wife in the dim candlelight. Could she ever have been different? Would little Augusta have brought a smile to her face, joy to her heart? Or would she only ever have stayed in the shadows, seeing only death in life? He had heard of some religious people who slept in their coffin every night to keep them aware of their mortality: he had a feeling Agostinella would have liked that, if she had not also been quite attached to a level of luxury appropriate to her standing in society. A silk-lined coffin, perhaps.

Should he try to find a Papish priest? he thought suddenly. She had been brought up under the rule of the Roman church, anyway. But she had never made much of the matter since her arrival in Letho. He had always had the impression that the de Cumae de Palaeopolitanis considered that their ancestry predated such modern nonsense as the church, and had their own systems of worship – chiefly ancestor worship – so that it mattered little where they went on a Sunday. He smiled, and then hurriedly made his face straight again: the maid would doubtless not approve.

The maid …

'Nina,' he said, reluctantly examining her wet face again. 'It's early to think of plans, I know, but have you considered what you are to do now? After all, Lady Agostinella was your sole purpose here. Will you want to return to Naples? If so, of course I shall meet the expense of your journey.'

The sobs grew harder, and the maid's shoulders vibrated like those of a bad rider at a trot. She drew near to the bed again, though she could hardly have made out Agostinella's features through her tears.

'I can never leave her dear corpse!' he managed to make out. 'I shall die here!'

'Not immediately, I devoutly hope,' said Murray politely. 'Well, let me know what you would like to do when things have settled down a little.'

He took a seat, and sat for a while in silence, as would be expected of him. Agostinella dead, he thought. He tried very hard to keep the word 'freedom' out of his mind. They had learned, to an extent, to accommodate each other, he supposed. And she had finally given him a daughter. He reflected on the shadow of their short marriage. She had had no kind of singing voice, only a reedy soprano, he thought, but she had at least been musical, playing the violin and the clarinet with unusual skill. When they had played the slow movement from Mozart's clarinet concerto together, he could almost persuade himself that he loved her.

Outside the shuttered windows, he could hear the rain beating harder now: the wind must be rising. The panes rattled as if in agreement. He hoped Blair would get back safely and not too wet. Mrs. Helliwell had told him that she had sent a message to her husband, so no doubt Mr. Helliwell would be at the house soon, offering times for a funeral, if the rain was not forbidding. Melville would no doubt oversee the opening of the grave in the kirkyard where Murray's mother and grandparents were buried, and his great grandparents, too, clustered together, companionable. What would they make of a resentful Neapolitan amongst them? Of course, she would never lower herself to speak to them anyway. He stifled a yawn. He was growing fanciful in his fatigue.

The room was chilly but somehow stifling, thick with the smell of the fusty old flowers Agostinella had used to fragrance it and the constant fires she had kept burning there even in the height of summer. At last he could bear it no longer: he rose and left, knowing he would have to spend hours there before the funeral, greeting mourners. He wondered if he could persuade the maid to open a window for a bit. Perhaps not just now, though, he thought, as the rain suddenly lashed the windows. He wondered how bad Thalland's house was, and decided he had better go and find Thalland for a full report.

Downstairs he was about to ring for Robbins to find out where Thalland was, when the doorbell rang. He opened the door himself, and found on the doorstep Mr. Helliwell, escorted by the angular form of Mr. Rintoul, their black shoulders smudged with white.

'It's turning to sleet,' said Helliwell crossly as he hurried past Murray into the hall. Robbins appeared and quickly took hats and coats. 'Very sorry for your loss, Mr. Murray, of course.'

'Sorry for your loss, sir,' echoed Rintoul quickly.

'Rintoul's last experience with a funeral was of course Widow Maggot, and he wasn't there at the kisting, so I hope you don't mind ...' Helliwell was businesslike: no doubt it was common knowledge that the laird and his lady had not been close.

'Not at all,' said Murray. 'Shall we go to the library? I believe the fire is lit. Robbins?'

'Yes, sir. I'll see to refreshments, sir.'

'Thank you.' Murray led the clergy into the library. 'You find us all in some confusion, Mr. Helliwell: besides Lady Agostinella's death and the birth of my daughter –'

'Oh, aye, congratulations,' interrupted Mr. Helliwell quickly, followed again by an echo from Mr. Rintoul. His hair was at all angles, and he seemed more subdued than usual.

'Thank you. You may have heard that a man was arrested yesterday afternoon for kidnapping Agnes, and perhaps also for murdering Mathilda Aytoun?'

'There are rumours, Mr. Murray, but no, I had not heard specifically. Who is the man?'

'We think he is the Glaswegian who committed the murder she came upon before she came here.'

Mr. Rintoul let out an unexpected sob.

'It's all my fault! I should have helped her when she came to me!'

'Aye, you should,' said Helliwell sourly. 'But it's no use greeting over spilt milk. Pull yourself together and try to be useful.'

Strangely this seemed to have something like the desired effect, and there were no more sobs. Robbins arrived with tea and tea loaf.

'I have let Mrs. Helliwell know you are here, sir,' he informed the minister, and left.

'Aye, aye,' said Helliwell, stretching his feet out comfortably to the fire. 'Well, you'll want to talk about the funeral, no doubt.'

'Yes, probably best,' agreed Murray. He was glad Mr. Helliwell was not being over-sympathetic: he was not sure he could have coped with that at the moment.

'Thursday would seem to be a good day,' said Helliwell. 'Unless the weather turns worse and the ground hardens. But at the moment I'd say that would be suitable, if you agree.'

Murray nodded. He could hardly hold any engagement above his wife's funeral, and in any case the place was so chaotic at the moment he had hardly an idea what was happening from one day to the next. Mr. Helliwell nodded back.

'A kisting at noon, then?' he asked, and Murray agreed again.

'We'll be there. I'll let the men know about the grave, too. Will you be wanting the best mortcloth or will you use your own?'

'We'll use our own,' said Murray. It had not been used since his mother's funeral: he could still remember it swish like her skirts as the coffin was lifted to leave Letho House. Helliwell was about to say something further when the door opened.

'Excuse me, sir,' said Robbins, 'but Mal Johnstone from the village is here. He says he would like to speak to you. And Mr. Blair has returned from Cupar.'

'I'm glad to hear it. The weather seems to have turned foul. Where have you put Mal?'

'Mr. Thalland has been working in the gun room, sir, so I put Mal Johnstone in the billiard room.'

There was a connecting door: something in Robbins' face implied that he had not wanted to leave Mal unsupervised. Robbins was occasionally dismissive of the tenants of Collessie. The staff he would have nothing to do with.

'Please stay here and warm up,' Murray said to Helliwell and Rintoul. 'I shall be back shortly.'

In the hall he met Blair, disentangling himself with William's helpless help from his various outdoor garments. With him was Macduff, apparently soaked to the skin. Blair bounced with delight when he saw Murray.

'We have seen Cahill again! He has told us all manner of things! Except he is very vague about poor Tilly,' he added sadly. Macduff nodded.

'I think he must have killed her, though, sir. He seems not to remember the actual deed, but there's an awful lot of blood on his coat for someone who just carried her away wrapped in a cloak. Sprayed, as well as soaked in.'

'But he admits to taking Agnes?'

'Oh, yes, very much so!' said Blair. 'And he – I think what he has been doing is that – well, I think he is the one who has been starting all the rumours about witchcraft.'

'What?' Murray had been edging towards the billiard room, but he stopped. 'He's the one who has set the village on edge?'

'I believe so, sir. He's quite proud of it. Thinks he's been gey clever.'

'He talks of nothing but witches!' said Blair. 'He said that Widow Maggot was one, and that she was friends with your Mrs. Dean and that was why he killed her, to stop her telling Mrs. Dean that he had been there. It was Mrs. Dean who told Widow Maggot that Agnes was at the house, and Widow Maggot told Cahill, and I think it must have been him Tilly Aytoun saw through the drawing room window that night and thought he was a ghost! He was up a ladder,' he added prosaically.

'So that must be where the ladder went,' said Murray. Blair blinked. 'Oh, Thalland's ceiling has collapsed, so he and the Robbinses are all camping upstairs for now. It'll be company for Robert Lovie,' he added. He had almost forgotten their prisoner on the top floor. He supposed he could be released now: his innocence of kidnap and murder had at any rate been established. Personally Murray would be glad to see the back of him.

'And he seemed to say – seemed to, neither Macduff nor I was very sure about it – that his sister, that Agnes worked for, was a witch, too!'

'Is there anyone he doesn't accuse of being a witch?'

'He's not accusing them: he seems quite happy that they are witches,' said Macduff fairly. 'He said the syrup was a witch recipe.'

'But Mrs. Dean made that.'

'Well, yes.' Blair looked innocently at Murray. Murray thought about his housekeeper, and some of her remarks, and decided to think about it in more depth later.

'Mal Johnstone's here,' he explained, nodding towards the billiard room.

'Aye, they said in the village he was heading here,' said

Macduff. 'That's what I came here for.'

'Well, apparently he has something he wants to talk to me about,' said Murray. 'Shall we go in and see him? Or would you like to dry off first?' he asked Macduff, who was dripping on the flag floor and starting to shiver. 'I don't believe there's a fire in the billiard room.'

Macduff looked torn. Murray knew he did not enjoy the best of health: catching a chill would do him no good.

'William,' said Murray, 'go quickly and fetch a warm blanket and a hot brandy and bring them at once to the billiard room. Take off your wet boots, Macduff, and come in to stand on the carpet, and at least we can fight off the worst of the cold till this matter is dealt with.'

Macduff looked relieved and sat on a hall chair to haul off his boots, then padded lopsided after them to the billiard room. Candles had been lit there against the day outside, though it was only past noon. Mal Johnstone was standing beside the billiard table, fiddling with the polished edge, his flat face riven with worry. He jumped when they entered the room, and his hand leapt from the table as though it had been burned.

'Mal, good day to you.'

Mal bowed jerkily.

'Mr. Murray, sir. Thank you for agreeing to see me.'

'You have something you wish to say?'

William interrupted, bringing the blanket and the brandy for Macduff. Murray waited until Macduff was comfortable in a chair, and turned back to Mal Johnstone who was gazing at the blanket and brandy with a longing look: Murray realised that he, too, was soaking. He caught William and told him to bring another blanket and brandy, and William hurried off. Blair curled himself into a seat beside Macduff, but Murray remained standing and so, of course, did Mal. Murray nodded to him.

'Sir, is it true? I thought you would be most like to know, but now here's Mr. Macduff, too. Is it true that a man has been arrested for taking young Agnes? And for killing Miss Aytoun?'

'That's right,' said Murray, with a glance at Blair and Macduff. 'A man is in jail in Cupar.'

'Is it – is it a man frae Glasgow direction?' asked Mal. Murray could see that he was shaking.

'Why would you ask that?'

'Oh! Oh, no reason!' said Mal. At that moment William returned and gave him the blanket and brandy. Mal made a great fuss of arranging the blanket around his shoulders, and took a moment to sip at the brandy with appreciation. 'Brandy's a thing I very rarely would have, sir. A fine thing, a fine thing on a day like today. Awful fine, sir.' He shuddered as he swallowed another large sip. It seemed to give him some courage. 'See, it was only that the other day I met a man with a Glasgow voice, like, on the Cupar road. He was putting some kind of bundle behind a bush – I didna see what, at all, sir.' He was suddenly emphatic, meeting Murray's eye firmly. 'I had my wee handcart with me – you ken I'm a carter, aye?' he said to Blair and Macduff. 'And I had my wee handcart, that can take a fair bit on it and at very reasonable rates, too. Well, the man stopped me and he asked if he could borrow my handcart. I said that it was my living and I didna lend it to just a'body. He said he could pay me, and he didna need me to push it, he would push it himself. I said I didna like to let the thing out of my sight, for it's a fine wee handcart, I built it myself before my father died, so it's stood me in good stead all that time and I wouldna want ever to lose it.'

'And negotiations no doubt continued,' said Murray drily.

'Aye, well, sir, they did. And at last he paid me a shilling – a whole shilling! – to borrow my cart and told me away home and he would bring it back to me that evening. Well, off I went back to the village, and that evening there came a knock on my door and when I came out there was the cart, all scrubbed, like, but not a sign of the man. So I wondered, ken, if it was maybe the same man? See, it gars me fair grue to think that a murderer and a kidnapper might have been using my wee handcart,' he finished innocently. His little front teeth settled again into his lower lip like a self-righteous fieldmouse.

'What day was this, did you say?' asked Murray.

'It would be Friday, sir. The day that Miss Aytoun's body was found out at Josie's Den.' The answer came glib and ready.

'And did you look back at all, to see what he was doing with the handcart?'

'No, sir, not a bit of it.'

'Your precious wee handcart, that you made yourself and had

given you such good service? And you didn't look back to see that a complete stranger was treating it properly?'

Mal considered that.

'Well, I might have given a wee look back to see … Whatever the bundle was he had behind the bush, he was loading it on to the handcart.'

'Ah, yes, the bundle. What did that look like?'

'Well, a bundle, sir.'

'What sort of size?'

'Quite big, sir, for something to be carrying by hand. Long – maybe about five foot?'

'Wrapped in what?'

'What?'

'What was it wrapped in? Canvas? Brown paper? Sacking?'

'Blue cloth, sir. A bit loosely, in blue cloth.'

Murray regarded him for a moment. Truth and fiction mixed together: a fairly sensible approach to trying to save yourself.

'And the Glaswegian gentleman –'

'I never said he was a gentleman, sir!'

'No, you didn't. Have you seen him before or since?'

'He was a stranger to me,' said Mal neatly, not quite answering the question.

'You didn't, for example, see him in the woods after church on Sunday? To tell him any local news you might have picked up?'

'Why would I do that, sir?' Mal's face had taken on a greenish tinge.

'Because you had arranged to do so, you and your friends? To help him with the witch hunt, perhaps?'

Mal's hand wandered out from his side, seizing the edge of the billiard table again in an uncertain grasp. He stared straight ahead.

'You have to get rid of witches, sir,' he whispered.

'Is that what he told you?'

Mal nodded, looking sick.

'Did he tell you to attack Lizzie Fenwick and imprison her?'

'He – aye, sir, he did,' said Mal, his knuckles white on the billiard table.

'Because you thought she had helped your father to his death?' Mal nodded very slightly. 'And Mary Robbins? What about her?'

'She – she talks a secret language to her wean,' said Mal, finding a little defiance from somewhere. 'I told him, and he said she was well-kent as a witch. You have to burn witches …' His voice faded again. 'The kirk burned witches,' he added faintly. Murray saw how weak he was: a strong will could have imposed on him easily enough.

'Would it surprise you to know that he had identified several witches, but was quite happy to let them continue their work? His own sister, for example, in Glasgow?'

Mal's gaze flicked up to meet Murray's, his eyebrows high.

'But – he said they had to be burned. He said he was sent to do it, that the kirk would burn witches. That they were everywhere, they had to be got rid of, just like they were in King Jamie's time. They're wicked, evil. It says … he said …'

Mal began to cry. Murray ran a hand through his hair, feeling sick himself. Despite everything, he felt sorry for Mal. He should send him home, but a glance at the window showed the sleet was thicker than ever. He caught a movement out of the corner of his eye and spun back towards Mal, but he did not seem to have moved. He frowned and turned to Macduff.

'Do you want to talk to him more about the handcart incident?' he asked. 'Are you any drier? Maybe it would be easiest if you took him to the servants' hall and sat by the fire there, and make sure you're both a bit drier before you have to leave. Get Mrs. Mack to give you some of her famous broth.'

'Aye, I'll do that,' said Macduff, looking pleased at the thought. He pushed himself out of the chair, and Blair bounced up beside him. There was a flash outside the unshuttered window, and they all stared as a low rumble of thunder murmured to itself in the distance.

'You're certainly not going out in that, anyway,' said Murray. 'Mal, go with Macduff and get warmed up.'

Macduff limped off chivvying Mal ahead of him. Blair and Murray looked at each other.

'Well, we seem to be making some kind of progress,' said Murray. 'Peter Cahill kidnapped Agnes, and killed Tilly, or you think he probably did.'

'That's right,' said Blair and as they walked back to the library he described the interview with Cahill in more detail.

'Tilly must have taken the wrong turning in the woods that night: poor girl, an unlucky mistake. Did you find out why he put her reticule in the hut? She must have told him she had been going there, otherwise why would he think of the hut at all?'

Blair was dismayed.

'We never asked. I must mention it to Macduff, when he has finished talking to Mal Johnstone.'

'It may well have been as you said, that he was trying to distract us.'

'But I also said that that was what he was doing with Agnes' cloak, and that turned out to be Mr. Rintoul,' said Blair.

'Well, just because he didn't do it once doesn't necessarily mean that he didn't do it the other time,' said Murray, trying to make it sound convincing. 'But if it wasn't for that, then what was it for?'

Blair shrugged elaborately, and shivered. Murray hurried him into the library to join Helliwell and Rintoul.

'I have been so busy thinking about Macduff and Mal Johnstone I forgot to see that you were comfortable!' he apologised. 'And we have been standing in the hall for ages. Rintoul, will you pull the bell, there, please? Oh, Mrs. Helliwell – forgive me!'

'Not at all, Mr. Murray.' Mrs. Helliwell had joined her husband and was comfortably settled by the fire, but hurriedly made way for Blair. There was a polite tussle for the armchair, which Mrs. Helliwell won: Blair sat down reluctantly but immediately stretched his limbs out to the flames.

'Oh, here is where you are!'

Isobel walked in and perched on a hard chair by the library table. She had changed into mourning clothes, too.

'And no wonder, too:' she went on. 'This must be the warmest room in the house! Charles, the parlour fire seems to be sucking heat in rather than sending it out, and the weather outside is wild! Have you seen the lightning?'

Mrs. Helliwell darted to the window and opened the shutter: outside was as dark as night, but in a flash it was lit by lightning, followed by an almost immediate crack of thunder. The lightning showed a world flooded with white: it was eerie to hear the storm in the silence of the falling snow.

'The Lord help all creatures out in that tonight,' murmured Helliwell fervently, joining her, and they all made an Amen. He pushed the shutters closed again and returned to the fireplace with his wife.

The door opened again and the Grants came in, followed, a little uncertainly, by Lady Aytoun.

'I hope we're not interrupting anything?' asked Mrs. Grant. 'Have you seen the weather?'

'Extraordinary, isn't it, Mrs. Grant?' said Mrs. Helliwell, and brought her over to sit with her. Mrs. Helliwell liked sensible women, being one herself.

'Very cosy in here,' said Cousin Andrew. He sat at the library table opposite Isobel, and drew the latest newspaper towards him, but seemed too unsettled to read. 'No reflection on your fine house, Cousin Charles, but is anyone else finding the day a little close? I have to admit to a longing to run outside, despite the weather.'

'I know exactly what you mean,' said Isobel. 'The whole place seems to be filling up. And that's not just in here,' she added, looking about at the company which was a large one for the library. 'Everywhere in the house feels too tight, somehow.'

'I think I should go up and see that Robert is in need of nothing,' said Mrs. Grant suddenly. She looked apologetically at Murray. 'I know he deserves nothing in the way of kindly treatment – but he is my son.'

'Of course, Mrs. Grant,' said Murray. 'And the nursery floor is probably not the warmest place in the house. Would anyone mind if we brought him down?'

He looked particularly at Isobel. The Grants waited anxiously, not ready to plead his case.

'I should have no objection,' said Isobel. 'It would not be entertaining to be up there alone tonight.'

'Well, the Robbinses and Thalland will be up there later,' said Murray, 'but no, it would not be pleasant. I'll fetch him, shall I?' he asked. 'I have the key.'

'I'll come with you, my boy, if I may,' said Blair. 'I am quite warmed now and someone else can have their turn in the old man's chair by the fire.'

Once in the hall, Murray remembered that he had wanted to

ask Blair something.

'The box and the bowl we brought from Widow Maggot's cottage – do you still have them?'

Blair frowned.

'Yes, of course: Macduff has not yet asked for them back. Why?'

'There has been nothing … strange about them, has there?'

'Nothing that I have noticed,' said Blair, his eyes wide. 'The box is as empty as the bowl. Why do you ask?'

'Well … I'm not very happy about the mirror,' said Murray, feeling that this was a bit of an understatement. He described, as best he could, what had happened with the mirror. Blair gave him a kindly look.

'And was this before or after what happened in the cellar?' he asked.

'After,' said Murray. He shivered at the thought of what he and Walter had seen in the cellar: the feet and the skirts appearing inch by inch, the hands … Blair gave his arm a little pat.

'It hasn't been an easy few weeks for you, has it, my boy?'

'Well, no, but – wait, it really did happen!' Murray suddenly felt ten again, as if he had been spinning tall tales to amuse the grown-ups. It had really happened, hadn't it? He and Walter had both seen that awful thing in the cellar. Something had certainly given the appearance of coming out of that mirror. Hadn't it? 'Look, let's bring the bowl and the box and the mirror all back down to the library, and we'll take a closer look at them.'

'Splendid idea,' said Blair, just as kindly as before. 'We'll collect them now, and then go and fetch young Robert.'

Blair happily pottered into his room and came back quickly, shoving the box and the bowl into his coat pockets. Murray tried to look as nonchalant as he fetched the mirror from his own room, but he kept the bright surface turned away from him, and away from Blair. They carried on up the next stairs to the nursery floor, where the storm seemed even louder. Mary and her little boy were just leaving their new room.

'All comfortable?' Murray asked with a smile.

'Very much so, thank you sir,' said Mary, curtseying appropriately.

'We're going to take Robert Lovie downstairs. What's the

matter?'

'Nothing, sir,' said Mary, frowning. 'I just thought I saw something move behind you.'

Murray spun round.

'There's nothing there,' he said.

'No, I know,' she said. 'I just thought for a second I saw something move, sir.'

'One of the dogs, maybe?' asked Blair helpfully.

'That might be it,' said Murray quickly, though he knew it was time for Flash and Bonnie to be in the kitchen having their meal. 'Well, let's go. I hope you are able to settle for a little, Mary – Mrs. Robbins, while we rebuild the house.'

'Aye, sir.' Her face was solemn, but he knew her eyes were laughing at him as usual. He nodded curtly, and led Blair along the corridor to Robert Lovie's room. Mary had disappeared down the stairs before they knocked on his door. There was an immediate 'Come in!' and they found Robert standing by the little barred window, gazing out at the storm.

'Isn't it splendid? I love a good storm – if I'm cosy indoors, anyway!' he said.

'Well, it's not too cosy up here,' said Murray. 'The company are in agreement that you may come down and join us in the library, which is much warmer than here.'

'That's extremely kind,' said Robert sincerely. 'If you're quite sure?'

Murray was not, but he could think of no good reason to leave him there when he was unlikely to do any further damage in this household.

'Yes, come along. Bring your book or whatever.'

'Just allow me a moment to make myself presentable,' said Robert. He slid off his coat and brushed his hair, then shook out his neckcloth which had been hanging over the back of a chair. He turned to them with a smile.

'I must say it will be pleasant to leave this room for a little. Just this afternoon I had the feeling it was starting to close in on me!' He flipped the neckcloth over his head, and began to tie it.

'Mr. Lovie, you seem to be injured!' said Blair suddenly. 'Aside from your black eye, I mean.'

'Injured?' asked Murray. 'Where?'

'It's nothing,' said Robert quickly. 'Just a scratch.'

'Let's see?' Murray was beside him in a stride, Blair right behind him. Blair reached out and carefully drew back the neck of Robert's shirt to show, just over the collarbone, a nasty narrow gash, a couple of inches long. Blair blinked.

'That's a little more than a scratch,' said Murray. 'How did you come by that?'

'Oh, it was very clumsy of me,' said Robert. 'I fell against the little shovel thing for the fire.'

'Really?' asked Blair. 'That's very curious. I've seen a scratch just like that somewhere else today.'

'Have you? I suppose other clumsy people have fireirons too,' said Robert. He did not quite meet their eyes. Murray waited for Blair.

'The other person explained his injury in a rather different way,' said Blair thoughtfully. 'He said that a young lady had attacked him with a tiny pair of scissors.'

'It was the shovel,' said Robert, almost in a whisper.

'The young lady in question was Mathilda Aytoun. The man was her kidnapper.'

'Would you like to review your story about your assignation with Mathilda Aytoun, Robert?' asked Murray. 'How did her reticule come to be in the hut where you had arranged to meet her?'

'Oh for goodness' sake,' snapped Robert. 'All right, then, she did turn up. She arrived and was very pleased with the whole set up, the candles and the picnic and so on. And then when I tried to claim my reward for all my hard work, she changed her mind! I mean, how unjust!'

'And she attacked you with her scissors?' Mrs. Grant's scissors, he thought, Robert's own mother's scissors.

'To be honest,' Robert winced at Murray's laugh. 'To be honest, I didn't see what she cut me with. I just let go and off she went, charging through the trees like a bolting horse. It does look a bit nasty, doesn't it?' He turned and examined the cut in the looking glass. 'I might need something on that.'

Murray's fist twitched, but he forced himself to relax. Robert was an arrogant little fool, but he had come off the loser with Tilly Aytoun. It was only a shame that in running from Robert she had met a worse fate. But how had she had Mrs. Grant's embroidery sharps? Murray had a feeling he knew.

They waited in silence while Robert arranged his neckcloth and brushed down his coat with the damp edge of a towel, and then declared himself ready to join the company below. Murray blew out the candles in the little nursery, and followed Blair's candle back along the corridor to the stairs, imagining shadows creeping behind them. He concentrated on Robert, and on not punching his handsome nose. No doubt someone else would perform that office very soon: it was only a matter of time.

The candles on the next landing seemed to have blown out, and he made a small nod of acknowledgement towards the room where Agostinella's body lay, guarded by the devoted maid. A little light rose from the hall, and they hurried on down through the shadows. Murray glanced back, and jumped. The maid was standing outside the room, in the passage, motionless. He looked more closely: it was not Nina, he realised. Who was it? And how, he suddenly thought, could he see her there in the dark?

The figure swayed a little, grew misty round the edges, then solidified again. He gasped. It was the woman from the cellar. He could not see her face, but he knew she was staring at him. He slid down the top step of the stairs, stumbled over the next few steps, regained his footing, and ran to the hall, catching up with Blair and Robert at the door of the library.

'What's the matter?' asked Blair. 'You've turned quite white!'

'Nothing, nothing,' panted Murray. 'Nothing at all. Let's go in.'

The library felt comforting, but stuffy. Murray saw to his delight that Augusta had been brought back: Mrs. Helliwell was holding her and Murray quickly took her, clutching her to him like a talisman. Augusta gave a little squeak of complaint.

'You're shivering, Mr. Murray,' said Mrs. Helliwell. 'Come up to the fire. It must be cold up there, then?'

'I was glad enough to come down,' agreed Robert with a pleasant grin, his composure regained. The man was astonishing.

'I was just saying, Mr. Murray,' said Lady Aytoun, 'that your little girl is lovely! Truly delightful, wasn't I, Mrs. Grant? Miss Blair?'

'Indeed you were, Lady Aytoun,' said Isobel in a level voice.

She was sketching again, and Murray wondered how cruel her sketches were this time.

'Thank you, Lady Aytoun,' he said. After all, Augusta was indeed lovely and truly delightful. Even silly people could be absolutely right sometimes. Lady Aytoun was clutching her large reticule closely to her, and he wondered if she had a supply of brandy in it. She did not seem too far gone at the moment, anyway, and was drinking tea.

He looked round at the company, Lady Aytoun, the Grants, the Blairs, the Helliwells, Mr. Rintoul admiring Isobel's drawings (presumably the pretty ones), Robert Lovie settling down beside his stepfather at the table, Blair decanting the Widow Maggot's box and bowl on to the table in front of them. He found he was still clutching the mirror, though unconsciously he had kept it away from contact with Augusta. He laid it down on the table next to the other things.

'What are those?' asked Isobel, poking the bowl with the end of her pen. It rang dull, a low, hollow sound. 'Oh, I don't like that,' she said.

'No, nor do I,' said Murray. 'The box is empty, you said?' he asked Blair.

'Completely. Not even a trace of mysterious dust,' said Blair with a mischievous smile.

'They were in Widow Maggot's cottage,' said Murray. 'Your father and I removed them in case they were stolen. We've been waiting for Macduff to find her relatives and return them to them.'

There was a knock on the door and everyone looked up. Macduff himself entered, followed sheepishly by Mal Johnstone. He looked around in awe at the quantity of the company in the library.

'Yes?' said Murray.

'Mr. Johnstone here has an apology to make, he says,' said Macduff, 'if we're not interrupting anything. Excuse me, sir, but are those the things you took from Widow Maggot's place?'

'That's right. What is your apology, Mal?'

Mal felt down the front edges of his coat with his hands, and up again, his little mouth twitching.

'I came to say, Mr. Murray, sir, that I'm sorry I was so misguided and foolish,' he said hesitantly, as if he had only just learned the words. 'I know now I was wrong. Of course there's no such thing as witchcraft. I ken fine that Lizzie Fenwick is a good woman, and a grand nurse, and I'm sure she did my faither no harm at all. And I'm very sorry I set fire to the house across the way, where the big lassie lives. I know now that she was talking her ain language to the wean, and not some devil's tongue. I've been – I believed all that fellow said to me, and I'm gey sorry.'

He looked it, too: he would not like to be taken for a fool amongst his fellow villagers, even if they had been nearly as gullible as he. Murray caught a flicker of movement beside him, and glanced round, but there was nothing there. What was wrong with his eyes?

The door opened yet again, and in came Robbins and Mrs. Dean. Mrs. Dean curtseyed to Murray.

'You wanted to see me, sir?' she asked.

'I don't think I asked … '

'Perhaps there's been a misunderstanding, sir,' said Macduff, who was looking as tired as Murray felt. 'I wanted to ask you a few questions, Mrs. Dean, about the Widow Maggot. Was she a friend of yours?'

'She – I knew her, well enough,' said Mrs. Dean, but her eyes were on the table. 'Mr. Murray,' she said, 'surely that looking glass should be covered in a house of mourning? Let me fetch one of the black cloths.'

She hurried out, as if relieved to be going. Isobel turned back to her sketching things, and looked confused.

'Has someone just moved my little knife? A silver one, for sharpening my pens?'

'What a curious bowl,' remarked Lady Aytoun, leaning over the table and clutching her vast reticule. 'It really is very pretty. Quite lovely! Oh!'

The last exclamation came as Macduff, with the least glance at Murray, lost his balance in his weariness, and lurched against her arm. Her reticule slipped and sprang open, the catch swinging, and there was an enormous clatter, as out of its gaping mouth sprayed forks, spoons, keys of different sizes, a pair of spectacles on a chain, and Isobel's silver knife. Mrs. Grant stared, and quickly worked out what was happening.

'Oh, so that's where things have been going! Did you take my embroidery sharps, too?' She started to hunt through the tangle of silvery objects, but Cousin Andrew met Murray's eye, his mouth open. He knew the sharps would not be there. Murray nodded.

'I don't know where they are,' said Lady Aytoun plaintively. 'Tilly was always taking things from me. I like shiny, pretty things, but she was always making me put them back.'

'Perhaps a reason for leaving Edinburgh during the season?' Murray murmured to Blair.

Mrs. Dean trotted back into the room, carrying a small sheet of black cloth. She stared at all the cutlery, and Murray could see her noting what was familiar from the Letho stocks. She passed no comment, however, but made her way to where the mirror lay on its back on the table. At that moment, there was an odd draught, and the candles blew out.

'Don't worry, sir, I have a taper if I can get to the fire,' said Robbins' calm voice, over the delicate scuffle of metalware that sounded suspiciously like Lady Aytoun scooping her loot back into her reticule. Beyond that there was silence in the room, but outside the wind was rising. Then: 'I can't seem to get to it, sir,' from Robbins, puzzled and slightly breathless. No one else moved.

'The mirror, sir, I must cover it,' said Mrs. Dean from somewhere near Murray's elbow.

'Not yet. You said it might go back in. Don't cover it yet,' Murray heard himself saying. The wind howled outside, but even the sound of cutlery had stopped. Murray thought the room was darker than it should be: the fire was lit, but the light seemed to contract, shrink into itself. He held Augusta tightly, as if they could somehow protect each other – but from what?

Mrs. Dean seemed to be the only one awake apart from him.

'Lizzie said,' she murmured, as if she were talking to herself. 'Lizzie said, when it comes, open the box and fill the bowl. Open the box and fill the bowl. Open the box and fill the bowl.'

He felt her reach past him, heard a tiny squeak of hinges. Then a dull ring from the bowl again, as she poured who knew what liquid into it. Then he felt her clutch his arm: she seemed frightened, but he found it strangely reassuring. She was still murmuring, 'Open the box and fill the bowl. Open the box and fill the bowl,' to herself. The wind shrieked in the chimney. Across the table, behind the dark bulk of Cousin Andrew, he could see a column of mist forming, collecting itself, glowing faintly in the blackness. Murray felt every nerve in his body tense.

Suddenly, over the wind he heard something new: a noise he could only describe as sucking, but louder than any sucking had a right to be. He half expected to feel it, but just as quickly as it had started, there was a sound like the swift licking of enormous lips, and everything stopped.

'If I can just get to the fire, sir, I'll light this taper,' said Robbins calmly, and in a moment the candles were being lit again, one by one. Behind Cousin Andrew there was nothing. Murray tilted his head to his daughter, and saw that she was sleeping peacefully in his arms. Lady Aytoun had a wild look, but her reticule was still open and the stolen items were half in, half out. Isobel had reclaimed her silver knife, and on the table in front of them all the box was slammed shut, the bowl was empty, and the mirror … the mirror was cracked straight across, the glass as black as coal. One look at it was enough to know that whatever had come out of it had gone back, and was not going to return.

'I'll cover it all the same, in a house of mourning,' said Mrs. Dean, and wrapped the black cloth around it. She took it, the bowl and the box, and carried them out of the room. No one stopped her.

In Mrs. Dean's own room, Agnes stirred on the bed, stretched, and sat up, looking around her in surprise. She opened her mouth and drew in a great, deep breath.

'See, that's what I mean,' she remarked out loud to herself. 'It's pure dead brilliant living here. I got to sleep in the housekeeper's bed! Wait till I tell my pal Dorrie.'

In Jennet's room, Lizzie Fenwick had been sitting up, but now she eased herself back down, exhausted. Thank goodness, that was that over. Silly man, Mr. Murray, taking something he did not understand. Anything could have happened. But Mrs. Dean was a sensible woman, and all would be well. For now, anyway.

On Tuesday morning, the snow lay like damp feathers in ditches and hedges, as if someone had burst an eiderdown. The sky was heavy, as if it could not quite make up its mind whether it wanted to fling down more snow, but over the course of the day it lightened and relaxed. Macduff went back to Cupar, without Mal Johnstone or Robert Lovie, though he knew he would come back for both. In Cupar the news met him that the guard who had gone to give the prisoner Cahill his breakfast that morning had found him cold and dead on his bed, the only mark on him that gash on his arm and an odd scratch down one side of his face, as if made by claws, but not large or sharp ones. Not a wound so much as a signature, thought Macduff as he sketched it, if only he could read it.

At Letho, Murray stood at the window of the parlour, holding Augusta up to look at the snow. As they watched, the white hare loped into view, still limping, looking tired but as always somehow reassuring. There's a thing, he thought. The hare's bad leg was on the same side as Lizzie Fenwick's. He smiled to himself. Still fanciful, he thought.

The household was busy: food had to be prepared and the drawing room tidied for all the visitors who would make their way there on Thursday for the funeral. Cards were sent, and letters received. Agnes chattered her way through it all, and Lizzie Fenwick sat on the kitchen settle, helping to chop vegetables. The mood was sombre but dutifully so: everyone felt a new lightness even as they sped about the house. Robbins returned the picnic hampers to the cellar: he looked about it and decided it was a useful enough storage space, if they cleaned it out a bit. There was no sense in wasting it.

Repairs were already under way in Thalland's house: the greater task of rebuilding the Robbins' house had to be considered more carefully, but Thalland had already drawn up some plans, based on the original ones which he had found in the estate office. Come the spring, work would start in earnest. Until then, Mrs. Chambers' old cottage was cosy, Mary said, and more appropriate to them than the nursery floor. Murray reckoned she liked her own roof over her head.

Thursday was still threaded with snow, though the sun shone. The neighbours and a few relatives had visited and commiserated and eaten oatcakes and drunk copious amounts. The ladies were now with Mr. Helliwell and Mr. Rintoul back at Letho House, no doubt drowning themselves in tea. The men, gentry, staff, and tenants, had followed the coffin down the drive and along the road to the village, then up the hill – doused in sand that morning to help the grip of the bearers' boots – to the kirk, where the Murray tomb had been opened. Snow lay in its secret corners and deceived the feet around its edges, but the coffin descended with all the grace expected of a de Cumae de Palaeopolitani. Whisky was shared between the mourners and the diggers, and deep breaths were taken of the cold, clear, sane air. Mal Johnstone held his hat to his chest and nodded to Murray, and members of the Kirk Session came and shook his hand. Their heads were misted with the fog of their collective breath, their eyes full of concerned sympathy for the laird. There was no talk of witchcraft.

Murray turned from Agostinella's grave, and felt a great weight lift from his shoulders, and from the whole village. It was a new start.

Scots words in *Out of a Dark Reflection*:

Assoilzie	(legal term) to clear of all charges
Begoyt	daft, foolish
Ca' canny	go carefully
Carlie	villain
Chap	to knock at, e.g. at a door
Compear	(legal term) appear in court
Crack	chat
Doitered	witless
Dominie	schoolmaster
Dreich	dark, damp and miserable (usually with reference to the weather)
Gar you grue	make your flesh creep, give you the creeps
Gey	very
Glumpsh	to complain
Greet	to cry
Guidman	husband
Heidyins	'head ones', people in charge
Kailyard	vegetable garden
Keek	glimpse, peek
Ken	to know (well-kent = well-known)
Kine	cattle
Kirk	church
Kist	chest or box. Kisting a corpse = putting it into the coffin
Pensit	puffed with pride
Quhilk	old spelling of 'which'
Raist	angry
Raivelt	confused
Redd	to tidy
Thrawn	stubborn
Wame	stomach

Lexie Conyngham lives in North-East Scotland and has been writing stories since she knew people did. The sequel to *Out of a Dark Reflection* is at the planning stage, but the next book by Lexie Conyngham will be *The Necessary Tale*, due to be published Easter 2016. Follow her professional procrastination on Facebook and at www.murrayofletho.blogspot.com, where you can also join a mailing list to keep up to date with new publications.

The Murray of Letho series:

Death in a Scarlet Gown
Knowledge of Sins Past
Service of the Heir
An Abandoned Woman
Fellowship with Demons
The Tender Herb: A Murder in Mughal India
Death of an Officer's Lady
Out of a Dark Reflection

Stand alone:
Windhorse Burning
The Necessary Tale (due Easter 2017)

Short Stories:
Thrawn Thoughts and Blithe Bits

Printed in Great Britain
by Amazon

45042905R00175